The Sword
of Destiny

BOOK ONE of the SPIRIT SWORD SAGA

Jonathan W. Thurston

A THURSTON HOWL PUBLICATIONS BOOK

ISBN 978-0990890218

THE SWORD OF DESTINY

Copyright © 2014 by Jonathan W. Thurston

First Edition, 2014. All rights reserved.

A Thurston Howl Publications Book
Published by Thurston Howl Publications
thurstonhowlpublications.com
Murfreesboro, TN

Mailing address:
4072 Hwy 200
Huron, TN 38345

jonathan.thurstonhowlpub@gmail.com

Cover design by Scott L. Ford

Printed in the United States of America

10 9 8 7 6 5 4 3 2 1

To all those who have been supporting me through my own darkest times, including my grandmother Debbie, Professor Tichi, Ken, Dustin, my sisters, and my ever-faithful Temerita, my dog who still thinks she is a cat, despite all the proof I have shown her to suggest otherwise.

A Shadow of the Flame

Thunder roared in the distance. Its brilliant flashes illuminated the dark of the night. The wind howled among the dark and naked trees to create a symphony of ceaseless creaking. The rain pounded on the soft ground and on the stone remnants of the dark tower. In the light of the storm, this place was a monster reaching up from the depths of the earth toward the ominous heavens. On this island of death, only the storm could breathe that arthritic motion into the trees and even the ground. The tower, however, was still.

It was a shattered and decrepit thing to the bare eye. It was a thin spire with bricks missing along its height, creating massive holes that swarmed the base of the tower, making it seem a spectacle that something so emaciated and crumbled could still stand, but it did, nevertheless. The rain poured into every orifice. Nature itself had condemned this unwanted scar on the planet. Although it appeared neglected, it persisted in its blasphemous announcement of presence. As this struggle between nature and spire continued, someone approached the colossus, and with his arrival he lit his way with a flame suspended in the air in front of him that burned unnaturally in the impregnable winds and flooding rains.

The man was as dark as the tower itself: he bore a robe just as ominous, just as black. It carried a hood that veiled his entire face. Leather gloves warded his hands from the maelstrom of the heavens that beat upon him. His bare and soiled feet splashed in the mud, which lathered the bottom of his robe. His broad shoulders and his extraordinary height foretold him to be a formidable and strong man. And yet, as he stopped at the foot of the tower and gazed up at its peak, the fire cowered and flickered. It lit his face and revealed a middle-aged man with red hair that covered the top of his head and some of his lower face. The greatest irregularity of the man was neither his red hair nor his bare feet, however. It was his red eyes: they burned with an intensity far more ferocious than that of his floating flame.

He lowered his head once more so that the hood hid his face again. He continued his walk to enter the base of the tower. Water poured from it as if it was trying to escape the tower at all costs. The man traversed each step of the crumbling spiral stairway. Each time he neared a gap in the wall, he pulled his robe tighter to him in an attempt to remove the icy daggers of the wind that impaled him.

As he climbed the stairs, a cloud of thin, black smoke appeared in a flash of lightning. He opened his mouth to scream as his body passed through the hazy image, but no sound escaped his lips.

A woman's shout... "Randir! Don't do this!"

The smell of roasting flesh and hair...

"Yes, Lord. I will do as you command..."

"My love, you are not so power-hungry that you would abandon all of us, now are you?"

The sound of metal meeting bone and the fleshy matter behind it...

"Ophelia..."

"...I didn't mean to hurt you," escaped his lips.

Those words echoed solemnly throughout the tower and loomed above even the din of the storm outside. The storm itself seemed far more distant than his own thoughts and memories haunting him now. The miniscule flame had diminished to nothing. Again, he pulled his cloak tighter around him and started to run up the remainder of the stairs.

He entered a small room which was in the top of the tower. There were no windows or holes, and therefore, no rain. In the back of the room there was a barren fireplace. Though he could not see it in the dark of the room, he knew it was there. Just as mysterious as his floating flame, the fireplace erupted into an enticing dance of inferno. The logs shriveled back against the heat and evoked an aroma that was all too familiar to him: the smell of burning trees. The room was now alight and warming itself. However, his eyes, blazing as they were, were not focused on the fireplace. In the center of the room there was a table with two chairs beside it. Another man occupied one of these chairs.

"Good to see you again. It's been what—70 years since our last meeting?" said the man at the table. He was also robed in black. His hood was elongated so that it covered even his chin. He wore the same gloves yet wore boots that appeared untouched by the flood outside. "Come, Randir. Have a seat."

The man called Randir stood right where he was and crossed his arms to illustrate his choice further.

"What? No 'hello' or 'how are you?'" chuckled the man at the table. "I'm almost disappointed by your blatant incivility."

"What do you want, Pullatus? Why have you summoned us?" demanded Randir.

Pullatus rose from the table, and though he was at least a foot and a half shorter than Randir, he appeared more intimidating. "What I have to say will be said in front of everybody or nobody," said Pullatus calmly.

"Hmph. Very well. While we're waiting for the others, why don't you tell me what you've been up to all these years?"

Pullatus walked over to the fireplace as he spoke, "Do you not remember what I told you I would do?" He paused to receive an answer, but when it was clear that he was not going to get one, he continued. "Very well. I started with Immyx at the Capital. I talked with Emperor Regin, and he has told me where his allegiances lie. Heh. That foolish king.

"After that, I went to some of the other worlds to see what resources we could use, but they are fairly complex and hard to mobilize."

Randir interrupted, "And what of Astra? Have you heard anything? Or perhaps, have you done anything with the people there?"

"I have heard things, yes. They are starting to get a little more rebellious, if anything. However, the biggest news regarding Astra is going to have to wait," responded Pullatus.

A voice called out from the stairway as another figure approached. "Heh, and I thought that I would be the first to arrive. Guess not, huh? Oh, well. I suppose that I should still count myself lucky that I'm not late."

This new person wore a blue robe without the hood. He had long, silver hair that reached far down his back and almost to his waist. His blue eyes shone a light of their own from the reflection of the fire. It was apparent that he was at least 80 years old. However, his voice was cold and raspy, commanding. Upon his arrival, the fire in the back of the room began to quiver.

Randir pulled back his hood to reveal his face in full. His red hair was very short and spiked. His face was marred with scars and was burned, especially on his right side where one large burn mark dominated from his eye to his chin. "Good to see you again, too, Xarden." As he started to smile a large grin, the fire crackled back to its higher intensities.

Xarden spoke back to Randir with an icy tone, "Randir, you know that you shouldn't play around with fire." The fire died down to a minute flame on the wood.

Pullatus said coolly before any more trouble began, "If the two of you continue this petty squabble, I may just have to inflict some form of punishment upon you both."

The other two grumbled to Pullatus, "Yes, master."

"When are the others coming? They should be here by now," said Pullatus.

Randir was the first to respond. "I know that Mali was still investigating a fortress he found at Macela, but I don't know what the others were doing."

"Some trouble was stirring up in Apolis, I think. I don't know who it was, however," replied Xarden.

At that moment, a flash of light exploded in the room, blinding everyone but Pullatus, who still had his hood hiding his face. A fourth figure had joined them. He was tall and wore a white robe and sandals. He had pale, small hands, and his face showed his young age. It was an immaculate, youthful face without any perplexities, except for his golden eyes. His ponytail of blonde hair went to touch the back of his robe lightly.

He bowed to Pullatus. "Forgive me, my Lord Pullatus, for being late to your summons. I got caught up with a few of the mountain atrocities. I apologize deeply for my delay."

Xarden grumbled, "Oh, boy. Someone needs to just lighten up." This comment was met by a glare from Randir.

Pullatus spoke proudly to the newcomer, "You have made not a grave error yet, Mali. You are not the last one to arrive. Your error is forgiven. The Shadow shall have mercy on you still."

"Thank you, my Lord," said Mali.

After a brief and awkward silence, Randir stated, "Well, three more left..."

From the bottom of the stairway, a voice echoed up to the four gathered men. "...so what do you think this is about?"

A second voice joined the first, "I don't know. I'm just ready for it to be over. We have one of these meetings about once every hundred years, and it's normally just a waste of time."

"Well, what can you expect? I mean, eventually they will have to find the Servants. It might as well be this time, right?'

Randir and Xarden chuckled. Xarden said with a grin, "May I, Pullatus?"

Pullatus nodded his head. Xarden muttered a couple of strange words which accompanied a flash of light again. Two more figures appeared in the small room.

They were both young women with blonde hair in ponytails and were obviously twins. They were the same size and wore the same facial expression of shock and utter embarrassment as they looked around the room.

One of them wore a brown cloak that just matched the mud that still dripped from it. She wore thick leather gloves and boots to shield her body from the rain. The other wore a black cloak. Surprisingly enough, neither her robe nor her boots bore one drop of water on them.

Together, the two chirped with a salute, "Forgive us for our tardiness, Lord Pullatus!"

This greeting caused Xarden and Mali to burst into uncontrollable laughter. The twins held their pose, and Pullatus stood still. The laughter died, and Pullatus gave them a significant nod. The twins relaxed.

Xarden said with an air of cheer in his voice, "'Bout time the two of you got here! We were starting to wonder when you two louts would arrive!"

Randir called out to Xarden, "Leave the two beautiful ladies alone, you old fool. They have done nothing wrong to you, so stop trying to cause trouble." Then, he appealed to the twins, "My ladies, please ignore the old coot. His malice is ceaseless." This caused Sarn to giggle into her hand, while Arnim merely smiled back at Randir. Xarden made no effort to hide the rolling of his eyes.

A voice came up from the stairway, "I'm here!"

A small man came from the stairs with his hood hiding his features. He too, like Randir and Pullatus, wore the black robe with gloves. He also wore the same boots that Pullatus did. However, a strange necklace dangled from his neck, bearing a green stone.

The fireplace erupted into fire, and thunder roared in the distance as Randir exploded into a fury. "Ixion! Why are you so late?! Can't you ever attend a meeting on time?" Of course, this unexpected outburst made many of the cloaked figures flinch. Pullatus and Xarden, however, remained calm. Ixion cringed the most noticeably.

"I was trying to research some secret reports in Pureau. I didn't mean to be late!" stammered Ixion. "Don't do anything harsh, Randir!"

The fire died down considerably as Pullatus said with a cold yet louder voice, "Enough, both of you. Ixion, you will have to be punished for this delay of yours."

"Yes, my Lord Pullatus. Anything you say," Ixion said with an extravagant flourish of his robe, though not without a timid fear in his voice.

Mali said coldly, "My Lord, might I ask what you have summoned us for?"

The tension that had steadily been increasing in the room broke as all eyes went to Pullatus.

"My friends. For 937 years, we have roamed this small world in the highest hopes of finding seven particular beings. Seven beings that have been marked by the Hand of the Shadows. Now, one of them is in our grasp."

At that, noise erupted. The twins, Xarden, and Ixion all voiced their own disbelief, while Mali and Randir just stood there, mouths gaping. It was only obvious that this news was unexpected, though the twins had hinted at it as they were climbing the stairs earlier.

"Silence. You knew that one day the Servants of the Darkness would appear. Why does it surprise you so?" demanded Pullatus.

Mali was the first to speak. "It does not shock us so much, sir, as it overwhelms us. Our waiting is at an end now."

Pullatus, even with his hood masking his features, seemed to smile beneath that veil. "My dear Mali, it is not quite at an end yet. This is one of seven. What's more is that I have made a change of plans now. The order was to obtain the blood of the seven. However, it will be far more advantageous to our cause if we can use these seven to help us gain control over Gevás."

The fire leaped in the background. Though the heat in the room increased, Randir's voice was as cold as ice. "Isn't that against our orders all the same?"

Pullatus replied just as coldly, "No. We will still kill the fools. It is just not our top priority. Also, we won't find all of the Servants at once, anyways. It will just be a way to pass the time, if you will. It will be nothing more than that. We are not disobeying, only prolonging the acting out of the orders."

The fire rose another few inches. "I refuse to abide by this plan of action. We will kill him. What is his name?"

"First of all, we will *not* kill him yet. Secondly, his name is Maris. He is from Astra. He started out as a simple sorcerer with grand ideas of politics and rebellion. Slowly, his society tamed him to their way of thinking. He grew as a sorcerer and became very powerful. He has always been well regarded there. However, upon meeting him, I introduced him to a new branch of *mysteria*: the Darkness. I have been training him these past couple of weeks so that he could easily cause extreme amounts of chaos in Gevás now under the right guidance. I told him what his powers could do for his nation and its possible rejuvenation if he rose up against Apolis...Needless to say, he believed me."

Xarden intervened, "My Lord, there's a Prophecy?"

Pullatus turned his head toward Xarden, "Hm? What prophecy?"

"Hmmm...I had thought that you had already been aware of it, honestly. Anyways, back when we were first inducted as Y'mordi, a sorcerer (I think her name was La Faye) made a Prophecy. It concerned the arrival of the Servants, though I did not know it at the time, nor did I find it accurate till now, anyways. It said, 'When seven come for seven coming, seven wake from seven sleeping. Seven lights for seven shadows.' Then, basically it goes on to vaguely and cryptically describe the seven lights and seven shadows. In essence, the interpretation is that when all seven of us meet to talk about the Seven Servants, seven Guardians of Light will awaken to their potential to repel us. When I first heard it, it was just comical. Then after the War, I thought that it was still a little iffy because of the use of the term, 'seven.' I figured that it would not help us until we actually got to this point."

Mali piped up, "And what of these Guardians? Do you have any idea who they are?"

Ixion commented, "Surely, they won't be able to stand

against us, though. Right?"

"Actually, the Prophecy made them out to be very powerful. I only know two or three of them for a fact, but I think I just discovered where three of them might be."

Randir roared at this, "What are you all talking about?! These Guardians don't matter! This Prophecy doesn't matter! What matters is that we follow our orders. We must kill this Servant. We have waited this long to play games with these ignorant fools? I don't think so."

Pullatus said calmly, "My word is final. We will use him to our advantage."

Ixion laughed, "Yeah, Randy. Why don't you just simmer down a little bit?"

"In that case, I refuse to be a part of this any longer. I will go and kill him myself without your consent," said Randir.

Upon hearing this, the entire room turned their heads at Randir. All of the faces in the room besides his own and Pullatus's turned pale. The fire dimmed at last. Darkness leaped out at the seven figures. The shadows danced on the floor. Outside, the rain pounded on the tower walls as the thunder provided it a solemn accompaniment.

Pullatus was the first to break this cacophonic silence. "Randir...you cannot and will not do this. It is against our laws."

Randir chuckled. "I will do this anyways."

The room exploded into the light of the now roaring fire. The red light branded the walls, and smoke filled the room. All the eyes were pinned on Randir as he erupted and disappeared into a pillar of flames.

Pullatus spoke quickly, "Sarn and Arnim, go to the Western Continent and see what the status is on their government. We haven't checked on any news there for a while. Mali, you shall be needed on standby, preferably at or near Apolis in case we need some work done near there. Xarden and Ixion, follow me. We're going to put an end to this nonsense now."

At that moment, the sun peaked through the atmosdome and pierce the horrendous rain outside. The dawn was here.

A Trio of Flames

The dawn filtered through the glass windows of the large, white house on the beach. The waves lapped delicately against the sand, and the white seagulls flew to extraordinary heights in the blue sky among the obscure fragments of the clouds. Their nonstop chattering joined the soft crash of the waves and the low howl of the wind to create an etude solely for the coast's welcoming first light.

Smells filled that house. The smell of warm coffee came first, and then the smells of other things like smoking bacon, eggs, and the never forgotten aroma of burnt toast followed. In this grand house, these were all enticing scents.

"Kids! Wake up!"

The sounds of groaning replied, and bare feet trudged to the location of the original voice.

It was a kitchen. It was not a fancy one, but nor was it a filthy one. It had a blue and white checkered floor with walls that bore a flower pattern repeatedly in seemingly infinite columns. The smells of the morning's breakfast meshed to give the teenagers a sensation of insatiable hunger. They walked to the table, which already held their individual platters with a scoop of eggs, three slices of bacon, one piece of toast, and a glass of orange juice each. The silverware and napkins were arranged around the plates in a meticulous manner.

Naturally, the first to arrive at the table was Dragenopn Helius (Drage, for short). He was a short, scrawny boy with short brown hair that spiked just slightly upward. He had often said that his brown eyes had been given to him to match what he called his "better-than-perfect" and "how-I-attract-the-ladies style" hair. Despite his petite frame, however, in school, he had tried out for nearly all the sports teams. He was always the first to go for meals and for anything that might earn him money.

"Wow, Mom. You actually cooked us breakfast today!" said Drage somewhat jokingly.

His mother Elizabeth gave him a stern look. Her hair was as brown as Drage's and went past her shoulders. Unlike Drage though, she had soft blue eyes that could turn to piercing ice if she wanted to pull off the stern look she was now. She was short but not quite as small as this particular son.

"Dragenopn, do you seriously have to be that way first thing in the morning? Ungrateful."

Drage's sister called out sarcastically from the back of the room, "Of course he does. He's Drage. What do you expect? Manners?"

Helen was only two years older than Drage but acted the same age most of the time. Drage had decided her lifetime mission was solely to pester him until the day he died. She was taller than both Drage and their mother and had the same brown hair and blue eyes as their mother. From a distance, Helen and her mother would have looked like twins.

A fourth voice joined the conversation. "Drage has manners. Sometimes, you just have to remind him a little bit." Drage's adopted brother Matthew gave Drage a subtle wink.

Matthew was easily the tallest one in the family. His hair was near pitch black, and his green eyes betrayed that he was not a blood relation to the Helius family. Though he was nowhere near as athletic as Drage, he was far superior in speed.

Racing each other up and down the streets of their little beach community always proved this fact. Often, Matthew would also prove to be the most mature of the siblings, despite the fact that he was one year younger than Helen and, therefore, one year older than Drage.

Elizabeth smiled at this remark. Helen waited until her mother turned her head so that she could stick out her tongue at Matthew.

"Listen, kids. I have a chore list on the refrigerator that needs to get done today. After you do all of those, I don't care what you do as long as you stay in town. Okay?" said Elizabeth.

All three of the children thought that their mom had the coolest job around: a criminal lawyer. They loved having a mom that convinced people that those who are accused of crime are not always the ones who committed the crime. They would often brag at their high school about how cool she was.

The three of them replied in unison, "Yes, Mother."

As their mother grabbed her briefcase and walked out the door in her professional lawyer attire, Helen rounded on the two boys. "Ok. Here's the deal: I want to go with Jamie to go see a movie and eat out before Mom gets back. You guys can do my chores, right?"

"No way!" said Drage. "I had plans with Matthew and Aria!"

Helen put on her innocent "please-oh-favorite-brother-of-mine" face. "Please, oh favorite brother of mine! I'll give you twenty bucks if you do it."

Matthew opened his mouth to protest the dishonesty of bribing their little brother, when Drage remarked cheerfully, "Deal!"

Helen smiled and gave Matthew a shrug. Matthew laughed. Helen said with a grin, "Thanks, Drage. Well, I am going to go freshen up!" She ran toward the stairs, a piece of toast in hand.

Drage and Matthew ate a while longer, and then went back upstairs to prepare themselves for the day ahead. When they were done, they came back downstairs to check the chore list. On it were several miscellaneous jobs like cleaning the kitchen, watering the garden, and washing clothes. Matthew said, "Okay, Drage. How about if you take the top half, and I will take the bottom?"

"Sounds good to me." He began searching for a broom while Matthew took the watering can to be filled up. Such was the usual summer routine. Elizabeth was a single mother, so the three of them did not hate doing chores every once in a while. Drage certainly minded it more than Matthew, however. Matthew usually had to convince Drage to actually do work. Otherwise, Drage could be as lazy as Helen.

Doing most of these chores lasted until about one o'clock when Drage went looking for Matthew. "Hey, Matt, you ready for lunch?" Matthew hungrily agreed. "Good. I was wondering if you would go on ahead and start. I was going to call Aria and tell her what time we should be done so that she could come on over." Matthew brightened at the suggestion and went to the kitchen to make their lunch.

Aria was Drage's girlfriend and had been since the beginning of last school year, Drage's freshman year. Drage had always loved Aria's soft brown hair and her dazzling blue eyes. The three of them had known each other since third grade but had never been good friends until about two years ago, when Drage and she had participated in a statewide fencing tournament.

She was the kind of person that just loved to participate in everything. With her good looks and skills in persuasion, she had been class president and homecoming queen at her middle school. This year, she was going to start freshman year, and she had spent most of her summer planning how to be the most active student in her class. In her free time, she had been hanging out with Drage and Matthew.

"Hello. Newman residence."

"Hey, there!"

"Who is this?" said a voice that sounded beautiful even through the other end of the receiver.

"Your one true love," said Drage with corny romanticism.

"Oh, this is Mrs. Newman, Drage. I'll go get Aria for you,"

she said with such amusement that Drage could not help but
blush.

A few seconds later, Aria came to the phone. "Hey, Drage!"

Drage had still not recovered fully from his blunder. "Oh,
hey, Aria. How are you?"

"I'm pretty good right now. I heard you decided to flirt
with my mom. Yuck!"

Drage stammered without direction until Matthew called
out from the kitchen, "Quit stuttering already!"

Aria chuckled at Matthew's outburst, though it was faint
through the phone. "Hey, I finished my freshman year plan this
morning. Do you want me to come over?"

Drage sighed with relief at the drop of the unpleasant subject. "Yeah. Bring the usual stuff."

"Well, of course. Is your sister going to bug us again?"

"No, she left with her boyfriend to do totally unromantic
and cliché stuff like going out to dinner and a movie. Aren't
you glad that I have a greater sense of romance than that?"

"Oh, yes. It is much more romantic to eat dinner at your
house with the rest of your family and having your mom sit
between you and me. And it is even more romantic that you
never take me *anywhere* anymore," said Aria with a mock scold-
ing tone.

When Drage stammered uncontrollably this time, Matthew
came out from the kitchen and took the phone from Drage.
"Hey, Aria. What time are you coming over?"

"I don't know. When can I come over?"

"Well, we are doing chores right now. Try coming around
three o'clock, okay?"

"Okay, sounds good to me. See ya!"

"Bye!"

When Matthew hung up the phone, Drage was sulking a
couple of feet away with a glare aimed at Matthew, who countered it immediately. "Hey, I was just trying to help you out
there, buddy! All that talking was wearing you out. Maybe you
should come eat? I just heated up some of last night's lefto-
vers."

The prospect of food made Drage forget his embarrassment instantly. The two went to the dining room to eat. Once they finished wolfing down their food, they completed their chores, finishing at two o'clock.

"Hey Matt, we still have time to have some fun before Aria gets here!"

Matthew eyed Drage suspiciously. "You sound like we don't have fun when Aria is here."

"No, I didn't mean it like that. I just meant that we could get some swimming in before she gets here. Race you there!" He ran toward the small pier on the beach. Matthew ran to keep up with him. As they ran, they started removing their shirts and shoes. Matthew beat Drage to the pier and cannon-balled into the small lake that connected to the ocean in the distance by a small stream. Drage followed suit once he reached the pier. Though it was both the middle of the day and the middle of the summer, the lake was relatively cold. Compared to the heat of the sun outside, this was a cool refreshment.

"The water is so nice," said Drage when he surfaced.

Matthew rubbed the salt water out of his eyes. "Yeah, it is. But the wind is a little chilly though."

They stayed in the water for about half an hour and then decided it was just too cold. They got out and walked into the house. They quickly dried off and changed.

"Hey Matt—did you tell Aria to bring the usual stuff? I can't remember."

"Yeah, I did. I guess we'd better get ready, too."

Matthew went into his closet to retrieve a long wooden pole as Drage went into his own closet to get a smaller pole. Matthew eyed his own pole, remembering all the times that their summer afternoons were spent this way. The idea was always to just beat each other brainless. They had always called it freestyle fencing because there were no rules. It was just a duel between a makeshift staff and a makeshift sword. They had been having these spars as far back as they could remember.

The dark tower loomed in the background. Though the sun

was high in the watery sky, the storm clouds turned the atmosdome into an ominous sight. Xarden and Ixion looked at each other unsure of the potential outcome of this venture. Pullatus stood a few feet in front of them. Several yards in front of Pullatus was a figure in a black robe: Randir.

Thunder roared across the blackened field. The mangled trees occasionally burst into flame from the lightning, depositing large amounts of ash onto the already dark soil.

The sounds of wood striking wood rang across the lake. Drage attacked Matthew relentlessly to no avail: Matthew blocked each flurry of attacks. He maneuvered his staff with ease, wielding it in two hands as he twirled it to parry away each attack yet was unable to make any attack of his own. Drage did not waste time on strategy or skill. He spent all his energies on cracking Matthew's defense. To Matthew's surprise, this melee did not tire Drage. This fierce onslaught had been one of Drage's common strategies, so over the years, Matthew's arms had become accustomed to this type of attack.

The attacks did start to overwhelm Matthew though. With Drage's ceaseless blurs, there was never an opportunity to strike back. Matthew leaped backward in the hope that Drage would reveal an opening.

Drage fell for it and charged at Matthew, realizing his error one step too late. Matthew struck his pole straight out to catch Drage's chest, but Drage had anticipated the move a half-second early and spun to avoid it, narrowly missing it while his momentum kept him moving toward Matthew. The attack would have hit Matthew in the head had he not ducked at the right moment.

Matthew rolled to avoid a combo he had not anticipated. He leaped upward and turned to block the next attacks Drage threw at him. He saw a hole in Drage's attacks and swung his pole toward it. It caught Drage off guard and sent him falling backward.

"One last chance, Randir. Obey my will, or you will suffer

for this disobedience," said Pullatus without emotion.

Randir's response came in the form of a large hammer that appeared from seemingly nowhere. Its metal handle was longer than Randir was tall. It had a cylindrical head about a foot long.

Pullatus whispered, "Now, Xarden. Put him in Stasis."

Xarden looked at Pullatus with shock. He had never been asked to fight another one of the Y'mordi, much less put one into Stasis. It was an ancient power that very few still remembered. It held the ability to hold something in both space and time, so that it was invincible and ageless, yet completely unconscious. Nevertheless, he summoned a blue and sparkling ball that hid a shining light. He focused the gaseous orb to charge at Randir, and the blue ball of energy shot toward Randir, who jumped superhumanly away. The jump's peak was easily several yards in the air. In midair, a ball of red fire shot from his free hand toward the dark trio. The three scattered to avoid the hot explosion as it hit the ground where they had just been standing. Randir landed on the ground without so much as flinching from the height from which he had just dropped.

Ixion spoke with a quick, high-pitched voice, "Lord Pullatus, I will take care of him for you." He charged toward Randir, brandishing a handful of small knives. He threw these at Randir once within a few yards of him. Randir swung his hammer to bat the knives away, but this small action gave Ixion the time to pull another set from his sleeve and throw those. A simple sidestep gave Randir the opportunity to dodge.

Ixion growled in frustration. Before he could prepare another volley, Randir held out his open palm and unleashed a beam of liquid fire to envelop Ixion. He leaped just in time to avoid it. Xarden made a move to assist, but Pullatus held him back, saying, "Let Ixion try to prove himself. He may yet surprise us." Xarden looked doubtful of this possibility, though he relished the idea of Ixion's possible failure.

Noticing that neither Xarden nor Pullatus were going to help Ixion, Randir charged at a high speed toward Ixion. Merely feet away from him, Randir leaped toward his body. Xarden barely saw the red glow of Randir's hand in front of Ixion's heart and watched it turn like a doorknob. Randir passed right through Ixion much like a ghost would through a wall. Randir froze a few yards from Ixion. Now, their backs were facing each other, and the world seemed still. Ixion froze with fear of what was going to happen next. Xarden and Pullatus did the same. Xarden and Ixion had seen this strange act done only once. Pullatus had been the only person ever to do it: the Heartlock.

Randir muttered one word, "Suffer." Then, the hand that had performed the Heartlock summoned a blazing fireball. Ixion screamed as his heart exploded into flames. Smoke rushed out of his mouth, ears, nose, and even eyes. He then fell to the ground, a smoldering and spasming body.

Aria had also entered the battle. Instead of poles, however, she preferred to use her small slingshot. Surprisingly, this meager weapon could inflict a lot of damage. She had always picked the sharpest and smallest stones she could find.

While Drage and Matthew batted each other with sticks, Aria would shoot her stone bees into the fray, adding an element of surprise into the mix. Sometimes, Drage or Matthew would attempt batting the stones back at Aria. Normally, the two boys would have qualms with doing even so small a violence to girls, but Aria had made it clear to them on her first inclusion that she was to be treated as if she were any other boy.

Matthew had just dodged another string of attacks when Drage prepared to lunge at him. Another of Aria's stones interrupted this attack, and Drage almost dropped his pole due to the nearly numbing pain in his hand. Matthew took advantage of this weakness and swung his pole to knock Drage's stick away. This move succeeded, and Matthew made a direct attack on Drage now. The pole hit Drage's arm hard, but it gave Drage the time to grab his "sword" and deflect an incoming stone. The stone whizzed past Aria's ear, almost nicking it. Aria took this retaliation as a sign to aim instead for Matthew.

Drage launched a more cautious barrage of attacks at Matthew. Matthew mistook this precision to be due to Drage slowing down or getting tired. Seeing this potential vulnerability, Matthew retaliated with his own attacks. Drage deflected all of these and noticed the height of Matthew's attacks. Thinking these to be too high and dangerous if one attack hit, Drage ducked and kicked Matthew's legs out from under him just as a stone flew over Matthew to where his arm had just been.

Xarden pulled his metal scepter out from his robes and shot another wave of Stasis out at Randir, but the red-haired man evaded it.

He called out to Xarden and Pullatus, "I will not surrender until you decide to obey your true orders."

Pullatus remarked, "I am the only one qualified to interpret our true orders."

All was silent except for the thunder's roar and Ixion's body still sizzling. Randir laughed at the sky. "You are all fools. I hope all of you suffer for it." His black robe exploded into fire as Randir transformed into an enormous dragon. His red wings reached toward the top of the atmosdome and pierced the gray clouds above. The crimson dragon reared its head back to roar and then faced the two cloaked figures below him. Steaming lava erupted from Randir's scaly lips down to the ground. Xarden held his staff high. A blue-tinted orb surrounded Pullatus and Xarden. The lava poured onto the shield but could not penetrate it.

Randir spared the two figures one final glance and then soared upward through the filmy shell of the atmosdome and into the oceanic world above, causing more rain to fall to the ground.

Pullatus turned toward Xarden. "What can you tell me about these seven Guardians of Light?"

The trio had decided that they had enough bruises for the day and went to put away their toy weapons. Drage and Matthew invited Aria to stay for supper, and she replied, "I would love to stay. I should probably call my parents and tell them, though."

At that moment, the phone rang.

Matthew answered it. "Hello?"

"Hey, Matthew, it's Mom. Don't worry about cooking dinner. I'm bringing home pizza for you guys. What kind do you want?"

Matthew called out to Drage and Aria, "Hey, guys, what kind of pizza do you want?"

Drage jumped in excitement. "Pizza! I'll take cheese!"

Aria responded more calmly, "Oh, I'll eat any kind."

Elizabeth had apparently overheard. "Oh, is Aria there? Tell her I said hi. What about Helen?"

"Oh, she said she was eating out with Jamie tonight. Hey, Aria, Mom says hi."

Elizabeth became instantly worried. "Did she tell you where?"

"No, she didn't. Do you want Jamie's cell number? I don't think Helen took her cell."

"Yes, if you can give it to me, that would be great."

Matthew went to go and find the number. He finally found it right beside the telephone. "Ok, here it is…"

"They are on Earth in a small community called Paradise Shores. One problem though, boss: The Emperor over at Apolis has been protecting Paradise Shores from the Darkness. We couldn't even get near the Guardians there. It would take a lot of power to break that barrier."

Pullatus considered this for a moment and then said, "Very well. We shall assemble the other four Y'mordi again then. Randir will have to wait. You go and find Mali and Ixion wherever he is respawning. I will bring the twins there. Listen. We need to just break the barrier for a second and allow some Shadows to enter to do the job for us. We cannot alert the Emperor as to what we are doing. We must remain hidden."

Xarden bowed. "Yes, my Lord."

After they had all eaten, Aria went home again. A couple of

hours later, Helen returned home and would not discuss her evening with anyone, except for her mother in private. While Elizabeth and Helen were having this particular discussion, Elizabeth called out to the boys, "Matthew! Drage! If you want ice cream, you can go ahead and get some!"

Drage took the opportunity immediately, and Matthew followed. After they ate, they both went back to the beach. They stretched themselves out in front of the lake. Had the tide been a little higher they would have been at least partially underwater. The clouds had dissipated and had left a beautiful night sky. The stars twinkled in their suspended positions, yet not one of those stars was able to outshine the spectacular pale moon that boasted its presence in the sky. It reflected its silvery image onto the water's surface.

Drage sighed in thought.

Matthew turned to look at him. "What is it?"

"I don't know. It's just that sometimes I wonder if this is all there will ever be."

"What do you mean?"

"I mean sure, life is good. But it is certainly not much of an adventure. I mean, look at it. You are born. You wait until you can go to school. You might hang out with friends, and you learn what you are going to need for the rest of your life. Then, you just keep switching to bigger schools until you get enough credit to get a job that pays you a lot of money. Then, you might start a family and watch it grow. What adventure is in all of that? There are no real surprises."

Matthew turned back to look at the stars. "Maybe for some people that is adventuresome enough. Maybe it is just the best way of life, and everyone wants that."

"Well, I know that I don't. I want to spend my life traveling. I want to do everything that can be done."

"Ambitious, much?" said Matthew with a grin.

"Shut up!" laughed Drage, elbowing Matthew in the ribs.

"Hey, that hurt!"

"Get over it. I mean, am I wrong for wanting something more in life? It seems that nowadays people are just...so content to let life lead them instead of the other way around."

Matthew nodded in agreement. He knew that in some ways
Drage had a point. "No, you're not wrong. It's just…you have
to know when to separate greed for a better life from gratitude
for your present life, I think."

Drage thought about this. Matthew always seemed to have
the right answer. So, why was Drage still not content with what
Matthew had just said? It seemed logical, and what's more, it
seemed *right*. "Matthew, what are you going to do with your
life?"

"I don't know. You know, I've always liked writing. Maybe
I could do something with that when I'm older."

"Yeah."

Matthew looked at Drage in pity. He knew that Drage was
still thinking about it. He could tell that Drage was not yet satisfied. They had both spent their lives reading so many books,
books about heroes, swords, dragons, treasures, and other fan-
tasies. Matthew had also felt the desire to have a storybook life.
The difference was that he was content with living a normal
life. He was fine with just creating those stories; he did not
have to be a part of them. "You know, it's too cold out here.
I'm going in. You coming?"

Drage stood up and brushed the sand off his back. "Yeah,
right behind you."

Drage sat up in bed, sweat drenching his body. It had been
a nightmare. The light of the moon shone in through his bed-
room window.

Strange sounds came from outside. He strained his ears to
make them out. For some reason, it made him think of wood
against metal. Then, he heard a voice cry out in the night.
Drage ran to the window. Outside, he could see several
strangers. They were all black and almost "misty." Where they
walked, small dark wisps of themselves trailed off for a moment. He saw another figure. Matthew. The men in black all
had *real* swords made of *very real* metal, while Matthew only had
his wooden pole.

Drage ran to his closet and grabbed his Christmas present from last year, a real sword. It was a long sword meant to replicate one from the Middle Ages, more of a dangerous souvenir than anything. He removed the sheath to reveal the bright, thin metal beneath it. His eyes scanned the silver blade for the first time in months. He had never thought he would be using this sword as a weapon. Was this moment the adventure he had been hoping for?

"What's going on?" he whispered under his breath.

He ran downstairs and out the door. He could see that Matthew was struggling in his battle against the dark figures. The taller boy looked tired, not exhausted, just tired. Matthew knew how to hold his own in a fight. However, something about Matthew's appearance made Drage uneasy as he stepped to Matthew's side to aid in the bizarre battle.

The pale moonlight guided the two of them in this struggle. The men in black seemed less and less like men and more like ghosts. Being near them inspired strange fears in Drage's heart. Drage could have sworn that he could see right through them. They swung their swords slowly and deliberately, making it easy to block and deflect. Drage was unsure whether he should strike back with his own sword. Regardless of what these things were, he did not want to kill them.

Slowly, Drage began to feel something strange come over him. As he watched his enemies very attentively, peculiar thoughts came to him. He felt as if the world was just a place of despair and lacked any hope whatsoever. He found himself believing that the journey he had always wanted would always be impossible.

Shaking his head, he removed the thoughts and focused on the fight. He looked back to Matthew who was looking paler in the moonlight.

"Matthew, what's going on here?"

"I don't know. I woke up in the middle of the night and saw them coming. I thought they were robbers or something. I was going to just call the police, but I realized that the police could not get here in time. They were practically at our door by the time I had the phone in my hand. There were just two or three at first, though. I was just going to sneak up behind them and knock them out. But more and more kept coming."

"What are they?"

To this particular question, Matthew had no answer. However, it was obvious that more were still coming. With each attempted slash, Matthew or Drage would knock the blade away. Occasionally, Matthew would make an attack and knock one or two to the ground.

Thunder rang out from the clear sky as lightning incinerated four of the black things instantly. They turned into wisps of smoke and then faded. A figure in a black robe fell from the sky and landed near Drage and Matthew. It was obvious, however, that this figure was a real person and not one of the hazy ghosts. He had a black robe with matching gloves and boots. His face was hooded fully. He wielded a sword similar to a longsword, but it had the length of a very long katana. He used this fearsome blade to obliterate several of the figures instantly. Their mists trailed off into the wind.

He called out to Drage and Matthew, "You have to get out of here! They won't stop until you leave or die!"

Drage and Matthew looked at each other in fright. Matthew responded, "Who are you?"

The figure destroyed several more of the dark figures and called back in a calm voice, "It doesn't matter. What matters is seeing your family again. You will die if you stay here, and so will they. And so will Aria."

That last comment struck a chord with both Matthew and Drage. "What have you done with her?" exclaimed Drage.

"Nothing. These things are Shadows, and they will kill her, unless I can get her out of here, too." The Shadows had diminished to just a few, though more could be seen approaching from a few houses in the distance. The man held out his hand toward the pier. A blue light shot from it and halted at the end of the pier. The light exploded to create what seemed like a hole in the air. Water poured from it instantly into a spiral that surrounded the hole, but the water never touched the pier or even the lake. The water always seemed to disappear as it fell from the hole, giving it the appearance of a vertical whirlpool. "Look over the pier. That is a Gate. Quick! Jump into it!"

Though they were already backing away to the only sign of safety, Matthew called out to the stranger, "How do we know we can trust you?"

"You don't. The only proof I have is that I have saved your lives by destroying those Shadows."

"What about Aria?" said Drage.

"I'll go and help her once you clear out. Hurry!"

Drage and Matthew exchanged glances. Drage gave Matthew a nod, and the two ran toward the pier. Once they reached the end of it, they looked back at their home. Drage said, "You know, portals normally don't take you where you expect them to."

Matthew looked puzzled at him. "What do you mean? You been in one?"

"Oh, no. It's just that they're in a lot of books nowadays. I never meant for this to happen when I was wishing for more adventure, y'know."

"I know. I think we've got to do this, though. If it is the only way to help Aria and the others, we've got to."

"Right." Drage looked at the portal. He closed his eyes and jumped. Then, the world vanished beneath him.

Water

"And the north?" said a voice.

"I couldn't see anything," said another.

Drage became aware of feeling both cold and wet. He opened his eyes and looked up through a shimmering haze to find the bright disc of the sun a lot smaller than usual. He sat up and realized where he was: in water. He grabbed for his throat, sensing death at his door, but his lungs did not hurt. He opened his mouth to find that water was already in his mouth, as if he had been breathing it. The strange thing was that he actually *was* breathing the water. He breathed: in, out, in, out.

"Oh, look, Aria. He's finally awake," said the second voice.

"About time, too," said the first.

Drage turned to face the distorted voices. It was Matthew and Aria. "What's going on?" said Drage, still surprised at his ability to speak at what seemed to be the bottom of the ocean. They were all on a vast, icy plain. The ground itself was not ice, but frozen soil. The cold of it affected them all.

Matthew shrugged. "There is no telling."

Aria looked at Matthew and said, "Matthew, should we start going over everything starting from last night, now that he's awake?"

"Ok, I'll go first since I woke up before Drage last night. It was the middle of the night, and I had just woken up. I went to the window and saw dark figures with swords. There were just a few of them at first. I thought about calling 911, but the figures were already at the house. I just grabbed my staff and went outside. They attacked with their swords, and I fought back."

Drage came in with his own information, "Yeah, and then I came out with my sword and helped a little. Some strange guy came and knocked the crap out of those things."

Aria looked puzzled. "What are you two talking about? You are both talking as if these guys weren't human."

Drage retorted, "That's because I don't think they were. They were sort of… I don't know…misty. And when that guy came and helped us out, each one he killed turned into little black wisps."

Aria looked to Matthew in disbelief, but he nodded grimly. Matthew continued, "He created what looked like a portal, and apparently it was. He told us to go into it if we wanted to save you, ourselves, and our family."

Drage interrupted, "That was after he had called the black things Shadows, too. Isn't that what he said?"

Matthew thought about it. "Yeah, I'm almost sure that that was what he said too. What about you, Aria? What happened with you?"

Aria began, "It started when someone woke me up. It might have been the same guy that you all met too. He was in a black robe, and I couldn't see his face. He told me the two of you were in trouble and that I was too. He said if I didn't come with him, you might die. I definitely didn't trust him, but he was threatening your lives. So, I followed him outside, and he opened up a portal. Then, I came here."

Drage seemed angry for a second then. "So, he tricked all of us into coming here by telling us that we were all going to die?"

Matthew shook his head. "If he had wanted to kill us, he could have done that already. We *are* still alive, after all. There isn't anyone out to kill us here."

Drage considered this idea and then said, "And where exactly is here?" He shivered in the cold of the water.

Matthew looked back at Drage, ready with information. "While you were sleeping, Aria and I looked around. It seems we are on an island. It is very small, but the whole area is cold as if we were farther north than back in Massachusetts."

Aria added, "Obviously, we are underwater, and we can breathe and move almost as fast as we could on land, which is even stranger. Swimming is possible but still a lot harder here, because you sink easier. Matthew checked around the north and west, and I inspected the south and east. It is very small, and cold ocean is everywhere. The whole island is sort of like a glacier suspended in the water. I peeked over the edge, and it doesn't look like it goes down very far."

"And what about food? And some heat?" inquired Drage.

This time, neither Matthew nor Aria had a good answer. Matthew was the first to speak. "Drage, we couldn't find anything here besides the ground itself."

Drage jumped up and exclaimed, "You mean we are just going to freeze to death here?!"

Aria tried to soothe him. "Drage, we can't do anything. Though we are on an island, there is no land anywhere to be seen. There is nothing here."

"We can't just do nothing, though."

"You're right," said Matthew. "We can't do nothing. We don't know what we can do to get back home. The only thing we can try to do is learn more about where we are and focus on staying alive in case someone comes."

Aria leaped at the chance to create some form of organization. "Okay, Drage, you scout around the island and try to find some fish, just anything that might be edible. You can swim fast, so maybe you can go a little bit away from the island first before you get tired, but remember that this water is somehow...less dense. So, it is a *lot* easier to sink. Matthew, you help me look around for some resources. Maybe we can create a fire, somehow. I know Matthew and I have already looked around, but maybe we missed something."

Drage looked perplexed at the idea. "A fire? In the water?"

Aria snapped, "Well, we can breathe in it, so why couldn't there be fire in it, too?" She did not like being called out like that, and her remark was more of a way of saving face. Still, a part of her believed that maybe a fire could be made in this water. If it was less dense, it just might work.

Matthew and Drage shrugged at each other and scattered to their assigned duties.

Drage started to swim out as far as he could. However, the farther out he swam, the colder it seemed to get to him. Out of instinct, he started to hold his breath and then realized the foolishness of the action. Eventually, he found something living in the freezing waters: a school of small fish. They did not look too different from those back at home. They were small but many. Their slick silver bodies evaded every attempt that Drage made to catch them. Eventually, Drage realized something: He had kept his sword when he went through the portal. It was tied to his side, which was confusing in itself. He felt embarrassed for not having noticed its added weight sooner. It was not that heavy, but nor was it that light. Everything felt different underwater here. He drew it and attempted to skewer the fish.

When he returned to the island, he noticed warmth emanating from it. Once his feet touched the icy ground, he realized just how tired his muscles were from the swimming. Aria was right: it was much harder to swim here for some reason. He walked to where he had first woken, assuming that the place would be where everyone would meet. What he saw stunned him: Aria had started a fire. However, the flame was an array of several shades of blue. Drage ran to it embracing the warmth that it gave. In a hurry to warm even his hands, he threw down his temporary skewer with its column of dead fish.

As he sat down in front of the azure flames, he let out a tremendous sigh and turned to Aria. "Hey, where's Matthew?"

Aria walked over to where the sword had been dropped. She picked it up and held it over the fire in an attempt to roast the fish. "He helped me build the fire and then said that he wanted to scout around some more."

Drage looked concerned but then inquired with a smile, "And how exactly did this particular fire happen?"

"Is that a question regarding the color or how we actually got it started?"

Drage hesitated. "Both, I suppose."

"As to the first, we have absolutely no idea why it turned out blue. The water is obviously different here, so maybe it has certain chemicals or properties that allow that to happen. And to the second, it was actually more of an accident. We had explored the whole island with no luck when we came back here to stop and think. When we got here, I stood up and started pacing. It's the only way that I can think straight sometimes. Then, clumsy me decided to slip on the ice. Matthew caught me before I landed flat on my face, though. I actually cut myself on the knee a little. When we saw the dirt my leg had uncovered in the frozen ground, Matthew and I realized that maybe we could just try igniting a piece of frozen soil. So, we used his staff and some of my arrows, and..."

Drage had particular trouble believing this. "So you just rubbed your sticks on the ice and made a fire?"

"Yes, actually. Matthew suggested that maybe the ice just had certain properties in it that increased the friction."

"Ok, fine. Whatever... Wait, you brought your arrows?"

Aria nodded. "Yes. When the stranger told me what danger we were all in, he also told me I might need to bring my arrows. I was really surprised as to how he knew I had those. They were under my bed, actually. Don't ask why I had them. That's a long story."

Drage was still gaping at the surprises he was getting but then shrugged off his confusion. "Do you think we should go and find Matthew? He's probably freezing his butt off by now. I mean, I think I can trust him not to get lost on this island, but I'm still worried about him."

Aria smiled. "Go on and find him. I am going to stay here and eat a couple of these. It looks like you got six, so two for each of us. Sound good, Drage?" She looked up at him fondly. The two were a close couple but not a physical couple by any means. They were really close friends who had admitted their love for each other.

Drage gave her a nod and a wink and ran off into what was becoming night.

"Hey, Matthew. You ready to come eat? I caught us some fish."

Matthew laughed at the idea of Drage being able to catch any kind of fish, but his stomach was eager to believe it anyways. "Really? And you didn't eat it all yet?" he joked.

"Of course not! I haven't eaten any of it yet, actually..." grumbled Drage at the accusation.

Matthew sighed and lowered his head in shame. "I'm sorry, Drage. I didn't mean it like that. I guess the cold is just getting to me. Let's go, huh?" He did feel a little bad for making the joke.

Drage brightened at the idea of warm food. The two walked back to the fire. Drage started, "So, what did you come out here for, anyways?"

"Oh, I just needed some time alone to think about everything. That's all."

"Hmm. Well, in that case, you need to think a little less often," retorted Drage with a wide grin. Matthew shook his head. They went about that way until they reached what they now called the "camp."

Aria held out the skewer to them when they arrived. "Hey, guys! Eat up. The fish actually doesn't taste too bad. Just make sure you don't burn your fingers on the metal, and don't let the sword melt."

Drage snatched at his sword. He stuck it into the fire and waited for the top two fish to blacken just slightly. He then proceeded to consume his crunchy fish before handing the skewer over to Matthew.

For the most part, they ate in silence with each of them in deep thought. Thoughts about the future, the past, and even what to do now. They had always had everything that they ever needed. Now, they had nothing except their clothes, a sword, a staff, a bow, some arrows, and each other's company.

Aria broke the silence after a while, "Drage and Matthew, I know it's a sensitive topic, but since we have nothing better to do…can you tell me a little more about your father? You guys never talk about him."

Drage looked up at her. "Well, I know his name, but that's about it. His name was John. Mom said that my dad and she loved each other very much."

"Then, what happened? Surely if they loved each other so much, they would have stayed together?"

"Mom…never really talks about him. She didn't *act* like he left us or anything. And she wasn't sad as if he had died, either."

Aria turned to Matthew. "Matthew, do you know your birth parents?"

"…No. I don't. Mom never mentioned anything about them, either."

The trio were silent again. They remained that way for almost an hour until Aria was just too tired to think anymore. "Hey, guys, I think I'm going to rest for a while, so just wake me up in an hour or two, okay?"

The boys agreed, though they knew that the first person awake would be Aria. As Aria rested, Matthew started to drift off, too, and he fell asleep. Drage stayed where he was, wide awake. His eyes gazed into the blue flames. Thoughts raced through his head.

Where are we? When are we going home? How are we going to survive? Will I ever see Mom and Helen again? …Maybe tomorrow will be better.

With those final thoughts, he looked up into the new night sky. Stars twinkled down into the water. If there was a moon, Drage could not see it, but the stars were enough for him. New constellations shone down. He smiled up at them.

Tomorrow will definitely be better. We can do this.

Then, he fell asleep.

Randir finally approached the young trio. He had been hiding in the shadows of the night on their small island. He had been watching them for a few hours. He did not notice anything that would set them apart as unique or even skillful in fighting. His first questions were of how these kids could pose a threat to the will of the Y'mordi. However, when the one boy stayed awake and looked at the stars, Randir could feel something inside of the boy burning brightly: the energy of *mysteria*. The boy possessed a small but strong amount of it. If he was trained properly, he could become a threat, though not to Randir due to his recent exile.

There is no way that Pullatus will allow me near this fool Maris. I cannot kill him myself, it seems. Maybe these three might be able to bring him down, though. Xarden mentioned Seven Guardians. These must be three of them. Otherwise, they would not be here. Regardless, the world has accepted them. Once Pullatus is aware of their presence here, he will surely send someone over to kill them. Maybe I need to watch over them. Just maybe they could destroy Maris. They will need to get to Apolis first, though.

Randir reared back his head and gazed at the stars himself. He remembered so many nights when he had sat and watched the magnificent stars in their static positions. Unlike Drage, however, every time Randir looked at these, he saw the memory of his beloved Ophelia.

"Should we wake up Matthew?" said Drage, who had woken up just seconds after Aria.

"No, let him sleep."

"So, what are we doing today?" Drage replied with an air of cheer and hope.

Aria sighed with exhaustion, "I don't know. The only thing we can do is just try to stay alive. I was thinking we might try to find out more about this world and whatever properties it has. I am finding it very interesting."

Drage smiled at her. "Y'know, Aria, even though we are at the bottom of the ocean, you still look very beautiful."

Aria's look of weariness melted and was replaced by a face

of fondness. Her face glowed with both embarrassment and affection. "Thank you, Drage."

"I'm glad that you two are in such a good mood this morning, but would you please give it a rest?" called Matthew. The three of them burst out laughing.

"Pardon me for interrupting your fun, but I am looking for three children from Paradise Shores," broke out a voice.

All three turned to face the stranger. It was a man in a white robe. He looked young and had blonde hair that was in a ponytail. His eyes were a gold color as bright as his own demeanor: his robe and hair gave him the appearance of a human version of the sun itself.

Drage was the first to speak, "Who are you?"

"My name is Mali, and I am an Y'mordi. Are you those whom I seek?"

By this time, Matthew had stood and joined the group. "Yes, we are. Are you here to help us? We want to get home."

Mali's expression did not change. "Good. Perhaps, I can help you then, if only you could help me as well."

Drage grew tenser and growled, "Give us some information first. We've been here for a day already and would like to know what's going on here."

Aria looked at Drage in surprise. She had never seen Drage get angry in all their time together, at least not this frustrated. However, the cloaked man sent shivers up Drage's spine and gave him an immediate sense of distrust.

"Well, you see, this place is not the world you are familiar with. This place is a world called Gevás. While your world Earth is attributed to the Element of Earth, Gevás is attributed to Water. This means the whole world is underwater. However, all worlds can only exist if they possess all of the Elements, so you can expect to find land here, though it is all underwater as this island is. There are even floating domes of air that normally contain islands called atmosdomes. I see that you have also discovered the differences in fire as well."

Matthew started, "Do you know why we are here?"

"Yes, I do, actually. A man named Pullatus tried to send

Shadows across a barrier that protected your small community in order to kill the three of you. However, someone was able to stop him and bring the three of you here."

Aria asked, "And what favor is it that you want from us?"

Mali eyed her. "I want to simply have one of your lives. I have been instructed to kill you all, but as long as one of you is dead, my master will be satisfied. In exchange for just one life, I can grant you passage back to your Paradise Shores."

The reaction was immediate. Aria stepped back in disbelief as Drage raised his sword. Matthew was against any struggle like this one, but he decided to trust Drage's judgment on this matter. He raised his weapon and joined Drage's side.

Mali reared his head back and laughed to the sky. He faced the two boys. "You foolish children. You think you could stand a chance against one of the Y'mordi? Since you refuse to give in to my simple request, I shall end all three of you right now." From beneath his cloak, he brought out a fearsome blade that was nearly two yards long. It was thin and bright but was deadly sharp at the point.

Drage's thoughts raced. He had never fought anybody who actually knew how to use a sword, and the idea more than scared him now. However, he was equally aware of the necessity of it. He overrode his thoughts and charged.

Mali blocked the first attack easily with one movement but then changed his leisurely attitude as he attempted to ward off Drage's notorious flurries. Matthew joined the fray with staff twirling. Mali sidestepped out of the commotion for a moment and used his free hand to pull another katana out of his robes. Matthew knew at once that he would have to change his normal cautious tactics to those of Drage in order to keep Mali's other sword busy. If the man in white had just one free moment, he could easily slice one of them in two. The extra weight of the second blade did not slow Mali in the slightest. Strangely enough though, neither Drage nor Matthew found much resistance from the water.

Aria watched from afar, wondering what she could do to help. When she finally realized that she could do nothing to help either Drage or Matthew, tears welled in her eyes. She could see how Mali was not getting any weaker or slower throughout the battle, while Drage and Matthew were.

A gloved hand fell on her shoulder. She wheeled around to face the stranger. It was another robed man. He was in a black robe very similar to Mali's. His hood hung from the back of his neck and touched the middle of his back. He had strange red hair and burn marks all over his face. Before she could scream, the man clapped a hand over her mouth and used his other hand to signal for her to stay quiet.

"I promise that I am not here to hurt you. I need to help your friends, or else Mali will kill them both. But be quiet."

Aria nodded when she glanced at the skirmish to her left. The man walked over to the battle. He held out his palm to the combatants. A red fire burst from his hand toward a small opening. It blasted Mali backward, setting him on fire. Drage and Matthew turned toward the newcomer with astonishment.

The man spoke calmly yet sternly, "Leave him to me. You three need to get off this island. I brought you a vessel last night. It is only a Helian Transport, but it will get you to where you need to go. Take it north to the kingdom Alerris. I cannot give you much more help than that, however. Hurry!" He summoned fireballs into both of his hands and started hurling them at the now enraged Mali.

He did not have to tell the trio twice. They ran for where he had pointed to indicate the transport's location. It was a strange machine to their eyes. It looked like a regular car from home but without wheels. They climbed in and found the keys in the ignition switch. Its interior was set up almost exactly like a car. Matthew was the only one with a permit, so it was decided that he should drive. They charged full speed into the sea and a few seconds later discovered that the vehicle had a compass built into the dashboard. They altered their course to go north.

The sea was vast and empty to their eyes. They saw not one form of life throughout the great blue. It seemed as if they were the only things that inhabited the entire ocean. They drove for hours in silence before any significant change was noticed. The temperature, read by a strange thermometer they had found in the vehicle, had raised a few degrees outside the vehicle. They started to get hungry, and Drage had volunteered to swim around and catch more fish. Aria sighed with hunger and allowed him to go. Matthew took a second to figure out how to park it. He wanted to make sure that the vehicle would not just sink to the bottom of the sea.

Drage went outside and began his hunt, while Matthew and Aria stayed inside the vehicle.

"Hey, Aria, so what do you think of this world? Excluding our circumstances, that is."

Aria thought for a second and said, "Well, it is a strange place. That's for sure. Still, it fascinates me. Maybe, when we get back home, I can try to research this place. It might exist in some culture's mythology or something. One day, we might be able to come back to it."

"So you don't just hate this place right now?"

"No, why would I? I've only met two people here so far, and I doubt that two people can represent the entire population. This place is kind of interesting."

"Hm, I think I agree with you. I just wish there was better access to food."

"Speaking of food…" started Aria, but a screen that they had identified as a small TV flickered on. It showed a woman in a brown uniform.

"Attention, all transports. There are serpents near the southern coast. I repeat: serpents are near the southern coast. If you are in the vicinity, park your vehicles and turn off all lights."

Aria's thoughts snapped into focus. "Matthew, that's where we're headed though. If Alerris is the closest kingdom, then their southern coast is where we are headed. What are we going to do?"

"We have got to get Drage back in here."

Even as this was being said, there was a pounding on the vehicle doors. Matthew and Aria jumped as they turned to see

Drage. Aria opened the door, and Drage rushed inside.

"Lock the door, Drage," she said.

"We need to shut off all the lights, so keep your eyes open for anything in the water." said Matthew.

Drage interrupted, "Guys—"

Aria snapped at him, "Hush, there's something out there. We need to be looking for it."

"Guys, that's what I am trying to tell you. I found something below the car. It looked like a huge snake, but it didn't move."

Aria and Matthew turned to face him. They said in unison, "Was it asleep or dead?"

Drage's face turned white as he realized what they were hinting at.

The screen came alive again. "Passengers of the Helian Transport, what is your status? You are in a hazardous area."

Aria pressed buttons on the screen until one gave off the static that told her that it was the button for the microphone. She pressed it again and held it down this time. "We're from Earth, and we have a serpent under our vehicle. What do we do?"

The uniformed woman responded, "Make sure all of your lights are off and your transport is parked." She looked to her left and appeared to be talking to somebody. She returned her attention to the trio. "Someone is coming over to help you. He will protect you, but do not engage these creatures. Do you understand?" Her tone was strange, as if this plan was not a normal procedure.

Aria whispered, "Yes. We do."

"Good. Over and out."

With those final words, the screen went black. Drage whispered, "Hey, guys. Look ahead."

Aria and Matthew looked forward and almost had to squint to see the long serpentine body that was coming toward them. As it came further into view, they could see its fierce, slit, red eyes and the fangs that extended from its jaws, each the size of one of the teenagers. Two more beasts joined the other. It was

Matthew who noticed there was one already behind them.

As the four serpents closed in on them, the teenagers' hearts raced faster and faster. The first sea serpent opened its mouth as if to devour the entire vehicle. "Are you Dragenopn Helius, Matthew Helius, and Aria Newman?"

The three looked at each other in surprise and fear. Matthew called out, "Yes, we are. What do you want with us, and how do you know our names?"

The two serpents behind the first chuckled in a raspy yet booming voice. The first smiled. "One of the great Lords of the Shadows has demanded your deaths. We were hired for the job."

The sea serpent behind them struck the vehicle. Its fangs tore through the metal from both the roof and the floor. Aria, Matthew, and Drage scrambled in their escape. The sea serpent took another huge bite and swallowed the entire vehicle.

The trio swam together to face the beasts. Matthew and Drage held their weapons ready to block any attacks, though they were fully aware of the futility against such humongous monsters.

They became aware of a fifth creature. He was different from the others. Instead of being long and skinny, he was shorter and had depth and real weight. His scales were a bright gold, and the creature had muscular arms and legs armed with five sharp claws at the end of each of these.

Before they could react to their impending doom, the newcomer opened his mouth wide, revealing several rows of sharp teeth. The golden beast bit down on the nearest serpent and broke it in half with his jaws. Blood poured from the snakelike corpse as he flung it into the sea. His mouth was crimson with the stain of the creature's life still dripping from his mouth. He aimed his razor claws at the next one. Hissing, the second serpent attempted to dodge, but still the talons raked its belly wide open and rendered its insides into the open sea.

The third snake tried to make an escape, but a humongous red fireball shot out from the gold monster's maw and roasted the serpent before it could go any further. Its black corpse fell into the dark abyss of the sea below.

The last sea serpent, seeing the pointlessness of trying to escape, attempted an attack on the trio. It had come within a few yards of them with its enormous fangs flashing when the golden creature dove down into it unleashing a torrent of blood as its back snapped from the weight and speed of the murdering fury of gold. The blood had clouded around the trio and made them feel noxious instantly.

Aria was the first to fade. She passed out and began to fall fast. Matthew dove to grab her but only found himself deeper in the filth and joined her in unconsciousness.

Overwhelmed by everything, Drage's eyes darted around, searching for some way out, while holding his breath against the red cloud and trying to stay up in the water. A patch cleared to reveal the monster that had attacked the serpents. He realized then that the creature was not like the sea serpents at all: it was a golden dragon.

Steam poured from its mouth and almost covered the enchanting and mysterious blue eyes. Its mouth and claws were tainted with the blood of the serpents, and its scales shone with their own beautiful light from the reflection of the sun.

Of all of these unique qualities, Drage noticed its eyes the most. They were almost human. Intelligence and wisdom emanated from those blue sapphires.

Water jetted from the dragon's nostrils as it breathed out into the sea.

This disturbance shifted the cloud tighter around Drage. He could not hold his breath any longer, and the dark blood entered his lungs. Vomit rose from his stomach, but before it could leave his mouth, his consciousness vanished. The last thing he saw was that pair of blue eyes staring deeply at him—into him.

The Emperor of Darkness

The cold woke him. It was his first observation about his surroundings. He could feel the cold icicles of frost piercing his skin in many places. He could not help but wonder if he had ever experienced such a cold before. His eyes looked upward through the shimmering water to glance upon a pale moon that hovered far above the ocean's unreachable surface.

A flood of memories surged through his mind all at once, and he struggled to get to his feet only to fall back down onto the hard ground. The pain in his head shot through his body much like a nail being driven into a board. He grasped his head with one freezing hand. The water seemed to swirl before him.

A voice growled from behind him, "You should not have tried to get up so quickly, boy."

Drage turned his head to face the source of the voice. The speaker was tall and skinny. He was gold-colored and glittering in the moonlight, but Drage's eyes blurred everything into colorful clouds.

"Who are you?" Drage managed, straining to keep his articulation clear.

He snorted. "My name is Rexam Draconis. I am the Guardian of the Emperor of Light and also his Loyal Servant. I have been instructed to deliver the three of you to his sanctuary," rumbled the deep voice.

Drage's vision started to clear, and he noticed the speaker was indeed golden and was armored with a multitude of immaculate scales. The body was long and wormlike. The head of the creature reminded Drage of a camel with serpentine whiskers. Even from his broken memory, Drage could have sworn that this reptile was a lot larger when they had been attacked. Then, it had not been wearing the white robe that it wore now. He became aware that the beast had a long tail that curled around his clawed feet and twitched with impatience.

"Excuse me, but what are you?" Drage stammered in full awe.

The creature smiled in amusement. "I am a Dragon, a Golden Dragon, to be precise. However, contrary to your popular Earthan belief, I will not devour the first human I happen to find. I am as intelligent as you, if not more so."

Drage recovered from his shock. "And what about Matthew and Aria? Where are they?" Drage took a glance around and saw only ocean around them along with a multitude of icy hills and a few small ridges.

"They will come back soon enough. They wanted to walk around. I think they were a little uncomfortable talking to a Dragon." He smirked. "This is not going to be an easy journey."

Drage eyed the Dragon. "What?"

"Sit down," growled Draconis. He pointed one clawed hand at the ground between them and muttered one word, "*Farus.*" The small spot of icy rock to which he had pointed combusted into a bright, blue flame. Heat emitted from it in a series of waves. Drage crumpled in front of the fire in order to obtain as much warmth as possible. He even went as far as to hold his hands mere inches from the tips of the flame. Draconis observed Drage.

After a few minutes had passed, Matthew and Aria appeared at the top of a hill empty-handed. When they saw that Drage was conscious, they ran faster to approach the fire.

Aria started, "Drage! Are you alright?"

Drage smiled. "Of course, I'm alright! Why wouldn't I be?"

Aria went to his side and punched him in the arm. "Well then, why didn't you get up a little sooner?"

"Ow! That hurt! I was just tired, that's all."

Matthew laughed.

Aria and Matthew sat down to enjoy the fire and then regarded Draconis. The Golden Dragon began, "Before any of you start asking me questions, I am going to explain as much as I can to you in as little time as possible. First, you need to know that there is more than one world. As a matter of fact, there are five. They do exist in the same universe, but the essences of each world reside in different realms. For example, Earth exists mainly in the Earth Realm, whereas Gevás is mostly in the Water Realm.

"Second, you need to know why you can breathe here. All of the worlds have a spirit or a soul inhabiting them. Therefore, when a Gate is opened to connect two worlds, the world chooses to allow people to enter and then makes any physical changes to them that are necessary to survive. Your bodies are presently different from when you were on Earth. Gevás has given you many abilities, chiefly the ability to swim better and breathe underwater."

Drage interrupted here, "So you mean something like all of the worlds are alive or something?"

"In a sense, yes. That does not mean that it is as mortal as you or I, and nor does it imply countless other possible implications. It merely means that the world thinks and feels and has dominion over what occurs between itself and other worlds.

"I need to give you a brief history of Gevás, so try to pay attention. About a thousand years ago, this world was first inhabited by two men from Earth named Lux and Dagan. Lux loved this world passionately and began moving people from Earth to Gevás. He set himself up as the ruler of the people. Dagan saw what Lux did and tried to claim some of the world for himself. When Lux refused to surrender what he had constructed, Dagan began gathering forces from Earth and battling Lux in what are now called the Obsidian Wars. It was horrible and caused thousands of deaths. By the end though, the final battle caused both Lux and Dagan to disappear from the face of the planet. However, they both left powerful legacies. This place is a world of both advanced technology and powerful enchantment.

"Alright, so I've given you an extremely brief summary of the world in about one or two minutes. Now it's your turn. Tell me exactly what has happened since you arrived on this world."

Matthew told the whole story to Draconis. He served as a good listener until Matthew mentioned Mali. At this point, Draconis growled deeply and loudly. Aria moved backward without thinking. She then felt ashamed of herself afterward. As Matthew concluded their tale, Draconis glared into the azure flames. "The Y'mordi, or the Lords of the Shadows as they are called now, were once Servants of the Darkness and Servants of Dagan. They aided him in the times of the Obsidian Wars as assassins and generals."

Aria looked puzzled. "But I thought you said that the Obsidian Wars were fought a thousand years ago?"

Draconis lowered his snout. "Yes. Dagan gave the Y'mordi immense powers. They could crush entire cities with a single blow. They murdered innocent people without so much as lifting a finger. Among their powers, they were blessed with a form of immortality. Age and sickness has no effect on them. In battle, they can be killed only to be resurrected moments later in the Dark Realm of the world. Dagan was well-known for his use of a power known as Darkness. Lux, being the opposite, used the Light. Here, there is a powerful force called *mysteria*. It is merely the essence of your heart. It connects emotions with the physical world and allows you to manipulate the world around you. The Y'mordi were each adept at using these powers and managed to 'disappear' after the Wars. I have suspected for a while that they still exist, though I have not known how extensive their activity was. They are on the move again.

We must hurry."

Drage responded, "Hurry and do what?"

"We must reach the Emperor. Only he can help you now."

As Draconis rose to begin their journey, Matthew and Aria rose to follow his lead, but Drage stayed back. Draconis turned on Drage. "Come, now! We have to hurry!"

"How do we know that we can trust you?"

Silence took hold. Aria showed a look of anger and shame simultaneously. She knew that Drage was being stubborn, yet she also acknowledged she had been placing her trust a little blindly. Matthew stared at Drage, not revealing any emotion at all.

"You don't. I saved your life, and I can only guide you with a promise of safety, but even that will be plagued by the Y'mordi trying to halt our progress. Besides, what you *want* to do is irrelevant to me," said Draconis with a grin. "I have my orders, and I will not disobey them, boy. You are coming one way or the other."

Drage looked to his two friends in hope of maybe some rebellion, but they all looked complacent with their present situation. Drage sighed and looked up at the mighty golden creature. "Fine, we will come."

Draconis smiled. "Good. I would not expect anything less from someone like you. Now, before we go, you are going to need preparations." From his robe, he drew three small bags. "There is food in here. Make it last." He handed these to each of them. "Also, you will all need some weapons in case we do get separated. Aria, what are your skills? Have you ever handled any type of weapon before?"

Aria shuffled her feet. "I am good with a slingshot."

Draconis smiled. "Good. You must have very impressive aim then. Do you think that you could manage a bow and arrows pack?" Aria nodded. Draconis handed her a pack also under his robes. Then, he turned to Matthew. "And you? What can you do?"

Matthew looked at him without expression. "I can wield a quarterstaff if you have one."

"I do. It is a cheap one, mind you, but a sufficient one nevertheless." He handed Matthew a staff.

Drage whispered to Matthew, "What all does he have in that robe? A whole store?"

Draconis heard this comment and grumbled at him, "And you, troublemaker? What weapon can you wield?"

"All I need is a simple sword."

A shimmer swelled in Draconis's large, blue eyes. "Ah, this choice comes as no surprise to me. Here is a sword." It was indeed a simple sword with a small iron hilt and hand guard with a strong blade. Drage did not find it too heavy and did not find it hard to use. Rather, it flowed through the water and felt little resistance.

Drage replied, "Thank you."

Draconis nodded his head once. "Let's go."

They began their journey but did not find many interesting things at first. The whole of this world was so icy and cold. After just half an hour, Drage took a bite of the foreign food in the bag. It seemed like a strange species of fish, but it tasted much blander. The landscape was so barren to him and uninteresting. It seemed very unusual to him that there would be a need for an Emperor in so desolate a place. Every passing hour only provided more of the same landscape.

The pit of the ocean always stayed to his right. They were traversing the sandless shore. He looked at each of his companions and wondered what was going through their minds. He lowered his head in thought.

Matthew could not believe the eerie, white beauty of this frozen desert. There was not a living thing anywhere to be found. There were no breathtaking landscapes. Ice was the only existence. Yet, he found this place to be full of amazement and natural wonder. He had always loved the water, but existing and breathing at its depths were amazing feelings altogether. However, the cold was far too unbearable. Even though most of his life had been in a cold climate, he had never really become accustomed to it. He wondered how people could actually live here in this wasteland of ice.

Aria herself did not mind the cold though. She could re-member several times when she had been colder than this. In elementary school, she had been in several of the state clubs such as mountain climbing and kayaking. Though most of the organizations found her to be too young, she had insisted on her participation and had made her parents support her. When the organizations saw her quick adaptability, they decided to let her participate. Even now, she could remember all of those ear-ly mornings of climbing several of the mountains in the south. She closed her eyes in reminiscence of that day. She had finally reached the peak of Clingmans Dome, and the clouds had formed a misty lake below her and had reached out toward the horizon. The sun had been reflected on the lake's thin surface. Though she had worn very heavy mountain gear, the cold had still nipped at her skin.

As she walked on, she opened her eyes, and the reality felt warmer than the memory did. She looked at Matthew for a moment as if she was about to say something, but she decided to savor the silence of the journey instead. She had always seen Matthew as an older brother. He had always given her the best advice when she needed it. Of course, Drage was the one she loved, but Matthew was in some ways a better comfort. She glanced at Drage and remembered when they had first talked to each other.

It had been at a tournament her fencing club had held. As it turned out, Drage had been going to the same school, but the two had never spoken to each other. The fencing club was the only club Drage had ever really participated in, though he had been in a different one on the other side of the city. So, the two had met with an épée at each other's throat. It was the first time Aria had been beaten at anything. Drage had proven to be too quick for her with a blade. After the tournament, Aria had sought him out, and the two had begun talking.

Two months later, Drage had found the courage to ask her out. Of course, he could not ask her out through traditional means. He was always gutsier than that. He had asked her out as he was getting his "diploma" for graduating middle school.

She could remember the event perfectly. He had walked up to the podium, grabbed the diploma, shook someone's hand, and said into the microphone, "Hey, guys, I have a poem I'd like to read to you as my words of farewell." Since this interruption had not been planned, many of the teachers had looked at each other with a look of "This isn't supposed to happen!" He went on regardless:

"Life can be short yet happy, or long yet sad
We've felt its ups and its downs throughout the years,
Yet even now, I cannot help but look back at it all and say,
'Wow, we're so alike: We had the same joy and tears.'

There is one regret I still have before leaving:
I did not love her because of her amazing body,
Or her amazing eyes, it was her amazing smile;
Aria Newman, will you go out with me?"

She had thought it was easily one of the corniest things he had ever done, but it was also the sweetest. She stood, looked him in the eyes, and said, "Sure, where are we going for our first date?" He had put her on the spot, and she had every intention of pushing the attention back onto him. He responded just as quickly, "Ok, do you want to go to a movie tonight?" The widest grin formed on his face.

He was always a jokester. She kept her eyes fixed on him and replied, "Yeah, what time?"

She could see the laughter trying to escape him then, because his smile only got larger. "Shall I pick you up at eight?"

She nodded once. "Yeah, see you then."

Content with the situation, Drage shook the man's hand again and walked back to his seat unable to remove his smile.

It was the first time she had said "yes" to any guy.

Now, however, Drage looked pretty sullen. As their feet marched on through the ice, he seemed to be looking inward far too much. It was not like Drage to be this quiet. To break the silence, she said to Draconis, "Hey Draconis, so can you tell us more about this world? I mean, is it the same size as Earth, or is this ice all there is?"

Drage and Matthew both looked at her, amazed at her curiosity in these circumstances. Draconis responded with a more indifferent tone. "Well, in Gevás, there are four continents that are all labeled based on their location. So, we have the Northern, Western, Eastern, and Southern Continents. Each Continent has a number of countries or kingdoms with their own capitals and cultures. Right now, we are in the Southern Continent in a country called Varyx. We are nearing its capital, Terin. Obviously, the Southern Continent is mostly a cold, arctic wasteland."

Aria replied, "So where are we going ultimately?"

"We are going to the capital of the kingdom Helio. It is called Apolis. The Palace of Light exists in its center. Once we pass Terin, we will have about one or two days before we reach Helio. Then, it will take about three or four days to reach Apolis." He looked back at the young trio. "I would typically use a Gate to get us there, but the Emperor has extended the barrier around Apolis until the Y'mordi threat lessens. We couldn't even get close right now." He glanced up at the sky. "Let's take a break for a minute. We'll reach Terin in a little over half a day."

As they stopped to sit down, Matthew expressed his curiosity. "Draconis, when you made the fire earlier, that was the force you called *mysteria*, right?"

Draconis nodded. "Yes, Matthew. Why do you ask?"

Aria responded, "How does it work, exactly? I mean, it doesn't exist on Earth, so how does it happen here?"

Draconis looked at her. "No, it is quite possible on Earth."

For the first time in a while, Drage spoke, "No, it doesn't. I would think we would know if people had learned how to spontaneously start fires or breathe underwater for an unlimited amount of time."

Draconis responded, "That is because it is against the law to reveal the presence of *mysteria* on Earth. As a matter of fact, there is a council in charge of the use of *mysteria* there. They are known as the Ring of Elders."

Matthew replied, "The Ring of Elders?"

"Yes, they are made up of some of the greatest mages on Earth."

Aria could not hold her curiosity any longer. "So, how could one actually use *mysteria*?"

Drage looked at her with a face contorted with anger and surprise. Before he could say anything, Draconis responded, "There are different ways of using *mysteria*. Some items like scepters or orbs exist to help fuel the spells. Also, words act as a focus for *mysteria*. Every Element depends on the mage to feel certain emotions. Advanced mages do not need any of these focuses, however." He pointed one claw at the ground and said, "*Farus*." A blue fire lit up the icy ground.

The trio were amazed at the skill. Aria asked, "And what emotion does Fire need?"

"Fire can require anger, love, loneliness, greed, hate, and almost any passionate emotion. Therefore, Fire is one of the easiest to use but the hardest to control. There are four other core Elements: Water, Wind, Earth, and Nature. They each have their own attributes and abilities."

Draconis walked around to each of the teenagers and said, "*Lami*." Instantly, the three lost all exhaustion, hunger, and thirst. "That was a spell of restoration. It is of the Nature Element."

Drage looked down in thought and then replied, "When that…Y'mordi attacked us, it used light. Is that an Element of *mysteria*?"

"Yes, but not the same kind. There are the five core Elements, but other higher-level Elements exist and so do sublevels. Each of the core Elements has four Forms to classify their uses. For example, when I make a fire to warm us up, that is *one* Form of Fire called Flame. There are also Heat, Lightning, and Lava. There are two socially approved higher Elements: Light and Darkness. Several mages have claimed to have discovered new Elements, but no others have been recognized by the Prophets." When Draconis saw the confused looks on their faces, he commented, "Oh, each Element has what is called a Prophet associated with it. A Prophet is what the greatest specialist in that Element is called. I believe that three of the Prophets are in the Emperor's Council, too."

"What about the higher Elements? Do they have Prophets too?" Aria inquired.

"Yes, they do. Also, if there are Elements that are neither known nor accepted, in theory, they too could have Prophets. It depends on who is the greatest mage in that Element. That is not to say, however, that any of the Prophets are extremely— wait..." Draconis sniffed the air.

Matthew asked, "What is it?"

Draconis pulled a large sword from beneath his robe. It had a golden blade and was easily as long as he was yet half as wide. The hilt was elaborately decorated with the crest of the sun and bore two long gold tassels at the pommel. "The Y'mordi have found us."

He took a fighting stance and spoke to the three as quickly as he could. "Listen, keep the ocean to your right, and you will reach Terin. I shall meet you there. Do not trust anyone there besides each other. The Y'mordi will be looking for you even there. Now, go!"

The watery sky grew ominous as black warheads of clouds swarmed the blue. The light dimmed as the clouds spread. Drage, Matthew, and Aria began to run, but a flash of light exploded a few yards in front of them, and with it came one of the Y'mordi. "I have been searching for the three of you for some time now. Now, I shall finish what I started. This time, however, I will not give you a choice," said Mali as he pulled back his hood. His blonde hair seemed eerie in the twilight. His golden eyes glowed with their own intensity. The most menacing aspect of him was the katana that flashed into his hand. Yet, equally menacing was the one that appeared in his other hand.

Drage attacked, swinging in small arcs with his new blade. Matthew was next to join with his whirling staff, while Aria prepared an arrow. Mali countered each attack and sought an opening. The whole battle was like a fast dance where the four participants were trying desperately to keep up with each other. Drage kept Mali on defense with his bombardment of slashes. Matthew attempted to protect Drage from the few counterattacks that Mali made and was able to knock a threatening point away from the both of them on multiple occasions. Aria's arrows always flew true, but Mali had almost catlike reflexes that enabled him to dodge each deadly bolt. Upon preparing another arrow, Aria looked back to where Draconis was.

The Dragon was engaged in battle with another man in black. This one had a medium-sized sword. There was nothing particularly interesting about him. In comparison to Draconis who looked much larger all of a sudden, the man was very small. However, the man looked crazed. His black hair flew wildly against the soft current. While this strange man would attempt to land a combo of attacks against Draconis, the Dragon would manipulate his position around the sword instead of using it directly.

The next thing she knew was that her feet were no longer touching the ground. An explosion of Light had lifted her several feet high, and she landed hard on the ice. She heard Drage call out her name, but her muscles were already sore. Then, Matthew was flung near her. In pain, she tried to sit up and observe what was going on around her. Mali now had the upper hand against Drage. She could see Drage struggling to match Mali's speed. Mali's gloved hands were so swift in wielding his deadly katanas. She could make out the fine lines in the leather gloves that probably constituted some design or another. Then, an idea hit her. She focused on both of the gloves and how much she hated this man for threatening her boyfriend. Dizziness came with the concentration. *"Farus."*

The Y'mordi's hands became alight with bright blue flames causing him to drop both katanas. As Drage tried to make a stab during this moment of opportunity, Mali shot a ball of white Light from his flaming hands at Drage and blasted him several feet high into the water.

Aria watched as a large hole appeared in the sea near Mali and Drage, and its consistency was that of red fire and molten lava. Another man in black stepped out of it and shot a red fireball from his open palms toward Mali. The ball exploded on impact, and Mali was now a charred crisp on the ground.

The man Draconis had been fighting became aware of this occurrence and disengaged from their battle. Though he was not screaming, his voice was loud enough for every one of them to hear, "Heh, this is not the end. All of you, bow to me. I am Maris, the new Emperor of Darkness!"

Drage, Matthew, and Aria could not believe what happened next. A thin tornado surrounded the man called Maris and grew to reach the layer of clouds. Draconis was sucked into it. Then, the whirlwind of death began its movement toward them. They ran fast and noticed that their rescuer, the wielder of flame, had disappeared. As the force of the wind began to increase, they could feel themselves being pulled into it. The wielder of flame returned and grabbed Drage and Matthew. The flaming hole reappeared right before they fell into it. It closed behind them, but they quickly noticed that the hole had transported them to about half a mile away from the tornado. Their location was close enough for them to see Aria float into the vortex.

Drage called out, "Aria!" However, the tornado began ascending into the clouds. After a few seconds, even the clouds were gone as if nothing had ever happened there. Even the wielder of flame had vanished again. It was just Drage and Matthew standing on an icy plane.

Stumbling and Salt

A s they walked, the sun descended into the aquatic horizon. Their bodies were adapting to the coldness of the
water. For a little over a day, they had been traveling
through the frozen country, always keeping the ocean to their
right and not saying a word to each other.

In Drage's mind, any hope of returning to Paradise Shores
was fading. They were too far away from home and might never see it again. They had lost their only guide to this world.
More importantly, they had lost Aria. This world seemed cruel-
er and more dismal with each passing hour. Even his usually
lively pace had slackened since they had been separated from
Aria and Draconis. He did not even look to Matthew for sol-
ace. He stayed deep in thought and wondered what would happen to Matthew and himself.

A part of him enjoyed this adventure, but he had never expected to lose Aria in the process. He let his feet propel him
forward, but it was a forced and deliberate motion. His mind
focused on what they were going to do next.

Matthew, on the other hand, tried to keep his emotions in a

more optimistic state. He, too, wanted Draconis and Aria back, but he was not ready to give up all hope yet. He tried to keep his head high and look toward the future, but it was a difficult task given their circumstances. He tried to imagine what was going through Drage's mind and simply could not. He had never had a true love, a girlfriend, or even a crush. In essence, he was a true romantic and was waiting for that perfect woman in his life. He had also never felt the true love of family. Though he had been a part of one, he was not blood-related and had never felt that he fully belonged. Despite his brotherly connection with Drage, he had never been fully comfortable with the other members of the family.

As if Drage could read Matthew's thoughts, he said, "Hey Matthew, what do you think Mom and Helen are doing right now?"

Matthew saw his chance to cheer Drage up from his dark stupor. "Well, I'm sure that Helen has taken over our rooms and probably has a new boyfriend living in each of them. Mom is probably wondering where we are and why the chores haven't been done."

Drage laughed at this simple joke despite his loss of hope. "I was being serious, you dope!"

Matthew smiled at him. "Oh, I know." He laughed, too. It had been a while since they had laughed.

Drage's face became serious but not depressed. "Do you think we will ever see them again?"

"Yeah, of course we will. I never pictured you to be the one that wanted to go home so badly. You're finally having that adventure you've been wanting, and all you can do is mope?"

Drage looked down in thought. "Yeah, I guess you're right, huh? Well, I suppose all I can do is keep going and not lose hope, right?"

"That's right."

Drage smiled. "Okay, I will try. What have I got to lose? We're on an adventure. Let's make the most of it. From now on, no more moping from me!"

Matthew nodded. "Good. You wanna stop for a while? Or

do you think we can make it a little farther?"

"Let's keep going! When we can't see the ocean at all, we'll know it's too dark."

Matthew had sometimes wondered if Drage had some strange mental condition, because he had always been able to switch between emotions so easily. Matthew had always been curious as to how Drage could perform such a trick.

They walked for about an hour longer until they saw lights out in the distance. It was a small town. Several of the buildings were tall, but the town itself was not wide. Though it was dark now, they saw no reason not to rest in a town instead of on the hard ice. As they came closer to the lights, they could make out the towering buildings against the last remnants of the fading dusk. The mini-skyscrapers had several windows and were made of a silver metal that reflected the twilight's orange glow. It seemed to be a futuristic city. It did not have the strange robot cars that Drage imagined. Nor did it have the alien creatures he pictured as they entered the city. It was a simple place that just used shiny materials in its architecture.

"Wow, the buildings are so tall. How did we not see these earlier?" Matthew exclaimed.

Drage shrugged his shoulders. "I'll bet you it looks amazing when the sun is higher though. Let's look around for a place to stay for the night." They walked over to the nearest building and knocked on the front door. The person who answered was a rather large man in a white shirt that was tight on his skin and leathery khaki pants. His hair was gray and thinning, while his face displayed several scars and his few remaining teeth.

"What do you want?" he grumbled.

Matthew spoke up, "We are just looking for a place to stay for the night."

"We have no more vacancies! Go somewhere else!" With that, the man slammed the door in their faces.

At each building, they gained about the same result. The only lights remaining came from the green neon lights at the front doors of most of the buildings. The sun was gone. There was not a single person roaming the streets. After they had traversed nearly half of the lifeless town, they found a person who was a little kinder.

"Yeah, we have a couple o' extra rooms and food for ya, if ya have any salt on ya."

Matthew and Drage looked at each other. Matthew said to the man in confusion, "Salt, sir?"

"Well, yeah, what else would I want? Doncha know what salt is?" He laughed with his hand over his gut.

Matthew apologized to the man, "Sorry, sir, we don't have any." Matthew prepared to leave in surrender at the same time that Drage realized that salt was probably the main currency here. However, the man stopped them before they could leave.

"Now, wait jus' a minute. I'm a reason'ble fella, so if ya can trade me somethin', that's fine too."

Drage brightened at this opportunity and with reluctance offered his sword. The man's eyes shone greedily at the simple offering. "If ya give me that, I'll give ya one of the rooms for three days and food, too. Deal?"

"Deal!" the two said in unison.

They settled into their room. It was a small place with stone walls and a floor that resembled wood. They lay on a small yet very soft bed that night. They did not say anything to each other before drifting off to sleep. They were too exhausted to even speak. It was the first time that they had had any real sleep on a real bed in days.

The meal had not been superb, but it had been warm. The old innkeeper had given them a plate of grilled fish. However, they were a different type of fish than Drage and Matthew had been used to eating. The fish almost had a sour taste.

In contrast to the cold water outside, the whole building had a heater that warmed the water inside. It was similar to living in a hot tub. Drage and Matthew particularly enjoyed this new experience of a Gevatian hotel. They slept well and without dreams.

When they awoke a little past noon, they felt restored. Matthew spoke to Drage, "So, you ready to go look for Draconis and Aria?"

Drage got up and yawned, "Y'know, we have no change of clothes, no toothbrush, no anything. I feel like a grub."

Matthew sighed, "Yeah, me too. Maybe we can sell my staff today or something, and we can get some 'salt' to buy some things with." He did not particularly enjoy this idea of having to learn a completely new currency concept, but he hoped it would work out.

"Alright, ready when you are."

They locked their room, went outside, and gaped at the bizarreness of the town. A light mist covered the streets. However, even above the layers of mist, they could just barely make out the towering heights of the buildings. It felt like being in Boston again. The only difference was that there was a significant lack of people and cars. The two of them were almost completely alone on the road. They could see only three or four others, and they were all robed in black robes.

They read the nearest sign. It read, "Terin General." The building looked like a convenience store, but Drage and Matthew did not think too much of it because of their lack of salt.

Matthew exclaimed, "We are in Terin! We are going the right way then. Maybe Aria and Draconis are here already."

Drage nodded in agreement. "I kind of figured it would be a more populated city though."

Drage and Matthew began looking for a larger store or a pub or just somewhere where there would be more people. The two hoped that someone had seen Draconis or Aria around here. They walked over to larger business that had a few people standing outside.

They entered the building and noticed it was an archive, similar to a library. There were several shelves of mechanical volumes. They could tell the pages were made of thin sheets of metal. Some people sat in chairs reading the rusty pages of old books. Drage approached the nearest person. "Excuse me, have you seen a Dragon around here?"

The person did not look up and instead moved to another

seat on the other side of the library. Drage frowned at this rudeness. "Wow, everyone is so polite around here."

Matthew said, "Well, let me try." He went to another seated reader. "Hey, I need some help. I'm looking for a Golden Dragon. Have you seen him?"

The person looked up at him, but the hood masked the upper part of his face. The lower part was pale and thin. His hand shot out and grabbed Matthew's arm. He growled, "Come with me, now." He stood up and pulled Matthew with him. Drage was about to do something, but then he saw an abnormally large knife in the man's hand was pointed at him. The three of them went outside and into a side alley.

The man growled again, "Now, where is the girl?"

Drage spoke, "Girl?" Then, realization dawned on him. "You mean Aria? Where is she?" he exclaimed.

The man held up a finger, signaling Drage to be quieter. "Tell me, or I'll break your friend's arm." To emphasize his point, he yanked Matthew's arm behind his back, but Matthew did not make a sound. Matthew looked at Drage and mouthed the word, "Practice?" He winked to emphasize *his* point. Drage made a subtle nod. The man saw Drage's gesture and said, "What? What are you whispering about?" When he looked at Matthew, Drage lunged for the hand with the dagger and managed to grab his wrist at the same time that he punched the man in the face. The force was enough to loosen the man's hold on Matthew, and Matthew wheeled around and was able to trip the man so that he fell to the ground.

A voice called out from the entrance of the alleyway. "Leave the boys alone. Do not touch them!" It was another man in black.

Drage and Matthew prepared to fight again. This new man held up one large claw and said one word, "*Lune.*" A strong ripple formed and blasted toward them, but nothing happened. They turned around and noticed that the original attacker was completely immobile. The strange ripple had arrested his entire movement. They turned back to the new stranger. "I've been looking for you two, but I am glad you made it here alright."

Another robed figure joined his side, though this one was considerably smaller. The figure pulled back her hood and ran to Drage. "Drage, you're alive!" She almost tackled him in her warm embrace.

Matthew and Drage both realized what had happened then. Matthew called out, "Draconis! Aria! You guys made it!"

Draconis signaled them to be quiet. "There might be more of the Y'mordi around. We do not have the time to be discovered right now. We need to gather a couple of cars."

Drage smiled in surprise. "Wait, you guys have cars, too?"

Draconis was already moving, and the others struggled to keep up with him. He stopped and turned back to the alley. "I almost forgot. *Farus.*" The Y'mordi's body exploded into flames. Aria gasped.

"Did you have to do that?" she said.

Draconis turned back and continued his fast walk. "Yes, but I told you they do not die that easily. Well, technically, they do die, but it will take him several hours to be reborn in the Dark Realm. He was actually how I found you, Drage and Matthew. I could sense that smell of Darkness that only the Y'mordi are evil enough to possess."

They finally stopped at what looked like a tall garage. It had several of the cars inside. They were much smaller than most Earth vehicles and almost comical. They were monotonous with their color selection of black and sable. However, Draconis approved of them. "Do any of you know how to drive?"

Drage volunteered. "I can! Is there a difference between these cars and the cars on Earth?" In truth, Drage had practiced driving as much as Matthew had. He simply did not have his permit yet.

Draconis nodded. "Yes, there is, albeit a small one. The wheel can be moved in four other directions. If you push it in, you will go faster: These cars do not have brakes or gas pedals. So, if you pull the wheel out, you will slow down. Also, if you push it down, that will make the car rise. Likewise, if you push it up, the car will sink. The cars do not sit on the ground but rather float above it as high or low as you want them to."

Drage looked inside one of them. "Okay, that makes sense. I can do this!"

Draconis chuckled, "Good. We will all take this one for now." He pointed to one of the dark vehicles. He looked at Drage, who was about to take the driver's seat. "No, you will not be driving just yet. If I need to ward off any following Y'mordi, I need to know that you all will be able to make it to the Palace in one piece."

Matthew looked around before he got into the car. "Don't we need to pay for it first?"

"No, I will just leave an Imperial Seal here." He held his hand up in the water. "*Eldra.*" A light began making a pattern into the water outside the car. It formed a large hieroglyph of light. As Draconis started the car, he said, "The Imperial Seal has a lot of weight to it, especially in the Southern Continent. Only someone who works directly for the Emperor, a Loyal Servant, can actually create that Seal. It is one of the Emperor's greatest tricks. Anyone who receives the Seal in place of services or items is remembered by the Emperor. All Seals made are kept track of by one of the Emperor's servants, and by the end of each month, the Emperor will repay all such debts. It is a very nice system, actually. Many people value the Seal over actual salt, because the Emperor usually assigns a higher value to the services or items, so the person getting paid gets a lot more salt than the person would have requested."

Once everyone was in the car, Draconis began driving across the frozen wasteland of the Southern Continent.

Later that night, Aria had fallen asleep. Drage and Matthew were still fully awake. They looked out of their windows, watching as the ocean went on and on for miles. They noticed the frozen soil was being replaced with snow on the ground. Being a few miles away from the coast was enough to get rid of the ice. Drage started, "So, are most of the cars here this fast?" The car had shot off at around a hundred miles per hour when they had left Terin. Now, it was well into the range of 130 to 140.

Draconis smiled at this question. "No, not most of them. We were lucky to find one that did, to be honest."

"So, what happened when that tornado got you and Aria? I mean, Drage and I were just so confused afterward," Matthew said.

Draconis sighed. "First, I need to explain a few things to you. The Emperor knew that you three were coming to this world. He had expected you, at least slightly, anyways. There is a Prophecy left over from the time of the Obsidian Wars. It says that the Y'mordi would find someone who would temporarily lead the Darkness out of its hiding. The Prophecy also implies that they would attempt to defeat the Emperor of Light. However, there was a caveat in the Prophecy that said that there would be seven Guardians of Light who could defeat this leader of the Darkness. The man who attacked me was not one of the Y'mordi. It was the man the Y'mordi are setting up to be the leader of the Darkness. His name is Maris, and by the looks of it, he is a demented mage. He is not particularly skilled at swordplay, but he knows his way with *mysteria*. Both Maris and the Emperor believe that you three are three of the Guardians of Light mentioned in the Prophecy. Someone helped to bring you here, but I was sent to find you and protect you until you were with the Emperor. Maris tried to kill both Aria and me in his tornado, but I was able to use a Gate to get Aria closer to Terin. When I did this, Maris attacked, and that attack was much more difficult to escape. But when I did escape him, I found Aria, and we began looking for you two."

Drage looked out at the open expanse of the sea. "You mean, we have to stop that guy? We could hardly fight the Y'mordi, much less their leader."

"I would not worry about it if I were you. You will have four other people with you besides Matthew and Aria. As a matter of fact, I am also one of the Guardians. We will be able to defeat him. I will not allow anything else to happen, and nor will you."

Drage smirked. "I'm glad you have such confidence in us and all, but I'm really not that good at fighting."

Suddenly, the car rocked. Drage and Matthew looked to the back window and saw two things that looked like deformed motorcycles behind them. On each motorcycle was a black-robed figure. One of the figures had a gun and proceeded to shoot at the back of the car, while the other person held one hand up and blasted spherical ripples at the car, causing it to hurl itself forward.

"Drage, take the wheel," growled Draconis.

Aria woke up then. "What's going on?"

Drage leaped into the driver's seat as Draconis smashed through the driver's window and gained a foothold on the roof of the car. He shouted several words, and Matthew watched as every bullet or ripple was deflected by some unseen force that he knew to be *mysteria*. He tried to explain the situation to Aria as she turned around and observed Draconis's aggressive protections. Drage struggled to keep the car steady at first. The wheel moved up and down too freely. Draconis was having a hard time maintaining his balance, but he managed to deflect all of the Y'mordi's projectiles.

Aria thought back to how she fought against Mali. She closed her eyes and thought about how much she wanted to help and protect her friends. She opened the near window, and her hand reached out to the Y'mordi as she called, "*Lune!*" A ripple emitted from her hand and engulfed the figure with the pistol. The person dropped from the motorcycle, crippled and frozen in the water. The moment of confusion gave Draconis the time to cast a fireball at the other Y'mordi, which sent it flying as well. As Drage moved from the seat, Draconis entered through the window and took over the wheel.

As he drove, he said to Aria, "Very good, child. You are a quick learner."

Because he had focused his mind on keeping the vehicle straight, Drage was clueless. "What? What happened?"

Matthew was astonished by what had just happened himself. "Aria, how did you do that?"

Aria smiled in embarrassment. "Draconis taught me a little bit about *mysteria* while we were looking for the two of you. I thought I would try that one out. It was Force of the Element Wind. You can use it to immobilize enemies by using pure wind to trap them where they stand."

Now, Drage was surprised. "You used *mysteria?*"

Draconis laughed. "Apparently, she did, Drage. Maybe the two of you will learn how to use it someday as well. For now, we are almost at the Palace. You will soon get to meet the Emperor."

A few hours later, they arrived at the golden gates of Apolis, the capital of Helio. They could not see anything of the city because of the colossal walls that surrounded it. The only sign of beauty was the golden part of the wall that contained the gate, which was guarded by a small man in white robes. The four Guardians exited the car and approached the guard. Draconis said, "Step aside. We serve the Emperor."

The man spoke with a high pitch, "Do you have your identification?"

Draconis roared back at the man in a fury, "I do not need identification! I am the Guardian of the Emperor and his Loyal Servant! Step aside now!"

"Forgive me, but I must obey my orders as you must obey his laws. Leave."

Draconis growled a final time before he grew in size and then proceeded to pick the man up and move him out of the way against his will and loud protests. Draconis opened the gates and allowed the other three into the city. "Now, tell me, guard, what is your name, so that I might speak of you to his Imperial Majesty?"

The man said, "My name is Ixion."

"Hmph, very well. Ixion. You shall hear about this again and will remember your error the next time you encounter a Loyal Servant." They all looked into the city and were amazed by what they saw. Here, it was truly a city of light.

A City of Light

The town was both immense and breathtaking. Many of the buildings shone with their own brilliant, golden walls and shimmering, multi-hued streetlights. The scattered houses were mere ants in comparison to the commercial buildings. Each one had its own little mailbox in the front yard that connected to the main road. Above them, cars swam through the city and parked at the lots on the upper floors of the building rather than the ground level. The people themselves were just as interesting to the trio. While most wore white robes that went to the ground, several of the people would wear tight clothing that looked similar to leather but covered the entire body and bore a wide array of colors.

The three stayed close to Draconis because he was the only person they knew. Everything was so different and bizarre, yet interesting and fantastic. This city so greatly contrasted the dull, metallic city of Terin.

Then, they became aware of something truly spectacular: the Palace of Light. It was a building both wide and tall and bore the resemblance of a skyscraper and a palace combined. It looked both modern and ancient. The design of the building seemed Indian in nature, with spires and domes, but the shining material was similar to what one might see in Tokyo. Its immense spires stretched above all the other buildings. Unlike the city, the Palace was not gold. Instead, it was entirely silver. It was solid metal from top to bottom, except for the grandiose stained-glass windows that were as tall as the rooms they concealed.

Matthew smiled at the beauty of the design, while Aria and Drage merely gawked at its unbelievable size. Draconis noticed their reactions and smiled to himself. Drage asked, "Draconis, is that the Palace?"

Draconis enlarged his smile as he said, "Yes, Drage, it is."

They continued to close the distance between themselves and the front door of the Palace. As they passed a building, a man called out to them. "Hey, Rex! How's it going? Where have you been?" The man seemed old yet not ancient. He was thin and had a bright, cheerful face.

Draconis turned to face the tall, old man. He maintained his smile. "Ah, Valdridge! All is well here. I have been out on errands for the Emperor. What are you doing in the city?"

Valdridge replied, "We just got out of a meeting with the Emperor, and he was wondering what was taking you so long to get here. He sent me to look for you actually, but I suppose that that is unnecessary, seeing as how you have already arrived."

Draconis nodded. "Ah, I see. Well, I must hurry if the Emperor is ready for me."

"Oh, please. I shall escort you in myself. And who are your guests, might I ask?" he said, bowing to the four of them.

"This is Dragenopn Helius, Matthew Helius, and Aria Newman of Earth."

Valdridge was taken aback by the names. "Ah, Helius, did you say, Rex? Well, if they're from Earth, I can see why the Emperor has been anxious to find you." Then, he addressed the trio. "I am called Master Valdridge of the Emperor's Council. I am pleased to meet all of you." With this introduction, he made a slight bow.

Drage, Matthew, and Aria imitated the gesture and responded, "Pleased to meet you."

Valdridge gestured for the four of them to follow him. "Come, let us hurry. No time must be wasted."

"Most definitely not," Draconis agreed. They continued the rest of the walk to the Palace.

Once they reached the main door, Valdridge said, "Wait here, and I shall announce your presence." With that being said, Valdridge opened the entrance to the palace.

Draconis proceeded to lecture the trio. "Now, I am quite confident that you have all been educated as to proper manners, but I must advise you to remember that he is one of the most influential men in this world. Remember to be civil, and watch your tongue."

Drage, Matthew, and Aria merely looked at the ground. They were not embarrassed or nervous as much as just unsure. This whole experience was foreign to them, and they did not know how to react to it all. They could clearly remember that last day on the beach they had spent together. They could see all the birds in flight, and they could smell the fresh sea air. Here, they could not even experience the sensation of air.

The door opened and revealed Valdridge. "Follow me, please."

As they entered the foyer, they were quickly impressed by the golden walls and chandeliers that hung along the ceiling. They could feel the heat the Palace generated. The water was the perfect temperature. As they stepped forward on the beautiful tiles, they became aware of a series of doors that led to other parts of the Palace, but the center door was the one they were approaching. Without ever touching the door, Valdridge opened it. He had waved his hand in front of it, and it opened before him. He stepped aside and gestured for them to enter.

Before they entered, Draconis said to them, "Drage, Matthew, Aria—I will not be entering the Throne Room with you. I have other matters to attend to before I can see the Emperor. However, I wish you all the best of luck."

"But, Draconis," Aria began, "When will we see you again?"

Matthew added, "Yeah, we don't know anybody here besides you and the Y'mordi, and I doubt that the latter will be too keen to help us."

Draconis responded, "You will see me again. Of this fact, I am confident. We will have to see each other again when we strike against Maris. Farewell."

Drage said, "Well, good luck to you too, Draconis."

Draconis bowed to the three of them and left with Valdridge. Aria looked to Drage and Matthew. "Well, are you ready?"

The two looked through the open doorway and responded in almost perfect unison, "Yeah." The three walked into the Throne Room. It was longer than it was wide, had no windows, and several mechanical lights that illuminated both sides of the velvet carpet. This carpet path led from the door to the majestic throne at the end of the room, which held an elderly man in a golden robe.

The children walked down the carpet and toward the man. Each step they took inspired new fears, causes for nervousness, and even memories of home. When they were a few yards from the throne, they stopped and bowed to the Emperor of Light. When they rose, they noticed no reaction and looked at each other, wondering what to do next.

The Emperor stood and then said, "Welcome to Apolis, and welcome to my Palace. Most of all, welcome to Gevás. Tell me, young ones, how do you like this world so far?"

Drage stepped forward and chose to speak for the three of them, "Sir, your city is beautiful, but all we really want is to go home."

The old man smiled down at him and finally could not contain his joy any longer. "Yes, I am sure you do, Dragenopn. However, what you fail to realize is that this Palace…is your home."

Drage stammered, "Sir…I'm afraid I don't know what you mean."

"Dragenopn, this Palace is where you were born. Elizabeth was my wife."

At this point, Drage was unable to work his mouth. Matthew said, "Your Majesty, Drage was born on Earth."

Drage managed, "But...that's crazy...I don't even know my father..."

The Emperor explained, "Yes, I know. My name is John Helius. Your mother was a mage here. She worked in the Palace as one of my Council. When you were born, we found out that your birth coincided with the words of a Prophecy that detailed the impending Darkness. Draconis may have told you about it already. Elizabeth and I felt that it would be better if you were raised without the knowledge of this world. We wanted you to be raised with something that might stand a better chance against the Darkness: a little bit of arrogance." He smiled at his last words but became more serious as he continued. "Elizabeth decided that you should be raised on Earth with her, while I stayed here and made sure that you would have a kingdom to come back to when the time was right."

Drage managed another word, "Whoa."

Aria said in surprise, "So, you mean that Drage is a prince?"

Drage's eyes widened as the Emperor continued, "Yes, he is. This throne is his birthright. When I die, he will inherit it along with this Palace, this city, and this kingdom. He will be one of the greatest men in this world."

Drage stammered, "This is quite a bit to take in right now."

The old man smiled. "Well, the first thing to see to is for you to all have a decent meal, a warm bath, and a nice bed for the night. Then, I shall have one of my servants give you a tour of the city tomorrow. After that, your training shall begin."

Matthew inquired with eagerness, "What training?"

"If you are all to stand a chance against this self-proclaimed Emperor of Darkness, you will need a little more skill and strength. When I receive Draconis's report, I shall be able to adapt your training." He called, "Servants, come!" Several people dressed in red outfits came out of a door into the room. They bowed and began to escort the three to the dining room.

As they prepared for bed, Aria said to Drage, "Hey Drage, so what are we going to do now? I mean, we cannot go back on our own, so maybe we do have to stay and fight Maris."

Matthew replied, "True, and I am actually starting to like it here." Drage and Aria eyed him. "What? You have to admit this city is pretty amazing. Besides, your dad is here anyways." He was in many ways shaken by Drage's news. Though Matthew was happy for Drage, he also felt a little lonelier because of it. Drage's father had not even acknowledged Matthew as his son, and now Drage was a prince. Matthew had in some ways been cut out of the picture.

Drage hesitated and said, "Yeah…he is, isn't he? Maybe we do have to fight Maris. I mean, besides the fact that we may never see home again, this actually doesn't look all that bad. We have our taste of adventure. I get to spend time with my dad. We have such nice beds, too." He smirked. "I never thought I would be praising a bed so much, honestly."

Aria sighed, "I guess I just really miss my parents."

Drage replied, "So do I, but I don't think that we can really do anything about it right now. There is not much we can do at all. Y'know what? Let's just get to sleep, and we can talk more about it tomorrow."

Matthew yawned, "Yeah, those beds really do look nice. Good night, guys." He left to his room.

Before Aria left, she pecked Drage on the cheek and said, "Good night, Drage. See you in the morning."

Drage replied with a smile, "Yeah. G'night."

"…and how did this happen?" asked Pullatus.

"I assure you, my Lord, I do not know," replied Xarden. "It was that fool Randir, I am sure. He helped them escape from Maris near Terin. I am sure of it, my Lord!"

Pullatus muttered, "Well then, Xarden, I shall trust the mistake shall not be made twice. Ixion is stationed at the Palace, so he shall have a watch over the Guardians' activities. He should be coming soon to give his report as well. I have the twins protecting the Great Servant, while Mali is suffering from his error."

Xarden remained kneeling and inquired with a delicate tone, "My Lord, can you tell me how it is that they escaped us on Earth exactly?"

Pullatus turned to Xarden as if to inflict pain, causing Xarden to cringe. "Yes, I suppose I shall. There was a man in a black robe similar to our own. However, he was *not* one of us. He was very skilled in the Darkness though. He was able to stun me...temporarily. I was apparently caught off guard."

"You? Beat by some stranger? This is an insult!" Xarden knew he might be pushing it a little too far. He enjoyed being sarcastic and appearing superior. Being lowly was what Ixion and Mali did. However, under Pullatus's angry eye, he could not afford such luxuries as being his regular self.

"It appears to be so. Nevertheless, the next time I see him, I shall annihilate him in the most painful way imaginable, and you know I can do that, Xarden."

Xarden felt a memory almost a thousand years old resurface. "Yes, my Lord, I do know that you can do that."

"Good. Do not forget it. Now, I need you to find these other Guardians before the Emperor of Light does. They are only aware of four as far as Ixion has told me. Oh, speak of the rat, here he comes..."

Drage awoke to the light of the sun peeking through his window. He rose wondering what time it was and then realized he had no extra clothes with him. Then, he spotted an elegant wardrobe on the other side of the room. He tossed off the thick covers and walked over to the wardrobe. He opened it and gasped in amazement. In it were several outfits of clothing, and all of them were his exact size. As he went through the outfits wondering what to wear, he spotted something that looked comfortable: a pair of spandex-like jeans, a blue shirt, and a white jacket. He put on the attire and exited his room.

When he went to look for Aria and Matthew, they were not in their rooms. Puzzled, Drage went to the dining room to find them finishing breakfast. "Wow, you guys really know how to wait, doncha?"

Aria smiled and responded, "Well, we were hungry, and you weren't waking up. So, we just helped ourselves."

Matthew commented with his own smile, "Yeah, and besides, you looked like you needed your beauty rest."

"Thanks a lot!" said Drage, acting offended. He joined them. The breakfast consisted of eggs, some unusual kind of fish, and pancakes. Apparently, the eggs were some kind of fish eggs, though there was hardly a difference in taste between these eggs and the breakfast eggs from home. No one even questioned what the pancakes were made of—they tasted even better than the ones from home.

A man in a red outfit entered the room. "Please, I will be your guide today. When you are ready, come with me." They slowly recognized the man to be the same guard from the day before, Ixion.

They prepared to face the day and went to him. "We're ready," said Matthew.

"Good," said Ixion with his high-pitched voice. "Follow me. I will explain the layout of the city first. Apolis is divided into four sections or Quarters, as they are often called. They are based on the four directions of the compass. I'm assuming you know what those are?"

Matthew answered this question. "Well, of course we do. North, west, east, and south."

"Very good. The North Quarter is for the business and merchant industries. That's where all the shops, businesses, and banks are. The West has all of the residential areas. It has homes and several hotels. We probably won't spend too much time there, but we might take a look at it. Then, the South Quarter is also known as the Imperial Quarter. All of the courts are there. Also, you can find the Imperial Gardens there. Some of the city's aristocrats' houses dot the Quarter as well. Finally, the East Quarter includes the entertainment and military divisions. It is not the most ideal combination, but it works rather well. There, you will see the disq stadium. That is a sight to behold."

Drage inquired, "Disq?"

"Yes, it is the major sport here in Gevás. Maybe one day you shall understand the rules of the game," Ixion said with a hint of a joke in his voice.

Drage pondered the prospect of becoming an athlete in this other world, and the idea was an enticing one. "Maybe I will…" he muttered.

Ixion ignored Drage's comment. "In the center of the Quarters is the Palace. It is arranged so that the Emperor can see any of the Quarters he would like just by walking over to a different window. Now, if you will follow me, I will take you all to the North Quarter to see some of the shops."

As they walked down the street, they became more and more amazed by the vendors and buildings they passed. Their eyes widened as their interests were piqued. Ixion's voice just droned on and on to the trio, and after the first few minutes of their tour of the Quarter, they had learned to ignore him and his high voice. Drage whispered to the others, "Hey, do you see that bookstore they have? It's amazing!"

Aria was quick to agree, "Yeah, it is. Look at all of these street vendors though. It's remarkable that they still get business even though there are so many stores around here. Typically, small private vendors will set up their kiosks a lot further from the main stores in an area. Now that I think about it, I wonder what the economy is like here."

"I know they use 'salt,'" offered Matthew.

Ixion overheard this statement and said, "Yes, in Gevás, the only real currency is salt. A couple of centuries ago, the idea of salt was recommended over the use of small metal circles that everyone used back then."

Aria thought about this idea for a second. "But isn't salt too easy to find here? Isn't this salt water?"

Ixion laughed, "Yes, but all salt that is used for currency is marked, of course. It is marked by the Imperial Seal."

Matthew added, "So that means that it would be easy to tell if the salt was worth anything or not too, right? And that also means that it is practically impossible to have counterfeit currency in the system."

"Yes, that's right. Of course, the Emperor has to make sure that the economy is stable by changing how much salt has the Seal on it as well. Some people actually make it a hobby to collect old salt. They can test how old the Seal is and sell the salt at a high price because of its age."

Drage commented, "That is what some people do on Earth, too." Then, he spotted a street vendor that had a kiosk set up with several fish laid out on it. The owner was boiling them there. Bubbles emitted from their soft bodies. His stomach grumbled. "Hey, Ixion, do you think we have time to grab a bite to eat?" It was a little past noon, and Matthew and Aria were also beginning to feel hungry.

Ixion followed Drage's eyes to the kiosk and said, "Oh, certainly. Here are a few Imperial Favors." He handed the three of them pieces of paper marked with the Imperial Seal.

Matthew asked, "What are these?"

Ixion replied, "Well, all official businesses are supposed to only accept salt payment, because they are owned by the government, but street vendors are private industries and therefore do not have to. Most street vendors are traders. You give them an object or a service, and they will do the same for you. People who work for the Emperor, however, have these Imperial Favors. They are slips of paper that offer the Emperor's promise of a service. These can be traded at banks for a decent amount of salt. The only tricky thing about using Favors is that the amount you get back from the bank for one fluctuates day by day. Also, some businesses accept a Favor in return for a standard service of theirs. For example, a Favor will grant you one or two nights at a hotel or maybe a nice meal at a restaurant."

Drage said, "Thank you!" and ran to the fish kiosk. Matthew and Aria both went their separate ways to find food. They all met back up near the fish kiosk and talked about how intricate and interesting this world was.

The three were even more entranced by the excellence of the Imperial Quarter. First, Ixion took them to several of the government buildings, such as houses of the Council, an enormous library, and a theatre that played movies in a more realistic format.

"…not that strange, is it? The screen wraps around each person in the theatre and emits sounds, smells, feelings, and lights. It is a film that engages all of the senses. There are some theatres across the world that actually display interactive movies where every viewer gets their own room, and they can move around to view it in different perspectives."

Drage was thoroughly impressed by the idea. "Really? Maybe we should go see one then."

Ixion shook his head. "Not today. I have orders to get you back in time to eat with the Emperor."

Then, Ixion showed them to the Imperial Gardens. In all their lives, they had never seen anything so beautiful. The Gardens had all kinds of plants, all of them colorful and different shapes. They recognized the Garden to be similar to an organized coral reef. However, some of the plants were as tall as trees. The whole setting was comparable to a jungle under the sea.

Aria exclaimed, "Drage, it's gorgeous!"

Drage was also enchanted by it. "Yeah. Just think: One day all of this will be mine, too."

Matthew half-joked, "Yeah, you're forgetting that I'm your brother too."

For a second, Drage was speechless. Then, he said, "Yeah…that's true. Maybe my dad knows something about you that neither of us know." Then, another thought hit him. "Oh, yeah! What about Helen? She's older than me. Was she born here too?"

Matthew tried to concentrate. "Hm…I don't know. She probably was, actually."

They spent the rest of the evening looking around the Gardens more. Then, Ixion took them back to the Palace.

"I hope you enjoyed your tour, children." Ixion said as they approached the front door. "I shall leave you now. If you need help with anything, don't hesitate to call for me."

Matthew said, "Okay, thanks, Ixion!"

Aria and Drage said their thanks, and they all said farewell to their guide as they entered the Palace. The Emperor was waiting for them in the main dining room. He stood as they approached. "Ah, you're back. I was wondering if your guide was running late."

"No, we're fine," said Drage.

"Sir," Matthew began, "Have you talked to Draconis yet? Do you know if we can see him soon?"

The Emperor eyed Matthew. "I have spoken with him regarding your journey here, but I have sent him out on another mission. He will not be back for at least a couple of days. I shall of course let you know when he returns."

Matthew smiled, "Thanks."

The Emperor held out his hands. "Please eat."

As they ate, the Emperor continued to talk to them. "Alright, now based on what Draconis has told me, it seems that this world is in extreme danger. The Lords of the Shadows are on the move again, and, this time, they have a man that they are using to wreak havoc on Gevás. This act means they are trying to remain a secret to the world, but not to me."

Aria asked after swallowing her food, "Why are they trying so hard to remain hidden though? If they are so powerful, it shouldn't matter, right?"

"That is where you are wrong. Because they have not announced themselves, that means that they are doing things behind the scenes, and they do not want people to be suspicious of them. They might be advising kings in other countries or teaching at schools or a list of other activities. If people became scared and more cautious, then it would make the jobs of the Lords of the Shadows a little harder."

Drage remarked with a mouthful of a fish known as skander, "Then, why don't we tell everyone that they are still around?"

"Dragenopn, if we tell the people, then they will be afraid and lose faith in the Imperial family for not keeping the Lords of the Shadows away. It is not our job to inspire fear. Besides, we need to take care of Maris and the Lords of the Shadows without involving the people. Everyone has their own matters and problems to attend to."

The rest of the meal continued in silence. When the three got up to leave, the Emperor said, "Be up and ready early tomorrow. We will start our training at dawn." The trio nodded to him and went upstairs to Drage's room.

Aria exclaimed, "This town is incredible! The people here are all so nice, and the Gardens were spectacular!"

"Yeah, and there is always so much to do here too. You could never get bored," said Matthew.

Drage was also ecstatic about their day's experiences. "It was pretty great, wasn't it? What do you guys think our training is going to be like tomorrow?"

Matthew said, "Well, it will probably just be practicing our fighting. It's going to be very difficult to fight Maris. You guys saw how much trouble Draconis had fighting him." Aria and Drage agreed.

That night, they looked around the Palace and discovered how large the place was. They found several ballrooms, dining rooms, bathrooms, bedrooms, a library, lounges, and more. Aria compared it to living in the White House. She had only been there once for one of her clubs in school, but it had been an interesting experience nevertheless.

"Wow," Drage said. "This place is huge. I've never been in such a large building."

Matthew and Aria both looked at each other and laughed. They knew that many of the buildings in Boston had been much taller than this Palace. They were simply not as wide nor had as many rooms.

Matthew turned to Drage. "Alright, well, I am going to bed since we are getting up so early tomorrow."

Aria agreed and kissed Drage goodnight. Drage spent another few minutes touring the Palace on his own. He could not help but admire the architecture of the building and the warm glow he felt being inside of it. It was nice and warm there. Finally, he yawned and went to bed also.

When Drage opened his eyes, Matthew was standing over him, shaking him. "Wake up, Drage! We have to meet your dad for training!"

Half asleep, Drage responded, "No, ten more minutes." He rolled over on his side.

Matthew shook him again, "Hey, get up!"

Drage groaned a final time and started to get up at last. "Okay, I'm up. I'm up. Just close the door on your way out, so that I can get dressed."

Matthew smiled. "Fine, but stay up. Don't go to sleep again."

Drage said, "Alright, I won't."

Matthew retaliated, "Are you sure?"

Drage responded with a poorly aimed shot of his pillow at him. Matthew left the room and closed the doors behind him. When Drage was ready, he met Matthew and Aria outside his room.

"Hurry up!" the two said in unison. They went downstairs to the Throne Room where the Emperor was waiting for them.

The Emperor looked sternly at the three and said, "You are late. Dawn was half an hour ago."

Matthew was quick to apologize, "Sorry, sir. We took a little bit longer than we expected to get ready."

Drage looked down at his feet, ashamed. Matthew normally took the blame away from him whenever he was in trouble. He did that even back at home. Drage had never felt comfortable with it though.

The Emperor responded, "For now, it is fine, but next time, show up on time. First of all, I am going to give you your new weapons." He walked up to the three and held out his hands. A white bow appeared in one of his hands, while a golden quiver filled with long white arrows appeared in the other. "Aria, these are for you."

Aria's mouth gaped at the gift. "Wow, they're very beautiful. Thank you, sir."

The Emperor gave her a warning, "They may be beautiful, but they are just as sharp and deadly as any other arrows could be, so do not underestimate them. They can be just as potent with a good aim." Then, a long bar of white light appeared in his hands which solidified into a staff of white wood. "Matthew, this staff is for you."

Matthew took it in both hands and whirled it around a couple of times, careful not to hit anyone. "It's very smooth and almost weightless. Thank you very much, sir."

The Emperor smiled. "My pleasure." Then, he turned to Drage. "My son, this is a very special sword." As he spoke, he walked over to the throne and retrieved a sword with its scabbard. "It is different from regular swords in that it is possessed by a spirit."

Drage looked at the sheathed sword with interest. "A spirit?"

"Yes. Back in the time of the Obsidian Wars, there was an entity known as the Great Spirit. Very few legends are left about the Spirit, but it is true that it did exist. One of the only things I know about it is the Spirit's fate. The dark lord Dagan planned to destroy it, but his plan, whatever it was, failed. Instead, the Spirit made Dagan's attack divide itself into five parts. These five pieces of the Spirit traveled away from Dagan and went to another part of the world. Eventually, the fragments of the Spirit found something of interest, a battle.

"They had never witnessed such emotions as those that were present on the battlefield. Nor had they experienced the strength of some of the souls there. Each piece of the Great Spirit became attracted to a certain person because of the characteristics of the person's heart. So, they bonded themselves with the weapons of those interesting souls in order to help them in the battle. The possessed swords became invincible and have not been destroyed to this day. Each sword is hidden somewhere across the world." The Emperor unsheathed the sword in a single grand gesture. The blade was of the smoothest metal and bore a perfect reflection of the world around it, making it resemble a mirror. The hilt was a simple silver metal. "This sword is known as the Sword of Destiny. It has an extraordinary power, the power to reduce friction."

Drage was confused. "Er…what?"

"In other words, this Sword can cut through almost anything with extreme ease. It can cut with no real force involved."

Drage smiled. "That is cool! With something like that, Maris won't stand a chance!"

The Emperor waved the Sword around, illustrating its weightlessness. "Hold on one moment. Strangely enough, it has its exceptions. Its power does not work on anything alive and nor will it work on other swords. Because it is possessed by a spirit, you will learn over time that it has its own personality. These exceptions are not weaknesses but choices of the spirit inhabiting it."

"Hm… It still seems very interesting."

"One more thing before I give it to you. Know that it chooses who wields it, and its power can only be used by those who appeal to what it wants."

Drage's grin widened. "Oh? And what is it that it wants?"

The Emperor responded, "That is for you to discover." He sheathed the Sword and handed it to Drage.

Drage accepted it and bowed to the Emperor. "Thank you."

The Emperor motioned for the three to follow him. "Alright, now come this way, and I shall introduce you to your instructors."

The trio followed him through the castle. Again, they were amazed by its splendid beauty. With each step, they tried to memorize their way through the castle's winding passages and twisting corridors. By the time they found the room, however, they had completely lost all sense of direction. The room was a small circle that was connected to three long, narrow hallways that led to their own individual chambers. The Emperor pointed to the room on the left and said, "Matthew, that's your room."

Matthew looked at his staff, unsure of what to do. Then, he turned to the corridor and walked down it. The Emperor turned to Aria and said, "Now, you must go down the middle hallway." Aria went without any visible expression on her face.

She was nervous about the idea of training, but she had no intention of showing that she felt that way. "Dragenopn, the one on the right is all yours." He patted his son's shoulder and walked past him to the previous room.

Drage was suddenly alone. The place seemed as cold as it was outside the city. He walked into the corridor one step at a time. He had always been confident in his abilities with a sword, but after fighting the Y'mordi Mali, he was not so sure of himself. As he stepped into the dimly lit room, he recognized the figure in front of him.

Draconis smiled down at Drage. "Hello again. Glad to see me?"

Drage returned the smile eagerly. *Draconis is my instructor?* he thought. "Of course I am! I was wondering when we were going to see you again. Actually, my dad said it would take you a few days to return."

Draconis chuckled. "Well, I am here now and ready to teach you."

"What is it you are going to teach me?"

"I am going to teach you as much as I have been instructed to do so. I am going to teach you one of the warrior ways."

"Warrior ways?" Drage asked.

"Yes. Basically, a warrior way is a form of fighting, acting, and sometimes even thinking, and these warrior ways are based off one of the twelve zodiac. Before you ask, the zodiac are different here than they are on Earth. There are different stars and planets here. You do not need to know all the zodiac though. I am going to teach you the Way of the Dragon."

Drage started cautiously, "Do you think you can tell me all of the zodiac anyways? I am a little curious…"

Draconis nodded. "Yes, the zodiac consist of the Raven, the Wolf, the Dragon, the Unicorn, the Sea Serpent, the Lion, the Phoenix, the Shark, the Fox, the Crane… What were the other two… Oh, the Dolphin and the Mermaid. Anyways, I only know a couple of those forms well. The Way of the Dragon is so applicable that one hardly needs to know the others."

"So, how do I use it?"

Draconis raised his massive golden sword. "Draw your weapon."

Drage pulled the Sword of Destiny out of its scabbard and took his normal position. Drage was surprised at how light the Sword felt in his grip.

Instantly, Draconis unleashed a flurry of strikes at Drage. As he struggled to block these, he tripped backward and fell. When he lifted his head, Draconis's golden blade was pointed at him. "Your starting stance was wrong. An aggressive position such as that is only useful when you know your enemy well. It is far better to be cautious and on the defense when combatting a new enemy. However, the form I shall teach you is neither a defensive form nor an offensive form." He stepped away from Drage and demonstrated. "Instead of holding your blade centered and angled toward your opponent, hold it lowered like this. Keep the hilt to one side and the blade angled downward to protect your legs. Doing this will confuse the enemy and make it seem easier to attack your center."

Drage stood and imitated the sword stance. "Like this?"

"Yes, that is right. Now, be warned that this form is showier than other forms. It uses a natural grace, speed, and rhythm. Spins, small leaps, advanced dodges, and sweeping strikes are common in this form. So, first, I shall show you how to attack, since you seem so eager to learn that skill. When you engage an enemy, do not waste time. Rush in with your first attack. Close the distance between you and the enemy. Sometimes, a strong leap and spin will take you there and simultaneously give you some momentum for a fierce attack. For all of your close attacks, try to keep your arm moving at all times. Yes, that means you will keep the one-handed grip for this form."

Drage spun at Draconis. He changed his thinking to what Draconis said and felt his arm attacking in a long combo that seemed to never end. It was a fluid series of attacks that wasted no movement. Each time, his blade met Draconis's own golden sword. Then, he saw an opening in Draconis's defenses. He lunged with his blade. Draconis spun, and for a moment, their backs met. Drage's momentum carried him forward still in the lunge, while Draconis's was still in spin. Drage found himself on the cold floor. He did not have to turn to know that Draconis's sword would be waiting for him. "What did I do wrong?"

Draconis lectured, "You tried to stab. That is one factor of the form you must learn. In the Way of the Dragon, you cannot stab. That will be your greatest downfall. Stabs require too much energy and force you to lose control of your body weight. Refrain from using them." He smiled then. "But overall, your attacks were very nice. It was a continuous flow of attack. Another thing: Do not be afraid to hurt me. This room is enchanted by his Imperial Majesty. Anyone here cannot be injured."

Drage's eyes widened. "Really? That's kind of neat."

Draconis chuckled. "Yes, it is 'kind of neat.'" He resumed his form and said, "Now, I shall teach you how to defend. It is the same concept for the most part. Focus on meeting my blade constantly. Use only one hand, and try to use as little energy as possible with your arm. As a matter of fact, if possible, you should try to maneuver yourself around the blade instead of the reverse. However, you will find it far easier and more effective to just dodge instead of block. When dodging, try not to move too far away from the opponent. It is fine to maneuver around them, though, strafing."

Drage then reset his form and said, "Ok. I'm ready."

Draconis was upon him so fast that Drage almost fell from the initial charge. It was a strong flood of attacks pressed at Drage. He had been accustomed to such attacks from Matthew before, but he had typically moved backward from them so as to have better control. He had never actually tried staying immobile. Suddenly, he saw Draconis pull his sword back. Instinct took over in an unpredictable way. He turned and leaped as Draconis stabbed the air where Drage had just been standing. As he finished the spin, Drage extended his Sword and attempted a slash at Draconis from behind. However, his Sword met the golden metal. Draconis had used the momentum from the stab to pull the sword over his head and behind him to block the blow: he had seen it coming.

Drage was dumbfounded. "How did you do that?"

Draconis turned to face Drage with a smile. "I was testing you. You are a quick learner. You managed to pull off the same evasion technique that I used when you tried to stab me. Now, let's combine attack and defense together."

Drage came back to his room covered in bruises. He saw his bed and collapsed on it. He looked up at the ceiling. *Ow-wwwwwwwww*...Exhaustion washed over him. Suddenly, he heard a knock at the door. *Did I even close the door?*

It was Aria knocking on the open door frame. "Hey, are you okay?"

Drage refused to even do as much as sit up in his bed. "Yeah. Just extremely worn out. How did your training go?"

Aria came over to the bed and sat down beside him. She had the widest grin on her face. "Oh, it was amazing, Drage! My instructor taught me how to use *mysteria*, and I can really use my bow and arrows now! Who would have thought magic could be so easy!"

"Well, I am glad you had fun. I spent the whole day fighting Draconis."

Aria gasped, "Oh, Draconis was your instructor? That had to be rough. My instructor is a member of the Emperor's Council. She is also the Prophet of Nature. She was a very nice lady. Oh, by the way, it's time for supper. Surely you're hungry?"

Drage frowned. "No. I am not getting up. Ever. I am going to stay here till we can go home. My body can't move another muscle."

Aria leaned over Drage and kissed him. His eyes opened wide. Then, he relaxed. He kissed her back. "How about now?" she asked. He did not respond, though, and kept kissing her. They heard a cough from the doorway.

Matthew stood there, grinning. "Oh, I'm sorry. Did I interrupt something? It's time to eat, you two." He turned and left without waiting for a reaction.

Drage and Aria looked at each other and burst out laughing. Aria smiled at him. "Alright, I'll help you up." She offered her hands, which Drage grabbed. Together, they went downstairs to eat.

"For the next few days, you will continue your training. At present, I have several of my Loyal Servants seeking the other Guardians. We have scoured this Continent countless times, and we cannot find them anywhere. We will have to search the other Continents."

Drage was discouraged about the training that he would have to be put through over the following days. Matthew commented, "Honestly, what are the chances of finding three specific people before Maris attacks?"

The Emperor continued, "Not very good. But the Prophecy left us a few clues. They just need to be deciphered."

Aria inquired, "Well, can we see this Prophecy? Maybe we can help."

He stood and said, "Of course. Hold on one moment, and I shall get it for you." When he returned with the large metallic scroll, he began reading it.

"When seven come for seven coming, seven wake from seven sleeping. Seven lights for seven shadows.

Each with secrets hiding, and each with Hearts unique. The Thirteen shall rise up then.

One, a traitor and loyal servant with shadows always in mind,

Two, a prince born of Light, bound to destiny,

Three, a protector born of Earth, bound to Light,

Four, a mage outcast from birth yet blessed by her own,

Five, an Earthan love with strong heart overflowing,

Six, an heir and self-made outcast dressed in gold,

Seven, a Prophet and wise man hiding eternal.

Seven the Guardians of Light be, seven chosen by the Light. Seven Lights to pierce the Darkness.

When seven come for seven coming, seven wake from seven sleeping. Seven lights for seven shadows."

Drage replied, "That's it?"

"That is all," said the Emperor.

Aria offered, "Is there a way that we could have a copy? We might be able to figure some of it out."

The Emperor chuckled at the remark and said, "Of course. Would you do the honors of copying it? With *mysteria?*"

Aria leaped up from her seat with excitement. "I'd be glad to!" She pulled a long stick from one of her deep pockets. She pointed the wand at the metallic scroll and said, "*Voe.*" Everyone saw bubbles of air emit from the wand and trace the letters. She asked the Emperor, "Do you have an extra scroll?" The Emperor rose and found one for her. As she moved her wand, the air retained the shape of the letters and lifted up from the scroll. She transferred the air letters between the scrolls and said louder, "*Lune.*" The words shot into the blank scroll. Then, the air disappeared, and the letters were imprinted on the scroll. "I did it!"

Matthew clapped. "Nice job, Aria! Very impressive!"

Drage did not say anything out of both shock and a slight bit of anger. He did not enjoy the idea of Aria using this world's magic. It was binding them slowly yet permanently to this world. The idea scared him.

Later that night, Drage stayed awake looking up at the ceiling, waiting. He had been waiting for several hours for everyone to go to sleep. Tonight was the night he was going to leave. He knew from the moment he had planned it out that it would be a bad idea, but he saw a necessity in it. He did not like the idea of staying there in the Palace and doing nothing while Maris came closer and closer to them. Also, it seemed that the Emperor was getting nowhere with the search for the remaining Guardians. Drage had it in his mind that it would have to be up to him to find them.

He yearned to ask Aria and Matthew to come as well, but he could not help but notice the great smile that had been on Aria's face when she had copied the Prophecy. He could tell that the two would be happy here until he returned with the other Guardians.

He remembered looking at one of the maps of Gevás after

supper that night and seeing places that struck his interest. One of those places was an island to the north of the Southern Continent called Heaven's Isle. When he had inquired about it, his father had mentioned that he had sent scouts there, but they had not returned. Heaven's Isle was known to have a similar reputation to the Bermuda Triangle back on Earth. For the past two to three hundred years, people have gone missing around that area.

To Drage, the island seemed the perfect place for a Guardian to be hiding.

Who knows? Maybe I will find more than one of the Guardians there. No...that is just wishful thinking. But if I can find even one Guardian, I am helping us a lot.

Finally, he decided he had been waiting long enough. He got out of bed and began packing his things: a few sets of comfortable clothes, a map he had managed to smuggle, some food from the kitchen, and his Sword. He descended the stairs, trying not to make much noise. His light backpack rustled with each step. He decided it was the map. Then, he reached the bottom and smiled. He was almost there. Suddenly, he realized what he was doing: he was leaving everything behind. His dad, his girlfriend, and even his brother were going to be here. When they woke up, they would just find an empty bed and a small note with "I went to go find the Guardians. Be back soon!" scribbled on it.

He sighed and kept walking. A voice whispered beside him, "Oh, you could have waited for me, Drage. Geez, I didn't know we were leaving so early." Matthew was right beside him.

Drage stopped and said with red showing in his cheeks, "No, I'm going alone, Matthew. You are not coming with me."

Matthew smiled. "Well, of course I am. I have a backpack too, see?" He turned so Drage could see the backpack that he carried.

Drage stammered, "Wait...how did you know I was leaving?"

"Oh, Aria said you were going to. She said she could see it in your eyes when the Emperor was talking about Heaven's

Isle. She said you had made up your mind and that I would not be able to change it."

"Wait, so that means…"

Aria appeared, coming down the stairs. She saw the look of dismay on Drage's face. "Well, of course I'm coming too. What did you expect? For us to just let you go off on your own?"

Suddenly, the reality of what was happening hit Drage. "So, you guys aren't trying to stop me?"

Matthew clapped his hand on Drage's shoulder. "Of course not. We think it's a good idea. But we are only going to have a shot at finding the Guardians if we do it together."

"Drage, Matthew is right. We are going to have to work together on this one. Besides, you did not even prepare properly. Matthew and I grabbed everything we will need."

Drage laughed. "Are you serious?"

Matthew and Aria kept walking all the way to the door. Aria turned back to Drage. "Are you coming or not?"

Drage laughed again and caught up with them. "Yeah, let's go."

Matthew opened the door and muttered, "Guys…are we sure about this?"

Aria and Drage nodded, and Drage repeated, "Yeah, let's go. We'll find the Guardians. I'm sure of it now."

On the Road to Heaven

It was their third day on the road. They had been traveling northward using a compass that Aria had acquired from the Palace. The three transports they were using were not very fast but were noticeably faster than the Helian Transport they had encountered when they had first entered Gevás. The man who owned the Transport Lot in Apolis had offered the transports to them in exchange for 5,000 salt. The salt had been gained from one of Matthew's ideas. They had left the Palace with most of their nice clothes from their rooms and had sold them. They had received a substantial amount of salt in return for them.

Drage pressed the button on his transport that displayed the image of a mouth. He started, "Hey, Aria, how much farther do we have left to go? I would have thought we'd be at the northern tip of the continent by now. We've been driving for a while. I'm getting tired."

Aria's voice came from a small speaker in the dashboard of the vehicle, and Drage turned his head to see her mouth moving from her own transport. "No, we are about three-quarters of the way through Mashan Telis. At the latest, we will be at its capital by tomorrow afternoon. From there, it's a straight shot to Heaven's Isle."

Matthew's voice came too. "Hey Aria, Drage has a point though. We've been driving for about eleven or twelve hours, and we didn't get much sleep last night."

Aria remembered the night well enough. They had experienced a very uneventful day and had still been riding around in Mashan Telis with the cold hills being their only company. On the rare occasion that they had found a small town, they had rested there only if they were hungry but otherwise had avoided it. Well into the night, they had stopped at a mostly deserted town to find an inn. The innkeeper had been an old man who was very polite and kind-hearted. He had been cleanly dressed and had two rows of polished teeth. Nevertheless, he had offered them a room for some salt. Throughout the night, the three had heard screams coming from somewhere else in the inn. Those screams had lasted all night long. After their broken sleep, they left early in the morning.

She nodded and said, "Alright, fine. We'll stop at the next town." She started looking ahead and noticed something odd. "Hey Drage, check the map for me. I think we passed all of the hills."

Drage pulled the map out of one of the inner side compartments of his transport and opened it. He traced his finger along the path they had traveled. They had started in Helio and had gone north, leaving Helio to enter Mashan Telis. Then, they had detoured to the northwest to run into more towns, though that also meant more of those colossal hills to cross. So, if they had gone through all of the hills now, then they were almost there. "Yeah, we should be out of them now. We need to be heading northeast, but there is a town if we keep going straight north. At most, it will delay us by three or four hours."

Aria sounded doubtful. "Well, that is a considerable distance out of the way."

"That is true," agreed Matthew. "But the fact is that we need to stop, and I am pretty sure that Heaven's Isle will still take a while to get to yet. I vote we go north."

"Me, too!" exclaimed Drage.

Aria felt left out in the matter. She retorted, "Fine, but we are going to get up bright and early tomorrow morning to make up for it."

Drage nodded carefully from his seat in his two-chair transport. So far, he felt emotionally exhausted. He had been glad to have his brother and girlfriend with him on this quest, and he certainly could not deny their helpfulness. However, he saw every mile they left Apolis as a mile closer to Maris. He was beginning to get tense now. The last thing he wanted to see was his friends getting killed. He thought back on Draconis's training. Remembering the form came as easily as the memory of his bruises did. By now, they were mostly healed. He sighed. The future was so daunting. He tried not to think of home. He did not know where those thoughts would take him.

Finally, some hours later, the town came into view. It was a livelier town than their last and had plenty of shops and inns. It took the trio a while to discover where to park their transports. Aria went inside and paid for the room.

While Aria was gone, Matthew walked over to Drage. "Hey, are you doing alright? You look kind of down in the dumps."

Drage nodded with a half-smile on his face. "Yeah, I'm fine. I guess I am just a little worried. It's not every day you're stuck in a foreign world looking for three specific people while some mad sorcerer is out to kill you."

Matthew smiled. "Yeah, that's true. But you know as well as I do that this isn't about what we want. It's not really much of a choice for us right now. We can either help this world and fight, or we can just go home and let these people suffer and die."

Drage nodded. "You're right. It just makes me feel a little helpless, I suppose. I don't like having no choice in the matter."

Matthew put his hand on Drage's shoulder. "You know, it's not that bad if you think about who is making the choices. If you can put your faith in the real choice maker, you know that you are always doing right. It makes it a lot more bearable."

Drage nodded in agreement and turned to see Aria returning. She had the key to the room in her hands. She said, "Okay: food or sleep first?"

Drage and Matthew exclaimed in unison, "Sleep!"

"...Drage...Drage...Drage! Wake up!" Aria whispered.

Drage opened his eyes in confusion. "You can't be serious..."

Aria continued to whisper. "I needed to talk to you for a second."

He sat up. "What is it?" He was still mostly asleep.

Aria looked doubtful for a second and continued, "I need you to promise me something. Promise me that no matter what happens, after all of this is over, you and I will still be together. Don't leave me."

Drage smiled and reached up to her. He stroked his hand gently through her hair. "I could never leave you. I promise." Then, he laid his head back down and drifted.

Aria smiled. "Drage, you really are too wonderful. Sometimes though, you can be rather stupid. I guarantee that I will make sure you keep your promise. You won't leave me. I need you too much. Tomorrow, we will start working on that Prophecy. Maybe we can figure some of it out." She leaned over, kissed his forehead, and returned to her own bed. She hoped she had not woken Matthew: Drage and he were sleeping in the same bed while Aria had her own. "Good night."

In the morning, Drage noticed they had slept a lot longer than they had overall anticipated. He left the room so as to not wake Aria and Matthew. He stepped out onto the balcony outside their room. Even the ground floor had lovely white extensions to its rooms.

As he looked out, he noticed the beauty of the world around him. This city was much like one he would see back home. Then again, most of the cities back home were not underwater. Still, he had always loved the water, and this world had exceptional merit. He noted that the water was warmer than it had been back at Apolis. So, the whole world was not a frozen wasteland after all.

Today, they would seek Heaven's Isle. The easiest way would be to get to the capital of Mashan Telis and get a boat there. While their car could float above water, it was not made to last with no ground beneath it, not to mention it was illegal. However, the acquisition of a boat would be a difficult matter on its own. Without even bringing up the topic, all three of them knew they might have to steal the boat. In many ways, they had already accepted that concept.

Drage's mind wandered to the future again. He realized he could have a future here in this world that might be better than his future on Earth. Here, he would be a prince and be trained in leading the people and using the sword. On Earth, he would live out just another normal life. This quest really was the adventure he had been so desperately craving.

He swam upward. This activity had so far been one of his favorite aspects of the world. Whenever he wanted, he could just swim. It was a little harder in some ways here, but he had gotten used to it. He had given up trying to understand the mechanics of a completely underwater world. The logic behind it defied him fully, even though Draconis had explained much of it. A part of him was fine with accepting it for what it was. When he swam, he could forget everything else.

"Drage, get down here!" called Aria from the room.

Drage allowed himself to sink back down to the room.

Aria looked tired and a little frustrated with him. "Are you not even going to put on some decent clothes?" Drage realized he had just swum outside wearing nothing but his boxers. He smiled innocently at Aria.

"Me? Oh no, I was just sleepwalking again!"

Aria tried to look serious, but a smile kept breaking her face. "I'll bet you were." She kept thinking about how much she loved Drage. She was still upset with him for trying to leave her that last night at Apolis. That was part of the reason for forcing that promise out of him. Her faith in him had wavered since then, but she wanted to always feel secure around him. In her mind, coming up with that promise was easily one of the best things she had ever done.

Sometimes, her boyfriend could be such an idiot, but that never seemed to stop him. Aria remembered how her mother had criticized Drage when the two had begun dating. Drage was never dressed "properly." Aria had fallen in love with his overwhelming confidence and his independent thinking. She realized these were not the best qualities to look for in a man, but Drage wore them well.

She walked to Matthew and said, "Hey, Matthew, wake up. We need to get ready to leave."

Matthew sat up without a word. Aria eyed him. She could not help but notice how handsome he really did look. He was tall and had nice dark hair. Even before she had met Drage, Aria had always viewed Matthew as a very sweet guy. They had been friends for a long time.

Drage headed to the bathroom. "Hey, when I get out, I'll go and find us some breakfast, okay?"

Aria nodded and replied, "Alright, while you get breakfast, Matthew and I will start getting our things back in the transports."

Drage went into the bathroom.

Aria first heard the sound of hissing from the bathroom. Small bubbles of heat came from under the door. She heard Drage call, "You guys have got to try this thing!" Aria and Matthew laughed.

Aria turned to Matthew and said, "Hey, is Drage alright? He seemed a little off yesterday."

Matthew nodded. "Yeah, I talked with him a little bit. I was worried too. He's just a little freaked out by everything that has happened to us so far, I guess. He'll be fine though. I think he is still working out how he feels about this place. It'll take him a while to adjust."

Aria sat down on one of the beds. "It will take all of us a while to adjust. But for now, thinking about home is not going to help us at all. We need to be focusing on what we need to be doing about these Guardians."

Matthew raised an eyebrow. "The Prophecy?"

Aria nodded, "Yes. I think that you and I can figure it out, at least a little."

"What? You don't want Drage to help?"

Aria sounded tense. She was still unsure of that decision herself. "No, not yet. You yourself said he has been preoccupied. I don't want to stress him out anymore. This Prophecy is one huge riddle. It will wrack our brains constantly."

"True, but couldn't that help to distract Drage a little?"

"It could, but it could just as easily freak him out if the Prophecy reveals something...bad."

Matthew was surprised now. Aria was going somewhere with this conversation; he was sure of it. "Bad? What do you mean?"

"Well...the Prophecy implies that the Guardians will have to face off against the Y'mordi. If there is a clue to the outcome of that battle, it might show that some of the Guardians will die. How do you think that will sit with Drage? He will try—"

"—try to make sure the Prophecy doesn't happen. He would try to not show up for the battle."

Aria nodded. "Right. If he does that, we are sure to lose."

"Good thinking, but I think I still feel bad leaving Drage out of this."

"We're doing it to help him."

Then, Drage opened the door, and several air bubbles left the bathroom. He came out wearing a half-robe that covered his lower half. "The showers here are so cool! They shoot out jets of warm air!" He walked over to the pile of clothes he had brought in last night. Aria took her change of clothes into the bathroom to take her shower. Matthew walked over to the balcony both to give Drage a little privacy for putting some clothes on and to give himself some fresh water.

He said, "The water is getting warmer, Drage."

Drage called out from the room, "Yeah, it is. Hopefully, it will continue. I am not fond of the cold."

Matthew laughed. "You were born in the Southern Continent and raised in Massachusetts. How in the world are you not used to the cold yet? If we go too far up north, you'll sweat to death."

Drage mumbled through the shirt he was putting on, "It's still cold!" Suddenly, he stopped trying to squeeze his way through the shirt. "Hey, Matt, could you help me with this? I give up."

Matthew laughed and walked over to Drage.

"Okay, so the first part says, 'When seven come for seven coming, seven wake from seven sleeping. Seven lights for seven shadows,'" Aria began.

Matthew said, "Well, the first seven would be the Y'mordi probably. According to the Emperor and Draconis, they were really the first signs that the Prophecy is in motion."

Aria agreed. "Yes, but it says that they 'come for seven coming.' So, maybe there is another group of seven people that we don't know about. This would mean that they were chosen like we were though."

"And the next two mentions of seven are both the same. They're the Guardians."

"Right. Seven Guardians for seven Y'mordi."

Matthew asked, "And what do we know about the Y'mordi? Besides what Draconis and the Emperor told us?"

Aria thought for a second and then said, "Well, my instructor is one of the Prophets. In my training, she told me a little about the Y'mordi. She said that each one is skilled at using a certain Element."

Matthew nodded. "And the Elements are Fire, Water, Earth, Wind, Nature, Light, and Dark, right?"

"Right. Some of them, we have already met. The one with the katanas, Mali, used Light. The one who attacked him on the island used Fire. One of the ones that chased us to Apolis used Wind. Each Y'mordi is very skilled at their individual Element. That makes them particularly dangerous. Also, my instructor told me that the Y'mordi were given new names when they became Y'mordi."

Matthew clenched his eyes in confusion. "Wait, so what is the story behind them before they became the Y'mordi?"

Aria shook her head. "No one knows. You would have to know their names before they swore allegiance to the Darkness. According to my instructor, the Y'mordi have changed their names since then, anyways. The original names were…hold on a second." She walked over to her own backpack and pulled out a piece of metal. On it were scrawled several names. "The original names were Y'tal, Y'dax, Y'ran, Y'lam, Y'mir, Y'nas, and Y'xon. Obviously, they all had a 'y' at the beginning, probably to match the name of their little group. Now, we know only one of their modern names: Mali. I didn't get the time to study them, though. We left too early."

"So the Y'mordi have had three names: their pre-Y'mordi names, their original Y'mordi names, and their modern names…" Matthew looked at the first metal sheet. "Okay, what does the next bit say?"

"'Each with secrets hiding, and each with Hearts unique. The Thirteen shall rise up then.'"

"That is going to be confusing. 'Each' could refer to any group of the seven or all of them. Besides, knowing that someone has a secret isn't very helpful anyways. It only helps if you know the secret," said Matthew.

"That is true. 'The Hearts unique'… maybe that means that each of the Guardians has a unique Element too?"

Matthew smiled at the idea. "You're probably right! What elements do we have so far? We know that Drage is probably Light because of his dad."

Aria agreed. "Probably. But there is no telling about Draconis, you, or me."

"Well, let's keep that in mind when we look at the next section. 'The Thirteen shall rise up then.' Hm…wait a second, why thirteen? If you have any two groups of seven, it would be fourteen, right?" He had never been the best student in school, but he had always done well enough in it to be fairly competent in multiplication.

Aria looked at the Prophecy again. "You're right. Thirteen doesn't make sense. The only way that that could be possible is…if there was one person participating in both groups."

Matthew hesitated, "You mean someone who is a Lord of the Shadows and a Guardian?"

Aria nodded. "I think so. That complicates matters by itself though. How are we going to find the right one? How will we know if he or she will fight on our side at the battle?"

Matthew leaned against his transport and sighed. "I don't know." He turned and saw Drage coming back. "Hey, Drage is on his way here now. You might want to put that away."

Aria stuffed it into her transport and turned back to meet Drage. "Hey, did you get us some good food?" She tried to put on her best smile.

Drage looked at her, thought about an appropriate answer to the smile, and shook his head. He had given up on understanding women a long time ago. He held up the food for her and said, "See for yourself."

Aria distributed the food as she said, "Alright, well, let's get going. Remember, northeast. We need to get to some boats quickly."

"I know where you can get some cheap boats, lady," said a raspy voice. The three turned to find the innkeeper. "If you go just straight north of here, there is a popular fishing village. They sell boats there for pretty cheap. I don't know where you are going, but the boats they offer you will be pretty nice."

Aria looked at Drage and Matthew before turning back to the innkeeper. "Thank you so much, sir. And thank you so much for the nice room. We enjoyed our stay very much!" The innkeeper made a primitive-sounding grunt and walked back into the inn. Aria could not help but wonder how much the man had heard. She wondered why no one thought it was strange that three teenagers were roaming the Continent. She faced Drage and Matthew and noticed Drage's Sword. Maybe that was why no one said anything to them. Maybe, everyone was scared of that Sword. "Alright, what do you think? Should we trust him?"

Matthew shrugged his shoulders and said, "I don't see why not. He gave us a pretty good deal on our rooms last night. I think we owe him a little bit of trust for that."

Drage nodded. "Right. Let's go north, then. It can't hurt us to try, anyways."

Aria shook her head. "No, it depends on how fast the boat we get is. If it is very fast, it will save us time. Heaven's Isle is just north of the capital. If we can ride faster than the time it would have taken us to ride the transport from here to the capital and then to Heaven's Isle, we will have saved time. Otherwise, it will have been a waste. It is very risky."

Drage retorted, "When we left the Palace, we knew it would be risky. Let's go for it. If there is a chance of us getting there faster, it's a chance we need to take."

Aria was surprised. Normally, he would suggest rather challenging routes simply for the challenge of it. Now, he was using his head. She smiled at him with pride. Her boyfriend was not a complete dolt after all, it seemed. "Alright, everyone get in your transports. We need to get to this city."

Before he entered his transport, Drage turned to Aria, "Do you think Draconis and my dad are missing us right now?"

Matthew and Aria looked at each other, unsure of a proper answer. "I'm sure they are doing everything they can to find us," Aria responded.

Drage agreed. "Good. If we run into trouble, it will be good to know that Draconis and my dad are right behind us." He entered the transport too late to hear Aria and Matthew sigh. They both laughed at their harmonized sighing. Then, they too stepped into their transports. The machines hummed to life as they buzzed through the city, leaving the inn behind them.

Port City was one of the most unique towns they had seen yet. Instead of the typical tall buildings, it consisted of several small huts and cottages. Most of the men walked around with their shirts off, while the women wore what looked like bikini tops and skirts. It was certainly warmer than Apolis but still cold to Drage, Matthew, and Aria, too cold to be wearing practically nothing. Most of the people were busy with some chore or another and carried buckets of fish across the town, while others mopped an area with Wind. The trio was amazed by how busy the place was and by how normal everything seemed to the people.

Matthew moved in front of the others. "Hey, we need to start looking for some boats for sale. By the looks of it, every person here already owns a boat or transport or whatever you want to call it." He was still partially confused by the terminology here. He began scanning buildings for a "For Sale" sign or some other indication of an unwanted transport.

Drage called out and pointed, "There! I see one!" Matthew and Aria both followed the path from his finger with their eyes and saw the boat. It was large and had a sticker labeled "6,000 salt."

Aria frowned. "That's actually not that much. Why would anyone sell a transport for that much?"

A voice replied from behind them, "'Cause everyone already has a transport 'round here. An' I don' have the youth to still use a fast un like dat."

They turned to face the deep-voiced man. He was not wearing a shirt and allowed his bulbous gut to extend over his aquatic jeans. They could barely see the tattoos on his chest behind the wall of hair that hid them. The man was missing several teeth and had a pale complexion. He did not look fearsome, just not somebody you would want to mess with on any given day.

He held out his massive hand and said, "Mirah's da name. Spelled Em-Eye-Ar-Ei-Eich, but said like 'mee-rah.' I'm jus' a simple merchant here an' have shop temp'rarily set up 'ere in Port City. What can I do fer ya?"

The three looked at each other, wondering what to do, and Drage replied while shaking the hand in front of him, "We would like to buy that transport you have there." He pointed at the boat.

Mirah glanced back to the boat. "Ah, you've found a nice, little beauty, aincha? 'Tis a pity no one wants her, y'know. I be's glad you like 'er though. So I do. O' course, I'll lower da price for ya. How does 4000 salt sound?"

Aria gaped. *Is he seriously lowering the price?* She exclaimed, "We'll take it!"

Drage, Matthew, and even Mirah looked at her, shocked. Mirah spoke a little softer, "Alright, get yer salt ready, an' I'll go get da deed." He walked over to the boat and began rifling inside of it for something. Aria started counting the salt until she had the right amount.

"This is going to be easier than I thought," she said. She feared what was wrong with it.

Drage brimmed with confidence. "He said it was a fast un too—I mean…a fast one too."

Matthew laughed. "Nice going, Drage. Sometimes, you really are such a goof."

Mirah returned with a sheet of metal. "'Ere ya go. Da deed." He handed Aria the paper and took the salt in return. "What are t'ree young uns like yerselves doin' all da way out in Port City anyhow?" he asked.

Matthew responded, "Oh, we're just looking for somebody."

Mirah nodded and cleared his throat a few times. It was then that the trio noticed his humongous mustache. "Well, then. If ya need any help, be sure to give ol' Mirah a call." He handed Matthew what looked like a business card that was comprised of a thicker sheet of metal. Then, he walked away.

Matthew turned the card around many times and said, "I wonder what this is supposed to be. All it has on it is his name, 'Mirah Silverpike.'"

Aria examined the card and shrugged. "He said to give him a call. Maybe they use cards to communicate here. We should ask somebody about that eventually." Suddenly, she realized she had the deed to the transport in her hands. She jumped up in glee and sunk back down. "We didn't have to steal one!"

Matthew gestured back to where they had parked their own transports. "And what are we going to do with those?"

Aria looked back to the entrance of the city. "Hm. I suppose we will not need them anymore. Maybe they will still be here on our way back, and we might be able to use them. Until then, we can't take them with us." She turned back to the boat.

Drage stood beside her and said, "Alright, let's do this."

She nodded, and they opened the doors to the transport and entered.

It was simple yet larger than expected. It had several areas. The pilot's station was at the front. The middle was divided into two rooms: a bathroom and a navigation room with a strange computer that Aria began trying to figure out immediately. The back of the ship was a small sleeping area. It also had compartments with enough food to last them for close to two weeks. Matthew discovered a panel that opened to the "basement" of the ship, which was only a couple of feet tall. Though it was considerably small, it had enough room for any of the three to squeeze inside and work on the wires and engine parts that were found under the panel. It was Aria who discovered the empty storage compartments that made up the ceiling.

Once Aria learned the computer's basic functions, she pulled up a compass. It was holographic and floated in front of the computer. Just by wishing it so, she could make the compass change its size and even color. For now, it was a green pointer with the four directions labeled and several tics used to show the different angles. She called out to Drage and Matthew, "Alright, I have the computer figured out. Who's going to pilot this thing?"

Drage leaped to the front seat in the pilot's station. Matthew joined him in the second seat. Drage flicked several switches. These seemed like the same controls as the smaller transports. There were only a few extra features to this one that he had yet to explore. A few more switches later, and the ship rose, taking off into the sea.

Aria watched the compass and exclaimed, "Hey, you are going too far west! Turn it to the east more!"

Drage retorted, "Aye, aye, Captain!"

Aria just shook her head. Just when she had started giving Drage some credit, he made the same old corny jokes. She smiled. Some things about Drage would probably never change. She was fine with that though. Looking through a window, she watched as the edge of the Southern Continent came out from under them, and they were over just dark ocean. After checking the compass a final time, she leaned closer to the window and stared down into the deep abyss. The difference between transports and boats made sense to her now. Transports relied on propulsion, pushing off from the ground for help. They could survive in the deep sea but not for too long. The Helian transport they had taken to the Southern Continent when they had first arrived had probably just been a stronger transport. This was a boat built to just hover in the sea. The ship darted through the water at lightning speed.

Two hours later, Aria pulled up a holographic map and zoomed in on their area. They were already halfway to Heaven's Isle. The ship rocked violently. Aria fell to the floor as she saw the lights flicker. Matthew called out, "Hey, Aria, are you alright?"

The ship lurched again. Drage yelled, "What was that?" Aria carefully stood and moved to the window in the room. Outside, she could see nothing.

Suddenly, a man in black appeared in front of the window. He held up his hand, and Aria saw his mouth move. The ship was forced backward. Aria fell to the ground. She called out, "There's someone out there. He's using *mysteria* to hit the ship!"

Drage appeared and helped her stand. "Well, then, let's get out there and stop him! We've all been trained, right?"

She nodded and followed him and Matthew to one of the doors. They opened it and exited the hovering ship. Together, the three swam to the top of the boat and stood there. They raised each of their weapons in anticipation. The dark figure leaped onto the opposite end of the ship. His hood hid his face.

"Well, well. Look what we have here. It's my favorite Guardians."

Drage stepped forward, raising his Sword. "Stay away from us." He tried to sound confident, though he knew he was terrified. This man put him on edge more than the Y'mordi did. Something in his deep voice foreboded a different evil.

The man chuckled, but the hood did not move. "You are

all fools. Bow to Maris, the new Emperor of Darkness." He
pulled his hood back to reveal his face. His raven hair fell back
on his shoulders, and his tight lips cracked into a smile. His
cold, dark eyes stared at them cruelly.

Aria whispered to Drage and Matthew, "This battle isn't
supposed to happen yet. There is supposed to be seven of us,
not three. He'll kill us!" She knew that if Maris fought them
now, their chances of survival were slim. Matthew and Drage
looked to the dark man with fear and some determination. The
two boys clenched their teeth.

Maris smiled at them.

The Behemoth

Whipping out her wand, Aria shouted, "*Lune!*" A blast of Wind shot from its glowing tip. Maris waved his hand in front of his body, and the blast dissipated instantly. She was stunned. Only an exceptional mage could use *mysteria* without ever having to use any aids. It could come so naturally to some people. Maris seemed to be one of those people.

Drage and Matthew attacked with their weapons spinning. Maris lifted his hand, and a ball of black mist shot toward Drage, knocking him backward and covering him in what looked like dark smoke. He began suffocating.

Matthew continued his assault, whirling his staff and trying to keep Maris busy so as to give time for Drage to rejoin the melee. Maris had not even drawn a weapon. He was merely dodging all of Matthew's attacks as if he knew every move that was coming. Aria shouted from behind him, "*Farus!*" A small ball of Fire erupted from her wand toward Maris. Matthew jumped back, while Maris sidestepped to avoid it.

Drage pulled himself out of the dark cloud and rose. He held his weapon ready to fight. He realized he had not even attempted the Way of the Dragon yet. He tried to empty himself of his panic and fear and tried to focus. He lowered his stance to the one Draconis had taught him. He approached Maris. Seeing Drage coming closer, Maris raised his hand again to blast him backward, but Drage held up his blade at the right time, slicing the ball of dark energy into several small wisps. The Sword of Destiny could even slice through Maris's *mysteria*. The Sword returned to its stance. Drage jumped and spun at the same time. He built the momentum into one large attack forcing Maris to draw his own sword. Sparks flew as the two shards of metal clashed.

Maris was surprised at first and lost his previous confidence. Drage did not stop at his initial attack, however. He kept the form continuous and did not stop the speed of his attacks while trying to save his own energy and reduce his movement. With Matthew attacking as well, Maris was hard pressed.

Aria watched the battle in terror. She tried to think of something she could do but came up with nothing. There was too much chance of hitting either Drage or Matthew, even with her arrows. She observed everything and noticed that Maris was tiring. He was not half as skilled with a blade as he was with *mysteria*. Perhaps Drage and Matthew could defeat him after all.

Maris realized the tides had indeed turned. The boy with the sword was swift and used the same form that the Dragon had used closer to Terin. He needed to come up with a strategy soon. Then, he noticed it. With every strike the boy made, sparks appeared. He tried to focus on these and realized that it was not just two metals hitting each other. It was something greater.

He said, "So, where did you get that Spirit Sword, boy?"

Drage hesitated. Maris tried to slash at him, but Matthew aimed an attack causing Maris to shift his blade to block that instead. Drage continued the assault as he said, "How did you know it was a Spirit Sword?"

Maris smiled. "Because my sword is also a Spirit Sword. This is the Sword named Behemoth. Which one is yours?"

Drage did not respond and persisted in his form, trying not

to lose focus. He did not want to risk Maris knowing more than he knew already. Drage became tired himself. He noticed that Matthew still whirled his staff, not breaking a sweat. Matthew's attacks matched Drage's own speed strike for strike.

Aria could not take it anymore. She noticed all three of the fighters were becoming exhausted, and the likelihood of accidents was increasing. She raised her wand and called, "*Lune!*" She directed the blast to come into the center of the struggle and divide. It separated all three of them. Before anyone could react, she focused on relaxing and contentment, emotions associated with Water. She whirled her wand a second time and yelled, "*Dlaez!*" A wave of Ice appeared in front of her and shot toward Maris. It was her first real attempt at freezing something. She had seen the Prophet do it once.

Maris struggled to rise and shouted, "*Inferum!*" The ice melted before it reached him, but barely. Drage had recovered and ran up to attack. Maris turned to him and held up his hand. He whispered, "*Serva.*" Another ball of Darkness left his hand. As it approached Drage, it expanded to form a large cloud. The edges of it became several thin and dark strands. The cloud enveloped Drage and constricted around him. He struggled violently as the black mists tightened. Then, as quickly as it came, it was gone. Drage's eyes were wide open. He collapsed.

Aria called out to him, "Drage!" She ran to him as Matthew ran to Maris with staff spinning.

Maris laughed and stepped backward. "Luckily for you, I have work to do, kingdoms to conquer. Until next time." A black portal appeared behind him, and he stepped into it.

As the portal closed, Matthew sighed and turned to Drage and Aria. She was leaning over Drage. "Is he alright?" Matthew asked as he ran over to join them.

"He's still breathing and everything, but he's unconscious. I didn't recognize what Element Maris used, either. It looked like it was just Darkness though."

Matthew pulled Drage up to an almost standing position. "Well, let's take him into the ship. Maybe you can find something on the computer."

Drage's eyes snapped open, and he reached for his Sword. He yelled as he slashed at Aria. Matthew pushed her out of the way and grabbed Drage's sword hand. As they struggled, Matthew noticed that Drage was growling, and there was something different about his eyes. They were wild and furious, but most interesting of all, the irises were black. Matthew called, "Aria, do something!"

Aria did the first thing she could think of. She grabbed Matthew's staff and hit Drage in the back of the head. He slumped back to the ground. Aria gasped at what she had just done and at what Drage had just tried to do. Matthew lifted him up again. "Let's get him back into the ship." Together, they were able to move his limp body inside. They went to the computer. "Alright, let's see if this thing has internet."

Aria pressed a few buttons and watched the screen. She pointed at an icon. "I guess this is it. There are several of these links to different...areas. I don't think there is a unique program for the internet. It's as if all of the knowledge in the internet is already on the computer. There is no real connection or signal. It's just sort of there."

Matthew added, "Like magic?"

Aria nodded. "Right." She spoke into the computer's microphone. Aria had learned the computers in this world had advanced voice recognition software. "Search for..." She thought about an appropriate way to word it. "Magical disorders?" The screen displayed a site labeled, "Disorders of *mysteria*." She whispered, "This is it." She noticed the disorders were listed by Element. "Search under Darkness." The screen changed to list several specified disorders. She browsed through them. "Matthew, this might take a while. We might need to take Drage to the nearest hospital."

Matthew raised an eyebrow. "Oh? And where would that be?"

"Open new window. Search for nearby hospitals." She did not know if saying that would work, but she assumed it was worth a try since the computer could do almost everything else. A new window opened showing a zoomed-in map of their location. To the north was a red mark. "There," she said. "A healer should be right there on that island. It's called…Macela."

"Macela?"

Aria pressed a few more buttons and then explained, "Yes, overall, it is said to be mostly uninhabited. There is one large castle in the eastern part of the island. A Prophet lives there too!" She read over some of the information to herself. "She is considered a queen there by the people who live in the castle. She might be able to heal Drage too." She was still a little worried though.

Matthew nodded. "Okay, so what is the problem?"

Aria frowned. "Well, it seems that Queen Daghda has not been in communication with the Emperor for several months. Scouts were sent here but never came back."

"Why didn't the Emperor investigate more? Couldn't a Guardian be there?"

Aria shook her head. "No. According to this, though I would not know how it knew, the Emperor believes there is no Light strong enough in Macela for a Guardian to exist there."

Matthew came closer. "I wasn't under the impression that the Guardians had been publicized."

"They haven't. I think that this computer…knows that Drage is here. That would give us more access since he is a direct descendant of the Throne." She still was not quite sure how the computer could know those things. She glanced over to where Drage was. A sigh escaped her lips. "It's our only hope though. We are going to have to try to get him there. It's not that far away, luckily. Do you know how to steer this thing, Matthew?"

He nodded and walked over to the pilot's station. The ship shot off faster than even Drage had managed to make it go.

"Mali, come to me."

Mali approached the leader of the Y'mordi showing neither fear nor bravery. He knew an order when he heard one, and he was never one to disobey…except when he had completely failed an objective. "Yes, my Lord Pullatus?" He stood near

Pullatus now beside a fresh hole in the top room of the tower. He had always despised this tower. Even for him, it seemed too dark and depressing.

"Mali, I am afraid that the Great Servant Maris has become far too independent of thought. Rather than going straight to the Palace of Light now and attacking the Emperor, he seeks support from other kings and queens across the world. He does not want an assassination. He plans to start a war." Pullatus sounded so devoid of emotion. Mali regarded him now with a fear and awe. In all their years together, Mali had never seen Pullatus's face. Still, the Dark Lord Dagan had granted him leadership of the Y'mordi above all of the others.

"Is this not why we had decided to use him, my Lord?"

Pullatus did not turn from his hooded gaze on the ashen plains outside the tower. "It is, yet we did not seek for him to throw us away in the process. He has already gained the support of some of the nations in the Southern Continent."

"Pardon me, my Lord, but is it not true that that means we have those connections now? Surely by now, the Emperor will expect an attack on his life and will have his Loyal Servants everywhere ready to protect him at a moment's notice. Due to my failure, they surely know of the existence of the Y'mordi now."

Pullatus nodded and replied, "Yes, you are correct. Nevertheless, I am not satisfied with not having the Great Servant fully in our grasp. Today, he attacked the three Guardians from Earth. He attacked them alone. He almost got himself killed."

Mali frowned and thought for a second. "You know, my Lord... I am willing to do whatever I must."

Pullatus nodded again. "Yes, I do know, Mali. You have always been the most loyal among the Y'mordi, which is why you were chosen to be among us. I shall not assign you another task yet though. I shall need you when the Great Servant must fight the Guardians. In that battle, you shall be very much needed. Until then, your skills will be of no further use to me. You have failed me too many times here."

Mali looked down in shame. "I know, my Lord. No matter

how many times I fail though, I shall always insist that I will not do so the next time. I will not quit trying."

"That is a good spirit to have. You shall have a chance to redeem yourself nevertheless. For now, you may return to the Dark Realm."

Mali stepped back and bowed. "Yes, my Lord. I shall arrive when the battle begins." A white portal appeared, and he stepped into it.

Pullatus smiled. Mali was definitely a useful tool, and he could be easily controlled. Though he had punished Mali for his last error, Pullatus knew the truth. Over the years, the Y'mordi had grown weaker and softer. Some of them had been out of practice for so long. However, he knew that there were a few who were stronger than they used to be, himself included.

For now, however, he had other issues to attend to, one of them being the rebel Randir. He had killed Ixion once, possibly aided in the escape of the Guardians from Earth, helped them escape the island Varyx, and had eluded all communications.

Something would definitely have to be done about him. Randir had gotten stronger. He was puzzled as to how that was true, however. Pullatus, Randir, and Xarden had all been in the Palace of Shadows in the Dark Realm for most of the centuries. What powers had Randir received to make him this strong? Pullatus shook his head. It would not matter. The Darkness would punish Randir far more severely than he ever could. It would not be his problem then. He smiled at the thought of Randir's suffering.

Later that night, Matthew called out, "Hey, Aria! I think we are at Macela now."

Aria ran from the sleeping area to the pilot's station. Through the glass, she could see the island. Mountains stretched as far as the eye could see. Each one was covered with a thick layer of snow. Aria frowned in confusion. The idea of having snow in this world was ridiculous in her mind. Nevertheless, when she looked up she saw several gray clouds masking the watery sky. Aria shivered at the thought of going out into the snow. "I bet you it's a trick of *mysteria*. I doubt this weather is normal."

Matthew agreed, "You're probably right. You said the east side of the island, right?"

"Right."

He steered the transport to the east a little further, and they caught their first glimpse of the castle. It was as large as the Palace of Light yet twice as tall. "Wow," Aria said. "Well, all we have to do now is find the Prophet."

Matthew inquired, "Do you know which Element this Prophet dominates?" He had remembered that each Prophet had a unique Element. He also knew that there were three that worked directly for the Emperor.

"She is the Prophet of Earth. That means she will more than likely personify the Element easily."

Matthew was confused. "What do you mean by that?"

Aria kept her eyes on the castle. *What had happened to the Emperor's scouts? And why had this queen not been communicating with the Emperor?* Something was off here, and Aria planned to find out what it was, but first she had to help Drage. "Each Element is associated with certain emotions and feelings. The Prophets were chosen for each Element because of their personalities and in some cases adeptness in that Element. If this Queen is the Prophet of Earth, then she will probably be prideful, arrogant, strong, and full of hope. If I remember correctly, she will have strong senses of duty, desire, and stress. More than anything though, she will want to be protected. Don't say anything that might offend her."

Matthew nodded. "Alright, I can do that. Can Drage?"

Aria's eyes were still red from crying earlier. "I don't know. He hasn't woken up since I knocked him out." She was really hoping that she had not given him brain damage or anything. She had not meant to hit him in the head so hard with the staff.

Drage moved in his bed and groaned. "Matt...Aria...what happened?"

Aria heard the faint sounds and ran to the room. "Drage? Are you okay?"

He sat up and rubbed the back of his head. "Yeah, but my head is killing me." His eyes widened. "What happened? Where's Maris? Did we beat him? I don't…remember…"

Aria smiled. She had not killed him then. "Drage…Maris cast some strange spell on you. He disappeared, and then you started attacking Matthew and I…I had to…knock you out."

Drage's eyes widened. "It was real? I had been hoping it was just a really bad dream…" He looked down at the floor. How could he have let himself try to hurt his two best friends? He had tried to kill them. "Where are we?"

Aria touched his hand. She wanted to let him know that everything was going to be okay and that she was there for him. "We are on an island called Macela. The Prophet here will help get rid of that spell for you." She looked into his eyes and noticed the same thing that Matthew had seen: black eyes. Drage was not back to normal yet. The ship rocked as Matthew landed it.

Matthew called out, "Alright, we're here."

Aria looked at Drage, concerned. "Do you think you can stand? Or are we going to have to carry you?"

Drage waved a hand. "No, don't worry about it. I can make it just fine." He groaned as he tried to stand. Just as he was about to fall, Aria grabbed him. He smiled up at her. "Well, maybe I could use a little help."

Matthew noticed that Drage was conscious. "Hey, it's finally awake," he joked.

Drage managed a weak smile and opened one of the doors. "Let's get going."

Matthew went to Drage's other side and helped support him. Together, the three walked toward the looming castle.

As they trudged through the icy snow, they became more and more exhausted. Drage was not very heavy in reality, but the dead weight of him was making it more difficult. Matthew looked at Drage and noticed he was unconscious again. "Aria, look!"

She turned and gasped. "No wonder he became heavier all of a sudden."

"I'll carry him," Matthew offered, taking Drage from Aria.

Aria looked at him with a raised eyebrow. "Are you sure?"

Matthew smiled and replied, "Yeah, he's light as a feather."

"If you say so." She smiled as she walked. These mountains were quite beautiful with their snowy landscapes. The only disturbing part about them was their lack of any life. No matter how hard she strained her eyes, she could not see trees, animals, or even grass. The only possibilities for life had to be in the castle. She shivered.

When they reached the castle door, Aria noted it was not a large door but an elaborate one nonetheless, with intricate carvings in its wood with a lion-head knocker in its center. Aria walked up to it and banged the knocker against the door. The hollow sound seemed to echo across the island. It was the only sound besides their own misty breathing.

Finally, a voice echoed around them, "Come in."

When Aria opened the door, the room beyond was in a wrecked state. Broken chairs and tables littered the hall, while the remains of the glass chandelier sparkled from the torchlight that lit the room. At the end of the wide room was an elegant throne. The woman that sat there wore a simple white cloak and had long, white hair. Her wrinkled face made her seem a relic that matched the antique style of the broken, burnt furniture. Her thin, pale lips twisted into a smile. "Come in."

Of Curses

Aria stuttered as she fumbled for the right words.

Matthew stepped into the room with Drage on his back. "Are you the Queen of this castle, my lady?" He tried to sound as polite as possible. If Aria was right, this woman would love any form of compliment, though he preferred not to get the better of somebody the first time he met the person. In fact, he already felt guilty, but he tried not to let it show.

The old woman spoke again, "Yes, I am the Queen of this castle. However, I suppose saying that is not saying much. Everyone else here is dead."

Aria's eyes widened. "Dead...your Majesty?"

The Queen smiled. "Yes, I am afraid that the Emperor of Darkness has killed every last one of them."

Matthew and Aria looked at each other in horror. *What happened here? Did the Queen have something to do with this?* Aria thought of which emotions she would need. She focused on fear, love, and even caution. They were simple feelings for now because they were natural for this situation. She lowered her hand to her wand. She was prepared to summon Wind if necessary.

"Stop, girl," said a voice.

Aria and Matthew looked around, yet no one was near.

The voice repeated, "Do not raise that pathetic stick."

That time they found the source of the sound. It was Drage. He was conscious again. Matthew put him on the ground in fear and worry. Drage's eyes were wild, but he had not drawn his Sword like last time. He looked at Aria and said, "You would stand against one of the Prophets? You are a fool after all." His voice sounded doubled. Matthew could recognize one part of it to be Drage's own voice, but the other was harder to recognize. Aria's face turned red, both at the insult and at her confusion.

Drage turned to face the Queen. He took a deep bow. "My lady, you have already sworn your allegiance to me, yet you do not prepare your armies. Why do your err here?"

The Queen's wicked face became one of terror. "Lord Maris, the chanti have been denying my requests. They will not respond. It is not my fault!" she yelled, hoping for mercy. She remembered what Maris had done the last time they had met.

Drage up closer. "I can tell you are lying, Linda Daghda. Shall I have to make you suffer once more?"

A smile spread on the Queen's face. "No...you are in a weaker form this time, Maris. You shall be the one to suffer here. I do not know what trick this is, but you shall die here." She stood and held her hands up to the dark ceiling above them. "My chanti! Now, you may feast!"

Aria and Matthew looked to the ceiling in time to see a thousand long, green tentacles fall from the darkness. One at a time, several balls of the tentacles splattered on the ground and squirmed toward Drage.

Drage held up his hand and yelled "*Serva!*" Spheres of Darkness left his hand and forced the tentacle creatures back. He repeated the incantation, and strange black humanoids appeared. Each one wielded a simple black sword. They wore black, misty robes, and their faces lacked any real definition. All of their eyes were closed. Drage motioned with his hand, and the humanoids attacked the tentacles. These humanoids were

Shadows.

The Queen held up a silver scepter. She pointed it at Drage. A lightning bolt shot out of it, while Aria drew her wand and yelled, "*Lune!*" The lightning bolt curved in front of Drage and caused the nearest tentacle creature to explode.

The Queen screamed out, "No, my chanti!"

Each one of Drage's black humanoids raised its blade and held the chanti at sword point. Drage did not lower his eyes from the Queen. "I am not Maris. I am like you, nevertheless, my lady. Tell me where he is, so that I may rip his throat out. Give me your knowledge."

The Queen stepped back shaking and sat down in her throne. "No, I cannot tell you where he is. I have been ordered not to." Then, Matthew realized in horror that the Queen also spoke with the doubled voice. The other layer to both Drage's and the Queen's voices was the voice of Maris.

Drage walked closer to the Queen. "Very well. I shall have to take the knowledge from you then." He held up his hand and said calmly, "*Serva.*" Suddenly, a black cloud began pouring out of the Queen's body and floated in the water in front of her. Her eyes and mouth went wide in a silent scream. The cloud drifted over to Drage and entered his body. He convulsed until the cloud was fully inside of him. Then, he fell to the ground.

Aria and Matthew rushed over to him, ignoring the black humanoids and the tentacles. "Drage!" shouted Aria. As they came up to him, the Queen rose and held her scepter high. A barrier hit Aria and Matthew, slamming them to the ground. Aria tried to reach Drage, but the barrier blocked him off from them.

The Queen muttered, "Do not try to touch him. He is even more infected now." She approached the three teenagers. She snapped her fingers, and all of the dark humanoids turned into mist that floated up to the ceiling. The chanti crawled aside and scaled the walls to reenter the darkness. She leaned over Drage's body. "It is a curse that Maris had cast on both of us."

Aria was puzzled and unsure whether to trust the woman

or not. "A curse?"

The Queen nodded without looking up from Drage's body. "Yes, it is an old spell known as the Heartbind. It allows the caster to have full control over another person's heart. It is a dangerous thing and hard to break. Luckily, however, Maris was not very skilled with casting it. Somehow, he created a midway point. It is like he started the curse and then broke it off before it finished."

Aria could not help but be intrigued by the idea. "What do you mean? It looks like it was pretty successful to me."

"No, it was far from successful. There was only a small piece of Maris's control in both of us. However, a heart cannot split into two, so the heart tried to combine them."

Matthew looked up and whispered, "So Drage and you were both half yourselves and half Maris."

The Queen pursed her lips. "I am afraid so. However, your friend here took away that piece of me in order to gain information on Maris's whereabouts. Therefore, he has a lot more of Maris in him right now. The farther away Maris is, the less control he shall have over your friend. So, your friend shall be more like himself then. If Maris is nearby, I fear that your friend will be easily controllable and will probably try to kill somebody. Strangely enough, however, both he and I wanted to kill Maris even while under his curse. Maris's strength is not as great as I had originally thought." She frowned and turned to Aria and Matthew. "Who are you, and what are you doing here?"

Aria stood and responded, "My name is Aria. This is Matthew, and he is Drage. We actually came from Earth."

The Queen raised an eyebrow. "From Earth? Hm, that is certainly of interest. That does not explain why you are here though."

Matthew and Aria looked at each other, wondering whether to trust the Queen or not. Matthew nodded to Aria and turned back to the Queen. "My lady, Drage is the son of the Emperor of Light. The three of us left the Palace of Light searching for the Guardians of Light. Our first plan was to go to Heaven's

Isle, but Maris attacked us, and we found out that a healer was here. We needed to help Drage."

There was silence for a moment. The Queen stood and muttered a few words. Drage's body floated in the water and headed toward a door in the castle. "Don't worry about him. His body is going to a Stasis room."

"A Stasis room, your Majesty?"

"Yes, Stasis is a very old form of *mysteria* belonging to Wind. In this world, there might be a small handful of individuals who can use it even slightly. I happen to be one of them. It is the ability to freeze an object in both time and space. The object cannot think, feel, breathe, live, or die. It is a total immobility. In that state, he shall at least be safe for now, and Maris will not be able to sense him no matter how close he gets. I happen to know the ability because I sought its usefulness. I actually specialize in Earth, you know." She walked over to one of the other doors. "Now, come with me to one of my chambers. I need to hear your whole story before I feed you and give you a decent place to rest."

Aria and Matthew followed with reluctance. They trusted her more, but she had recently tried to kill them, so it was still awkward. Aria stole one last glance at the room and was amazed to see the furniture was repairing itself. Tables pieced themselves back together, and the chandelier pieces lit up again.

Draconis approached the Emperor and bowed before him. "Your Imperial Majesty, I have not found them yet, but I found a man in Port City who sold them a Bermuda 600 ship. By the looks of it, they headed north."

The Emperor frowned for a moment then said, "So, my son is trying to reach Heaven's Isle then. He thinks a Guardian will be there. He is clever yet. The place will surely be dangerous though." He had been surprised when Dragenopn left him. He had been even more surprised to find Aria and Matthew gone as well.

Draconis raised his head. "Shall I go and stop them?"

The Emperor raised his hand to quiet Draconis. "No. The

Prophecy said that the Guardians would face Maris. If this is true, then I have no doubt that they will return safely. Knowing that they are also searching for the Guardians is a worry off my mind now. I know that they will return alive. I just hope that they will return intact and ready to fight." He stood up from his throne, and his golden robe straightened. "No, we must let them do as they will. We can only help them by finding the other Guardians. Draconis, go to the Western Continent. We shall try to find the remaining Guardians there."

Draconis stood, replying, "Yes, your Imperial Majesty." A Gate appeared behind him as he stepped into it. It closed behind him.

The Emperor began to walk to the library when a high voice reached out to him.

"Your Imperial Majesty, have you heard from the Guardians yet?"

The Emperor turned to see one of his servants. It was the short man named Ixion who had been moved multiple times over the past couple of weeks. He had proven himself to be quite capable at each of his jobs so far, even as a guard, though Draconis had disapproved. The Emperor had not begun to trust the servant yet though. "That information is not for you to know," he replied and turned to walk to the library.

Ixion stood there and smiled. He had overheard the conversation between Draconis and the Emperor. He had only asked to test the Emperor's faith in him. He had much to tell Lord Pullatus.

"First, I shall have you call me Linda and not this 'Your Majesty' business. I am hardly a Queen anymore, though I suppose I still bear rights to the title of Prophet," started Linda.

The three of them sat in one of the numerous studies in the castle. It had been one of the only rooms that did not have dead bodies littering the floor. It was still a dark place, as the rest of the castle was. Linda had used a few quick spells to restore much of the room. The only light was the floating fire she had put in the middle of the room in the center of the triangle formation of chairs. Unlike most flames in this world, Linda's spell was colored red and yellow, similar to the ones on Earth.

She continued, "Now, I must tell you what happened to this place. Before I can help any of you out, even your friend in the Stasis room, I am going to have to help you know my story so that you can trust me.

"A few months ago, this castle was brimming with life. It had about as many people in it as a small town would. I had begun teaching a number of apprentices here as well. Being a Prophet who does not work for a king has many benefits. Everything was fine here. My people loved me. I had my own students. My army of chanti could ward off unwanted visitors. I had no problems.

"One day, Maris came into the castle. He told me he was trying to raise a rebellion against the Emperor of Light. He was trying to gain allies and wanted to know if I would support him. The list of reasons for the rebellion was outrageous, and he sought to overthrow the Emperor completely. I was against his thinking fully. Then, he offered me a position in the Emperor's Council if he became the new Emperor. At first, I wanted to heavily consider his offer, and then I just declined it again. I remember that I sent him away immediately. His reaction was not so kind, however.

"He cursed me and made me kill all those around me." Tears filled her eyes then. "He made me kill every last person here. When he left, my heart quit trying to fight him as much. I had nothing left. Not even my husband, the King, escaped the slaughter."

Aria felt sympathetic. *It had to have been hard killing everyone she knew and not having any control of herself.* She muttered, unsure what to do, "I'm very sorry to hear that...Linda. It must have been hard."

Linda looked Aria in the eyes and said with the slightest hint of a smile, "I'm fine. However, in order to help your friend, you need to know some of the conditions of his curse." Her scepter lit up. Strange lights whirled around it. The light dimmed to create several colors, and the colors separated around the scepter to make holographic images. They formed a multi-colored ball. "This is a typical heart. It has many different Elements and emotions involved in it, as you can see. Assuming that your friend has as much Light in his heart as his father does…" Some of the colors faded to leave white light replacing them. "There. That's better. This is similar to what your friend's heart should have looked like before the curse." Suddenly, a black cloud formed and surrounded the ball. "This is the curse. As you can see, even though that Darkness is very large, you can catch glimpses of his heart beneath it. That is what creates the mixture of Light and Darkness in him now. In some ways, he has control over that Darkness. Also, that means that Maris has some control over his Light." The dark cloud tightened on the ball and wrapped around it. "However, the closer Maris becomes, the more Darkness your friend shall experience and hence lose control. I am convinced now that this strange combination will lead your friend to want to kill Maris more than anything else. It will be his highest goal, but you must not let that happen if he is held by Darkness. Observe." The cloud squeezed tighter on the ball of color. Then, a light from outside the model heart came closer to the darkness and hit it. The cloud disappeared, and the heart underneath writhed in place. "If he kills Maris, it will remove the curse too quickly and likely destroy parts of your friend's own heart. It could kill him."

The whole display disappeared. Matthew raised his eyes to Linda in fear. "So, what can we do to help him then? If we can't let him fight, then Maris will only tighten his control, won't he?"

Linda nodded. "Well, that is partially correct. Maris can be killed, just so long as your friend is not under the influence of the Darkness. If you can get him to be himself for that while, he will be safe. Doing that will slacken the grip of the Darkness on his heart, making its elimination easier."

Aria inquired, "So, basically, the curse cannot leave Drage until Maris is dead?"

Linda nodded. "I am afraid so. However, I am going to

help you both as much as I can. You used some pretty powerful *mysteria* back there, you know. You were able to deflect a lightning bolt, and that is saying something. If you travel with the Prince of Light, I have reason to believe that you have great potential as a mage. Would you be interested in being my apprentice?"

Aria blushed at the idea. "I would love to very much. Only, I am not sure that now is the best time. We still need to find the other Guardians." She was surprised that a Prophet and Queen would consider her worthy of apprenticeship. She was overjoyed at the idea, but she saw the importance in finding the Guardians.

Linda smiled at her. "In that case, allow me to help you find the other Guardians. Do you have any ideas of where they might be?"

Matthew spoke, "We have an idea that there might be one on Heaven's Isle. We were trying to get there before we came here."

"Ah, I see. I suppose I can provide you with a Gate. It will take you straight to the coast of Heaven's Isle. Would you like for—"

She was interrupted as another figure entered the room. Matthew and Aria stood with their hands moving to their own weapons. As the figure came closer to the floating fire, they recognized him as Drage. He had his Sword in hand. He whispered in his doubled voice, "He is at Heaven's Isle then? Maris shall suffer this time." He turned and ran out the door.

Aria turned to Matthew in horror. "If he kills Maris like that, he will die too! We have to stop him!" All three of them ran in pursuit. Somehow, Drage had increased in speed. When they got to the front hall, Drage turned and unleashed a wave of Darkness. They had not seen this attack coming. Linda struggled with dissipating the cloud. She could not fathom how the boy had escaped Stasis like that. It was physically impossible to do anything while under its tight grip. Matthew did not need his eyes, however. He kept running and followed Drage out the door.

The snow whirled about them in their speed. Matthew became closer and closer to Drage but always just beyond reach. "Drage, stop! What are you doing?"

Then, Matthew saw where they were going. Drage was headed back to the ship. He intended on leaving. Drage gained an extra boost of speed and made it to the ship several yards ahead of Matthew. He opened one of the doors, ran to the pilot's seat, and started the ship. Just as it began moving, Matthew leaped through the open doorway. The transport moved quickly and went higher in the water to avoid the mountains and even the castle.

Matthew got up to find Drage's Sword pointed at his face. Drage spoke in a soft voice, "If you dare interfere with me, I will kill you. Know that." He sheathed his Sword and returned to the pilot's station.

Matthew stood the rest of the way and looked out the window. That ice-covered castle still had Aria inside its walls. He could not help but wonder when he would see her again.

Drage and Maris

Aria stood outside, watching the ship leave. They were gone. Tears welled up in her eyes. She hoped they would both be alright. The cold of the snow bit at her skin, but she did not care. The metallic dot disappeared into the distance.

"My dear, come inside," called a voice from the castle. Aria turned her head and went back inside the ruined castle. Linda stood there dispelling the remains of Drage's dark spell. Aria approached her.

"Please, can you make me a Gate to get me inside of that ship?"

Linda shook her head. "I'm afraid that is not possible. I could easily create a Gate to the inside of the transport but not without creating further risk."

Aria was doubtful. "What risks? I've been through a Gate before."

"That may be true, but Gates are more complex than you could ever imagine. In essence, a mage is taking matter from two separate places and creating a connection between the two of them. The Gate itself is made up of the collision of the matter. It is possible to enter it, but think about the space in which it is created."

Aria's eyes widened in recognition. "The space would be...destroyed."

"Precisely. If I was to create a Gate, there is too much chance that either of your friends could be in that exact spot. Do not worry though. I have something better in mind, if it suits you."

Aria stared at Linda, puzzled. The Prophet was so wise and seemed to have an answer for everything. "What is it?" she inquired.

Linda smiled at her. "If the three of you are the true Guardians of Light, and you are searching for the others, then I have no doubt that the other Guardians will be revealed soon. With your two friends scouring Heaven's Isle and who knows where after that, and with the Emperor probably searching as well, it stands to reason that the Guardians will all be found, with or without your help." She paused and walked closer to Aria. "I would like to prepare you more for the battle with Maris. I would like you to be at least a temporary apprentice. A sword and a staff can be extremely effective in a close battle, but a bow and arrow set will not be half as useful. Are you as confident with that wand as the others are with their weapons?"

"No," said Aria as she lowered her head. She agreed with the Prophet completely. There really was not a thing she could do for Drage and Matthew. Even if she was with them, she was not strong enough to help that much. One of the last times she had tried to help Drage, she had been unable to stop Maris from cursing Drage. She needed training. "You're right. I'm ready to be your apprentice." She held her head high. It was the only reasonable decision she could make.

Linda smiled. "You will do well. I am never good with names though."

"Oh, my name is Aria."

"Good. Aria is a nice name. Now, let us begin your training. We do not have a moment to lose. First, we shall practice Fire..."

Matthew was lying down on the bed, staring emptily at the ceiling. He could not believe this was actually happening. Aria was gone, and he was here with Drage-Maris on the way to Heaven's Isle. He felt pity for both Drage and Aria at the moment. In one battle, everything had changed.

With each passing mile, Matthew noticed his breath was no longer misting. The water's temperature was increasing. The thought of swimming outside now was comforting, though he did not have a chance to actually go outside at the moment. He figured Drage would just leave him behind in the dark depths of the sea.

Drage had changed for the worse. Now that Maris had a small form of control over him, Drage was far more heartless. When Matthew had tried talking to him earlier, Drage had just glared at him and turned back to steering. Though Matthew thought it would be a good idea, he just could not bring himself to knock Drage unconscious. The fact that Matthew was still alive was proof that Drage still had partial control over the Darkness inside him. Matthew was sure of that. The only thing he could do was wait for them to arrive at Heaven's Isle. From there, maybe Matthew could get Drage to snap out of it. The farther Drage got from Maris, the weaker the control would be.

Matthew rose from the bed and approached the pilot's station. He entered and took a seat next to Drage without saying a word. The ocean seemed to expand infinitely in front of them. There was water as far as the eye could see. Several schools of fish passed by the windows. To Matthew, the scene was breathtaking. He had swum in the ocean before but had never been to the depths of the sea in a vehicle that sped through the water like a fish.

Drage spoke without looking, "I can sense him. Maris is at Heaven's Isle. I can feel it."

Matthew became alarmed. If Maris truly was at Heaven's Isle, the search for the Guardians would be even harder. He would have to worry about keeping Drage safe, stopping Drage from killing Maris, and trying to find a Guardian if there truly was one there. That uncertainty worried Matthew. They could simply be going on a wild goose chase and not know it. "Drage, if you kill Maris, you will die too. It's that curse he put on you."

Drage's doubled voice was solemn yet powerful. "It sounds like a pretty lousy curse, don't you think?" He folded his arms. "I must kill him to become the new Emperor of Darkness. I cannot allow him to possess such a title."

Matthew became shocked at these words and protested, "Drage…if you kill him, you will die. There is no avoiding it. The only way to stop him safely is to find the Guardians. Drage, remember the Light. If we can work together, I am sure we can stop him, but you can't let Maris take control of you. You have to resist him!" He spoke a little louder than he meant to at the end. He was desperate to get his point across to Drage.

Drage turned to look at Matthew. His eyes were still black, but Matthew could have sworn that he saw a bit of the Drage he knew deep within those eyes. The second voice faded. "Matthew, I am trying everything I can to stop him, but he is so strong. I'm not sure that I can do this." He looked back to the rest of the ship. "Where is Aria? What have I done?"

Matthew felt sad and happy at the same time. Drage was back, at least for a little while. "Aria is back at Macela with the Prophet. She will still be there for us when we come back though. I'm sure."

Drage glanced back at Matthew. "So we're still going to Heaven's Isle?"

"Yeah. We're almost there now. We need to find the Guardians if there are any there."

A wide grin appeared on Drage's face. "We'll find them, Matt. I know we will. It will be hard though. I can feel him now. Every time I close my eyes, I see him standing in front of me. It's like he's waiting for just the right moment to attack me and take over." His eyes became watery.

"It will be okay. You just have to focus on your Light. You are the Prince of Light. You can't let yourself fall to Maris's Darkness," Matthew explained with a tone of sympathy.

Drage nodded and turned back to face the open sea.

"Right. I will try my best, but promise me something: If he does take over, I need you to knock me out or something. Don't let me do anything stupid, okay?"

Matthew said, "Okay, it's a deal." Drage was back for now. Knowing that fact removed some of Matthew's worry already. "I wonder if Draconis and your dad have found some of the Guardians yet."

"It's possible, I suppose. There is no way for us to know though. We can only keep searching. The Guardians are the only way that we can stop Maris."

Matthew studied Drage for a moment and then broke into a smile. "Since when did you become so stern?"

Drage smiled back and gave Matthew a shove. "Oh, shut up!" For a second, the dark in his eyes faded to a lighter gray. "Last time I checked, you didn't have to worry about some guy taking over your heart. It's not easy, y'know." He laughed.

"True, but you don't have your brother nearly trying to kill you, do you?" Matthew retorted.

Drage widened his smile. "Good point. I haven't killed you yet though, have I? Besides, I normally came after you with my sword even when we were back at home. Nothing has changed, right?"

They exchanged looks, and Matthew replied, "Right. Nothing has changed. Any day now, we'll be taking a Gate back home. You know what? I'd be willing to bet that Mom is making a nice warm breakfast for us right now. When we get back, it will be hot and steaming."

Drage looked out into the distance. "Yeah, that sounds nice. I miss the fresh air too. I miss feeling the wind in my face."

They were both silent for a while, sharing the beautiful view of the sea in front of them. The ship continued to carry them through the endless water. Though it was night, the moon shone with a pale light above the world. When fish passed by, the light reflected on their bodies, making them appear like bars of silver light streaking across the depths.

Drage broke the quiet, "He's gone. He's not on Heaven's

Isle anymore. He must have used a Gate. The change was so sudden. It didn't fade. It's just gone."

Matthew smiled. "That's good. It will make it easier to find the Guardians now."

"Right. You know, I am starting to wonder if after we check out Heaven's Isle, we could go back to the Palace. Of course, after we pick up Aria too though. I mean, we are definitely way out of our league out here, and there's no telling what could get at us. We have to be ready at the battle anyways. There's no point in spending the whole time adventuring. We could be training instead," Drage explained.

Matthew replied, "That actually doesn't sound like a bad idea."

"Plus, if we get back to the Palace, maybe my dad can do something about this curse thing."

Matthew's eyes gleamed. "You might be right for once."

Drage gave Matthew another playful shove and laughed. "Oh, thanks!" Drage was becoming more relieved. He could feel Maris's presence slipping away into the crevices of his heart. Then, he saw it in the distance. "Look out there! I think I see Heaven's Isle!"

Matthew focused his eyes ahead of him. He also could see the small black dot out in the distance that appeared similar to the island they were seeking. As they approached the island, the two realized that dark clouds formed above them. Matthew was the first to comment on the strangeness of the snow that fell from the clouds. "Hey Drage, does that snow look...red to you?"

Drage peered against the window, and his eyes widened as he whispered, "It's not snow...It's fire. The clouds are raining fire."

No sooner had Drage spoken than the flakes of fire grew into larger blazing balls. Soon, the two could hear the heavy orbs of flames bounce off the roof of the ship. They hoped the ship was not going to catch on fire. Matthew said, "We need to get to that island quicker. Can we make this thing go any faster?" He scanned the dials around him for one that might reveal an answer.

Drage seemed pensive for a moment and replied, "We might not have to." He turned to meet Matthew's inquisitive look. "I might be able to use this Darkness of Maris's. Whatever this curse is, it gave me some of his power, so I see no harm in using it. Did I ever say a word that summoned it?"

Matthew looked unsure as he said, "Yeah. *Serva.*"

Drage closed his eyes and concentrated. *What emotions are associated with Darkness? I don't even know.* He focused on the Darkness he could feel covering his heart. "*Serva,*" he whispered. A black cloud surrounded the ship, causing the fires to fade before they ever touched the ship. Drage smiled. "I did it!"

Matthew ran to the computer and pulled up the radar to look around the ship. The firestorm above was getting worse, but it had no effect on them. The island was drawing closer. Then, he saw them. A line of five or six serpents was headed in their direction. "Drage, I think we have some trouble coming this way."

Drage came to look at the radar, and his face paled. As the serpents came closer, the fire clouds dissipated to allow them to attack the ship. Drage had an idea then. "Alright, Matt, do you think you can steer the ship for a while?"

Matthew's rushed over to the controls as he said, "Got it!" Matthew knew what Drage was planning but saw no better plan of action.

Drage opened the door and clambered onto the top of the transport. The cloud of Darkness faded beneath his feet. He held his arms in a fighting position. He closed his eyes and focused again. "*Serva!*" he roared into the sea. Several balls of dark energy appeared around him. He motioned his hands forward, and the spheres shot toward the approaching serpents. Two of them became enshrouded and sank, still struggling with the tight clouds that had ensnared them. The remaining three dove under the transport to avoid Drage. "Where did they go?" he asked.

Both Drage and Matthew felt the ship rock as one of the serpents attacked the bottom of the ship. When another revealed its presence to Drage, he blasted it with another ball of dark energy, causing it to sink.

Two more were left.

Before Drage could prepare another spell, the remaining serpents swam back to the island. Drage was puzzled as he entered the ship again and asked Matthew what had happened, but Matthew was not at the pilot seat.

"I'm over here!" Matthew called from one of the basement compartments. He was trying figure out the inner workings of the ship. "That last attack really messed up the engine. We might be having a crash landing."

Drage ran to the pilot seat and attempted steering the transport so that it did not crash right into the side of the floating island. They were very close now. He tilted the steering wheel down so as to make the transport rise higher in the water. They barely missed the edge of the island.

"Matt, you might want to get out of there. We're about to crash!" Drage yelled as he pulled the steering wheel toward himself to try to slow the ship down, but it would not obey his command in time. The ship hit the ground, and both of the boys felt the force of it knock them forward. The ship jumped and hit the ground once more. This time, the two of them lost consciousness. They had reached Heaven's Isle.

Anima

Hightime always seemed to be the best season in the Western Continent. It was easily the warmest season as well. Because of this amazing warmth, many of the coral reefs were in full bloom. Draconis had often visited this Continent at this time of year just to watch the colors spread across the open sea.

Though he preferred the nice chill of the Southern Continent, he found many personal joys in the Western Continent. Along with the breathtaking coral reefs, the Continent held most of the world's atmosdomes. Many children in Gevás would delight in visiting these atmosdomes and playing in the bubbles of air. Air-running was what many people had called it several years ago. Draconis had learned in his studies that the people on Earth had a complete reversal of it just called swimming, where people would move through the water, which was a lot denser there.

The reason Draconis loved these atmosdomes so much was due to their reminding him of his own home. Like most dragons in Gevás, he had been born in another world called Sharl Vran, the world of Wind and Dragons. Sharl Vran was a place unlike any of the other worlds. It was a world of clouds, rainbows, and grassy plains suspended in the air by ancient forces.

His wide smile faded as other memories came to him.

He did not need the past, however. When he had first come to this world, Draconis had been only a child. He was lost and confused by the knowledge of another world. His coming here had only been an accident, but he had found guidance under the present Emperor's great-grandfather Bral Helius. Bral had been the first Emperor of Light who bore the name Helius. Remembering the old man made Draconis's smile reappear. For protecting Draconis, Draconis had promised Bral to protect the Emperors of Light for the rest of his life.

He stepped away from the soft beach and the stunning display of coral. His golden scales shone in the light of the sun above him. He approached Rulia's ancient forests. The faded green giants loomed above even him. Rulia was a peaceful kingdom as most of the kingdoms in the Western Continent were, and it was the home of many of the world's most powerful mages and aristocrats.

Draconis had decided to avoid the capital Pureau for now. If a Guardian was there, he or she would be nearly impossible to find. He needed to search the rest of the country first. The Emperor had told Draconis it might be possible for a Guardian to sense when other Guardians are near just by opening himself to the Light. Supposedly, the Guardians had a unique aura to those who could see through the Light.

"Three more Guardians..." he grumbled.

Maybe Dragenopn and the other two will find one or two of the Guardians while I am searching here. If they can manage to do just that, then we will be a step closer to destroying this false Emperor of Darkness.

Then, a Green Dragon appeared from behind a tree. She had blended into the surroundings so perfectly that Draconis had not even noticed her at first. Her long wings stretched down to cover her tail, and her three horns were elongated as well. "Are you the one called Rexam Draconis?" she asked in a meek voice, or at least as meek as a Dragon's voice could be.

The Golden Dragon nodded, hoping that this particular

Dragon did not try to make any connections that would cause any discomfort. "I am Rexam Draconis. How is it that you know my name?" he inquired.

The Green Dragon lowered her eyes. "Many Dragons here know of your reputation as the Loyal Servant and Guardian of the Emperor of Light. You have been regarded as the Golden Hope by many of the Dragons here."

Draconis's eyes widened. "The Golden Hope? And what is it that you all hope for?"

The Green Dragon's eyes met Draconis's own. Her eyes matched the emerald color of her scales. "Freedom."

Draconis shook his head in denial. "No, that is not my responsibility. That was before I came here, before Bral Helius."

A small dragonet ran from a tree to grab his mother's leg. The child's horns had not developed yet, but his wings had already reached the top of his legs. The Green Dragon put her hands around the child in a soft embrace.

"You cannot be serious, Rexam. You are the only nonhuman who is truly free in this world. The leader of Rulia has begun removing our space and making the boundaries even tighter."

Draconis gaped at her. "Tighter? Is he crazy?" he growled.

The Green Dragon felt a secret joy that Draconis had revealed that much care. "He is no crazier than other humans. Rexam, can you not see? It has been a little over 150 years since Mentiris's rule. Why does your Emperor insist on maintaining this segregation?"

Draconis did not have a ready answer though. "Has it been that long? Yes, I suppose it has. I had to have arrived here around 130 years ago." He had always held duty higher than his personal wants and desires. The Emperor of Light Mentiris had ruled before Bral had. One of the things that Mentiris's era had been known for was the Griffin's Rebellion. History shows that the Dragons, griffins, and even the anima had started a rebellion against all mankind. Emperor Mentiris had started a form of genocide of the nonhuman populations to counter this rebellion and had eventually settled for three marked areas of the world where nonhumans were allowed to live: the Northern Continent, Rulia, and Saldir.

Bral had made Draconis an exception, stating to the public that Draconis had entered Gevás after the Rebellion. Because of Draconis, the Dragon's Clause—which stated that nonhumans who came to Gevás after the Rebellion had already ended would be exempt from the exile—had been created. However, few nonhumans had arrived in Gevás since that time.

Due to the fact that Draconis had felt a debt to Emperor Bral, he knew he could not protest the exile. He had no right to question the actions of the Emperor, and no human ever spoke up for the rights of the nonhumans, not even the later Emperors of Light.

"Rexam," began the female, "There is another name that is mentioned among us now: the Black Hope. He is an anima from Astra in the North. He wants to lead the exiles against your Emperor."

Draconis growled. *Now both Maris and the Black Hope are trying to kill my master?* "You would defy the Emperor of Light, Dragon?"

The Green Dragon snapped back in her own growl, "I would if he does not care for us already. The Black Hope is the promise of a new Emperor, an Emperor of Darkness."

Draconis's heart skipped a beat. Maris *was* the Black Hope of the exiles. This meant that Maris was from Astra, and he was also an anima. If this was true, then the Guardians were in a greater danger than he had originally suspected.

He turned to leave the Green Dragon and her child. "I must see the Emperor."

Now, it was the Green Dragon's turn to be frightened. "You will not tell him of what I have told you, will you? You will not tell him of me or my child?"

As Draconis summoned a Gate, he turned his head to the Green Dragon. "The information you have given me is important, and I must relay it to the Emperor, but fear not. You and your dragonet shall be safe. I serve the Emperor of Light now." Before he stepped through the Gate, he held his hand back to the Green Dragon and said, "*Eldra.*" The mark of an Imperial Seal etched itself into the water. "Take care of your dragonet," he said as he stepped into the shining Gate back to the Palace.

Sarn yawned.

"You can't be ready to leave already? We just got here," said her twin, Arnim.

Sarn snapped back, "Well, we have been doing this for the past few days. Every day, Maris just wants to go and negotiate with some ruler or another. And every time, he just expects us to wait outside for him. Aren't we supposed to be guarding him anyways? He seems a little pushy to me."

Arnim nodded in consideration. "True, but you must be patient. Your impatience almost got us killed outside of Terin." Arnim had been very angry that day when the girl and that foolish Dragon had disabled both of the twins. The plan had been to get ahead of the Guardians and stop them at the Palace where Ixion would be able to help the twins, but Sarn had not been able to wait and had attacked far too early. Arnim had had no choice but to join her sister in combat.

Sarn's feet shuffled. She had apologized countless times after that particular disaster.

"You have a point though," Arnim continued. "I, too, have noticed that Maris does not want us around. It seems that he is attempting to simply use us. If he succeeds, he wants to be able to credit only himself and leave the Y'mordi out of the picture."

"If we are going to have to kill him anyways, what does it matter?" asked Sarn.

Arnim stayed silent. Then, she whispered, "That is not the best question here. Why is he trying to influence leaders on the Eastern Continent? Nonhumans are not allowed here, and as a matter of fact, Mentiris was from the Eastern Continent. Most of the people here absolutely despise anything that is not of man. They are often against the use of *mysteria* as well. Maris is an atrocity to them, especially if he reveals that he is an anima."

Sarn nodded in agreement. "You're right, so let's just grab him and take him to the next place. We are just wasting time by staying here."

Before Arnim could protest this suggestion, Sarn had already stepped through a Gate. Arnim shook her head. Her sister was always so impetuous and anxious. She needed to slow down. Nevertheless, Arnim held a fond smile for her sister's innocent and almost juvenile personality. Then, she too stepped through the Gate.

Draconis opened the doors to the Throne Room and ran to the foot of the golden chair. He knelt before the Emperor and started, "Your Imperial Majesty, I have new information regarding this self-proclaimed Emperor of Darkness."

The Emperor replied, "Rise, Draconis, and speak to me of your new information."

As Draconis rose, he became aware of the third person in the room, the Emperor's new personal servant, Ixion. He snarled in anger, "Are you not that foolish guard who tried to bar my entrance into the city?"

Ixion paled with a fear he did not have to fake. The Emperor replied to Draconis, "Have no worry. He has done well here in Apolis and has recently been promoted to be my personal servant. Nevertheless, I know that you are not fond of the man." He turned to the servant saying, "If you could please excuse us."

The servant bowed as he left the room.

Draconis snarled, "I truly do not trust that servant, your Majesty. He reeks of a strange scent. I wish you would hire someone with whom you are more familiar."

"I will do no such thing, Draconis. He is a fine servant. Now, tell me of your news."

Draconis's face would have reddened if it were not covered in golden scales. He bowed once more before the Emperor. "Forgive me, your Majesty. I meant you no disrespect. I merely desire your safety."

The Emperor stepped down from his throne and put a

hand on Draconis's shoulder. "All is well, Draconis. Now please, say what you came to tell me." He walked a few steps farther, gesturing for Draconis to walk with him.

"I have discovered that Maris is an anima from Astra. He intends on freeing the exiles from the Griffin's Rebellion."

The Emperor turned to Draconis as they walked. "An anima, you said? That is serious." He recited from an old book he remembered. "'Anima are animals blessed with the powers of *mysteria*. At will, they can transform into a human, and they are powerful mages.' Being an anima would explain how Maris became as powerful of a sorcerer as you have claimed. It also accounts for his preference of *mysteria* to the sword."

Draconis shook his head. "That is true, but somehow he has learned how to use a sword anyways. He might be using *mysteria* as a way to do that. With each passing day, he is only becoming stronger and stronger. We must prepare to fight him with or without the other Guardians."

The Emperor forced, "No, Draconis, we must adhere to the Prophecy. Besides, this news that you have brought me is a good thing as well. It means that Maris is not completely evil. He is not obeying the Lords of the Shadows. He is going to try to use them. That is very good news indeed. His heart may still see Light once more."

Draconis replied, "If what is said is true, then he will not listen to you. He will bear too much hatred for you and have too much love for freedom to be able to listen to reason. I am confident the Y'mordi are only feeding his darkening heart with more and more lies."

The Emperor snapped back, "Are they lies, Draconis? Do you think that they are? Or are you just saying that to please me?"

Draconis opened his mouth to speak of his loyalty to the Emperors of Light, but then he stopped. Deep down, he felt the exiles deserved to be free. He thought back to the dragonet he had seen earlier. It had been born in this world after the exile. The Dragon's Clause did not protect such creatures. He knew it was not right, but he said, "My loyalty is to the Light and whatever laws the Emperor of Light dictates. I am your Servant." He lowered his head in commitment.

The Emperor sighed. "I know, my friend. You have always been faithful to me and my whole family. I do not doubt your loyalty. Forgive me, Draconis." He turned to enter one of the side hallways and looked out one of the windows. He waved a hand over it, and the stained glass became clear, enabling him to look out upon his city. "Maybe you are right, Draconis. Maybe we should get ready to fight here if need be. Now, the three children are our only hope of finding the other Guardians. If Maris is going to go about this affair as a politician, he will have armies when he arrives. Alert the military."

The Emperor was in charge of all three of the military divisions: the navy, the terra, and the Enigma Brigade. While the navy were the aquatic troops, and the terra were the ground troops, the Enigma Brigade was a secret organization of the Emperor's strongest fighters and sorcerers. It was a small handful of individuals. The Enigma Brigade had been around since the end of the Obsidian Wars. It had been founded by the remnants of Lux's army, the Light Brigade. Now, the Brigade, along with the rest of the military, needed to help protect Apolis.

Draconis bowed as he left. "Yes, your Majesty. As you wish." The Gold Dragon formed a Gate in the middle of the Throne Room and went through it to enter the streets of Apolis. He headed toward the military's headquarters. If Maris was bringing armies, there would be war soon.

In the Palace of Shadows, Mali stood tall in the central ballroom. It was a dusty old room that had been used as a practice room for the Y'mordi since the Final Battle of the Second Obsidian War, when the Dark Lord Dagan and Lux had completely disappeared.

Mali focused on keeping several Lights shining brightly in the room. He could count twenty of the glowing spheres in the room. It was difficult to focus on the high amount of spells here. Light seemed to be one of the most harmless Elements to an outsider, but Mali had learned how to make it dangerous. The first time he had obtained this ability, it had resulted in one person gaining skin cancer. Since then, he had been able to magnify the ability so that objects could literally explode at the high frequencies he emitted. For Mali, Light was a weapon.

"Mali," called a voice from behind him.

Instantly, the twenty orbs vanished, and the room fell into darkness. "Pullatus, my Lord, what is it that you desire?" said Mali as he bowed to the leader of the Y'mordi.

The short figure in black spoke again, "The battle is about to begin, but first I need you to bring Ixion to the ruins at the Obsidian Plains. I believe Maris fixed one of the holes in the atmosdome, so it does not rain as much as it did last time. In a few more days, we shall all regroup there. Maris has almost finished his political negotiations. Apolis shall soon be taken."

Without rising, Mali summoned a Gate behind him. "Yes, my Lord." He stepped backward into the Gate and closed it once he could feel the ground of Helio beneath him.

Heart of Fire

"And the emotions associated with the Element of Nature?" continued Linda.

Aria answered, "Nature is associated with courage, wonder, freedom, competence, pain, innocence, indifference, and generosity."

Linda nodded. This girl was clever. She had a certain aptitude for memorization. "Very good, and what about its forms?"

Aria looked up in thought. "Nature is made up of the forms Poison, Growth, Medicine, and Wood."

"And in relation to the other Elements, what are its strengths and weaknesses?"

This question had been Aria's greatest problem. She could remember the common sense ones, but some of the others were harder to remember. "Nature is strong against Liquid, Air, Force, and Dirt. However, it is weak against...Lava, Lightning, Flame, Ice, Gravity, and..." She paused.

Linda realized she was taking far too long to finish this one and smiled. It was good that the girl realized she was not perfect. A person who knows their mistakes can fix them easier. "Force, Aria. Depending on the strength of the Nature and the strength of the Force, Nature can be weak or strong against Force. Sometimes, summoning a tree can shield you from a blast, but anything weaker will be swept away. Do not forget that."

Aria nodded, ashamed by the fact she had not known the answer. "Alright."

The Prophet of Earth stopped questioning her. "Very well. Why don't we practice using *mysteria* again?"

Aria nodded again and held her wand in a ready position.

Once the stream of Fire billowed from Linda's hands, Aria waved her wand, shouting, "*Lune!*" The fires fanned out around her instead of attacking her. "*Dlaez!*" She breathed out as the flames chilled into nothingness.

Before Linda could prepare another attack, Aria repeated, "*Lune!*" The blast from her wand shot at the Prophet, but Linda dissipated the spell before it reached her. She counterattacked with Lightning, and Aria defended, "*Gejman!*" A wall of Dirt appeared in front of her, shielding her from the Lightning. The Prophet had taught her on the benefits of the Element Earth. Aria did not stop there, however. "*Nexum!*" The Lightning bolt left her wand, traveling through the dissipating wall, and Linda barely shifted the bolt in time.

Linda smiled at the force of the attack. "Very impressive, girl. You are getting much quicker. Remember not to hold onto your thoughts. Distractions are the last things you need when casting such spells. You need to be able to switch between emotions so thoughtlessly that any spell will be possible for you at any given moment."

Gratitude washed over Aria. She was glad to see she was progressing already. Linda had begun their training by testing Aria's present abilities in *mysteria*, and Linda had not been impressed. Her method for teaching was a lot stricter than the method of Mistress Leona, the Prophet who had trained Aria in the Palace of Light.

After this testing, Linda had quizzed Aria on her knowledge

of the Elements, but when that had failed, Linda had begun her instruction of Aria in that knowledge. "Now, I want you to try to divide your emotions. Try to control two spells at once. Attempt two simple balls of Light."

Aria focused her heart on the concept. It was like trying to look at two things at once. The problem was that she had to see those two places with her heart. "*Eldra*," she whispered, still trying to hold her focus. Then, one small Light appeared to her right, but she did not lose her control.

Linda urged her on, "Don't give up. If you cannot summon another one, then divide the one you have created. Focus on the Light."

Aria closed her eyes to deepen her concentration. Gradually, a second glowing sphere illuminated the space to her left. Her eyes opened, and the lights moved around her, appearing to chase each other in their relaxed circle.

Linda's smile grew. "Very good, Aria." She used her own *mysteria* to dissolve the spells of Light. "Let's take a break."

The massive dining table was long enough to seat around thirty or forty people. Since the Prophet had not yet been in there, the furniture was still repairing itself. It did so at a hurried pace when she entered the room with Aria at her side.

Linda tried not to allow her sadness to take over her now. Though she knew there was a decaying corpse under the table, she did not look and only sent a wave of *mysteria* around the room to take care of the body along with the damages to the room.

Aria's curious expression revealed her amazement at how the room pieced itself back together. "Excuse me, but what Elements are you using to do that? It seems very advanced."

Linda shook her head, delighted she had such an interested apprentice. "A lot of it is using several spells of Gravity. It pulls the materials closer together, and then I use Growth and occasionally Lava to fix the items. It is not as complicated as it may seem. Soon, perhaps you will be able to perform the act."

The dust scattered into an enormous cloud as Linda used

Force to clean the table. The cloud escorted itself outside as the two sat down on the fully mended chairs.

Aria smiled. "You know, I am really beginning to like magic."

Linda was puzzled for a moment and then showed a look of realization. "Magic is what they call *mysteria* on Earth, is it not?" inquired the Queen.

Aria nodded. "That is right. We call it magic."

"Such an interesting term. It makes it seem more trivial, less ancient. Well, let's eat." Food appeared on silver platters that shone in the light of the glimmering chandelier that had just repaired above them.

"So," Aria began. "Do you think that Drage and Matthew are going to be okay?" She had hid it well during her training, but she was extremely worried about the two boys since they had left. She hoped that both of them were alright.

A look of fondness appeared on Linda's face. "I am quite confident that both of your friends will be perfectly fine. The one with the curse in him—Drage, correct?—had a strong light inside of him. When you open yourself to *mysteria*, you can sense the Elements around you, and I could sense Light in his heart. He is definitely the Prince of Light, and he will remove his curse. I have faith in that. The one with the staff will make sure of it too."

Aria turned toward the Prophet at the mention of Matthew. "And what about him? Could you sense anything in him?"

"He, just like you and Drage, has a strong potential of *mysteria* inside his heart. However, his heart lies more in the Element of Earth. He exhibits many of the emotions associated with it as well. Perhaps one day, he will learn how to use his abilities."

Aria looked down at her food. "Maybe. I hope he finds out soon though. It would help him a lot if they ran into any trouble." She ate her food mechanically, still thinking about what Drage and Matthew were doing at that moment.

Linda began, "Do not worry about them. They will be fine. Besides, I do not think that Maris is looking for them. He is trying to rally support from the other leaders of the world. He wants to start a battle against the Emperor."

"But he cannot do that until all of the Guardians of Light are there."

Linda nodded in agreement. "That is true, but keep in mind that the Prophecy will be fulfilled. If you realize that, then you will see that neither Drage nor Matthew nor any one of the Guardians will fall until that battle. They are guaranteed that safety."

Her heart felt reassurance at those words. She had been worried of the answer and had not asked Linda about the accuracy of Prophecies, but now she saw that it could not hurt. "Linda, are all Prophecies true? Are they always guaranteed to happen?"

With a sigh, Linda explained, "That depends on who made the Prophecy. Prophecies are very difficult to explain, actually. Only a Prophet can make a Prophecy, though no one is quite sure what one's affinity for an Element has to do with the ability to create a Prophecy.

"A Prophecy comes to a Prophet at random and is, in essence, *mysteria* speaking through the body. It is a strange event, but these Prophecies are often very true. However, some Prophets have made false Prophecies in the past. Theories behind this phenomenon range from bad interpretation by the individual to possession by the Darkness. Regardless of the cause, not all Prophecies are to be taken as fact, but if a Prophecy begins coming true, one can assume that the rest of the Prophecy is true as well."

Aria understood and nodded. "I see…Have you ever made a Prophecy, Linda?"

The Prophet's eyes shone with remembrance of a time when she had made a Prophecy. "Yes, I have, but it was only once, and, to be quite honest with you, I would rather not discuss it as of yet. Please, enjoy your meal." She smiled at her apprentice and at the same time wished that the girl was not so inquisitive. Linda admired Aria's curiosity, but she felt that that interest in everything around her was a little too strong. Aria needed to learn her boundaries. She needed to understand that not everything should be learned.

"Aria, before we move on in your training, I would like to know your heart's true Element."

"My heart's true Element? What is that?" asked Aria with a puzzled expression.

Linda explained, "Though it has the potential to change, every heart is made up of mostly one idea, one feeling, one Element. This Element is known as the heart's true Element. There have been cases in the past where people have had two true Elements, but I have not heard of a time when someone had more than that amount."

"And how does one discover his or her true Element?"

"Relax your mind and what control you possess over it. Allow whatever emotions you have flow free throughout yourself. Do not try to direct your feelings. Let the essence of *mysteria* pour from your body. Then, I will be able to identify your heart's true Element."

Aria nodded and closed her eyes. She relaxed and felt almost tired. Her heart released every feeling she had at that moment.

Drage's black eyes no longer held that spark of life as she looked into them. She missed the old Drage, the one that did not take everything seriously and did not try to kill her and Matthew...

Mirah's hearty grin...

The light reflected from Apolis's golden walls and shimmered in her eyes along with the amazement at the unbelievable beauty of the city.

In the storm that Maris had summoned, Draconis had held Aria in his claws protectively. "Everything will be alright," he had said...

Matthew's thoughtful smile spoke softly that first morning, "Let's let Drage sleep. Why don't we try to explore the island a little bit? This place is so strange. I can't figure out how we are able to breathe in this water..."

Weeks before they had arrived in Gevás, Drage and she had been swimming in the sea, and she could not help but marvel at his physique. He had risen from the water and glanced up at the sky with a twinkle in his eyes. Those amazing brown eyes reflected the blue sky, the clouds, and the sun so perfectly. Drage had always been scrawny, but she loved his body sometimes anyways. Many women would have said that seeing a man's skin cling to the bones like that was just gross, but she did not see it like that. The drops of water that clung to his torso were little pinpoints of light that surrounded him and almost gave him a warm glow. She loved him…

Linda felt Aria's emotions shifting. She could sense fear, comfort, determination, sorrow, and mostly love and passion. Those two emotions filled most of Aria's heart. The Prophet had discovered Aria's heart's true Element, though it was counterintuitive. She had personally hoped that the child's Element would be Earth as her own was.

"Aria, you are Fire, it seems."

Her eyes opened, and she understood what the Prophet had told her. "Fire? That is my heart's true Element?"

Linda nodded. "Yes, you have such strong passion and love inside yourself that Fire is your strongest Element."

Aria was proud that she knew her heart's true Element, and then a thought hit her. "Wait, I think you just revealed a part of the Prophecy…No, you revealed two, if not more!"

She ran to her backpack and retrieved the sheet with the Prophecy inscribed on its silver surface. "Matthew and I had decided that the segment that says, 'Each with Hearts unique' meant that each of the Guardians of Light and the Y'mordi will have their own Elements. Also, it means that no two Guardians or Y'mordi will have the same Element. It must refer to the heart's true Element. So, this means that I am Fire, Matthew is Earth, and Drage is Light. We are still missing Nature, Wind, Darkness, and Water." She continued scanning the Prophecy. "'A prince born of Light and bound to destiny' must refer to Drage obviously. 'A protector born of Earth and bound to Light' is probably talking about Matthew since his Element is Earth… He is bound to Light because his brother is the Prince of Light. He is bound to the Sword of Destiny!"

Linda smiled. "And that means, Aria, that you are the 'Earthan love with strong heart overflowing.'"

Aria turned her head toward the Prophet. "Linda, how is it that I can use *mysteria* the way that I do? My parents were from Earth. They had no ability, or at least I don't think they did."

"You told me your name was Newman, did you not?" Linda pondered for a moment. "If the ability is not in your blood, then it was given to you. There is another ancient, forgotten spell that utilizes *mysteria* and also focuses on all five of the core Elements. It involves giving all of your ability in *mysteria* to another being. This spell is known as 'gifting.'"

Aria was astonished at the idea. "Someone…someone gave me their powers?"

"It could be, though I could not imagine why." Indeed, Linda was just as perplexed by the idea as Aria was. Why would somebody gift an Earthan child? Linda knew that some piece of information had to be missing. She just did not know what that information was. She sighed in frustration and decided that maybe it was not for her to discover.

Aria was fascinated by the idea. Someone had given her their powers of *mysteria*, and she wanted to know who had been so willing to sacrifice such capabilities to a young girl and when it had happened. How long had she had these abilities? Had her parents known something of this underwater world? The questions seemed endless.

"Aria, I am starting to think that we should continue our training elsewhere."

Linda still felt the aroma of death that filled this broken castle. No matter how much *mysteria* she used to repair the place, the fortress would be a graveyard in her mind. A part of her kept expecting her tender husband to come in through the front door to embrace her once again, but the once lively castle was only dark and melancholy now. The life she had cherished was gone, thanks to the sorcerer Maris. Her fists clenched in anger.

"Oh?" questioned Aria. "And where will we go? What if Drage and Matthew return?"

"The Guardians will reunite at the Palace of Light. That is where we must go. It will at least give the Emperor some reassurance, and there are others there who can teach you. I have not spoken to his Imperial Majesty in a while. I think it would be best if we went there."

"Are you sure that Drage and Matthew will be okay?"

Linda sighed. "You truly do love them, don't you?"

Aria nodded. "I do."

"They will be fine. At some point, all of you will be together again at the Palace of Light. The Prophecy says the Guardians of Light will fight Maris. I know that everything will turn
out right. We need to continue our training in Apolis. Besides, I
would like to see what the Emperor is planning to do next.
Here, I have lost track of the happenings of the world."

"Do you have a ship we can use?"

Linda shook her head in exasperation. "You have too many
questions, girl. No, we will not use a transport. You forget that
I am one of the Prophets: I will simply construct a Gate. It is a
medium-level spell that can theoretically be created using any
Element: it requires focusing on making a sort of bridge of that
Element connecting two points in space. A world's main Element is usually the easiest Element for transporting around that
world."

A blast of Sand left the Prophet's reaching hand and transformed into a vertical whirlpool of light and dirt. Aria walked
to the Gate and entered it without fear this time. The last time
she had been in a Gate, it had taken her to a new world.

Linda took one last look at her castle. She glanced up at the
chanti that were still attached to the ceiling. "My dears, please
flee to the mountains now. It is time for you all to return. I may
not be back."

With that request, the slithering tentacle creatures exited the
castle through the shattered windows. A tear left Linda's eye.
Even before her castle had become populous with traveling
mages, Linda had had her husband and the chanti to keep her
company. Suddenly, she felt alone.

When the last creature left the castle, Linda broke the spell
that had preserved the castle's existence over the decades. As
she stepped into the Gate, she could hear the relic building collapsing on itself. The graveyard was burying itself, it seemed.

The Gate closed behind her, along with everything she had
ever loved.

Heart of Water

The scent of flowers woke Drage. He groaned in pain as he struggled to rise. He tasted blood in his mouth and saw blood lining a few cuts on his hands. Drage ran one bleeding hand through his hair and winced as he felt another scratch on his forehead. He turned to Matthew, who appeared to be in no better condition. Drage shook his older brother's shoulder. "Matt, get up. Get up."

Matthew stirred and hissed in a breath. "Are we alive?" He sat up and looked around. He turned to see Drage's bloody figure and said, "Are you okay?"

Drage nodded. "Yeah, I'm fine. We're both alive too. I think I'm going to check on the ship from the outside, though. We are going to need to use it to get out of here."

Matthew's head ached from the crash. "I will see if I can find some med supplies or something on the ship. My head is killing me."

Drage unbuckled his seatbelt and went to the door. When he found it would not open, he used the Sword of Destiny to slice through the lock. The Sword slid through the metal with ease. He smiled at the power of this Sword. The door slid back, and the warmth of day rushed over him with the brilliant sunlight. Drage stepped into an immense field.

Once his eyes adjusted to the brightness, the vivid red of the surrounding flowers flooded his vision. The exotic birds swam far above him and sang beautifully. It was the first time he had encountered animals other than fish here in Gevás. In the distance, Drage could see several low buildings. "We really did make it. We made it to Heaven's Isle…" he muttered to himself. Then, he turned back to the ship. "Matthew! We made it! We're here!" he called with a smile spreading across his face.

Then, he saw the state of the ship. The whole front was wrecked. The cuts that Matthew and Drage had suffered had likely come from shards of the windshield glass. The back half of the ship was fine, but the front would definitely need some repairs before they left.

Matthew came out with a small medical kit. It held several bottles labeled with minimum information. He pulled out a small tube called "Stitch-All." The directions on the back stated that this medicine was used on cuts of all types. Matthew shrugged and squeezed a small amount into his hand and rubbed it over his abrasions. To both their amazement, the skin stretched itself together, healing on sight as the medicine evaporated. Matthew grimaced at the tickling yet almost itching sensation he experienced.

Drage equipped the same medicine, and Matthew surveyed both the damage to the ship and the beauty of the landscape around them. "So, this is Heaven's Isle? It's a nice place. Do you think we will find any Guardians here, Drage?"

Drage shrugged as he watched his wounds heal. "I hope so. I would hate for this whole journey to have been for nothing."

Matthew pointed to the houses in the distance. "I suppose we should check there first. It's the only sign of people that I can see." He stuffed a few of the medicine bottles in his backpack.

"Yeah, let's go," Drage agreed as they walked through the exquisite red flowers. The water was so much warmer here, and the scent of the flowers filled the boys' noses. It was a sweet smell that reminded them of home and the trees that thrived in the heat of the sun and the rain of summer.

They were halfway to the houses when a deep and slow voice resounded over the crimson meadow. "I am honored to have the Prince of Light and his brother in my presence. However, I would like to know what has warranted such a visit."

Drage and Matthew spun around to find that no one was near them. They were alone in the field. Yet, they could still hear the long breathing through the currents of the water. Matthew responded, "We are looking for the Guardians of Light. A man named Maris has tried to kill us and will probably attack the Emperor of Light, unless we find the Guardians."

The voice rumbled, "The Guardians of Light? You will not find them here. I am the only one here now."

The two boys turned toward each other in confusion. Drage called out to the voice, "Well, can we at least see you? We came a long way to get here, and we can't just leave without having met at least somebody."

The voice was silent for a while, and then it responded to Drage. "Come to the buildings ahead, and I shall meet you there."

The two walked faster. Though they had not seen the person, he was certainly a demanding individual, and they did not want to keep him waiting. As they neared the buildings, they became aware that no one was there. The buildings were short, metallic structures without windows, and only one of them had a door at its side. They ventured closer to this particular building and opened the door, making a loud, creaking sound.

Inside the building was a long, spiraling stairway that wound straight down into the darkness. The two looked at each other and descended the stairs without a word. After a few minutes, they came across a door, but the stairs had not stopped. They continued for as far as the eye could see. The impatient voice came from somewhere behind the door. "Yes, open the door."

As Drage put his hand on the doorknob, Matthew felt unsure. Something did not seem right. The Emperor had said that no one had ever come back from this island. Had anyone ever gotten past the storm of flames and the serpents? What secret hid on this island?

The door opened, and a humongous silver room was revealed to them. It reminded them of a hangar at an airport. The ceiling probably touched the surface of the island. Standing in the middle of the room was an old man in a gray robe. The boys approached him, and they saw his silver hair reach down past his shoulders. His face was old and gaunt, yet his posture was tall and straight. In his right hand was a tall metallic scepter with a clear orb at the end of it.

Once they approached him, Drage raised his Sword. Drage laughed, and his doubled voice echoed around the room. "So, you were hiding here, old man? You knew that I was on the surface then. Tell me: Will you aid the Emperor of Darkness? I fight against the Light of Helio. Where do you stand?"

The orb on the old man's staff glowed a bright blue as a wave of cerulean light shot out to engulf Drage, but the boy did not react to the flash. He did not move at all: He did not even breathe.

Matthew turned to his brother, worried. "Drage? Drage?"

There was no response. Matthew turned to the old man and exclaimed, "What did you do to him?"

The old man spoke in his deep and deliberate voice. "I put him under Stasis."

Matthew shook his head. "That won't work. He's escaped Stasis before."

The old man laughed. "That is impossible, boy. The only way a person can be freed from Stasis is if somebody releases the spell for them. Stasis freezes someone in both time and space. Do you not know anything of ancient spells?"

Matthew swallowed. "I honestly don't. Neither of us are from here. We are from Earth."

The old man was quiet.

Matthew continued, "Drage is under a curse that the sorcerer Maris put on him. It is the Heartbind but a mutated form of it."

The old man sighed. "Before I trust you, boy, I am going to need you to prove yourself to me. I need to know that you truly are Matthew Helius."

Matthew stepped back in surprise, ready to raise his staff. "How did you know my name? I never told you."

"My name is Marqest. I am one of the Ancients, a group of people who were able to survive the Obsidian Wars and used *mysteria* to keep themselves alive. However, I am one of the last of the Ancients. I have held this island as my fortress and have protected it against the rest of the world for about a century and a half now. However, I have watched Gevás carefully over the years, and I have even watched your journey since you arrived here."

Matthew retorted in frustration, "Then, why did you act as if you did not know us at first?"

"I needed to test Dragenopn to see if he was being influenced by the Heartbind. Because he is in front of me and under Maris's control, I suppose that is reason enough to believe that you are Matthew as well." He turned and walked away from the two. He gestured with a finger for Matthew to follow him. Matthew took one frightened look at Drage and walked after Marqest.

As they walked to the other end of the room, Marqest said, "Now, boy, I shall try to help you as much as I can, because I, like you and your brother, serve the Light—"

Matthew interrupted, "Out of curiosity, sir, why are you here? If you serve the Light, could you not have done it better by serving the Emperor?"

Marqest snorted. "No. Ever since Lord Mentiris, the Emperors of Light have misunderstood the meaning of the Light. I will serve no one person. After the Wars, I made it my goal to serve the Emperors of Light, and I was raised to the role of Guardian of the Emperor of Light. However, Emperor Mentiris did not trust me and branded me a traitor to the Light and then banished me. He had some nerve, banishing a Prophet…"

Realization dawned on Matthew then. His eyes widened.

"Sir, excuse me, but I think you are one of the Guardians of Light."

Marqest turned to Matthew. "You were not supposed to figure that out. Now that you have, you will make sure I come with you to fight in this battle, will you not?"

Matthew winced at the suggestion. Was he really going to make an old man fight? He had to though. "'A Prophet and wise man hiding eternal,' said the Prophecy. You are an Ancient and a Prophet. You are the Guardian of Light that the Prophecy speaks of. It is not about what you want, what I want, or what anyone wants. It's about fate. We're all caught in it." Gradually, Matthew began to realize that was what their entire journey had been so far. They were all stuck in one Prophecy. At that moment, he felt helpless.

The old man chuckled. "Do not worry, boy. I knew that this day would come. My master almost a thousand years ago was the Prophet La Faye. She taught me everything about *mysteria* and the ways of the world. Before she died, she created the Prophecy of which you speak. Then, she told me I was one of the Guardians of which she had spoken. I have long known I would face this battle, and I have not feared it." Now, Matthew was awed. He could not imagine this elderly man fighting in the prophesied battle. "You saw how quickly I put your brother into Stasis. Do not underestimate me, boy." The man smiled as he clicked his scepter into a tile in the floor. The walls opened, and massive screens replaced them, and a chair appeared in front of a long keyboard. "This is what I have called the Compendium of Myriads, or COM, for short. It is the largest database among all worlds and has ultimate knowledge. It has recorded almost everything that has occurred in this world since around 900 years ago. I have fed COM hundreds of thousands of books, and I have given it something unique, a mind. It can reason, and decide, and think, just like you and I."

Matthew stared up at the goliath machinery in front of him. It stretched to the ceiling. *How could technology think?*

Almost in answer to Matthew's thought, Marqest spoke. "COM, locate Matthew Helius." Every screen displayed Matthew in the room as he stared up at the screens, and the image created a mirror effect that went on to infinity. Marqest turned to Matthew. "Ask it any question. Ask it a riddle, if you wish. It enjoys a good riddle."

Matthew gaped at first, and then he pondered for a hard riddle. Then, he began:

"The black child of a white father;
A wingless bird that flies even to the clouds of heaven.
I give birth to tears of mourning in pupils that meet me,
and at once on my birth I am dissolved into air."

Marqest snorted at the riddle. "That is a clever one. It does sound Earthan. Did you understand it, COM?"

The screens cleared, and a face appeared that covered all the screens at once. It had features but not necessarily unique or distinguishable ones. The face was constituted of hundreds of blue numbers. "Yes, I understood. Matthew Helius, is the answer 'smoke?'"

Matthew was dumbfounded. The computer was smart indeed. "Yeah, that is the answer."

Marqest smiled with pride at his ancient invention.

COM interjected, "Marqest, Maris has arrived. He has killed our remaining serpents and has dissipated the fire storm. What shall I do?"

Marqest growled at the news. "It appears that Maris intends to take me away from my own sanctuary." He turned to Matthew. "Listen to me, boy. I will be able to hold off Maris for a while, but you and Dragenopn must go to the Northern Continent. You have two more Guardians to find. I will meet you there after I take care of things here. Prophecies are funny things. There is a good chance that one of the Guardians will exist near Maris's old hometown."

"Maris was born in the Northern Continent?" asked Matthew.

"Yes, he is an anima, and you shall soon learn what that is." Marqest pointed his scepter at Drage, and the frozen boy's body was pulled toward it like a magnet. Marqest allowed his scepter to create a Gate in front of them. "I will be there soon,

I promise," assured the old man.

Matthew nodded. "Be careful." He stepped into the Gate. Marqest clicked his scepter, unfreezing Drage, and then pushed him into the Gate behind Matthew, and the two boys found themselves in Astra of the Northern Continent.

Marqest opened a second Gate, traveling to the top of the island. His eyes scanned over the field of dead flowers. The birds no longer sang above him. "You killed everything."

Maris smiled. "If you had approached me as an honest man would, I would not have seen the need to teach you a lesson, old man."

"I am the Prophet of Water."

Maris's grin faded. A pang of fear stabbed at his heart for a moment. The Y'mordi twins at his side took a step backward. They had seen Maris defeat the Prophet of Earth at Macela, but she had not been prepared for the attack. This Prophet was already in anger, it seemed. This battle would be far more dangerous.

Marqest allowed his feelings of sorrow wash over him. The orb of his scepter took on a light blue hue. Thin tendrils of mist crept across the island that had once been Marqest's small paradise. "It is wrong to deprive an elder of the small things in life. Were you never taught that?"

Maris grunted, "I was taught that old men had a tendency to be a little crazy and stayed inside all day."

A wave of Stasis left Marqest's scepter and attempted to freeze Maris, but he saw it coming and moved out of its path just in time. "You will have to be quicker, old man." Then, Maris saw the second wave that had already been released. He held up his Sword hoping it might prevent the spell from hitting him. To both his and Marqest's surprise, the spell failed against the blade.

Marqest smirked, "You are lucky I did not make that stronger. I figured a quick, weak spell would do the trick."

These words boosted Maris's confidence. "Luck is all that matters to me."

Marqest's eyes squinted in frustration. "Hmph, the sword in your hands is none other than the Behemoth, the legendary Spirit Sword that brings the user luck in its finest form. Its greatest setback is the weight of the blade. It would require either a strongman or a gifted mage to lift it."

Maris clenched his teeth. *How does this old hermit know so much about the Spirit Swords?*

Sarn had had enough. She held one closed hand up, and several tiny rings of wind appeared around her. When she opened her hand, each ring transformed into a metallic link. The links formed an immense chain. She charged at the Prophet, and her spells of Air made the chain straight and solid, not flexible as a chain should be. Using Air in this manner made the chain more similar to a staff. The metal weapon crashed down above Marqest's head, but it met only Marqest's scepter.

Marqest pushed her away and summoned an icicle from the ground. It stretched in an attempt to pierce Sarn's heart, but she leaped away, laughing.

Maris roared, "Stop this! You are both my guards, not my warriors. Leave him to me!" He summoned Darkness and wrapped Sarn in it, constricting her life.

Arnim growled behind Maris and raised a pistol to his head. "Let her go…"

Marqest watched all of this unfold, interested. The binding force of the Y'mordi was strong still, but it seemed the Y'mordi truly were just using Maris as Maris strove to use them.

Sarn summoned Force to remove Maris's dark hold on her. She fell to the ground, coughing. The Y'mordi had the ability to breathe in both water and air, regardless of the world. However, breathing pure Darkness was only something that Pullatus could do.

A portal opened behind the Y'mordi, and Xarden entered the area, a hood masking his face. "Sarn, Arnim, Lord Pullatus wishes your presence. We are preparing to fight."

Maris smiled at Xarden's appearance. "Good, Xarden. Tell Pullatus that I have almost gained enough support to start the war. I would still like to visit Hurale and Astra before we make our final preparations."

Xarden bowed deeply to Maris and stepped backward into the Gate he had created. Sarn and Arnim followed without looking back at Maris. In that moment, both of the twins had wanted to kill Maris. His Sword truly did give him luck. Maris was counting on that luck to bring him to victory.

Maris turned toward Marqest with a chilling smile on his face. "Well, it looks like it is just you and me, Prophet."

Shadows and Lies

The traitor...
  The loyal servant...
    With shadows always in mind...
  That is what it says about me...

Randir had been considering the words of the Prophecy multiple times over the past few days. He was both an Y'mordi and a Guardian of Light according to that Prophecy. He had never meant to be a part of it, but it seemed he had no choice in the matter. He wanted that fool Maris dead, and if that meant helping the Guardians of Light, he was willing to do it. He could remember the specific orders from almost a thousand years ago: "Bring me the blood of the seven Great Servants." Pullatus twisted those orders to serve his own ends, and Randir did not like it.

He had been searching for the two remaining Guardians of Light since he had rescued Matthew and Drage from Maris's whirlwind. The Southern Continent had proven to have no other Guardians, however. It made sense. That Continent was where four of the Guardians had already been found. It would not make sense for there to be any more there. There was enough oddity in the fact that four *had* been found there.

Around the time that Drage, Matthew, and Aria were moving toward Heaven's Isle, Randir had transported himself to the Eastern Continent, the kingdom of man. His feet carried him across the grassy plains of Immyx. Memories came alive all around him. Before he had ever become an Y'mordi, he had been a King. His name had been Lord Victor Ferro at the time. His land had covered most of the Eastern Continent during the Obsidian Wars, and all of present-day Immyx had been his as well. This area had been where his castle had stood. It had never been as great a castle as the Palace of Light or the Palace of Shadows, but it had been a monument to Lord Ferro's own power.

Power. That particular quality had been Randir's goal since he had learned its meaning. Even when he was King, he had envied the Dark Lord Dagan and his unsurpassable power in politics, battle, and in overall influence. That was why he had left his kingdom to become one of the Dark Lord Dagan's elite: Dagan had promised immense power and semi-immortality to those who could pass his Trials. Randir remembered how his eyes had lit up with greed.

The Trials had proven to be very difficult, however. The Trials had consisted of the Trial of Body, the Trial of Heart, and the Trial of Will. The first two had been relatively easy for Randir to complete, but the last one had been the hardest challenge he had ever faced. The Dark Lord Dagan had filled his mind with Darkness and made him feel the greatest pain of mind that could ever be felt. In his mind, he had seen himself killing his beloved queen Ophelia over and over again.

While he had been shaking in fury of the vision, Randir had bowed to the Dark Lord Dagan and pledged an eternity of loyalty to the one true Emperor of Darkness. He had been given the name, "Y'ran."

Randir kept walking across the plains. He needed to find the other Guardians; at least one had to be here. He sighed. The Eastern cities always had so many people, but, luckily for him, no one believed in the Y'mordi. To the Eastern Continent, he was just a legend, a myth. He smiled at his own misty reputation. If the men here looked back at their history, they would remember Lord Victor Ferro, and they would know him as one of their most powerful Kings ever, but they also saw him as a deserter and a traitor.

This thought made him sick. Now, he had nothing. His power was worth nothing to him, and his wife and kingdom were gone. The only thought that kept him going now was that once the goal of the Y'mordi was fulfilled, he would no longer have his immortality: He would be free at last. His greatest wish was his own death. It was not a morbid thought to him. He had lived over ten times the normal life span of a human. The end was a welcoming idea to him.

The hum of an approaching transport reached his ears. He turned to the sound and saw two men riding on a very large motorcycle that floated above the ground. Perhaps, the men would not think anything was odd about his red hair, the long scar that crept across the right side of his face, or his black robe. But then again, robes and cloaks were things of mages, and the Eastern Continent specialized in technology, not *mysteria*.

As the transport stopped in front of him, a man stepped out in a strict, militaristic uniform. "Excuse me, sir, can I help you?" asked the uniformed man. The man's name was Jangal. He had spotted the strange, cloaked man from the Capital. His red hair was definitely foreign as well. Seeing a sole, peculiar figure in the night outside the city made him curious.

Randir smiled warmly at the two men. "No, thank you. I am fine. However, I must ask you: does the Capital still require a permit to enter?"

The two men from the motorcycles looked at each other and then turned back to the stranger. "Yes, sir. You can buy a permit relatively cheap though. It costs around 1,000 salt right now."

"Gentlemen," began Randir. "That is too expensive even for me, I am afraid. May I have yours?"

The men took a step backward and drew their small rifles. "What?! We're not going to just give them away to you."

Randir flipped up a hand and allowed a stream of Lightning to attack the man who had spoken. The weak current roasted the man's body as Randir gradually increased the Lightning's power. The smoking, half-liquidated corpse fell to the ground. "Such a waste," smirked Randir. He turned to the other man.

The gun fired and pierced the Y'mordi's side, but he did not even flinch. "My turn," Randir said with a smile. Summoning his long hammer in an instant, he swung it once, hard. He knelt over the two bodies and retrieved a permit from the second body. It was not a form of identification: it was only a person's ticket into the Capital.

He looked down at the fresh corpses. He did not feel any pity for the men. One fact he had learned over the years was that life was cheap. "Count yourselves lucky. At least you have the luxury of death."

He tilted his head to the sky and stared at the hundreds of stars above him. One of the aspects he loved about this world was that there were hardly ever any clouds. At night, almost every star was visible, and every constellation told its tale to him. He used to gaze at the stars with Ophelia.

A tear rolled down his cheek. No matter how much he wished for it, he could never have the past again. He could not save her. It was too late.

A scream roared from the depths of his lungs and filled the sea for miles. The ground around him exploded into passionate flames, but his anger stopped there. In this patch of inferno, he glanced at the stars one last time and whispered a promise to the water around him.

"One day, I'll find you again, my love. Just one more time. I promise."

The city was immense and rivaled the grandeur of even Apolis. The futuristic city that Dragenopn Helius had imagined when he had entered Terin more closely matched this place. The Capital held massive skyscrapers and hundreds of vehicles traversing the spaces in between the titan towers. Earsplitting music boomed throughout the city, and though it was a nuisance to foreigners, this music, with its drums and guitars and beautiful vocals, was a link that connected the young and old of the Capital, bringing life to a person regardless of his or her age.

Randir looked around, examining people to see if they had a significant amount of Light in them, but everyone here seemed the same. He realized that finding a Guardian here would be harder than he had previously thought. The heavily populated city seemed to have grown since he was last here. He wanted to use *mysteria* to destroy everyone around him, and he would know that any survivors had the potential of being a Guardian, because the Prophecy had to come true. However, he knew that such a commotion would only call attention to himself, and the other Y'mordi would find him.

Randir became aware of another person in a black robe. His mind flashed back to what had occurred back on Earth. Pullatus was still probably looking for the person who had rescued the three Guardians of Light on Earth, the one who wore the black robe as if he was one of the Y'mordi. It was not unusual to see a person in Gevás wear a black robe, but the robes that the Y'mordi wore were not made up of a particular fabric. They were made of pure Darkness. The mysterious stranger had not made another appearance yet however, and perhaps that fact had calmed Pullatus. The person in the black robe, perhaps a hiding mage, disappeared into a side alley.

He exhaled. The world was a brutal place. He entered the nearest pub and sat down by the bar. He called to the bartender, "I'll have just a small draft."

There were no such things as alcoholic drinks in Gevás, but the drinks at the pubs had spells on them that helped alleviate feelings of depression. As Randir sipped the small glass in front of him, a lightly armored soldier sat beside him. "Bartender, I'll take a bubbler, please."

Randir murmured to the soldier, "Had a rough day, huh?"

The soldier's head turned to Randir, and he realized the

soldier was actually a girl. Her hair had been cut to a short length, and somehow the girl had found a way to hide her maturity. The girl had the appearance of a young lad, yet Randir could see she was indeed a female. The bartender had not noticed, however.

"It was a little rough, I suppose. That air-crazed mage has been bringing Shadows to the Continent, though the Emperor Regin has told the sneak we will not house him or his party here," explained the deep voice.

Randir grinned at the imposter. "Oh? I was never under the impression that they allowed people like you into the army."

The girl retorted, "What is that supposed to mean? I am one of the Captains of the Emperor Regin's army. What is wrong with a drink every now and then?"

Now, Randir was astounded. "A Captain? Well, may I have a word with you?" Then, he whispered in her ear, "My lady."

It was the Captain's turn to be surprised. Her look softened into a faint smile. "No, I do just fine right here. My name is Terrell, Captain Terrell, though my birth name is actually Stehl. However, I am sure you can understand why I do not want the latter name to be advertised."

Randir nodded his head. "I can indeed. I am assuming you know the penalty for your crime, Captain?" Randir knew the law well. He had been the one to first make the rule that stated that women could not serve in the military. It was not that he had thought that females were necessarily weak. His own wife Ophelia had been in the army before he was King, but he did not want to see her get hurt.

The soldier snickered. "I know the penalty, but so do the scores of others that fight in the army."

Randir's eyes widened. "Others? How many are there now?"

She turned back to her drink. "What does it matter to you? I don't even know who you are."

"My name is Randir. I was born here several years ago, but this is the first time I have come back in a while."

"It's changed, hasn't it? To answer your question, Randir, at present, I would guess that at least a third of the army is made of just females." The words had accidentally slipped. The bartender turned his head, surprised.

Randir growled and jumped over the bar. He grabbed the front of the bartender's shirt and threw him to the ground behind the bar. As he knelt beside the terrified man, he performed the Heartlock. He held one hand up and allowed a fireball to fill it. His other hand covered the man's mouth as the man was set ablaze from the inside. Wisps of smoke escaped his eyes and ears. After a moment, he stopped struggling. He stood to find the Captain pointing a knife at him. "What did you do to him? Who are you?"

No one else in the pub had noticed any of these events. Randir murmured, "I think I must admit something to you, Captain: I am different from you people. Do you remember the old stories about the Lords of the Shadows?"

The Captain nodded her head, "Yeah, I know them. So—" Then, she understood Randir's point. "Wait, you're telling me they're real?"

"Yes, I am."

"Why are you here?"

Randir explained, "There was a Prophecy made about a thousand years ago that said the mage Maris would be protected by the Lords of the Shadows and that he could be defeated by seven Guardians of Light. I happen to be both a Lord of the Shadows and a Guardian of Light. The others want to use Maris to take over Gevás, but I simply want him dead, so I came here hoping to find one of these Guardians of Light. All seven have to be there in order to defeat him."

The Captain stood then. "You've got some guts. This is one of the largest cities in Gevás, and you thought you would check here for one of your seven Guardians? You're crazy!" She turned to leave.

This girl was proving to be more and more interesting to Randir. He grabbed her arm, stopping her. "I would like your help, Captain. If anyone can find these Guardians of Light, it would be a Captain in Regin's army. I am a traitor to the Lords

of the Shadows. I mean no one here any harm." Then, he remembered the men he had killed outside the city.

Captain Terrell hesitated and then said, "Fine, but I want
payment, whether we find your Guardians of Light or not."

Randir raised an eyebrow at this remark. "Payment? And
how much would you be requesting from me?"

She considered and decided, "10,000 salt sounds appropriate."

"10,000 salt! Are you mad?!"

The Captain responded with an equally forceful voice. "I
am a Captain here! With the threat of Maris's Shadows, I have
orders to follow. If you are giving me a job searching the entire
city, then I had better be well compensated for it. It's 10,000
salt, or you are out of luck!"

Randir frowned. *Why am I even putting up with this nonsense? I
have worked too hard and gained too much power to have problems like
these. But she can help me look for the Guardians here...* He sighed.
"Fine, I will give you the salt, but I can only give you 5,000
now. If you find a Guardian, I will give you the rest."

Captain Terrell eyed Randir. Was she ready to make a deal
with one of the Lords of the Shadows? 10,000 salt was a lot of
money, and she knew she needed it too. It was hard work getting one of the black market mages to keep the spell that made
her look more like a man maintained. It was very expensive.
"Fine, you have yourself a deal, Randir." She held out her hand,
and Randir shook it firmly.

Randir agreed, "Deal."

The Captain pulled Randir's arm, dragged him outside the
pub, and instructed him to walk with her. "Alright, now the
first thing that you are going to do is help me get rid of some of
these Shadows." She pulled a sleeve back to reveal a gadget that
was strapped to her wrist. It was a small computer that all Captains in the Emperor Regin's army had. She began to press several buttons on its shiny surface.

Randir exclaimed, "That was not part of the agreement!
You need to help me locate the Guardians!"

As she finished her sequence on the gadget, she replied,

"And I am doing so right now. I am tapping into the census records of the city. It will take a minute, however. I will analyze the list when it is finished loading. For now, you can help me. If you do this favor for me, I will pay you."

Finally, he understood. "And that will decrease the amount of salt I have to pay you, in other words."

Captain Terrell nodded.

"You can go back to the city, now," said the Captain in her masculine voice while placing a hand on the soldier's shoulder.

The two men she had relieved saluted the Captain in gratitude and headed toward the Capital.

Terrell looked to Randir. "Now what are we going to do about all of these Shadows?"

Randir smiled as he looked out at the scattered groups of Shadows. They regarded him in slight fear. The Capital's guards had been shooting at a few of these creatures hoping they would not attack all at once, but Randir knew group thinking was not the way of the Shadow.

Shadows were simply spells of Darkness that had been given the slightest amount of life. They could not think independently and were therefore the perfect minions, but they were not by any means masters of swordplay. However, an army of Shadows could stand against any army of man with ease. The most interesting skill of a Shadow was its ability to cause despair. For some, Shadows can force a person to relive their darkest memories, and Randir had many of those.

Randir spoke to the Shadows in front of him with a voice of power and authority. "Go to Terin now, and await Maris's orders there. You will only prove yourselves to be nuisances here. Leave." He shot a fiery Gate into the center of the area, and the Shadows obeyed.

Captain Terrell was amazed. "Wow, how did you do that?"

Randir stood proud and tall. "When I was first inducted into the Y'mordi, I was assigned the second rank and was given the position of General of the Shadows. I was the one who mobilized the Shadow Armies in the Obsidian Wars."

Terrell gaped at the man. "That is impressive. For now, I am only a Captain, but I hope to reach the position of General at some point."

"A female General? That is unheard of!" exclaimed Randir with a grin.

"That may be true, but I could be the first. You keep forgetting that no one knows I am a woman." She turned back to the city. "Now, I shall help you find your Guardians. If they are in the Capital, I shall find them."

"Thank you, Captain. I shall return to the Capital tomorrow night. I must continue my search elsewhere." Then, Randir realized what all had occurred over the past few hours. *What am I doing?*

"Very well, I suppose I shall meet you at the same place again?"

Randir nodded and opened another Gate. As he left, he decided he would have to kill the girl after this whole mess was over. She knew too much already. A part of him was fine with that. It would not be the worst thing he had ever done. Still, he felt remorse over the idea. He promised himself he would kill her quickly.

As the Lord of the Shadows vanished into the Gate, Stehl, or Captain Terrell as everyone knew her, sighed. Randir had been so handsome, but she knew in her heart she would have to kill him once he paid her. She remembered that Randir had never given her the first 5,000 salt, either. Her fists clenched in anger. That was good though. Anger would make it easier to kill Randir when he returned tomorrow. She would still have to try to find the Guardians, or else Randir would not give her the salt. However, she did not want to kill him. He had not been rude as most guys were. He had also been the first person ever to figure out she was not a guy just by looking at her. It had to be those dark, ancient powers of his. She shook her head. She knew better. All men were pigs. She had seen the way they ate and slept. She had heard the way they talked about women behind their backs. All men were vile creatures that deserved to suffer. It made her wonder why she was trying to act like one sometimes. Feelings of disgust washed over her every day after working with those men.

Even above the Emperor Regin, I serve the Light. If Randir is a Lord of the Shadows, then I will have to kill him. That is my true duty...

The Beast of the Mountain

D rage and Matthew had entered a humongous forest, and the sky was hidden from them by the tops of the trees. To the boys, these woods were even more spectacular than Marqest's field of flowers. The water was cooler than Heaven's Isle, but it was still warmer than most of the Southern Continent. Occasionally, a squirrel would dart back and forth among the branches above them, ignorant of the presence of the two people below it. Drage's feet paced back and forth through the green grass of the sea. Matthew leaned against one of the almost lime-colored tree trunks. Their hair swayed in the rippling current.

"Where is he?" asked Drage. They had been waiting there for hours now.

Matthew kept his head pointed at the sky in fascination. He marveled at the extravagance of the aquatic forest. He muttered, "I'm sure Marqest will be here soon. Be patient."

Drage snarled in exasperation. About an hour ago, his heart had sensed Maris near them. It was very faint, but it still required a slight amount of control on Drage's part. It put him on edge.

Kill the boy…You only need to strike once, and it will be over with…

The voices in his head were strong and compelling. Drage sat down and gripped his head with crooked fingers. "No, not that…" he murmured. "Stop it." However, Maris's voice repeated the command in his heart. Though Drage's mind knew the idea was illogical, and deep within his heart, he did not want to hurt Matthew, his heart thought it was an enticing prospect. Maris was manipulating his heart.

Matthew escaped his daydream and looked at Drage in deep concern. "Drage? Are you okay?" He walked over and knelt beside his brother. "What is it?"

Then, he saw Drage's hand move to grab his Sword. Matthew sprang backward as the Sword slashed the water where he had just stood.

The little girl with the white, flowing hair and silver eyes began her song at the mouth of the eerie cavern. The mountain towered over the girl, but she felt no fear. If she felt fear, it would be for the creature she was summoning.

A few months ago, a villager had stumbled upon this cave and had ventured into its ominous depths only to disturb a slumbering beast.   Since then, the beast had demanded the sacrifice of small children to sate its bloodthirsty appetite.

Though no one in the village knew it, the monster was a remnant of the Obsidian Wars, a creature that Dagan had sealed into the mountain and had never released. It was one of the five Demons that Dagan had created to be destructive behemoths in the Wars.

The little girl knew that the villagers had not asked her to be the sacrifice this time: she had begged them to allow her to come to the cave and face the beast.

"I can do it!" she had pleaded. "I can defeat the beast of the mountains!" While many villagers had scoffed at the thought, others, including her father and the village elder, believed her. Her father had finally allowed her to go, though tears had filled his eyes. He had faith that his little girl had what it took to challenge the beast.

Her father had, for years, been a friend of the sorcerer Maris before he had disappeared. When he discovered that his daughter had extraordinary prowess with *mysteria* as several of their kind did, he had requested Maris to be her master and to teach her the ways of *mysteria*. Maris, of course, had accepted the request and had begun teaching the girl. He had always had such a way with children, and that was one of the reasons the little girl's father had asked Maris in the first place.

Now, the little girl was prepared to use everything her master had taught her. Her heart was calm, and her eyes were shut to allow her to focus. She could remember what her master had once told her: "What you see with your eyes can be deceiving. See with your heart." She brushed the memory away. Her heart needed to be free of feeling, so that she could prepare any of the Elements she needed. Thinking of her master made her feel both happy and sad at the same time. She had longed for several weeks now for his return, and it had brought her a form of loneliness.

The beast opened its gleaming red eyes from the back of the cave. The little girl's song sent tremors through the muck-lined walls and alerted the beast to her presence.

His sacrifice had arrived.

"Drage, snap out of it!" exclaimed Matthew in fear. It was not a fear for his life but a fear for Drage. *What's going through his mind right now? What is Maris doing?*

Drage had risen from his sitting position and had pointed the Sword of Destiny at Matthew, but he had not moved from there. Inside, he could feel his heart fighting itself: Drage's Light against Maris's Darkness. He had to regain control of himself. "Matthew...please..." he managed.

Matthew approached him, eager to help. "What? What is it, Drage?"

Drage's raven-black eyes watered as they looked up at Matthew's face. "I don't want to kill you, Matt."

Matthew shook his head, torn. "Drage, it's fine. You can

control it. You can beat him! Use your Light, and you'll be fine. You have to resist it." He put a hand on Drage's shoulder in an attempt to comfort him.

Drage's tears began to leave his eyes, making salty rivulets on his face. "Matthew... leave..."

The hand tightened on Drage's shoulder. "Drage, I can't do that. I won't leave you here!" cried Matthew.

Without a word, Drage lifted his hand and emitted a black sphere of Darkness that blasted Matthew several feet into the water and away from him. Drage looked straight ahead and summoned a Gate. He closed his stinging eyes and screamed, "I'm sorry!" He left Astra and Matthew behind.

The little girl ended her song when she heard the booms of each step of the approaching beast. *Mysteria* had become such an enticing thing to her. Its sweet light always gave her a warm feeling inside that reminded her of her greatest dream: freedom. It had been a dream she and Maris had shared, but she knew as a nonhuman that freedom was impossible. She was merely an exile.

"You are not much of a meal, little girl. Is this the best your pathetic village could do?" roared the raspy voice from the depths of the cave's shadows.

She did not respond to the beast. Her heart needed to be free of all feeling, clay ready to be molded into something greater. Her eyes remained closed to the monstrosity that trudged toward the opening.

I must remain calm, she thought.

It was time to confront the beast. Her eyes opened without taking in the nature of the beast. She observed it with a critical eye.

It was as tall as the mouth of the cave itself, and its body and eight spindly legs were covered in slender black hairs. The enormous globe of its body held a red design on its belly, while the head was a small box that contained several minute eyes and two acid-dripping and razor-sharp fangs.

The little girl found no trouble in feeling a twinge of fear at the arachnid beast. She held her hands up and allowed nerv-ousness to dominate her as she summoned Earth. Small for-mations of rock emerged from the mouth of the cave piercing the beast's body and trapping it in the cave. It shrieked, pierc-ing the calm of the cool water with its high-pitched cry.

"How *dare* you?" it screamed at the top of its lungs.

Before it could do anything else, the little girl reacted with a rapid change of emotion. She felt alertness. Her heart concen-trated on Force, and the spell shifted into a mental lance. Her hands reached out to the beast, forcing the mystical weapon to unleash itself. The invisible pike of Force went straight through the beast, destroying its head and drilling a gaping hole through the rest of it.

She waved a hand in front of her, and Fire lit up the re-mains of the beast. Her long, white hair undulated with the in-creasing current. Her head turned to the west. Something strange was happening in the world, and she could sense it. Ma-ris had said she had the ability to feel the most minute changes in the current. She had known when the beast had first awoken, when Maris had disappeared, and when the Werewolf had come to haunt their small part of Astra.

Though many children in Astra did not believe in the leg-ends of the Werewolf, most adults and the little girl believed in them. They said that the Werewolf was a wolf anima that trav-eled with a pack of real wolves across the world, though many who believed in the specter thought he only stayed in the Northern Continent. Seeing the flayed bodies had been enough proof for many skeptics to believe, but others decided that it was just some wild animal.

They also said the Werewolf preyed on the flesh of inno-cents and the blood of children. This particular story had terri-fied the little girl, and even Maris had warned her to avoid the Werewolf. Nevertheless, as she followed the current with her heart, she could hear the howls of wolves in the distance. How many monsters would she have to deal with in a day?

Matthew landed hard on the ground and groaned from the

pain it brought him, but that pain was nowhere near the agony he felt at having lost his brother and best friend. He was alone in these woods. He shivered at the coolness of the water.

He heard a surreal howling that echoed throughout the forest. He looked around, his head shifting from left to right and back to the left again. *Where is Marqest? He needs to get here soon.* Matthew did not know how to create a Gate, and he would not know where to go anyways. *Where is Drage, and what's happened to Marqest? I have to get out of these woods and back into civilization. At least from there, I should be able to contact the Emperor of Light.*

The howls grew louder. Matthew walked in a direction he felt would take him out of the forest. However, the howls moved closer to him. His feet picked up their pace as he realized he was running away: the animals were chasing him. As he ran, he noticed that the sound reached a maximum: though he could tell that the animals were close, they never came into view.

Dusk was approaching. He could see shades of red and pink shimmer on the horizon. Above the obscuring treetops, the stars and moon were becoming visible. The night was upon him.

Her bare feet ran to catch up to the Werewolf. He was approaching her village, and she could not let that happen. She could sense the Werewolf, his wolves, and another being in the spectacular forest that had been her playground and training area for as long as she could remember. Now, however, the forest reeked of a strong Darkness. It was nowhere near as powerful as the beast that had resided in the cave, but this Darkness had its own scent.

Then, she found the source of the Darkness. In a part of the woods was a Dark aura: A Gate had been created using the Darkness. Whatever it was, it was gone now. Did the Werewolf have something to do with the aura?

She shook her head. She did not have time for questions. She needed to catch up to the Werewolf, the pack, and that other person. Those wolves were fast.

The first wolf came into view. It was large and had silver fur with streaks of black running through it. Its eyes glimmered a brilliant shade of gold. As it approached Matthew, it sniffed the air, curious. More appeared from behind the ring of trees that surrounded Matthew.

In unison, the wolves sat back on their haunches and tilted their silvered snouts toward the tops of the trees and the obscured stars above them. From their throats rose high-pitched howls that echoed through the forest. Matthew felt engulfed by a forest full of wolves, but in reality, there were perhaps seven or eight wolves at the most.

Though the figure that came next was not a wolf, his appearance seemed to possess many of the same lupine qualities and almost fit in with the wolves. The fur that made his coat was clearly made of wolves, and his own hair was old and grizzled. The man's wrinkled face revealed no emotions, but his pupil-less eyes of pure white shimmered with a glowing intensity in these mystic woods.

He opened a heavily fanged mouth and spoke in a scratchy voice to the boy in front of him. "Why do you carry the scent of the Darkness, human? You have no strong Darkness in your heart, yet you still bear its scent. Why?"

Matthew was bewildered by the wolves, the man with no pupils, and the whole scenario. He managed, "I suppose it's because I was with somebody who was possessed by the Darkness, possessed by a sorcerer named Maris."

When the grizzly man smiled, a jagged fang curled over the edge of his mouth. "Heh, yes, I knew that Maris had discovered the power of the Darkness a while ago. I would have stopped it had I known sooner, but by the time I found him in the Western Continent, he was too strong for even me to confront."

Matthew stuttered, "You knew Maris?"

The man tilted his head back to the sky and laughed long and deeply. The wolves around them seemed to smile back at Matthew almost hungrily. When the man finished, he exclaimed, "Everyone here knows Maris, human. Maris came from here. He was one of the best mages, but then he got funny ideas in his head from that filth of the Shadows, the Y'mordi. A more interesting idea is what he has to do with a human such as yourself."

Matthew shuffled his feet. "That's kind of a long story." He was not sure if he could trust this stranger who knew Maris as well as he did.

The man sat down on a nearby rock and looked at Matthew with those piercing eyes. "I have all the time in the world, human."

Matthew sighed as he began his tale.

The wolves had finally stopped. She decided to walk the rest of the way. She did not want her rushed breaths to alert the Werewolf to her presence. She crept up to the pack of wolves and the two other figures in their center. She relaxed her heart in order to focus for *mysteria* when a wolf stepped up beside her and growled. She jumped in fright.

A voice called, "Show yourself, anima! I shall not harm you, so long as you will not harm me or my pack."

Matthew looked around the forest, wondering whom the man was talking to. Then, he saw her, a little girl of probably around nine or ten with a long white gown on and no shoes to cover her bare feet. The oddest thing about the girl was her completely white hair. *What had he called her? An anima?* For some reason, that term was familiar to Matthew. *What is this girl doing this far into the forest, anyways?*

The little girl said to the man, "Are you the one they call the Werewolf? The one who has killed several innocent people and committed numerous other wrongs?"

The man smiled his toothy grin and boomed, "No, that could not be I, my lady. For as long as I have run with the wolves, I have helped to maintain the integrity of the Northern Continent. I commit no wrong."

The girl shook her head. "If you have killed innocents, then you have committed a terrible wrong."

The man turned back to Matthew and sneered. "Those I

have killed were not innocent. Me and my wolves can smell Darkness. We have only attacked those who had just committed a wrong themselves. Their bodies reeked of their guilt until we ravaged their flesh. Now, if you don't mind, girl, this human was telling me a story. Somehow, he got mixed up with Maris these past few weeks."

The girl's eyes found Matthew and widened. "May I listen?" she requested.

The man grunted his approval and awaited Matthew's introduction of his journey into Gevás.

Matthew left out nothing to the story. He did not trust these people, but he had a lot on his mind, and it felt good talking about his adventures thus far. It helped clear his mind by simply addressing what he and Drage had been through.

The listeners were quiet, and then, the man spoke. "My name is Kibou Gerlach. Many people in this Continent know me as the Werewolf. The people in the East know me as a mercenary, and the people in the South and West know me as an assassin. To me, though, I am just a hunter of the Dark."

The little girl had never thought the Werewolf would be this interesting of a character. She had imagined him to be fearsome and aggressive, but all she had seen was a friendly, old man. "I am Lilian. I come from a village not too far from here, but I feel that I should tell you something of what I know of Maris, Matthew: I was his apprentice before he left Astra. He was not always evil. You have described him to me, and I know it was he, but he seems to be quite different too. The Y'mordi have twisted his mind, so that he now believes the Darkness is the only hope for saving us."

Matthew inquired, puzzled, "Saving you?"

The man nodded. "Apparently, you have not learned of our plight yet, human. About a century and half ago, the Emperor of Light Seth Mentiris accused nonhumans of starting a rebellion against humans. It was a false accusation, but he gained the support of most of Gevás, and he forced all nonhumans into a few small areas. Since then, no Emperor of Light has intervened with those laws. We have all stayed in exile here."

Lilian continued, "Yes, and Maris wanted more than anything to one day free the nonhumans from those laws."

"So, is Maris not a human?" asked Matthew. He had paid close attention, but he still did not understand what an anima was.

Kibou elaborated. "Neither the girl nor I are humans, Matthew. Nor is Maris. We are beings known as anima, half-animal, half-human. Anima have the ability to change at will between the two states of being."

Matthew's eyes took in the two people in gradual understanding. "Neither of you are human?" He had noticed that both of them had physical oddities, such as the old man's lack of pupils and the little girl's white flowing hair.

Kibou grinned and turned to Lilian. "Do you want to show him first?"

Lilian closed her eyes, and Matthew watched in awe as the little girl glowed with a white radiance. The light from the aura became blinding. When the light dimmed enough for Matthew to see, the girl was gone.

In her place stood a dazzling young mare. Her mane was as snow white as the rest of her coat, and her eyes were deep and mesmerizing. "Matthew, it's me, Lilian." Her words echoed only in his head. Her mouth never moved.

Matthew's eyes moved to Kibou, but the old man had disappeared. There was just an abnormally large and muscular wolf sitting on the rock. Then, Matthew noticed the white eyes. He muttered, "So that must be you, Kibou?"

The seasoned grey wolf bowed his head deeply in confirmation. "It is I," said the voice then. Though the words had not come from the wolf's mouth, Matthew knew Kibou the wolf was speaking to him.

Lilian spoke solely to Kibou, so that Matthew could not hear their thoughts. "I think I should take him to my village. Perhaps, this Prophet he seeks will come there. At least I can provide the human food and shelter if need be."

Kibou nodded. "Yes, he will need protecting, but I am

afraid I cannot go near your village. They would kill me if I came near. There is still evil left in this country, so I shall remain here in these woods."

Lilian regarded the anima cautiously. "You are strange, Werewolf. You kill others yet claim you walk in the Light. You live with wolves, yet you hunt the Darkness. What are you truly?"

The wolf snarled, "The wolves came centuries ago, by an Earthan. Wolves are not so greedy and bloodthirsty as you would make them out to be. That was why they were brought here in the first place."

The white horse stomped a hoof on the ground. "You are an Ancient, are you not? You have been playing games with the people of Astra for ages. You plague them with your reputation, but you still do what you feel is right for them? Why will you not obey the laws then?"

"Because not all laws are right!" growled the old wolf.

Matthew watched their physical reactions but had no idea what they were saying. Even though he had met new people, he felt alone. Aria was gone. His brother was gone. His whole family was gone. Not even Marqest or Draconis were there to comfort him. He put a hand up to his eyes and found them filled with tears. He felt no anger at what had happened to him, but he still felt as if he had been cut out of everyone's lives. Now, his only value was as a Guardian of Light. Was that his only purpose?

He found his mind wandering back to that night on the beach he had spent with Drage. Matthew wondered then if he would really have been content with a life of just writing. Looking back at his life, he realized he had never been truly happy. He had just always been content with the way his life was. Drage had been right all along.

Lilian turned to face Matthew. She could sense his sorrow and, beyond that sorrow, a shimmering potential of *mysteria*. The boy was more than he knew. She approached him in her human-like form. "Matthew, I would like for you to come back with me to my village. Perhaps, you will be able to do something from there. You need a place to rest for tonight any-ways." Though her tone did not reflect it, she pitied him. She had been able to see his pain as he had told them his story that had started on the beaches of another world. Her heart had found a particular interest in that feeling of freedom in the Earthan air. It was magical to her, yet she knew that freedom was not her right.

Matthew nodded, deep in his own thoughts.

The Werewolf approached the human, still in his lupine form. "I bid you farewell now, human. Shadows lurk in every corner of this world, and I must find them yet. Good luck to you." Before Matthew could say a word, he ran into the depths of the forest, and his pack ran alongside him with deepest devotion.

Lilian spoke to Matthew. "If you would like, you may ride on my back."

Before Matthew could respond, a wave of exhaustion flooded his body, and he collapsed beside the rock.

The aroma of a boiling potion, a foreign scent to him, was what woke him. He had never slept so soundly in his entire life, and it had revived him, even in mind. He found himself in a straw hut, and sunshine poured into the room through a crack in the wooden door. As he rose, he became aware of the soft-ness of the bed on which he had rested. That softness along with his own fatigue had likely contributed to his satisfying rest. It was much colder here than it was in the forest though. He walked to the door, noticing he was wearing only a pair of den-im pants. His curious eye peeked through the crack in the door and saw an amazing world of animals and humans outside his cozy hut.

Horses, lions, birds, and foxes were only the first creatures to be caught in his interested gaze. Occasionally, one of the an-imals would be surrounded in a colored aura and would trans-form into a human. The memories of the previous night came to him like a storm, but a part of him felt more alive. It had been his first real rest in days.

His eye found the girl with the white hair, Lilian. She was talking to an older man. The two were smiling, and then the man picked up the girl and swung her in the air. The man must be Lilian's father, because his hair, though much shorter, was also colored white. When he put her down, she whispered something in his ear, and they both looked straight at the door through which Matthew was examining the world outside. They approached him.

Matthew stumbled backward in surprise. He shivered from the coolness of the hut, and he looked around to see if he could find his shirt, but the small house was too dark for him to make out anything. Within seconds, Lilian and her father had made it to the hut. She opened the door and found Matthew still looking for something warmer to wear. "Are you well rested now, Matthew?"

Matthew turned to greet them. "Yes, thank you very much for bringing me here. I guess I had just been so exhausted when you found me. Sorry if I was too much of a burden. I can leave as soon as I figure out what I am going to do next."

Lilian noticed Matthew shivering in the room that felt a comfortable temperature to her. She had cast a spell to make sure it would stay warm, but perhaps the human had a lower tolerance for the cool Northern water. "Are you cold?"

Matthew nodded. "Just a little." He tried to stop his teeth from chattering.

Lilian's father said with a deep yet kind voice, "Here, human." He handed Matthew his bulky, brown denim coat. The inside was lined with a cotton-like material.

"Thank you," exclaimed Matthew as he received the coat. He put on the coat and found it fit him perfectly. When he tried to zip it, he discovered the coat did not have a zipper or anything that would even serve the same purpose. Perhaps, anima did not get as cold as humans did. He left his coat open, revealing his toned chest.

As the three of them stepped outside, Matthew felt the strong ripple of the current. It seemed in the Northern Continent the current could become more forceful. Matthew had a clear view of the village now. People everywhere laughed and cheered. In the sky, the sun shone brilliantly, yet elaborate fireworks traced the clouds.

Lilian began, "I recently defeated a monster that had been haunting our village for several months. Now, everyone is celebrating its defeat. They are going to have a festival tonight. You are welcome to stay if you like."

The father interrupted his daughter. "No, they are celebrating *your* victory, Lily." Her father beamed at his daughter, and his daughter smiled back at him.

Matthew smiled as well, but it was for a different reason. He had just discovered another of the elusive Guardians of Light. Then, he saw the complications of it this time. "Excuse me, but I need to tell you something, Lilian."

She turned her pensive eyes to him. "Yes?"

Matthew stumbled for words for a minute and finally managed. "Lilian…you are one of the Guardians of Light I have been looking for."

Though her face revealed no surprise, Lilian was shocked by this revelation. It seemed unbelievable. "Are you sure?"

"Yes."

Lilian's father looked at Matthew. "Does this mean she will have to leave here?"

Sadness welled up inside Matthew, but he knew he had to say it. "I'm so sorry. If she doesn't fight with the other Guardians, this whole world could fall."

"I understand," replied the father. "Please, enjoy the festival, Matthew. I would like to spend some time with my daughter."

Matthew noticed that many of the male anima went around the village wearing only a pair of pants. Though the water was not freezing, the occasional current made Matthew tremble under his coat.

He ran a hand through his black hair, wondering what to do. Since he was no longer with Drage or Aria, the best idea would be to go back to the Palace of Light, though he knew that was far away. The Gate from Heaven's Isle had saved them several miles. Still, looking back on it, he realized this world was a lot smaller than Earth. The Continents together were probably only the size of North America.

His mind flashed back to the way Lilian and her father had looked at each other. It had reminded him of how Drage had looked at his father those last few days they had spent at the Palace of Light. He tried to think of a time when he had been able to look at someone that way, with fondness and a completely unconditional love, but he simply could not remember such a moment.

Then, he felt a hand on his shoulder. He turned his head to see an old man standing before him. "Marqest!"

He smiled faintly, forcing his wrinkles to crease. He wore his silvery robe that almost touched the ground, and his gray hair flowed behind him. "Matthew, I was wondering where you had run off to. Where is Dragenopn?"

By the time Matthew finished the account, night was falling. The fireworks became more intricate over time as the lights in the sky became massive, sparkling dragons that chased after one another.

"Matthew," began Marqest. "When you left, I fought the sorcerer Maris and discovered the power of his heart. His *mysteria* is very strong, and I question if even the seven Guardians of Light will stand a chance against him, though I suppose there *must* be a chance if the Prophecy declared it. I could not defeat him even with my vast knowledge of spells."

"So, why did you come here after he beat you?"

Marqest's face revealed his uncertainty. "Well, I could not actually remember where in the forest I had brought you, so I just went to the closest village, deciding that you would probably be there soon, but when I heard you had finally arrived, you were passed out. No one knows who I am, and no one cares anyway due to the festivities." They looked around and observed the anima, dragons, and griffins as they danced around the bonfires. "Lilian is the 'mage outcast from birth yet blessed by her own,' correct?'"

Matthew nodded. "Yes, I think so. Though she was born an exile to the rest of the world, everyone here adores her. She is a hero. I am sure she is one of the Guardians."

"Well, that means we have found six of them then. There is still one more out there."

"Right," Matthew agreed. "Where could the last one be?"

"You, Drage, Aria, Draconis, and even the Emperor have scanned the Southern Continent in search of the Guardians but have had no luck. Before all of you came to Gevás, I believe the Emperor had been scanning the Eastern Continent for any signs. The South and East have always been close allies, so if a Guardian was there, I think we would already know about it. I guess our best bet would be to search the Western Continent. No Guardians have been found there yet, so maybe we could find one there."

Matthew brightened at the idea. "I like the idea, but what about Lilian and Drage? We could drop Lilian off at the Palace of Light and then look for Drage first. He has to be at the battle against Maris, right?"

Marqest nodded. "That is true...However, we have no idea where he is, and regardless of our efforts, he *will* be at that battle. In fact, I think Lilian should come with us. She seems capable enough if she could defeat whatever beast was in that cave on her own. Plus, we will not be doing anything dangerous. I was honestly thinking of visiting an old friend from Rulia. He is the Prophet of Wind, and I think he will be willing to help us."

Matthew was doubtful. He could see how much Lilian cared for her father and how much her father cared about her. He did not want anything to happen to her. Mainly, he wanted to go after Drage. He had to make sure nothing happened to his brother too. Still, he knew Marqest had a point. The Prophet was wise and knew the best course of action, he was sure.

"Alright, let's do it, but we need to get to this Prophet as fast as we can."

The little girl appeared and walked over to Matthew. "Is this the old man you told me about, Matthew?"

The old man's face turned red in bewilderment as he turned to Matthew. "Old man?"

Matthew replied, "Yes, this is Marqest. Marqest, this is Lilian."

Lilian did not pay much attention to the older man. "Matthew, when do we leave?"

"As soon as you are ready."

The Werewolf ran in a craze with his pack that night. They had caught onto the scent of a murder in a nearby village and were hunting down the criminal who had killed the innocent.

These were dark days. The Werewolf knew Maris had returned to Astra a few hours ago. He had not seen him, but he could sense that familiar presence tainted with the stench of the Y'mordi. After hearing the youth's story about the Prophecy, however, he had decided against trying to kill his old acquaintance. He had a pack to take care of, after all.

That human had told a strong story. The most peculiar thing was that it was all true. The Werewolf had not sensed a single lie in his words.

If Maris had taken control of a boy's heart, then that boy would be in particular danger. The Werewolf had heard stories of the Heartbind and knew how monstrous it could be. It was a dark power indeed.

He wiped these thoughts away and focused on the hunt. The grass crushed beneath his swift paws, and the others in his pack ran beside him, creating silvery blurs in his peripheral vision. The current swept through him as he closed his eyes and opened himself up to the world around him. Every tree, every rock became clear in his mind's eye. Sight was for those too weak to feel. He angled his head to his mate on his right.

She was a pure wolf and not at all an anima, yet the idea of such interbreeding was not uncommon. Many anima had a strong affection for their specific animals. The animals felt the same way, too. His mate looked like most of the other wolves in the pack, but she also had a white scar that ran over her left eye. Humans had given her that years ago.

The Werewolf growled at the pain the memory brought him. He felt such passion now, and it was why he had always hated the part of him that was human. He wanted to be forever free from such emotions and be a natural factor of the world, not an exile, or murderer, or even an anima.

He tilted his grizzled muzzle to the sky and pierced the silence of the forest with a shrill howl, his call to the crescent moon and to the mournful past.

Turning back to his mate, he smiled. He had love, and that was an amazing feeling to have. He had a loyal pack, a kind mate, and the cool night to guide him. He felt as if everything was perfect, but then he would remember the evil he had dedicated his life to pursuing. He remembered Lilian, the human, and that sorcerer Maris who had been foolish enough to trust one of the Y'mordi.

The Werewolf growled again. If he were an animal, he would not have such complicated feelings. He would have instincts and only the will to survive. His mind wandered back to thoughts of the possessed boy. Maris was defying the order of the world. Every being had the right to act of its own accord, and Maris was breaking that right.

A sound erupted from a nearby bush as their prey screamed and ran further into the woods foolishly. The Werewolf bounded after him, prepared to crush the life out of the criminal.

Stranger in Black

Aria stared out from one of the floor-to-ceiling windows to view the amassing troops below her. They were all donned in well-polished silver armor that covered most of the body, arms, and legs. Each soldier had a scabbard with a sword and a quiver full of arrows and a bow. Some soldiers also had a lance, a flag, or even a rifle. The army was not large, but she decided Maris's own armies would probably not be that great either. "Can they win?" she asked.

"I do not know," replied the Golden Dragon who stood behind her. "It's why we must hope that Dragenopn and Matthew find the other Guardians of Light."

She nodded. She wished more than anything that Drage and Matthew were beside her. She had missed them the past few days. "How many allies does Maris have right now? I remember the Emperor mentioning that Maris is gathering armies."

Draconis responded, "Well, Maris has gained favor in the two kingdoms to our west: Alerris and Varyx. He has also obtained the loyalty of two kingdoms in the Western Continent: Rulia and Saldir. I know he has not gained any aid from the

East, and I am not sure about the North. The chances are high that he does have several allies there, since that is where he lived."

"Even if they don't come, I want to fight anyways. I think I can do it now."

Draconis turned toward the girl. He realized she had grown since he had first rescued her in the icy sea below the Southern Continent.

"Can you explain to me how the military is arranged here, Draconis?" she asked.

The Golden Dragon came closer to the window and gestured to the troops before them. "These are soldiers of the terra, the standard military organization. The terra is comprised of warriors, archers, riflemen, and sorcerers. Speaking of which, did you know that a sorcerer is a mage who specializes in battle spells?"

Aria frowned. "Only battle spells? Maybe *I* should be focusing on those."

"I believe that Mistress Daghda has been teaching you those spells specifically. Has she been dueling with you?"

Aria considered Linda's training. "Yes, it has been mostly dueling, but are those sorcerers not going to face several enemies at once who can't use *mysteria*? Isn't that considerably different?"

Draconis shook his head. "Not necessarily. In a battle, sorcerers have to focus on protecting the army by deflecting spells and projectiles around the battlefield. Most massive spells could affect both sides equally, so sorcerers are trained to aim for one or two targets at once."

She let all of this new information sink in. She knew she needed to know as much about the military as possible when Maris came. "What about the rest of them?"

Draconis gestured to a few uniquely uniformed soldiers. "Those men are of the navy. The members of the navy ride in small transports and fight above the battlefield. These transports have weapons of varying strengths. Some will have cannons that are meant to destroy the enemy terra, while others will have guns that take down enemy navy transports. These naval transports are the greatest concerns for a sorcerer: a sorcerer must protect the terra from falling transports or projectiles sent from those transports."

"Will Maris have a large navy? Can Shadows pilot these transports?"

"I do not know," shrugged Draconis. "Perhaps his allies will provide a navy or two. Regardless, there is a third force in the Emperor's army, the Enigma Brigade. To most of the world, their existence is but a myth, but I can assure you they are very much real. The Enigma Brigade is the Emperor's finest warriors and sorcerers. The last time I checked, they only had nine members. You see, during the Obsidian Wars, the Lord of Light Lux named his great army the Light Brigade. The remnants of that army became a group dedicated to protecting the Emperor, and they called themselves the Enigma Brigade."

"And what will they be doing in this battle?" inquired Aria.

Draconis kept his sapphire eyes on the troops below them. "The Emperor has not told me of his plans for the Enigma Brigade. I have insisted that he use the Brigade to protect him during the battle, but he revealed to me that he intends to fight in the battle."

Aria detected anger in Draconis's voice as he explained the Emperor's intentions. "Isn't it a good thing that the Emperor wishes to fight? He could probably help out quite a bit, right?"

"No. I have been with the Emperor since he was a child, and I can tell you now he has never known a battle in his life. I trained him myself in the ways of the sword, but he would not last an hour on an actual battlefield. Mind you, he could do well in a one-on-one duel, but in a massive battle like this one, I lose confidence in his ability to survive."

Perhaps, Draconis was right: Maybe the Emperor would not do well on the battlefield. Besides, it would be unfortunate if Drage lost his dad as soon as he had found him. "You really care about him, don't you?"

Draconis breathed, "I do. I have protected the Helius family for many generations now."

Aria felt another spark of curiosity. "Draconis, what were you before you were the Guardian of the Emperor? What would you be doing if you didn't have the Helius family as your responsibility?"

Draconis turned from the window. He had not been prepared for this question. It was the exact question he had hoped the Green Dragon from Rulia would not ask him. "I would rather not talk about what I was before I came here. I am different from what I used to be. My duty is to protect the Emperor of Light. That is all that matters." He spoke with force as if he were trying to convince himself more than Aria.

Though Aria's natural instinct was to react in fear of the Dragon's growls, she walked in front of him and looked straight into his sapphire eyes with her own blue eyes. "Draconis, you have a right to your own life, your own thoughts, your own heart. You don't have to keep feeling like you owe Drage's family your entire life."

Draconis did not respond. The two merely looked each other in the eyes and said nothing. Blue gazed into blue. In his heart, Draconis saw the truth in Aria's words, yet he knew he had a strong obligation to the Emperor of Light. He could remember multiple occasions on which he had saved the life of the Emperor. Draconis was needed here, and he had promised Bral all those years ago that he would protect the Helius family for as long as he could. Could he really break that pact now?

Aria saw Draconis's confusion. She did not know how she knew it, but she felt as if she could see all of Draconis's emotions as she stared into his deep eyes: sadness, longing, duty, strength, and most of all, regret. The emotions played through that sequence like a story unfolding before her. She could not take it anymore and broke her eye contact.

The Golden Dragon shook his head. "Forgive me, Aria. I was in deep thought. You've a rare gift."

She turned in surprise to Draconis. "Oh? And what would that be?"

The Dragon smiled. "Getting a Dragon to think deeply." He chuckled and put a rough claw on Aria's shoulder. "I am fine. I know my duty, and that is all that matters to me. What I think and feel contrast greatly from what I actually do, and that is the way it was meant to be. I am content with my obligations to the Emperor."

Because Linda had cancelled training for the evening, Aria decided to take a leisurely stroll through the Imperial Gardens. She came here often when she was not busy at the Palace with training or talking to Draconis. Along with her worry for Drage and Matthew, she felt a unique fear: she was scared she could not control what was happening here.

On Earth, she had been a dominating participant in many activities and organizations. Though she was intelligent, she had prided herself most in how active she was and how she leaped at any opportunity to experience the world. Now, she just felt a sense of waiting. Intense training and fierce politics raged around her, yet she felt as if the world was silent to her. In her mind, she had reached the eye of the storm. She cried out in frustration and kicked a nearby rock. Her eyes found a bench, and she sat there, burying her head in her hands.

"Do not cry."

Aria looked up to find a black-robed figure standing beside her. "Who are you?"

"I am an illusion. Someone who should not exist," replied the figure.

Aria opened herself to the warm sensation of *mysteria,* and she sensed only Darkness in the man beside her. "Are you one of the Y'mordi? Have you come to kill me?"

"The answer is no to both of your questions. I do not serve the Darkness as the Y'mordi do. I do not obey the laws set forth by La Faye's Prophecy. Why would I kill the very person that I saved just a couple of weeks ago?"

Aria's eyes widened. "You were the man from Earth who saved us from the Shadows."

The man nodded his hooded head without a word.

"Who are you really? Why did you help us? Why are you here now?"

The man did not move. "To the first, I have already told you I am an illusion. I should not even be here, but I wanted to see you, Aria. At least one last time. To the second, I helped you because I had to allow the Prophecy to happen. Had I not saved your lives, the Prophecy would have been nearly entirely false. To the last, I came with an intent to inspire you. You have lost faith in yourself."

Aria retaliated, "I haven't lost faith! I just have nothing left to do! I've been training for days, but I can't do anything else!" Though she knew she would not do anything to the stranger, she raised a wand from her white robe anyways. It gave her a special comfort.

The man, however, did not react to Aria's drawing of the wand. He repeated, "You have lost faith. On Earth, idleness was the thing you loathed the most. Now, you turn from what your heart and instincts are telling you to do. The Prophet Daghda has already told you multiple times that you are a fast learner and that you are quickly becoming a skilled mage. Why do you not use your abilities for a greater cause than waiting?"

The wand in Aria's hand trembled as she yelled the word, *"Lune!"* Before the wall of Force hit the stranger, the shimmering wall shattered before him. Aria took a step back, astonished. "How did you do that? You didn't even use words, or a wand, or anything! I couldn't even sense any strong spells."

"You would raise your wand against me, Aria? Perhaps, you still have that fire within you. To think that you would use that power just for training…" He put a fist to his forehead in mock concentration.

Aria's emotions ran rampant as her wand released scorching fireballs with every movement of its slender body. Despite each blazing sphere, the stranger remained still, watching the fireballs dissipate into balls of black smoke within seconds. Aria ceased the fiery barrage. Her wand was still smoking from the heat of the spells. The stranger waved a hand, using Air, to clear the water of the remaining smoke. "Aria," he began. "What are you going to do now?"

Her blue eyes looked to where his face would be if his

hood were not blocking it. "I am going to help lead the terra."

The man smirked, "Now that is more like it. You will likely meet resistance with this new idea, but you have something that most of them have never seen: the will of an Earthan. That will come in handy against those who would believe you are not capable. The Prophet Daghda and the Emperor of Light himself will likely be among those who will protest your command."

"I want to know who you are," demanded Aria. "Perhaps, I will find that out once this is all over."

The man smiled beneath his hood. "You very well may discover my identity at some point, but that day shall not be today."

Aria stormed past the stranger who had saved her life on Earth and had brought Drage, Matthew, and herself to this new world.

She had work to do.

She stood in front of the building that housed the headquarters for the terra. She entered with her head held high. The man at the front desk saw her approach and asked, "Can I help you?"

"Yes," responded Aria. "I am looking for someone in charge of the sorcerer division of the terra?"

The man at the desk smiled. "I'm sorry, but I cannot just introduce you to her. If you would like, I could see if she has any openings for a later date." He prepared to look at his paper-thin computer screen.

Aria interrupted, "No, I would like to see her now. I have an interesting proposition for her."

A voice called from behind Aria, "Oh, and what proposition would a learning mage have for me?"

She turned in surprise to find the Prophet Mistress Leona before her. "Oh, Mistress Leona, I had no idea you represented the mage division." Red flooded her face.

The middle-aged woman looked down at the girl she had taught almost a week ago with her green pensive eyes. "Yes, I do. However, I am anxious to hear this proposal you have. What brings a Guardian of Light to the terra in this time of war?"

Aria had not expected the leader to be the Prophet of Nature. Nevertheless, she explained, "Mistress Leona, I want to help lead the sorcerers into battle."

Now, Mistress Leona was the one surprised. "Aria...I have no doubt of your abilities, but you are simply too young. The higher ranks of sorcerers have earned their spots through years of training and of real battle. You cannot take that away from them."

Aria's head shook. "Mistress Leona, you do not believe in my abilities, and I will not allow my fate to be decided by your faulty assumptions. I demand to be tested. I do not seek a permanent position within the terra. I only want to hold the position until this battle is over." She spoke in a commanding voice. The man at the desk pretended to be busy with his screen, but in reality, he was utterly shocked by what he was hearing. A young girl was giving demands to the Prophet.

Though Mistress Leona's initial reaction was to gape at the girl's insolence, she grinned at the wisdom of her words. "Very well, Aria. I shall allow you to be tested, but you must understand that the test to reach any level of authority will be both advanced and complex. Many mages study for years and still fail this test."

"I will not fail the test," said Aria with pride.

"Very well." Mistress Leona turned to the man at the desk. "Can you schedule a dueling trial at the ring for tomorrow?"

The man bobbed his head. "Yes, Mistress Leona."

The Prophet turned back to Aria. "Am I right to assume that the Emperor advised you to do this? Or perhaps it was that other Prophet who has pledged her services to the Emperor? Mistress Daghda?"

Aria brushed her brown hair out of her face and replied, "No. This is just me. It is quite likely that if the Emperor or Mistress Daghda knew I was here asking you this, they would be furious with me."

Mistress Leona's expression turned pale. "You are brave indeed. Not many would so blatantly go against the Emperor's wishes or even the wishes of a Prophet. Though you have had the fortune of meeting many of the Prophets, many would deem it a greater honor than you realize to have the opportunity to even see one. To those same people, it would be nearly a crime to openly defy them. I shall not lie to you, Aria: your bravery makes me hesitant."

Aria shook her head. "No, as you said, Mistress Leona, the Prophets are greatly respected. If the Emperor gets mad at anyone, it shall be me. It would take a lot more for him to be angered by a Prophet, especially one who is a member of the Emperor's Council."

Mistress Leona warned once more, "Aria, be cautious. Review your spells tonight. It shall be a tough trial tomorrow. I shall pray to the Light that your heart remains steadfast. One with half a heart to do this would fail." She turned to go into another part of the building, while Aria said a quick "Thank you" to the man at the desk and left.

She whispered to herself, "No, I pray to Fire I can do this."

Traitor in the Palace

D rage felt a chilling draft sweep over him. Because of his wet clothes, the wind felt a lot colder than it actually was. He was back in the air. As he looked behind him, he could see a wall of water that reached to the sky. His eyes scanned the area. He was in a massive bubble, yet there was ground beneath his feet.

Lightning struck only a few yards from where he stood, and the roar of thunder hit him like a wall of sound. Above him, the behemoth storm clouds rained down on his skin. Though the brilliant flashes of lightning lit up the entire atmosdome, the island was pitch black between the thunderbolts. Against the midnight horizon, Drage could make out a lonely spire that stretched to the top of the atmosdome. There was a flare coming from one of the higher windows. In the darkness, it was the only light visible as far as his eyes could see. Yet, even in this blackest of darkness, he found he *could* see. There was no light, but he did not need it.

Groaning, he thought about Matthew. He felt miserable for leaving his brother behind in that forest, but he knew he had had no choice. If he had stayed, he might have killed Matthew.

The freezing rain mixed with the tears on his face and dripped down to the ashen ground.

Though he had no idea where he was, a part of his heart felt that the place was familiar. He figured perhaps it was Maris feeling through him. Perhaps, Maris had meant for the Gate to end up on this hideous island. He lifted his Sword and trudged through the blackened muck toward the lonely spire.

Another lightning bolt hit the ground near him, and he slipped in the mud. He landed flat on his face, and the Sword of Destiny slid from his hand. He struggled to get back up, but he did not fall again. He retrieved his Sword and sheathed it, its blade making a squelching sound in the scabbard.

As he continued walking, he raked one grimy hand through his mud-caked hair to get it out of his eyes. He tried to focus on the Darkness that bound his heart and sensed Maris's presence miles away. The instinct that drove him told him the sorcerer was to the southeast. He was too far away for him to be a concern.

His thoughts turned to Matthew and Aria. He decided Aria was probably still with the Prophet at Macela. The Prophet would be sharpening Aria's new skills in *mysteria*. Drage could not understand why Aria was so fascinated by those mystical powers. Drage had learned how to manipulate Maris's Darkness, but it was only a dangerous cheat, similar to any gun or poison. A sword was an honest weapon. Its structure allowed people to defend themselves. *Mysteria* was only a means of destruction.

Matthew would be searching Astra for Marqest and the remaining Guardians. They were still missing two of them. If one of them was not in Astra, then Drage was willing to bet that there would be at least one in the West, since no Guardians had appeared there yet.

He folded his arms against his body to retain some warmth. The rain pounded against him, and the wind slowed even his walking. Though the rain froze his skin, he was grateful that the mud was being rinsed from his face. Another flash of lightning revealed scattered trees that were as coal-black as the rest of the island. Each tree looked as if the bark had been burned clean from it. The sable branches forked upward, creating the image of a monstrous claw.

As the colossal tower came closer into view, Drage noticed the black outline of a figure close to the tower. He drew his Sword with one hand and held out his other hand ready to use the dark powers of *mysteria* if need demanded it. Drage softened each step, but with every movement of his feet, the mud sloshed and squished. The figure paced in front of the tower and muttered to the air.

When Drage came close enough, he felt something in his heart. He believed, due to some foreign instinct, that the figure had an immense amount of Darkness inside of him, a Darkness that only resembled the heart of an Y'mordi. Drage clenched his teeth. The Y'mordi were the reason for his very existence in this world. They were behind everything. The Y'mordi and Maris.

He closed his eyes and allowed his heart to accept and welcome the Darkness. The torrent of dark power flowed through him. When he opened his eyes, the world became fully visible to him. It was as if his eyes suddenly saw only in black light. Grasping this much *mysteria*, he could see through even the purest of darkness.

The cloaked Y'mordi felt this grasping of *mysteria* and turned his head to the boy.

Drage released a web of Darkness, ensnaring the small man. The net became ropes that bound the man's arms and legs and covered his mouth, stifling his screams. Drage bent over the figure and lowered his hood to reveal the servant from the Palace of Light, Ixion.

When he took a surprised step backward, the man in the mud manipulated his own *mysteria,* and the web was stretched apart by verdant vines of ivy that sprung up from the ground. He stood, and a long dagger appeared in each hand at lightning speed.

Drage took another step back and muttered to himself, "That can't be...Ixion?" Then, he recognized the daggers and remembered the robed figure that had attacked Drage and Matthew in Terin. Ixion had been the one Draconis had set ablaze in the alleyway.

Ixion snarled at Drage, "How did you get here, Guardian?"

Drage held his Sword ready to fight. "Ixion, you're a liar and a traitor. How could you?"

Ixion smiled. "I serve only the Darkness. We needed to know what was happening in Apolis, however. Your idiot father fell for the trap perfectly. We know much about his armies and even your friend Aria."

"Aria?" exclaimed Drage. "What have you done with her?"

However, Ixion did not respond and leaped at Drage with his daggers flashing in the glow of the lightning. Drage held his Sword with both hands and placed the blade in front of him so it blocked Ixion's weapons.

Ixion was quick with his daggers and wasted no time between attacks. Drage felt his defense weakening as the flurry of blows continued.

His mind reached out for the only thing he thought could help him: *mysteria*. The Darkness further engulfed his mind, and a ball of Darkness forced Ixion back several feet, giving Drage a moment to reset his stance and recuperate. He shot another more powerful blast at Ixion, but the Y'mordi evaded it with a swift jump to the side.

Ixion bent low to the ground and placed hands on the ashen mud. A green glow surrounded his hands. As soon as Drage threw another blast of Dark energy, an immense tree sprang up from the ground in front of Ixion, shielding him from the attack at the cost of some of its bark.

Drage roared above the din of the storm, "Enough, Ixion! Quit the tricks!"

He lifted his Sword to strike down the tree, but as soon as his arms were lifted high, Ixion spun from behind the tree, threw one of the knives, and prepared to strike with the other. The first knife hit Drage squarely in the shoulder, piercing through the flesh and bone. Drage curved his slash to block the second knife just in time.

Drage found it easier to deflect the attacks of one dagger, but Ixion was still just as dangerous and allowed no opportunity for attack.

The sounds of the metals clashing rang across the Obsidian Plains and even resounded throughout the tower. Their breaths became ragged as exhaustion overcame them, especially Drage, who had not had rest, food, or water for a while now.

As the attacks decreased in strength throughout the battle, Drage became aware of a numbing feeling in his shoulder. Though the dagger had stung at first, he could now no longer feel the protruding blade. The numbing feeling was spreading.

Ixion changed his fighting tactics. Instead of aiming for killing strikes, he made frequent slashes to Drage's side, cutting his arms and chest with tiny, shallow nicks. Though these were not too agonizing, he could feel each cut spread a loss of feeling into those areas of his body. Then, Ixion attempted another stab. This time, it was directed at Drage's left hand, his dominant hand. The dagger pierced straight through his hand in burning pain. His fingers opened reflexively, and the Sword of Destiny fell to the mud below, splashing a large amount of mud on both of them.

Ixion removed the dagger forcefully and pushed Drage over into the mud. By this time, Drage had lost most feeling in his body. Weakness and exhaustion washed over him as much as the falling rain did. Ixion leaned over the boy and prepared to make the final blow when a voice called out from the entrance to the tower.

"Ixion, stop."

Ixion turned his head to the voice and saw Pullatus standing there. "Oh, Lord Pullatus. I found one of the Guardians of Light. Shall I kill him now?" he squeaked.

Pullatus waved a hand. "There is no need, Ixion. This boy has caused us too much trouble for us to just kill him so casually. We must approach the situation more subtly, would you not agree?" inquired the head of the Y'mordi.

The traitor Ixion bowed his head in agreement. "Yes, my Lord. What would you have me do?"

Pullatus gestured to the tower that loomed ominously above them. "This spire was once a part of a grand castle, was it not? There are dungeons beneath this ground. Take the boy there and lock him up well. I will have to make sure that his cell is enchanted, so that he cannot escape it."

"Yes, my Lord."

Ixion put a hand in front of Drage's face, and a green gas clouded Drage's vision. Then, the world faded to black as his consciousness slipped.

Later, a short man in a white robe entered the Throne Room and bowed before the Emperor of Light. "I am sorry, your Majesty. I had family in Varyx and wanted to see them before the war started," the man pleaded.

The Emperor stood and glared down at the servant. "Ixion, you have responsibilities in serving me. You shall not disappear like this again," he commanded.

"Yes, your Majesty," replied the man with a small bow.

The doors to the Throne Room opened again to allow a Golden Dragon to enter. Draconis had just finished talking with Aria a couple of hours ago. Then, his blue eyes spotted the servant in front of the Emperor. His peaceful mood changed to a snarling state. "What is he doing here? I thought he disappeared days ago?"

The Emperor folded his arms in equal anger. "Yes, he did, but he has returned with excuses."

Draconis walked up to the side of the servant and looked toward the Emperor. "He has shown bravery in defying you, your Majesty. However, he has shown even more bravery by returning. Shall I have him arrested for his injustice?" He placed a forceful claw on Ixion's shoulder.

Ixion was terrified. Throughout his years as an Y'mordi, there were only three people that had been able to scare him: Pullatus, Randir, and Rexam Draconis. "Please, your Majesty! I shall not falter in my servitude again! Can't you have pity on me? I am a lowly servant who only wanted to see his family and warn them to hide. I warned them to pledge their loyalty to your Majesty! Please, do not punish me for this!"

Draconis snapped, "Silence!"

The Emperor held up a hand, ordering both the Dragon and the servant to be calm. "Ixion, you left your place of work without notice and have failed to allow my Guardian and Loyal Servant entrance into the city recently. You have openly committed acts that go against my wishes. I must sentence you to ten days imprisonment. Draconis, you may take him now."

Before Draconis could respond to his new orders, Ixion threw a dagger at the Emperor and leaped away from Draconis. The Dragon released an instant burst of Force that knocked the flying dagger away from the Emperor, and it buried itself into the wall beside the throne.

Ixion's white robe faded to its true color of black. Another dagger appeared out of nowhere into Ixion's empty hand. Draconis drew his immense, golden sword with the sun-crested hilt and shimmering tassels. He held his sword low and in front of him. "You were a spy then? An assassin?" growled Draconis.

"Far worse than you could know, Draconis," said Ixion with a grin.

He threw one of his deadly daggers at Draconis, but it stopped midair, fell to the ground near the Dragon, and made a loud clank as it hit the ground. Before Ixion could show his bewilderment, the wall behind him distorted, and a fist made of the wall itself reached out and crushed into Ixion, holding him to the ground.

Draconis and the Emperor looked to the doorway to find the Prophet Mistress Daghda standing there. Draconis sheathed his sword and snorted, "Hmph, I had it under control. He is an assassin, Prophet."

Linda strode across the massive hall and approached the unconscious figure beneath the rock fist and arm. "No, Draconis. This is something greater. Remove your veil of anger and hatred. Look at his heart: it contains a unique form of Darkness. This man is one of the Y'mordi of legend."

Draconis snarled, "I knew there was something that smelled wrong about him."

The Emperor was also shocked by this news. "Mistress Daghda, can you identify this one?"

She bent over the dark assassin. "Perhaps. He used daggers and specialized in the arts of the assassin. It is likely that he is the Y'mordi Y'xon. Y'xon served as the spy for the Y'mordi and on more than one occasion had slipped into the graces of the Lord Lux. It is guessed by many scholars that he was born in the West due to his knowledge of many Nature spells. That is all I know, however, besides the stories, of course."

Draconis inquired, "And how did you disable him? It is a small matter, but I wonder how you did it. Was it Earth?"

Linda nodded. "Yes, when I came in and saw his dagger fly, I merely changed its density, so that it fell like osmium. Warping the wall was no problem either. Manipulating structures is just using Rock."

The Emperor nodded his head to the Prophet. "Thank you very much, Mistress Daghda. Draconis, if you would, please take care of this monster. Now my lady, I'm assuming you were needing to speak with me?"

"Yes, your Majesty. I am assuming that you encouraged Aria to do this?"

The Emperor was puzzled. "Encouraged her to do what exactly?"

Linda shook her head in frustration. "The girl has spoken to the Prophet Mistress Leona and has requested to be a leader of sorcerers in the battle."

The room was silent for a moment, and the Emperor broke it. "That is impossible though. She is not strong enough yet in *mysteria* to be able to lead any amount of mages. Besides, she is too young."

"That is what I thought too," agreed Linda, face flustered. "Nevertheless, the Prophet has decided to give her a trial tomorrow that will prove if she has the necessary strength to command. I believe that if the girl passes the test, the Prophet will make her a Wand Master 3rd Class, which is a promotion of three ranks, an unheard of thing in this world's history."

The Emperor nodded. "You're right, Mistress Daghda. Oc-

casionally, a cadet recruit might prove himself or herself in battle and be promoted one or, in rare cases, two ranks, but three
for a trial is absurd."

Linda replied, "It is illogical that the Prophet would see this
much potential in the girl, but perhaps it is for a reason. It may
be possible that Aria can accomplish this feat."

"Let's pray that she can," said the Emperor. "The Prophet
will make this trial Aria's most challenging experience yet."

By this time, Draconis had reached the prisons with the
filthy Y'mordi in one hand and the keys to Ixion's new cell in
the other.

When Drage awoke, the darkness had surrounded him.
There was not a single light, and he could make out nothing in
this world of night. Then, he realized he was starving. He was
rested, but he still felt near death. Wherever he was, it was extremely cold. His body convulsed with shivers.

He remembered the events of two days before. He reached
out for the Darkness and embraced its power. The world became visible to him through the black light screen. He found
himself in a tiny chamber with an iron door sealing the exit. He
rose and staggered to the door. On its smooth surface were no
knobs, knockers, locks, or anything. To him, it was merely a
rectangle of iron that would not budge.

He pounded on the metallic surface and screamed, "Hey,
open up! Is anybody there? Hello?" However, he found no response. Only the sounds of his fists pounding against the iron
and his echoing screams met his ears.

After his fists were covered in bruises, he slumped to the
ground in defeat. He rested his head against the wall of metal
that separated him from the rest of the world. His black eyes
wandered around the room and discovered he was not alone in
this cell. Four decaying skeletons in the back of the cell revealed how often this dungeon was visited. These people had
simply wasted away in here. Fear stabbed Drage's heart. He was
trapped.

"Wait…" he muttered to himself. "Where is the Sword of

Destiny? I could slice right through the door." He surveyed the room further and was disappointed to find the Sword was nowhere to be found. The Y'mordi had probably taken it after they knocked him unconscious.

He reached out to the Darkness and tried to test the strength of the door. Though his body was racked with pain, he crawled to the other side of the room and summoned as much Darkness as he could. He shot one powerful blast at the iron door, but the spell dissolved once it touched the iron: The door had a spell on it that was meant to resist Drage's *mysteria*.

Drage slammed a fist into the ground in anger, forgetting that his hand was already bruised from pounding the door. He winced from the pain and let his trembling hand relax on the cold floor beside the grinning skeletons.

A Madman's Revelations

The small copse of trees had been burned to the ground. Scattered everywhere were the bodies of men in uniform. Each corpse had large holes in its body, and blood still leaked from the fatal wounds. This battle had been recent.

Lilian was frightened. She had never seen such a massacre before now. It seemed so gruesome and violent. Her heart felt the echoes of *mysteria* all around her, but the battle seemed to have been very one-sided.

Matthew bent over one of the bodies to inspect the wounds and asked Marqest, "What happened here? These men were just destroyed. What kind of gun did this?"

Marqest shook his head. "It was no gun, Matthew. This battle was one of *mysteria*. I believe that Rulia has taken a turn for the worse. It is likely that Maris drove the exiles to rebel and take over Rulia. These men were soldiers for the King here. They were probably supposed to take out any exiles they found, and then they stumbled against the Prophet. We will have to be extremely careful approaching him then."

"What can you tell us about this Prophet?" inquired Matthew.

"Well, the Prophet of Wind is one I have not spoken to for a while. There was a time when he served the Emperor of Light, but that servitude was short-lived. He specialized in one particular form of Wind, Time."

Lilian cocked her head sideways. "Time? I have never heard of that form."

Marqest responded, "That is because it is a less known form and a far more dangerous one as well. The form Time allows a person to manipulate the flow of time itself. Saying this, however, is very vague, because control of time creates almost endless possibilities."

Matthew shook his head in disbelief. "Isn't messing with time impossible though? I mean, how can a person move through time without creating some paradoxes?" Matthew had read enough science fiction on Earth to believe time travel was unfeasible.

"Manipulating time is a tricky thing," explained Marqest. "There are rules for it, and if you break a rule, you could lose your mind, your heart, or even your life. The closest explanation to the existence of the paradoxes created by moving through time is this: When something is being created, typically the creator has some images in his or her mind of what the thing is going to look like when it is finished. An artist knows a few elements he wants to integrate into his painting. A musician has played a few themes that she is going to combine to create a symphony. A writer knows a few scenes of his story before he or she even starts writing it. So, when time was created, some instances were predetermined. The people in those instances might not have been known, and the steps it took to connect the two time periods are also a mystery, but they exist all the same."

Matthew ran a hand through his black hair and said, "Strangely, I think I actually understood what you just said, Marqest."

Marqest called, "Get down!" A blue light flashed out of his scepter and created a wall of solid ice in front of the three of them. As soon as the wall had been erected, it shattered into a million pieces by some unseen force.

"Someone is there," Lilian whispered.

Matthew took a step forward and called out, "Who's there? Are you the Prophet?" Marqest motioned with a finger for Matthew to be quiet. A high giggling erupted on the other side of the clearing. A shabby wooden cottage shimmered into view. "Is that the home of the Prophet?" asked Matthew.

The old man beside him nodded. "Yes, it is, Matthew. We must be cautious around him though. He did not hesitate to attack us."

Matthew nodded.

As they crossed the clearing, their feet snapped the occasional burnt branch. They curved their path around the bloody bodies that littered the forest floor. Lilian became concerned as they approached the cottage. She knew whatever had killed these men resided in that house. When she realized how scared she was, she concentrated on emptying her heart of emotions. She needed to be ready to use any spell at any given moment.

Matthew raised his staff. He was not scared of who was in the cottage, but he still wanted to be ready in case something did happen.

The cottage was made of wooden walls and had a tiled roof. The trio could only see a single window with blue curtains, hiding the room beyond it. The door was a simple red rug that hung from the entranceway and swung in the current. Then, a voice called from the tiny house. "Oh, you can come on in now. Beth is putting on the tea now, so you can have a seat." The same high giggling followed this unusual greeting.

The crimson rug lifted of its own accord, and the three entered the single room that was the cottage. To their left was a tall basin that reminded Matthew of a sink. A woodstove was past the sink and held a rusty teapot on its black surface. The steam from the teapot filled the room with hot bubbles. On the right side of the room was a comfy hammock suspended by two poles that had been driven into the hard wooden floor. Across the room were two bookshelves that stretched from floor to ceiling and held a massive collection of rusting metallic books. In front of these bookshelves was a small table with three white chairs. In one of the chairs was a middle-aged man in a fancy button-up shirt that matched the white of the chairs and what seemed to be his white sweatpants. His hair was turning gray, but dark streaks could be seen across the silver.

"Please, have a seat," he invited. "Beth is making the tea, so we can chat for a while, while she gets that done."

The three looked around and reaffirmed the idea that the man was the only other person in here. Marqest whispered to Matthew and Lilian, "Maybe he broke one of the rules. I think he might have gone somewhat mad." He ventured forward and took a seat near the Prophet of Wind. Matthew and Lilian followed his lead after exchanging glances.

"Allow me to introduce me and my wife to you," exclaimed the man. "My name is Derek, the Prophet of Wind and once known as Master Janus of the Emperor's Council. This is my wife Beth, who was also in the Emperor's Council." He gestured to the stove and teakettle, but only the hiss of steam replied. The man giggled as if he had heard his wife tell a joke. "As you can tell, she has quite a tongue on her. Our two children are probably outside playing in the grass right now. So, who is it that has come to visit the Prophet of Wind exactly?"

Marqest began, "It's me, Marqest. Don't you remember me, Derek?"

Derek's bright face turned dark. "Oh, yes, of course I remember you, Marqest. You still don't look a day over eighty," he retorted. "It's been a few years though. The last time you came to me, it was to ask about the Guardians of Light." Remembering the past had always been painful for this Prophet. He had gone back and forth through time far too often.

Marqest nodded, "Yes, Derek, and now I have brought two of the Guardians, well, three, if you count myself."

Derek's eyes widened at first and then softened in realization. "That explains much, Marqest. The world has been growing tenser and tenser over the years. Kingdoms no longer seek their usual allies' aid. They keep secrets and hire assassins to do their dirty work. Even Rulia has turned. The exiles have finally risen against the human government. The sorcerer Maris seeks to liberate the exiles and wage war against Helio. If the Guardians of Light are being revealed, then the Darkness too shall rise. We are entering a new age, are we not, Marqest?"

The old man nodded. "I am afraid so, Derek."

The Prophet of Wind roared, "Beth, hurry up with that tea! We have guests!"

Marqest interrupted, "Derek, we are still looking for one more Guardian though. I came to you, hoping that you might have found something out with your abilities."

Derek's head shook. "No, I have learned nothing new, and I refuse to traverse the tunnels of time any longer. I have kept that promise to myself. That was why I left his Majesty's service in the first place."

Realization dawned on Matthew. He turned to Marqest in embarrassment. "Hey, Marqest, I just remembered something. Aria and I had discussed some of the Prophecy, though I think the Emperor and others knew what we discovered already. It was not that much of a puzzle, but I had completely forgotten it. One of the Guardians is supposed to be an Y'mordi too. That is the Guardian we have overlooked."

Marqest nodded. He too had forgotten that piece of the Prophecy. He had spent years analyzing it and had not even remembered it when he went out into the world searching for the Guardians. He turned to the Prophet of Wind and said, "Forgive us, Derek, but we must leave now. I am sorry to have troubled you...and your wife." The three got up to leave.

"Wait!" exclaimed the Prophet. He rose, banging his chair against the back wall. "Boy, are you a mage?" He pointed one long and bony finger at Matthew.

When Matthew realized the Prophet was indeed pointing at him, he stammered, "No, sir. I am not. These two are though."

The middle-aged man laughed. "Boy, you have *mysteria* inside of you as well. I can sense it. You have a heart of Earth, though I sense a particular affinity for Wind in you. Marqest, did you never tell the boy?" He frowned at the older man.

Marqest's face turned bright red in frustration. "I do not have time to teach him. We are busy seeking the Guardians."

"Nonsense!" bellowed the Prophet of Wind. "We have plenty of time. As a matter of fact..." He snapped his fingers in the water, and the bubbles of steam stopped moving.

Matthew looked around and saw that everything else had stopped as well. Marqest and Lilian were frozen solid. Not even the current rippled his open coat. Though he knew the answer, he asked, "Did you put them into Stasis?"

"No, Stasis involves time and space. I merely stopped time for you and me. Come outside with me, please, boy. Nothing will happen to your friends, I promise." Matthew allowed the man to grab him by the shoulder and lead him back into the clearing.

The Prophet continued as he put some space between him and Matthew. "Now, I feel obligated to tell you that your heart has the true Element Earth. This just means it is the most dominant Element in your heart. However, you have a sufficient amount of Wind, too, which is my specialty. I cannot fight this battle with you, but I want to help you out as much as I can. It has been a long time indeed since I was ever involved in the world, and as I am sure you can tell, I am a little on the crazy side. I broke some of the rules when I manipulated time several years ago. Please, allow me to share my knowledge with you."

Matthew was still surprised from the freezing of time and the fact that he did have the abilities of *mysteria*. He looked back at the cottage and decided. "Okay, I'm willing to learn."

The Prophet smiled. "Excellent! Now, the first thing you have to learn is to open yourself up to the Element of Wind. Different Elements require different emotions. Wind requires you to be modest, loving, alert, and especially cautious. Choose one of those and allow it to fill your very being."

Matthew closed his eyes and concentrated on caution and alertness. Those were feelings he had experienced often over the past couple of weeks. "Okay," he said once he had the emotion firm in his mind.

Derek frowned. "Hm, you are not grasping it strongly

enough. Here, take this," he said as he threw Matthew a clear glass ball from one of his pockets.

The ball almost slipped out of Matthew's grasp when he caught it. "What is this?"

"That is an orb, an object that magnifies the concentration of your *mysteria*. However, it does not make your powers stronger. It only makes it easier to cast spells."

Matthew felt silly holding the glass orb and focusing on feelings he did not naturally feel at the moment. "Isn't there a word I can use?"

Derek shook his head. "No, I don't believe in using such unnecessary handicaps. Focus on those emotions, boy."

Matthew allowed his eyes to shut once more and focused. Suddenly, he felt a strange sensation overcome him. It was an almost dizzying feeling that made him feel as if he were soaring through the clouds. He imagined the wind pushing against his face. Though he could not see it with his sealed eyes, the orb in his hand glowed a light greenish hue. The Prophet of Wind grinned as the orb shone.

"Now, as strange as it may sound, exert that feeling that you are experiencing outward. Let it go, but not all at once. Stream it into the physical world."

Bubbles emitted from the orb and spun around Matthew. The water in the clearing began to mimic this pattern and orbited Matthew, creating a weak whirlpool. Matthew opened his eyes and beheld the aquatic wind he had created.

Derek continued, "Hold it. Don't let your focus fail."

Matthew could not help but smile. "Wow, this is amazing!"

Derek stepped closer to Matthew, allowing the artificial current to pull him in to the boy. "Now, I am going to explain a few things, but I want you to keep this wind going, understand?"

"Yes, sir." Matthew nodded.

"Using this ability, you can manipulate the flow of time. However, I will not teach you about moving *through* it now. I want to teach you how to use the simpler spells. You can release a burst of Time, and the world will freeze around you.

This spell will give you the chance to rush an enemy. Unfreeze time, and you are ready to attack. Use Time on yourself to increase your own attack or defend speed. It is an amazing ability, boy."

Matthew bobbed his head in understanding, still focused.

"You can drop your wind. I want you to unfreeze time."

The orb dimmed as Matthew reset his emotions. He closed his eyes, concentrating on time itself. When the orb glowed green this time, the trees swayed with the current, and Marqest and Lilian exited the house with puzzled expressions.

"Reverse it," demanded Derek. "Freeze the world again."

Matthew obeyed, and the trees became still once more: Marqest and Lilian froze in their tracks. He exclaimed, "Wow. I can't believe I just did that."

The Prophet giggled in his high voice and replied, "You will do a lot more after you have had some more practice." He snapped his fingers, and the world continued again. Marqest and Lilian finished their approach.

"Derek, what are you doing to the boy?" Marqest roared.

The Prophet crossed his arms. "I taught him how to use *mysteria,* as is his right. He needed to know how to protect himself. So, now he knows."

A fireball flew across the clearing to where the four stood. Marqest's scepter glowed blue as it cooled the fireball into nothingness. Lilian reached her heart out to sense the surrounding area. "There are men in the woods. They have guns and hearts of Fire."

Marqest snarled, "They are probably more of the Rulian soldiers. They are going to try to avenge their comrades' deaths. We need to leave now." He lifted his scepter to open a Gate when Matthew responded.

"No, we need to fight them here. We can't just leave the Prophet here to fight them off. The four of us can easily handle these guys. Come on, Marqest. Show some compassion."

Marqest replied, "I have known compassion to be rather useless. It has gotten many fools killed in the past."

Matthew did not want to argue with the older man. He

closed his eyes and allowed fear and alertness to fill him. The orb in his hand glowed once more, and everything froze. The world was silent.

"Good job," said Derek as he approached Matthew and put a hand on his shoulder. "Now, let's take care of these soldiers who would try to have me killed."

The two walked over to the edge of the woods where the heads of the soldiers became more visible. Derek eyed Matthew's wooden staff, interested. "You intend to bludgeon these men to death then?"

Matthew looked at the staff with fondness. It had been his weapon of choice all his life. "No, I intend to just knock them out. When they wake up, they will be so scared that they will not want to push the attack. Imagine if you woke up and all you saw were all of your friends still knocked out. Kind of scary."

"It won't matter. They will keep coming," replied the Prophet of Wind. "We should just kill them now."

Matthew shook his head in disbelief. "That can't be right. Once we defeat Maris, Rulia will go back into a state of order."

"No, this battle will make everything go into chaos. This battle shall break the tensions in the world, and the fighting might never stop, boy."

"It's still not right to take advantage of these men like this. If they died in an honest battle, that is one thing, but I can't do this. It is too wrong," Matthew explained.

The Prophet sighed. "Fine. I will help you though."

Matthew concentrated and sent a wave of Time to unfreeze the flow of time. The soldiers stepped backward in shock as Matthew came at them with his staff whirling, and the Prophet blasted them into the trees with Force.

Within seconds, the platoon had been defeated, and Marqest and Lilian had reached Derek and Matthew.

Marqest sighed, "Nicely done, I suppose. Matthew, we really must go though. We must go to the Emperor of Light's Palace and find out if he has discovered anything new." He held his scepter out, and a Gate appeared before them. Lilian stepped into the portal first. Marqest turned to Derek once more. "Derek, it was good seeing you again. I hope you, your wife, and your kids have a great life."

The Prophet of Wind bowed to the Prophet of Water. "The same to you, Marqest. I hope the winds of change are favorable to you until we next meet. Next time, perhaps it will be under better circumstances."

Marqest smiled and stepped into the Gate.

Matthew turned to the Prophet, but he had already turned back to the clearing. Matthew stepped up to his side. Then, he noticed the tears that flowed down the Prophet's face. Still, he was smiling.

"Boy, do you see them?" he whispered.

Matthew looked at the clearing and could not see another living being on the corpse-littered ground. "No, sir. There is no one there at all."

The man giggled. "Then, you are blind, boy. That is a shame, I must say. I live a perfect life now. I have a nice and comfortable house, a loving wife, and two gorgeous children. The girl over there is so strong-willed. She is so full of life, just like her mother."

"Beth?" inquired Matthew.

Derek nodded. "Yes…Beth. The boy that the girl is playing with is my son, my other wonderful child. He tries so hard to be strong…'like my dad,' he says to me, but they are both so perfect."

Matthew decided to humor the older man. "How did you meet your wife?"

The man brightened at the question. "Oh, Beth and I met at the King's castle here in Rulia about thirty years ago. We both used to work for the King here, you know. I was the King's adviser, and she was one of the King's personal healers. We met at one of the King's many balls. Most of his staff was there, so the two of us met there. I remember that night well. She had looked so stunning in that dress.

"Of course, she has not aged very much, as you can see. Using *mysteria* as much as we do makes you age a lot more slowly. That also shows how ancient I am though, too."

Matthew thought back to all the people he had met so far who had used a lot of *mysteria* throughout their lives. The Prophets were the first people to come to mind: Queen Daghda, Marqest, and Derek. Then, he thought about people who worked as mages here. In Gevás, it seemed that judging ages based on how they looked was near impossible.

Matthew looked back at the Gate. He needed to hurry up and follow Marqest. Still, he pitied this Prophet. "Sir, what are your kids' names?"

The Prophet responded without missing a beat. "Helen is the girl, and Matthew is the boy."

At first, Matthew did not think it was that strange, but then he realized another perplexity. *Beth... Elizabeth...* "What?" said Matthew as the world spun before his eyes. "How old is Matthew right now?"

"Well, let's see..." Derek appeared to do some calculations in his head and replied, "He must be around sixteen or seventeen years old now. Heh, I can't believe I forgot my own kids' ages." He rubbed the back of his head in shame.

Without having to use any spells, the world seemed to stop for Matthew. He could not believe what was happening. The possibility of the whole idea eluded him, yet it was staring right at him in the form of a middle-aged Prophet with black streaks in his graying hair.

Marqest came back through the Gate. "Matthew, hurry up! We need to go!" he exclaimed.

Matthew turned his head to Marqest. "I think the Prophet might be my dad."

The Enigma Brigade

The nine men in golden hoods and robes stepped forward into the Throne Room of the Emperor Regin. Eight of them had their swords drawn, many of the blades bloodstained. The man in the middle of their formation had the image of a great red bird emblazoned on the front of his robe. He motioned with a finger, and the remaining eight scattered to different areas of the room, so that each of them held a sword to the neck of one of the Emperor Regin's guards or servants.

The Emperor Regin stood from his throne, and his silver crown glimmered in the light that came in through his windows. He spoke with a deep booming voice, "So, the Emperor of Light would resort to this treachery?" His face was now a beet red that matched his red outfit.

The man with the red bird on his front stepped forward. As he stepped barefoot across the white tile of the Emperor's floor, he pulled his hood back to reveal a young man with red hair that flowed down his back and touched his waist. His eyes shone bright green. When he stood a few yards from the Emperor, he bowed. "It is a pleasure to meet you, Emperor Regin," said the young man, his serene voice almost chilling.

"I would say the same had you not just killed several of my most loyal men, you monster," snarled the Emperor.

The young man rose. "A monster? Emperor Regin, surely you do not believe I am a monster, do you? I come with the desire to spread my Emperor's Light to the rest of the world. Our goal is not to kill, to fight, or to destroy. All we want is to do what the Emperor of Light has asked, to save this world from drowning in the Darkness."

The Emperor Regin growled, "Who are you?"

The young man smiled with perfect composure. "I am Maksimilian, Captain of the Enigma Brigade."

The Emperor's eyes widened. "The Enigma Brigade, huh? I thought that was just a myth. What do you want with me?"

Maksimilian's grin stretched. "The Emperor seeks your aid now. The self-proclaimed Emperor of Darkness is preparing to wage war against the Emperor of Light and his allies. Now is the time to see who serves the Light and who serves the Darkness. Where do you stand, Emperor Regin?"

The Emperor Regin was flustered by the question. "I have always served the Light, and I shall continue to do so now! I would always lend aid to the Emperor of Light if he requested it. Immyx is my kingdom, and it will serve the Light and prepare to fight Maris as well!"

"Then, tell me this, Emperor Regin," began Maksimilian. "Why do you exhibit such anger and hatred toward the Enigma Brigade?"

The Emperor roared, "Because you killed most of the people here! You slaughtered innocent people! Why would you do that? How dare you!"

The young man shook his head. "No, their deaths are on your hands, Emperor Regin. Do not blame their fates on the Emperor of Light. You did not welcome us into your humble palace, and nor did you ever communicate to the Emperor of Light asking if he needed your assistance. You are to blame. Now, bow to me. Swear your allegiance to the Emperor of Light."

The Emperor Regin clenched his teeth. Shaking, he went to one knee with his head lowered. "I pledge my loyalty to the Emperor of Light. In times of war, I serve. In times of peace, I serve. I remain loyal to his Majesty, and the will of the Light is my witness."

Maksimilian turned to leave. "That is sufficient, Emperor Regin. You are bound to the Light now. However, I can sense your anger. If you need more justification for those deaths, here is another reason: I hate politics. If I had come here with solely words, you would have spoken in riddles to me. With blood, I have made you an honest man. Be grateful that I hate politics as much as I do."

As Maksimilian headed toward the door, the Emperor Regin pounded his clenched fist into the tiles. "You monster! I'll kill you for this!"

Maksimilian turned his head in the Emperor's direction. His smile was gone. It returned as the Captain turned his head back to the door and approached the exit. When he finally stood in the doorway with his crimson hair flowing down his back, he snapped his fingers, and each of the eight other members of the Enigma Brigade ran their glistening blades through the bodies of the last living guards and servants of the Emperor Regin. The eight fled the hall to leave their Captain and the Emperor remaining.

The Captain said as he closed the doors behind him, "That was for threatening the Captain of the Enigma Brigade. However, I have forgiven you."

The nine approached the next door. It burst open and standing there was an armored man. The formation halted, but Maksimilian stepped forward.

"Sir, I am going to have to ask you to step aside. We serve the Emperor of Light."

The figure in the doorway had tears on his cheeks. "So did all those people you massacred. You won't make it out of this palace alive."

Maksimilian sneered. "We most certainly shall. May I be so bold as to ask your name, soldier?"

The young soldier retorted, "Your boldness is matched by your cruelty and idiocy. I am the Captain Terrell of the Emperor Regin's military, and you are all under arrest for committing murder in the Capital."

Maksimilian took another step forward. "It is a pleasure to meet you, Captain. I, too, am a Captain, as it so happens. However, I must deny your request, though you did make it such a polite one. We have other matters to which we must attend. I hope you will accept my apologies, Captain Terrell."

Terrell raised her mechanical rifle. "I hope your Emperor will accept mine." A barrage of white-hot bullets struck the nine members of the Enigma Brigade. Gates appeared, allowing the Brigade members to escape. Two of them fell to the ground, bleeding.

However, Maksimilian just stood there, concentrating on the warm light of *mysteria*. Each bullet that came near him turned into a jolt of pure light that had no effect on him except the occasional bleached spot on his robe.

When Terrell's attack ended, one of the fallen men was motionless, while the other groaned in pain. Maksimilian extended empty hands to both of the men, and white bolts of bright light shot from his hands and blasted the two men into ashes.

Terrell put a hand to her mouth in utter horror. *Who is this guy?*

"Captain Terrell, you are now responsible for the deaths of two of my men. I shall have to take your life for this crime."

He pulled a lengthy katana from his golden robe and held it as he had been taught, in the way of the Phoenix. He charged and struck at the same time. His attacks were fused with *mysteria*, a spell that made him move at the speed of light itself. The slash cut through the Captain's side, spilling blood onto the floor.

Before the Captain could retaliate, a fireball blasted through the doorway toward Maksimilian. The young man sliced through the fireball with his katana. In the next hallway, a man in a black robe stood with an elongated hammer. The man had hair almost as red as Maksimilian's hair, though it was much shorter.

The Captain of the Enigma Brigade grunted, "Hm, who are you? Will the interruptions never end?"

Randir matched Maksimilian's smile. "Believe it or not, I am actually responsible for Captain Terrell's actions. If he did something rude, I am to blame."

Maksimilian turned from the wounded soldier on the ground and faced the man with the hammer. "You did not answer my question, sir. Who are you?"

"I am called Randir nowadays, though I suppose you might know me better as Y'ran. I am General of the Shadows and a member of the Y'mordi or Lords of the Shadows, whichever title you respect more," he explained with a wide grin.

The sword in Maksimilian's hand moved into an aggressive position. "An Y'mordi? I cannot respect any of your titles then. As a matter of fact, I should kill you now. I have long believed the legends of the Y'mordi were true, and now that I have the proof in front of me, I shall remove your red head from your neck. Do not move too much, or my task shall become more difficult."

Randir had had enough of the idle chatter. He released another immense fireball and swung at the man in gold. Maksimilian sliced through the ball of pure heat and slashed again to deflect Randir's attack.

Though her vision was blurring, Captain Terrell reloaded her rifle. Randir was late, almost three days late. Where had he been all this time? All the same, he had come at just the right moment, it seemed. She found herself wondering if Randir could defeat the Captain of the Enigma Brigade. Randir seemed much stronger with his sporadic power strikes, but he could not match the speed of Maksimilian's rapid slashes.

Randir held the Way of the Dragon with his weighty hammer. He minimized the movement of the weapon and focused on moving himself around the hammer instead. It was the form he had practiced for the past several centuries, and he had mastered it well. Still, Maksimilian's Way of the Phoenix proved to be a tough challenge. He began to sense something strange in the Captain of the Enigma Brigade. His heart was strong in *mysteria* and the Light, yet the man had killed many innocents in this palace. Something was not right.

Randir dodged a powerful slash from Maksimilian and rolled closer to Captain Terrell. He grabbed her hand and sent the two of them into a Gate that took them back into the city.

Maksimilian stood there disappointed. He hoped one day he would find those two again. The Y'mordi and the Captain Terrell owed him a debt of life. He could not help but wonder why one of the Emperor Regin's Captains was teaming up with the Y'mordi. He believed the Emperor Regin had been honest in his allegiance, so that meant that there were people under his command that secretly served the Darkness. This city was filth.

He summoned a Gate and stepped into the plains outside of the Capital to find the six remaining Brigadiers. One of them asked, "Hey, Maks, what about Fend and Warbrix?"

Maksimilian eyed the man who had spoken. "The soldier killed them both. I managed to attack the Captain, but one of the legendary Y'mordi took her away. It appears the Capital is under the influence of the Darkness," he explained.

The man responded, "What are we going to do about it, Maks? Do you want us to burn it down?"

Maksimilian turned to face the man. "No, Tilgé. It would simply cause too much chaos in the world for it to be deemed in the best interest of the Light. Besides, we have other people we must see. However, if you would like to take one or two other Brigadiers with you, you may scour the city a few times."

Tilgé responded through the veil of his hood, "I would appreciate that very much, Captain." He made a bow to the Captain and gestured for two of his comrades to follow him into a Gate.

Maksimilian stopped the man. "Tilgé, be warned that the Y'mordi are real and extremely dangerous. The chances are high that you shall find at least one of them in the Capital. The soldier's name was Captain Terrell, in case you forgot it. He serves the Darkness. Kill him on sight, understand?"

"Yes, Captain," he responded as he used the Gate to reenter the enormous mechanical city.

The five remaining men before Maksimilian stood in solemn silence, awaiting their Captain's orders. "The Emperor also wishes for us to go to the heathen kingdom Astra. It is completely overrun with exiles, but we must speak to their Queen nevertheless. His Majesty seeks the knowledge of which side the kingdom of Astra has chosen."

One of the men exclaimed, "But the exiles are all monsters! Why does the Light need their alliance?"

Maksimilian turned to face the man. He drew his stainless steel katana, pointing its curved tip at the man. "Bryco, it is not your place to question the orders of the Emperor of Light. Do you doubt his Majesty?"

The man became frightened and answered, "No, Captain."

The man with the long red hair narrowed his eyes. "Do you doubt me, Bryco?"

Bryco shook his head and stood erect with a salute, "No, sir!"

Maksimilian released a ball of light, creating a Gate. "To Astra then," he said. The five men entered the Gate leaving the Captain behind for a moment. Maksimilian turned his head back toward the Capital.

The Enigma Brigade had changed so much under his new rule, he realized. When the Brigade had first been created, it had been just a group of skilled fighters and sorcerers used for spy missions and scouting ventures. Then, a century and a half ago, a miracle had happened: Emperor Mentiris. He had seen Maksimilian's potential and had promoted him to Captain. The Emperor had used the Enigma Brigade as assassins. For the first time, the Brigade had been a weapon. That feeling of intense power had given Maksimilian a great sense of purpose.

However, when Emperor Mentiris had fallen, the Brigade was used for dangerous and highly covert missions, involving unexplored regions of Gevás or political rivalries. The Helius family had abused the nature of the Enigma Brigade greatly, but Maksimilian made sure that the Brigade remained in practice.

Of course, Maksimilian was the oldest in the Brigade, though he appeared to be the youngest. He was an Ancient, though an unusual form of one. While the remaining Ancients had survived through hidden spells that could prolong life by a few centuries, Maksimilian had a phenomenal secret, and it was still in hand, the Steel of Life. The blade itself had been his for ages, though it had only been given the piece of spirit when the Great Spirit divided itself during the Obsidian Wars. The Steel of Life had the ability to grant its user agelessness and immunity to disease. However, it had one flaw: if it killed or was even responsible for someone's death, it would lose its power for that wielder. Maksimilian had had to learn how to fight without delivering killing blows. He learned to weaken his victims and then finish them with a spell.

He had desired the powers of the other Spirit Swords and had searched for them over the centuries but had had no luck in locating them. He had known of the Helius family heirloom, the Sword of Destiny, but that Sword held no interest with him. There were three more out there somewhere, and he intended to find them.

He stepped through the Gate into cooler waters. The five golden-robed men were already in formation in front of him. His phoenix-adorned robe was a magnificent symbol for all of them. Bryco watched his Captain, the man he had often referred to as the Phoenix, step forward to greet the guards of the Queen's castle.

Bryco could barely hear the conversation.

"We seek a visit with the Queen. You would do us a great kindness by escorting us," said the Captain.

One of the guards replied, "What is your name, sir? We shall announce your presence to the Queen and see if she will have you."

Bryco could tell that the guards were being polite, more so than the guards at the Capital. He hoped that Maksimilian did not kill them. They were just doing their jobs. Bryco had always disagreed with his Captain's methods but had never said so.

"My name is Maksimilian. I come under the orders of the

Emperor of Light. I must see the Queen immediately."

The other guard responded, "Sir, the Queen is very busy right now. She——"

A bodiless voice resounded in front of the castle. "Let the men in. I am not busy at the moment. Plus, I would like to hear from the Emperor of Light now. News does not often travel this far."

Maksimilian stepped forward as the guards opened the doors for him. His face was blank.

Bryco knew, however, that the Captain had been about to give the order to kill those guards. He hoped these negotiations did not end in bloodshed. He was willing to do the Emperor's bidding, but he hated killing others, especially innocent people.

Maksimilian sniffed the air. He could sense the taint of Darkness here. It did not come from any of the individuals he had seen so far. It was more likely that someone who had a heart of Darkness had just been through here. He intended to ask the Queen about this disturbance. He grinned then: the one thing he enjoyed more than killing was interrogating.

Into the Labyrinth

They could not help but notice there was much more room now that Randir was gone.

The storm outside the spire had increased in intensity. The rain poured harder, though Sarn's Wind spell had created a barrier around the top room of the tower, preventing the chilling rain from entering. The lightning continued its rampage of the blackened plains.

Xarden commented, "This storm has gotten a lot worse. The atmosdome is breaking. Before long, this whole island will be underwater." He looked out through one of the holes in the wall, watching the violent storm.

"You're right," observed Arnim. Her brown cloak was still sopping wet from the rain. She was not one to let small things annoy her, yet the rain was a damper even to her mood. The torrent had soaked straight through her robe and hood. "The atmosdome is breaking. The pressure of the seas is crushing it. Your spell was not as strong as you had hoped, Sarn."

Her twin giggled. "It has served its purpose. With the changing of the times, this island will be found again, and it shall serve a new purpose. We still have the Palace of Shadows anyways."

Xarden responded, "Yes, this atmosdome has served its purpose, Sarn. However, we still have a long way to go. Maris is only the first of the seven. If you can strengthen the atmosdome, it would be worth the effort."

"No," said the voice from the chair by the burning fireplace. Pullatus's voice was soft, barely audible over the storm. "After we are through with Maris, we shall return to the Palace of Shadows. Many of you have weakened over the centuries. We need to return to our original training. We do not know when the next Great Servant shall reveal himself to us."

Mali stepped forward and bowed to Pullatus. "My Lord Pullatus, when is Maris going to strike at Apolis? When we met a few days ago, I assumed his attack would be soon, yet the world has only been building itself into a tighter tension. When will this battle occur?" he inquired.

Pullatus explained, "He has removed us completely. I approached him after our last meeting, and he tried to attack me. Nevertheless, he has won the allegiances of many nations now. With his new powers, he is creating an army of Shadows in the Southern Continent and trying to make them stronger."

Xarden did not turn from the window as he spoke, "Training the Shadows has not been done since the Dark Lord Dagan fell. You do not think that he can do it, do you, Y'tal?"

Pullatus noticed that Xarden used the name Pullatus had been given when he had passed Dagan's Trials of induction during the Obsidian Wars. "He just might be able to accomplish this feat. His will is iron now. Even if he only partially succeeds, the Emperor's armies will not be expecting Shadows with this much intelligence."

Mali rose, his white robe glowing from the light of the fire. "What of the Guardians?" He swallowed and also decided to use Pullatus's induction name. "Lord Y'tal?"

Pullatus's hooded face turned toward him, and Mali could almost feel the man's eyes burning into his skull, though he had never seen those eyes. "The last time I heard from Ixion, the

Dragon and Aria were at the Palace of Light. Matthew is likely to still be with the Prophet of Water from Heaven's Isle and is still probably looking for one of the Guardians. The Prince of Light is under the tower as we speak. Somehow, the boy ended up here through a Gate he created. I suppose that that has something to do with Maris's curse on the boy."

Xarden responded to this news with a question of his own. "Y'tal, have you killed him yet? If you have, then the Prophecy has been proven false."

"No, Xarden, I have not killed the boy." The warmth of the fire heated the room gradually, and it cast shadows across the five of them. "He is dying. I sent Ixion to lock him in the dungeon beneath these ruins. If he does not die from hunger, then the collapsing atmosdome shall crush him underground."

Sarn interrupted the conversation. "Speaking of Ixion, where is the rat? He should be here by now."

Pullatus was silent for a moment and said, "I believe Ixion has been captured by the Emperor of Light. He made his betrayal known to them, and it is likely he shall not be joining us for a while. It is very possible the Emperor has him in a cell that dispels all *mysteria*, so he will not be able to even communicate with us. However, I am confident he shall commit suicide as soon as he is able."

Arnim commented, "I do not mean to sound rude, Pullatus, but what makes you think that he will do that? You know the rat as well as we do: He cares too much about his own life to be willing to do that."

"That is precisely why he will do the deed: He knows that if he accidentally reveals any information, then when I see him next, he shall suffer more than he ever has before. I shall not be angry with him for the mistake of revealing his identity to the others. I suppose that it had to do with his disappearing to meet us," Pullatus explained.

The five of them were silent, each taking into deep consideration what had happened over the past few days as they stared into the red flames of the air. They all knew which topic was going to come up next, though they were hesitant to bring it up.

With a deep sigh, Pullatus began, sparing the others their fears, "I have come to the realization that Randir is one of the seven Guardians of Light. As the Prophecy foretells, one of us must be a Guardian, and he has played the part. When this battle is over, he shall come to us once more, no longer a rogue. Instead, he shall take his place as General of the Shadows. Of course, he shall be punished for his actions, and I am sure he is well aware of this fact. Until then, he is not our problem. We must prepare for the battle as well."

Xarden, Mali, Sarn, and Arnim straightened to receive their orders.

"The battle shall occur in the morning. We must prepare to aid Maris. He needs to kill the Emperor and the Guardians of Light. Arnim, I need you to protect him from any of the other sorcerers there. The Emperor's terra is armed with several strong mages. Do not let their attacks get past your barriers, understand?"

Arnim nodded with a bow, "Yes, Lord Y'tal. I shall fight at Maris's side tomorrow." A Gate appeared behind her, and she left the island.

Pullatus continued with his orders. "Sarn, I need you to see if you can free Ixion from the Palace of Light before the battle. I would like him to be able to fight, as well."

Sarn bowed and left the atmosdome. The barrier vanished, and rain poured into the room. Outside, the storm worsened, and the island began to flood.

"I need you to keep the Guardians away from Maris, Mali, so that he can eliminate the Emperor first. That is our highest priority now."

"Yes, Lord Y'tal, as you wish." He disappeared in a flash of Light.

Xarden started, "And what would you have me do, Pullatus?"

His ancient hair flew wildly in the gale that shook the tower.

"Xarden, I need you to return to the Palace of Shadows.

You and I shall not be participating in this battle. If something goes wrong, only then shall we make an appearance."

Xarden swallowed. "To take Maris's blood. 'With blood of the Great Servants,' read the other Prophecy, the Prophecy made by the Dark Lord Dagan himself. I understand, Pullatus." He retreated into his own Gate.

Pullatus was alone in the rotting spire. He released the spell of Fire that animated the fireplace with flames and walked to the massive hole. He surveyed the black land that had given the island its name, the Obsidian Plains. A memory tickled the back of his mind of when the island was beautiful centuries ago. It had possessed a different name back then, but it did not matter now.

He was satisfied with his work. The world was entering a new era, an era of Darkness. Maris was forcing the nations of Gevás to go against one another and strive to meet their own selfish goals. Chaos had begun its domination of the world.

Despite this progress, Pullatus knew he had other matters to worry about. Randir was one such complication. Though he would be complacent again after the battle, he could rebel at any later point. He had always been unpredictable, which made Pullatus question why the Dark Lord Dagan had chosen Randir to be second among the Y'mordi.

Another pressing matter was the whereabouts of the stranger who had ambushed them on Earth. After the mysterious figure had rescued the three Guardians, he had come after Pullatus personally and had spoken with him in detail.

"...pretty strong, Y'tal. I thought Elizabeth's barrier was nearly impossible to shatter, yet you have been able to do it. I assume you did it with the help of the other Y'mordi, wherever they are."

"Who are you?" Pullatus asked the stranger with the Sword of Destiny in hand. Somehow, the figure had immobilized Pullatus completely, in both body and heart. He could neither move nor channel mysteria.

The figure hesitated. "I...am an illusion, Y'tal. For years, this moment shall haunt you. You shall be reminded constantly of the man in black who allowed the Guardians of Light to escape your grasp and held you immobile the whole while."

Pullatus clenched his teeth in fury. "Can an illusion die?"

The man chuckled. "I bet you're anxious to prove that, aren't you, Y'tal? However, I shall not grant you that privilege. Instead, I shall make you this promise. One day, you shall come across another like me, one who is younger and less experienced. Nevertheless, he shall prove to be far more annoying to you and your goals. Fear him, for it is he to whom I have given my blessing."

Then, the figure did something even more unexpected. He Teleported. Pullatus had known that Teleporting was one of the ancient arts, an ability to cross through space, time, or even realms without the use of a Gate. It was one of Pullatus's own abilities that he had kept secret for centuries. Now, the man before him had vanished entirely, yet his words echoed on.

"I am an illusion…"

Pullatus snapped out of his thoughts and heard a distinct roar over the storm. The atmosdome had broken. The world outside became a roaring ocean. He summoned a Gate and left the island as the tower crumbled beneath his feet, and the Obsidian Plains were once again submerged in the seas of Gevás.

Mali stood on the top of the Palace of Light. He was on one of the lookout roofs of the gigantic castle. He knew that only secret passages in the Palace led to these rooftops, and so it was unlikely that anyone in Apolis, even the Emperor of Light himself, knew of the place.

When he had served the Lord of Light Lux before the Obsidian Wars, he had become familiar with the entire castle and had learned every tunnel and passage that there was to know. The memories still made him bitter toward his present circumstances.

Lux had been his master, and Mali had served him every day faithfully. It had been his entire life, yet the Lord of Light had never repaid him for his efforts. Back then, his name had been Hector Lavriahm. He had always considered his greatest quality to be his undying loyalty, but when he was ignored by the person he had spent years serving, he had reconsidered where his loyalties lie.

He had gone to the Dark Lord Dagan and had given him

information regarding the Lord of Light's military plans in return for a position in the army. However, he had not felt the same being in the army, so he sought a position closer to the Dark Lord, one of the Y'mordi. After months of training, he undertook the challenges of the Trials and passed them, earning the fourth rank among the Y'mordi with Xarden ahead of him and the twins below him.

His loyalty had been strong with Dagan and then just as strong with Y'tal, the mysterious leader of the Y'mordi, whose face he had never seen. Mali had beheld the strength of Pullatus only a few times throughout their thousand years. He had witnessed Pullatus's Trials and had gaped at the way he handled himself on that nightmarish battlefield.

He sneered, his white robe swaying in the soft current. Pullatus had been a fool for ordering Sarn to fetch Ixion. Mali knew the castle so well, yet Sarn was the one to search the colossal Palace. He was well aware of his orders, yet he felt the desire to help Sarn with hers while he waited for the battle. He leaped from the top of the Palace and allowed himself to fall to one of the lower balconies.

He looked onto the golden city. The street lights made it golden even in the middle of the night. The glimmering walls, the brilliant streets, and the friendly people had always enticed him. Over the past millennium, he had found himself wondering if he was on the right side, if maybe he should not have made that one fateful betrayal.

He shook his head to clear his thoughts. He was beginning to think like the rogue Randir, he realized. Randir was not a person he needed to imitate. The vows the Y'mordi had made were too strong for any of them to break. Once an Y'mordi, always an Y'mordi. Because there was no hope of leaving their dark organization, there was no point in possessing any treacherous thoughts. Such ideas would be futile.

The door to the balcony opened before him, and he entered the Palace of Light. He needed to get to the prisons below the castle. The stairwell at the back of the room was long and went down several floors but not to the lower levels of the castle. Still, he began the descent and tried to remember which floors he was passing.

He thought to himself, *If they found out that Ixion was one of the Y'mordi, then they will likely have extremely strong security over the area, maybe even guards. I doubt that Sarn will care though; she will probably walk right into any of the Emperor's traps. What was Y'tal thinking by sending her? And since when did he decide to allow us to call him that again? He was the one that told us to use other names.* "To remove the connections between us now and what we used to be. We do not want the world seeing those connections anymore," *Pullatus had said. I hate the name he gave me, "Mali." I know that he used the letters in our given names to create them though. Y'ran became Randir, Y'tal became Pullatus, and Y'lam became Mali. Still, he is too powerful to argue with now. The Dark Lord Dagan favored him so much.*

He arrived on the lowest floor that the stairs could take him, the ground floor. He stepped out into the main hall and noticed the bright lights were still on throughout the Palace. It was late at night, but everyone was still preparing for the next day's war. Pullatus had been two-sided on that matter as well. Earlier, he had said he did not know what Maris planned to do, and then he had said that the battle would be in the morning.

The light of *mysteria* surrounded him, and all light bent around him, rendering him invisible to the eyes of others. He walked across the hall but found no one there. He made it to another set of stairs and continued the descent to the dungeons. The golden splendor faded from the walls the further down he went.

When he stepped into the lowest floor of the Palace, he stood in the midst of the great Labyrinth, Lux's most magnificent structure. Its spiraling metal walls held infinite secrets, traps, and even the prisons in its winding depths. Torches lit by *mysteria* illuminated the curving halls. He had always hated this place even when Lux had sent him here. Besides the enchantments that were built into the Labyrinth, such as the torches and traps, a person could not use *mysteria* in the prison cells.

He remembered the way to the prisons and stepped forward, allowing the dim corridors to engulf him. The stairs behind him vanished, one of Lux's old tricks. His invisibility still held as he traversed the maze, and after several minutes, he could see the iron bars that enclosed the prison cells. Guarding them was a sleeping woman. She looked old with her white hair and white cloak. Still, he could sense an immense amount of power in the woman. He turned to the bars and saw two of the cells occupied. In one was Sarn, pacing. It was obvious she had been caught quickly. In the other was Ixion, leaning against one of the stone walls.

Mali tried not to wake the woman with his spells. He concentrated a small amount of powerful light into the locks that bound the cells both physically and with *mysteria* as well. The locks snapped open, yet the woman remained asleep. Sarn and Ixion looked to where Mali was but could not see him. Mali removed his invisibility and gestured for the two to follow him.

Ixion saw his daggers beside the woman and snatched them away from the woman. Before Mali could say anything, Ixion slit the woman's throat.

"Why did you do that?" roared Mali when the three had made it back to the top of the Palace.

Ixion snapped back, "She was one of the Prophets and had been helping the Guardians! She had caused enough trouble for us."

Sarn was eager to agree. "Yeah, she is the one that got both of us locked up. It's her fault she fell asleep. What do you care anyways?"

Though Mali was in a group that specialized in doing these kinds of things, he still felt it was wrong. He lowered his head in both anger and shame. "Both of you, prepare to fight in the morning. Maris's armies are on the move," he demanded.

The two Y'mordi nodded in agreement and disappeared into their own Gates.

Mali brushed a pale hand through his blonde hair. Though the murder of that woman had seemed so natural and effortless to Ixion and Sarn, he had felt utter horror at the injustice. At that moment, Mali felt an indignant resentment toward Ixion.

What he had done was unforgivable.

His tear-lined eyes surveyed the marvelous city Apolis. He wondered if it would still be standing tomorrow night. Below him, the troops of the navy and terra practiced their formations. He could barely see the lights of spells being practiced and hear the clash of the practice swords striking one another.

As his eyes closed, he examined his heart. Fused to every inch of his heart of Light was the Darkness, the Darkness of an Y'mordi. That Darkness was the spell of the Dark Lord Dagan that gave the Y'mordi their phenomenal powers.

However, even with that overwhelming Darkness, his own Light had remained. Perhaps that Light had been what allowed him to survive the Dark Lord Dagan's Trials. It certainly seemed that way.

Mali's teeth clenched at the unfairness that he saw happening around him. That woman had not deserved to die such a death. It drove him nearly to madness knowing there were people like Ixion who could murder so easily. He found himself wishing he had not come to Ixion and Sarn's aid.

"You'll pay for this, Ixion. One day, you will pay for this," he promised.

Then, he lay back on the roof and gazed up at the stars. It reminded him of Randir. When Randir had been much friendlier, before the end of the Obsidian Wars, the two of them had spent a lot of time together just staring at the night sky and reminiscing like two old friends.

That had all changed when Pullatus had sent Randir on that one particular mission, the one where Randir lost his wife Ophelia. However, Mali had been fairly certain that the Dark Lord Dagan had been behind the mission in order to test Randir. Mali had been saddened by the event as well. He had lost his best friend.

The stars twinkled in the sky. Mali sighed and decided to rest for a little while. In the morning, he had a battle to fight. In the morning, the world would tear itself apart.

Back to the Palace

That night, Matthew decided to stay with his father. The idea of it was comforting to him. It was the first time he could associate a warm sense of belonging with the word "father." He sat down with his crazed father and helped him finish his tea. The old man seemed to be thinking clearly.

"So, Helen is my sister, and Elizabeth really is my mother?"

Derek nodded with tears streaming down his cheeks. "Yes, she is, Matthew. When you were really young, she left. The last thing she told me before she said goodbye was that she was pregnant, but that the baby wasn't mine. Sure, I was shocked, but I was not mad necessarily. I loved your mother." He began pouring the hot drink into two small cups on the table. "The real surprise came when she left in the middle of the night with both of you."

Matthew sipped his tea in deep thought. He lowered the warm cup. "The Emperor of Light was the father."

Derek did not look at Matthew. "Are you sure?"

He nodded. "Yeah. Mom wanted to raise all three of us on Earth, so we've spent our whole lives there. We just came to

Gevás for the first time a couple of weeks ago. The Y'mordi have been after us."

"She never mentioned me, did she?"

The courage to find the words evaded Matthew. He just sat there in silence. "Dad, she told me I was adopted, that I didn't have the same blood as her or Drage and Helen's dad. My whole life, I felt like I didn't belong."

Derek frowned in puzzlement. "Now, why would she ever do that? It would have made at least some sense if she had said that to you and Helen, but to exclude you solely makes it even odder."

Matthew shrugged. "It might have been something as simple as looks. Drage and Helen both look a lot like her, while I don't look anything like her."

"You may be right," started Derek. "You may not be. Beth had a habit of doing things she never explained to others. If I were you, I would not think too much on it." He managed a meek smile and continued, "How has the Emperor treated you?"

"Like I was a Guardian of Light, or at the most, Drage's friend." Matthew replied.

Derek's smile faded. He reached over the table and put a comforting hand on Matthew's shoulder. "Matt, you're here. You have a right to be angry but not for now. I have my son again, and this time he is not one of my delusions." The grin returned, warmer than ever.

Matthew returned a half-smile. His emotions were scattered. For the first time, he did not feel so alone anymore, yet he felt betrayed and hurt. A part of him felt angry too, and he never became angry.

The Prophet could see that Matthew was not really feeling any better. "Matt, even though your mother lied to you, I know without a doubt that she loved you just as much as she loved Helen and Drage. You should have seen the way she looked at you when you were younger. She did love you, Matthew, and that will never change."

Matthew raised his green eyes to meet his father's own faded green eyes. "Alright, thanks, Dad."

A feeling of immense pride and happiness overcame Derek at that moment. For the first time in decades, he was ready to break his promise. "Matthew, I want to show you something, and I would rather you not try to imitate the spell just yet, okay?"

Curiosity rose above Matthew's other emotions as he nodded.

Derek raised his hand, and the world shimmered a thousand bright colors before returning to normal. He stood from the chair and gestured for Matthew to follow. "We are like ghosts now. We can traverse through the barriers of even matter here. Come," he implored.

Matthew followed his father to the door and watched in amazement as he stepped right through the red rug that hung over the entrance. Matthew stepped forward and closed his eyes as his body went through the rug without moving the fabric in the slightest. Outside, the trees had grown back to life, and bright yellow flowers traced the swaying grass. Matthew could see the effects of a medium-strong current but could not feel it at all.

Then, he saw four people running among the trees. Two of the considerably shorter ones approached Matthew and Derek and then collapsed in the grass a few feet away. He could see their faces and realized who the two toddlers were: Helen and himself. Helen had short brown hair, baby blue eyes, and a chubby face. The younger Matthew still had dark hair and green eyes too. The two were so little, and it was the youngest that Matthew had ever seen himself. His mother had never shown him any pictures of when he was younger. She had claimed not to have any.

Matthew whispered, "What is this?"

"This is the past," his father responded. "This was the day your mother told me she was pregnant with Drage."

Two more people came over to the collapsed toddlers who were roaring with laughter. The woman picked up Matthew, and the man took Helen. The two toddlers rode their parents' shoulders in utter joy, as if it was the most thrilling activity in the world. Everyone was smiling.

Matthew wiped his eyes as he felt an unusual feeling fill him. He could not deny what he was seeing: he had a family.

"Dad, I've got to go back to the Palace. Marqest and the others are waiting for me. I have to get ready to fight Maris."

Derek did not turn from the single window in his cottage. "I know, Matthew. I just wish that...I don't know. I just wish that we had met before now, before you were *forced* to be here."

"Me, too," Matthew agreed. Then, he had a stroke of inspiration. "Hey, why don't you come with me? With two of us using Time, Maris's armies would be gone before they knew what hit them!"

"Matt, you have no idea how much I would love to," he said with hesitation. "But you must know that I am not as strong as I used to be. My powers have dwindled over the years. I would not last a minute on the battlefield against Maris."

Matthew did not press the issue, and a part of him wanted his father to stay here in this cottage. He did not think he could bear losing his father to this battle. "Alright well, I will be back when this is all over."

Derek turned his head to face Matthew. His eyes had traces of red around their lids. "Will you, Matthew? If everything goes well with this battle, are you sure that you won't go back to Earth with your brother and friend? I finally found my son, and now he has to leave?"

His son crossed the room and put his arms around his father in a warm and loving embrace. "No, I promise I'll come back, even if it is on the way out. Maybe you could come with me back to Earth. I'm sure you'd like to see Mom again anyways, right?"

A smile spread across Derek's face as he hugged his son. "I just might, Matt. I just might." The two of them, father and son, stayed like that for a minute, and then the older man exclaimed, "Oh, and before you leave, I would like to try something. May I see your staff?"

Matthew went back to the table, grabbed his wooden weapon, and brought it to his father. Derek held a hand over the wood, and a hole appeared in the top of the staff. He placed his miniature orb in the hollow and used Wind once more to warp the wood so that it held the orb into place. Another spell sliced at the body of the staff, etching designs over its rough surface.

When he had finished, he returned it to Matthew to examine. Matthew traced his fingers along the carvings in the wood. "They're ravens," Matthew said.

"About 600 years ago, an organization was formed known as the Keepers. I do not know much about the original organization, but it lasted about 500 years. It officially ended a little before the Griffin's Rebellion. They were comprised of mages who specialized in not just Wind, but Time itself. I saw only the end of the organization, and I was in it, as was your grandfather and his father. The symbol of the Keepers was the raven."

"And the orb?"

"Even though you hold the staff and not the orb, your power will still be concentrated. Do not worry about the staff or orb breaking: I enchanted the staff a little. However, my power with Nature is somewhat limited, so I cannot promise it will last forever, but it will last a good deal longer than you would expect, so don't be afraid to give it your all in a battle."

Matthew ran up to his father and hugged him. "Thank you, Dad," he whispered

"Don't forget your promise," muttered the older man. "Come back to me."

Matthew smiled in their embrace and stepped back. "I'm ready."

Derek summoned a Gate in the middle of his simple cottage, and his son walked through the portal without a second look back. Derek had faith Matthew would come back soon. He knew his son would. He had his son back.

Matthew was outside Apolis. Even the thought of the golden city gave him a feeling that reminded him of home. He knew it was against the rules to summon a Gate so close to the walls, but Derek had managed it anyways. He ran to the front gate and noticed no one was there. "Hey!" he called. "Is anybody there?" Someone came to the gate.

"No one is allowed into the city at this time," the guard responded.

"No, my name is Matthew. I am the brother of the Prince of Light, and I must see the Emperor! If you won't let me in, at least find Draconis, and tell him I'm here," he pleaded.

The guard raised an eyebrow at him. Matthew glanced down at himself and realized how suspicious he appeared. He still wore an open coat that revealed his chest and pants that were foreign to the Southern Continent. It did not help that it was already the middle of the night.

Matthew continued, "Please, sir. I am to help him fight Maris."

At last, the guard responded, "I will find the Dragon and let him decide if you are to be trusted. On the eve of a battle, I do not want to be held responsible for a bad decision."

He left, leaving Matthew surprised. Was the battle going to happen so soon? He had expected time to find the Y'mordi Guardian of Light and to train. They needed to find Drage too. With luck, he had already returned to the Palace.

A flash of gold revealed Draconis's presence as the Dragon soared through the water in his serpentine manner. The gate opened, and Draconis gestured for Matthew to enter.

"Are you well?" he asked with concern.

Matthew smiled and rushed at the Golden Dragon, embracing him. "Yeah, I'm fine." He released the Dragon and asked, "What about Aria and Drage? Have they come back yet?"

Draconis frowned in confusion and looked past Matthew, shocked. "Aria came back with the Prophet of Earth, but Dragenopn has not returned yet. We thought he was with you." Matthew clenched his teeth. "The Prophet of Water and Lilian did not say anything about your story. They wanted to wait for you." His voice was a deep growl that displayed his irritation yet joy to see Matthew again.

Matthew lowered his head. He had really hoped Drage had made it back to the Palace.

The Golden Dragon noticed and offered, "You know, you look like you have gone through a lot though."

Matthew raised a brow. "What do you mean?"

Draconis eyed him. "For one, you wield a rather interesting staff now. I can sense the enchantments on it, though I cannot tell what they are. Also, you are wearing very fine Astran clothes, you must know." He smiled.

Matthew laughed. "Thanks, Draconis. Where's Aria?"

Draconis gestured for Matthew to follow him. "Come with me, and we shall talk. It seems that Aria has decided to try to become a leader of the sorcerers in the Emperor's terra." He saw Matthew's expression become puzzled at the mention of the word. "The terra is one of the segments of the Emperor's military. They are the ground troops."

"Oh," said Matthew still piecing together what had just been said. "She's become that strong in *mysteria*?"

The Dragon sighed. "Well, that remains to be seen. She did it against the Emperor's wishes, and we have no idea what makes her think that she can do this. The Prophet of Earth suspects Aria might have a chance, albeit a small one. In order to be raised to that rank, Aria will have to pass a trial, and in this case, it is a dueling trial, one where she must duel another mage. In the trial, both of them will be protected by the arena's enchantments so that neither can be hurt, but when enough damage has been done to one person, the other will be labeled the victor."

"Do you know who the other mage is going to be?"

Draconis shook his great golden head. "Unfortunately, I do not. However, I think that before we let her see you, we should let her perform this trial. We do not want her to be distracted. We can still watch, of course." The two were quiet for a moment as they traversed Apolis's troop-filled streets. "I apologize, Matthew, but I must ask you: do you have any idea where Dragenopn might be?"

Matthew's bright mood dampened. "I don't. Draconis, near Macela, we were attacked by—"

"Maris," Draconis interrupted. "Yes, I know that far. Aria told us."

"Oh, yeah, right. Anyways, Drage's curse got worse when we went to the Northern Continent. Maris had to have followed us there. Drage tried to kill me for a second. He realized he could not control the curse, so he...he just left. He summoned a Gate and disappeared. I have no idea where he is now."

When Draconis saw the tears that welled in Matthew's eyes, he pulled the boy close. "Matthew, it is not your fault. I am quite confident that Drage is fine, and he will be here soon. When he does come back, he will have his own stories to tell, and he will be glad to see us again. Do not lose hope yet, Matthew."

The young boy with the dark hair nodded. He knew that Draconis was right. The events of the past few days had been so emotionally overwhelming. He realized then that he should never have gone along with Aria's plan. He should have made all three of them stay in the Palace. That would have been the sensible thing to do.

They arrived at the headquarters of the terra. The building was not as extravagant as many of the other buildings, but Draconis knew the place well. They entered and went to the first elevator they found. A camera in the elevator inspected Draconis and Matthew, and finally the voice of the elevator said, "Floor?"

Draconis grumbled, "B8."

This building must have had an immense underground, Matthew realized. He found himself wondering how much of Apolis was beneath the city. The fact that the Palace had lower floors came to his memory.

When the elevator opened, they were in a vast stadium filled with people, all wearing the armor of sorcerers. The rows of seats surrounded a dirt circle in the center of the stadium. White boundary lines created another circle that was divided in half.

Matthew marveled at the amount of people here. "Are these trials always such a spectacle?"

Draconis shook his head. "No, but Aria could mark a record in the history of the terra. I have no idea why the girl wants a leadership position though. She must know she will need to be fighting Maris, not his armies."

"Will the military rank benefit her in other ways, Draconis?"

The Golden Dragon crossed his arms in thought. "It could. She would be recognized as a fully-grown mage, and even eligible to be a Prophet by some standards."

Matthew frowned in interest. "Draconis, you once told us that Prophets were the greatest wielders of an Element. How does one actually become a Prophet?"

"A Prophet is chosen by the Elements. Bad things have happened to people who told everyone they were Prophets but really were not."

"Whatever she plans to do, she has a crowd for it. If there is any recognition to be gained, she will get it one way or the other here," replied Matthew.

Finally, a door opened on one end of the stadium, and Aria stood in the doorway. She wore an elegant, white robe adorned with several bright red phoenixes. A black blindfold shielded her eyes. She stepped forward into the glaring light of the stadium and walked to the center of one of the half-circles.

Matthew had been so focused on Aria that he had not realized that the other duelist had arrived. The man turned to face the audience. He wore a simple golden robe and had a gaunt face with white hair streaming behind him. Matthew recognized him as the man who had shown the three teenagers to the Throne Room when they had first arrived in Apolis, Master Valdridge.

"Aria will be competing against him?" Matthew inquired in disbelief.

Draconis nodded in fear, "Yes, did you know that Master Valdridge is married to Mistress Leona? He is the Prophet of

Light. Why is Aria wearing that blindfold? She will get herself destroyed in a heartbeat."

A voice replied behind them, "It was not my doing."

The two turned to find Mistress Leona standing there. Draconis rose from his seat. "My lady," he said as he offered a small bow to the Prophet of Nature. Matthew imitated the motion.

Mistress Leona made a dismissive gesture. "Sit down, you sillies. The girl is definitely brave. I will give her that. As you can see, Rex, she has done her research."

Draconis squinted his sapphire eyes in memory. "The phoenixes are the symbols of the original Light Brigade and now the Enigma Brigade, but I cannot remember the significance of the blindfold. Would you enlighten me, Mistress Leona?"

"Certainly," replied the Prophet, always eager to spread her knowledge. "It is the trial that a student must pass at the Academy in Gryphos if they are to earn a mastery in the Elements discipline. Of course, the trial is more of a thought-based trial and not a duel, but the girl is definitely brave. She wants to prove to herself she can do it as much as she wants to prove it to everyone else."

They heard voices behind them. Marqest and Lilian had entered.

Mistress Leona turned to Draconis, "Rex, I shall leave you for now. I would like to get a closer look. You might want to move closer as well." She left them.

Marqest whispered into Draconis's ear, "Draconis, I have some bad news for you from the Emperor. The Prophet of Earth, Mistress Linda...she was murdered a little while ago. Apparently, the Y'mordi escaped and killed her."

Heart of Darkness

"I still don't understand why you didn't just kill him," complained the Captain Terrell for the hundredth time that afternoon. She had faith that Randir with his countless powers as an Y'mordi could have killed that filth who had massacred all those people in the Emperor Regin's castle.

Randir sighed. "Something was strange about him, I told you. I sensed something uncanny. When you are fighting something that you can't grasp mentally, sometimes, fleeing is the better option. Trust me, I love a good fight, but that man was different somehow. One doesn't just walk into the Emperor Regin's palace and kill all his guards just to make a point."

They were back in the city at the same pub where they had first met. A new bartender had already been hired and had served them their drinks with a smile. The pub had a lot less people now. Everyone was preparing to mobilize for battle. The Emperor Regin, though furious, intended to keep his promise and readied his troops to fight Maris and his armies.

"You were late, Randir," she added.

Randir slammed his glass down on the bar. "It seemed like

I showed up at just the right time! You're lucky I came when I did!"

Terrell's eyes softened. "I know. I am grateful too. It's just…I hate those men, the Enigma Brigade, for what they did. I am not mad at you at all for this, Randir." She traced a finger around the rim of the glass. "I know why you came back. I am sorry, but there were no Guardians here. I promise you that if there were any, I would have found them by now. No such Guardian of Light exists here."

The Y'mordi turned back to his drink and sipped some of the warm liquid. "I know. The other Guardians have returned to the Palace of Light, I believe. The battle will be tomorrow, and I will fight alongside the Guardians of Light."

Terrell's eyes narrowed. "Won't that get you into some kind of trouble though?"

Randir nodded his head. "It will. Y'tal will probably torture me for days. I have evaded him for centuries, but I knew I would have to face him when I betrayed him. I cannot stay a rebel forever though. At this point, all I want is to die, but I cannot have that wish. If I remain a traitor, then my fate will be one far worse than death. Not even Y'tal's torture of me will compare to that fate. I have to return to him."

Terrell pitied the Y'mordi. "Randir, have you not thought that maybe there could be a way to remove the powers that make you an Y'mordi? If ancient spells still exist, then there has to be a way to break those. Every spell has a weakness, right?"

"Perhaps, you are right," Randir responded. He had often considered the idea of breaking the bonds of Darkness that connected him to the other Y'mordi. In his mind though, he had labeled it as impossible, but now that this Captain had mentioned the idea, it seemed a little more doable. "I suppose I shall leave you now, Captain Terrell. I have plagued you long enough." He stood to leave when she grabbed his arm.

"You were going to kill me, weren't you?" she demanded. "I could see it in your eyes." As she looked into his flaming eyes now, she could see only the slightest trace of guilt. She turned back to her drink. "Don't feel bad: I was going to do it too. I had decided it when you left me last time. When you saved my life, though, in the castle, I knew I owed you. I couldn't kill you."

Randir smiled. "I couldn't kill you either."

"Why?" Terrell asked after she had taken another drink.

The seat creaked as he sat back down. "I don't know, to be honest with you. There are so many reasons to do it, but I just couldn't do it."

Terrell allowed a smile to come to her face. "You know what? For one of the Lords of the Shadows, you aren't half-bad. Call me Stehl. After this battle, it won't matter who knows I am a female anyways. I am going to transfer to the Emperor of Light's navy."

Randir's eyes widened. "You are not staying here?"

She shook her head. "No, I have a new goal now: killing those scum that slaughtered the innocent people in the Emperor Regin's castle. They will all pay for this, especially their Captain. The easiest way to do that will be to work in Apolis. Hopefully, having been a Captain here will grant me some benefits. That was just too much for me to bear. First, we have to get through tomorrow's battle though."

"Stehl," Randir began, trying to use the Captain's real name. "You know—" Then, he stopped.

"What is it?"

He turned his head to the entrance of the pub. "I smell blood, and it's strong too."

Stehl and Randir ran from the bar and exited the pub. "Which way?" she demanded.

Randir darted in the direction from which the smell was coming. The morbid scent filled his nostrils and clouded his thoughts. "There," he said, pointing to one of the shadowy alleys of the Capital. Several Fires sprang up to light the way.

In the back of the alley, they found the source of the smell: a young man's body lying in a pool of his own blood. At this point, even Stehl could smell it, and she covered her nose with one arm and investigated the body with the other.

Randir commented, "It looks like just another murder. That

is the major crime in the East, anyways, right?"

"Right," started Stehl's muffled voice. "But I know this man, and I know that he should not have been in one of these alleys. Something is wrong. He has sweat mixed with the blood. That means he had been running and was cornered here." She stepped back from the body. "You have a good nose, Randir. Do you think you could smell out whoever did this? I am in a punishing mood right now."

He sighed. "I might be able to track the person, but it will not be by smell. This city stinks enough without me opening my senses up too much to it. As strange as it sounds, I can follow the heat signals."

"You can actually see heat?"

He closed his eyes and allowed the warmth of *mysteria* to wash over him. Through the lids of his eyes, he could feel the different levels of heat. He found one large enough to have come from a person not too long ago. The person had left the same way he or she had come. Randir traced the person's tracks, following them step by step.

Stehl followed him without another word. She did not want to interrupt whatever he was doing. Her arm fell from her face, allowing her to breathe in the fresh water. Randir was becoming more and more helpful, it seemed. *Are the other Lords of the Shadows anywhere near as interesting as this one?*

Voices came within earshot. "Where is he? If you tell me, perhaps I will spare your life!" hissed the voice.

"I-I-I don't know!" stuttered the second voice between sobs. It was another dark alleyway, and Stehl could not see anything, but Randir seemed to see it all.

Stehl muttered to Randir, "What's the weapon?"

"The same knife."

She drew her rifle, and the small screen near the butt of the gun flickered to life. Her fingers glided across the surface to specify the target. She fired one white-hot bullet into the dark and heard a clink as the bloody knife in the dark clattered onto the ground.

"Randir."

The Y'mordi did not hesitate and flew down the alleyway at lightning speed. She heard a man cry out, and suddenly, the alley lit up with Randir's Fires. She rushed inside, observing the three men. One cowered in a corner in fear and confusion. Randir stood over the other he had knocked to the ground. The man had received a bloody nose from Randir's attack.

This same man had a robe of pure gold.

"The Enigma Brigade..." Stehl whispered to herself as she approached the men. She spoke in a distant voice to the man cowered in the corner. "What was he asking you?"

The man straightened and made a shaking salute. "To be honest, sir, he was asking about your whereabouts, Captain."

"Very good, soldier. Return to your post, and spread the word that anyone found wearing similar attire as this man is to be regarded as an enemy of the Emperor Regin and is to be executed on sight."

"Y-y-yes, sir," said the young soldier as he fled the alley.

The Brigadier looked up at the Lord of the Shadows and the Captain in terror. "You are the Y'mordi the Captain warned us about!"

"He is not the one you have to worry about," replied Stehl as she lifted her rifle to point at the man.

The gunshots accompanied screams for a few seconds that echoed throughout the backstreets of the Capital that night, but then, they ended.

The man with the long red hair had just sat down when one of his soldiers came to his side. "Captain, Tilgé is back."

After discovering that the queen of Astra would serve the Emperor of Light, Maksimilian and the rest of the Enigma Brigade had returned to Apolis, to the Palace of Light to inform the Emperor himself. Now, Maksimilian was ready to enjoy a nice meal. "Send him in, then, Sume."

Tilgé entered the room and bowed. "Captain, the other two were killed in the Capital. I have failed you. Please forgive me."

Maksimilian's eyes flickered. "Who is responsible for the deaths of these men?"

"Sir, the Captain you sent us to find, his name is Terrell, and he killed Seryl in cold blood and immediately ordered his soldiers to kill either me or Grenn if we were found. Well...they found Grenn. I barely escaped their Captain, sir. He had the Y'mordi with him still."

"We have lost four men today, Tilgé. I am not pleased. Nevertheless, the Emperor is satisfied with our work, so the risk was well worth it."

"What about the Y'mordi and Terrell, Captain? Are we just going to let them go?" Tilgé was becoming more and more enraged. His hatred for the Darkness was what had made him want to join the Enigma Brigade. He had always approved of Maksimilian's to-the-point methods.

"Forget about them, Tilgé. From now on, they shall be my concern alone. They have increased their debt to me, and they shall pay it in time."

Tilgé knew better than to question his Captain. "Yes, Captain," he replied, making a final bow as he left the room.

Maksimilian was alone. He realized Tilgé was becoming independent, but he favored the man all the same. Everyone in the Brigade had come to see Tilgé rise as Maksimilian's second. However, Maksimilian knew the younger man still had much to learn. He stared into the flickering candle that lit his table. It was a small blue flame that cast an ominous glow on his food.

It reminded him of the Y'mordi he had met earlier in the day. Before then, he had never seen physical proof that the Y'mordi still existed.

"He had used Fire..." the Captain whispered to himself. "...and a hammer..." Memories of the Y'mordi swirled in his mind. "Y'ran, did you really not recognize me?" He smiled then. "Of course not. You thought I was dead...like poor Ophelia."

"Why are we doing this again?" asked Stehl.

After they had disposed of the Brigadier, they had left the city, and Randir had suggested they relax under the stars. Stehl, however, thought it was just an excuse to be lazy and had never done anything like stargazing in her life.

Randir sighed. "Just relax for a few minutes, okay? It's been a while since I've done this, and after this battle, Y'tal will probably not even let me see the sun again for a while."

Stehl complied and looked up at the stars. "This is probably going to sound stupid, but I never knew there were so many stars up there. I've never had the time to just stare at the sky at night. Besides, in the middle of the city, the sky gets pretty mucky."

Randir turned his head in surprise. "Are you serious?"

She punched his arm. "Yeah, I'm serious! My whole life has been about the military. That's how I got to where I am now. My biggest goal in life has just been the next promotion."

"What about your family?" asked Randir as he turned his back to watch the sky.

"Don't have any. My dad died in some battle or another, and my mom abandoned me. That's a common story now though. A lot of orphan girls joined the military. It's the best life to have here. People respect you, and with promotion, your salary increases tremendously. We have to do what we can to survive."

Survival... Randir thought. *Is that what life is all about? I have managed to stay alive, and now, I wish I wasn't. Life is not worth living if you have to spend it alone.*

"Randir, are you okay?"

He snapped out of his thoughts and replied, "Yeah, I'm fine, just thinking."

"What do you see when you look up at the stars?"

"I see memories...haunting, miserable memories."

Stehl turned to look at Randir's face with its scattered burns and scars. "What memories could be so terrible that you see them in the stars?" She wanted to learn more about the man who had saved her life.

"I became an Y'mordi because I wanted the power of it. I was so greedy and wanted only to become stronger. I was once known as Lord Victor Ferro—"

"Lord Ferro?" she interrupted. "You were the ruler of Immyx?" She could not believe what she was hearing. If he was Lord Ferro, then it was he who had first started that ridiculous law that women should not be allowed in the military.

Randir did not avert his gaze from the stars. "I was, though it was not called that at the time. The area was much larger too. I had everything then: a kingdom, a loving wife, and no enemies. Somehow, I still wanted more. The Dark Lord Dagan promised immortality and the power to shape the world, so I took his Trials. The Trial of Body tested my strength in battle, and I proved myself competent there. The Trial of Heart was to see how strong my ability in *mysteria* was, and as you can imagine, I did quite well in that. The last Trial was the Trial of Will..." he did not finish the explanation.

Though Stehl was curious as to what had happened in the Trial of Will, she did not push the matter. Randir's pain was obvious, and she owed him her life.

The two lay there on the grass-covered hill, allowing the current to ripple through their hair, and watched the stars twinkle above them. Out here, the only sounds were the chirps of various aquatic insects resounding throughout the water. Both Stehl and Randir gazed at the stars and wondered if their lives were really what they wanted them to be.

"What are you doing here?" said a voice.

Randir bolted up and summoned his hammer. The two of them watched the new figure in black robes, muscles tensed. Randir asked, "Are you not the one that was messing with Y'tal earlier?"

"Yes, that was me. I thought he took it rather well, don't you?"

"How did you get here without me sensing you? No one has ever come that close to me without my knowledge."

The man in black folded his arms. "Teleporting is much quieter than using a Gate, Randir. I thought you would have known that. Besides, here, I am not real. I am merely an illusion."

Randir softened and lowered his hammer. Stehl relaxed when she noticed Randir had done the same. "I couldn't beat you even if I tried, could I? Y'tal couldn't. So how could I?"

The man smiled beneath his hood, though Randir could not see it. "No, you could not beat me. I have learned most of the ancient spells, and I have mastered one of the Dark Ways. To me, you are a mere mortal."

Stehl said, "Why are you here?"

The stranger hesitated and then said, "I am looking for someone. He has been in evasion of me, and he plans to erase the Guardians of Light, even you, Randir. Perhaps, he does not yet understand your invincibility. Regardless, be careful."

As the stranger prepared to leave, Randir swung his hammer to attack, but it froze in mid-swing. Randir was held immobile yet not in Stasis. Stehl noticed the spell and drew her rifle to shoot the stranger, but her own finger froze on the trigger.

"What are you trying to prove, Randir? Are you so eager to test your own strength?" He released Randir but not Stehl. The Y'mordi swung again and, this time, it met solid metal. The figure had drawn his sword, a stretched version of a longsword. The hilt was also made of steel. Randir recognized the blade at once.

"That is the Sword of Destiny. It looks different though," he said through clenched teeth as he tried to force the figure's Sword back.

"You are right, Randir. This is the Sword of Destiny. I made a few modifications to it, however. It simply was not long enough for my purposes." The Sword slid right through the hammer, cutting it in two. Randir fell forward to the sharp edge of the Sword, but the stranger pulled it back at the last second and held up a hand instead, sending a blast of Darkness at Randir. The Y'mordi flew backward several feet and landed hard on the ground.

When Randir rose, the stranger was gone.

"Who was that?" demanded Stehl, able to move again. "Look, your hammer is fixed."

Randir approached the hammer that had likely been repaired by the aid of *mysteria*. "What did he mean by he's an illusion?" He shook his head. "I don't think we will see him again though."

A beep emitted from Stehl's wrist device. She looked down at it and pressed a few buttons. Her head turned to Randir. "I have to go now. The troops are preparing to move to Apolis. I have to help with the mobilization."

The Y'mordi raised his hand, and a gleaming fireball erupted from it, creating a Gate. He explained, "This Gate will take you to the front gates of the Capital." For a moment, they stared at each other, each waiting for the other to do something, yet nothing happened. Randir managed, "It was nice meeting you, Captain Terrell."

Stehl smiled and replied, "It was nice meeting you, General Ferro. I hope we see each other again." Her feet stepped backward until her back touched the edge of the Gate. Without another word, she slipped into another place, and the Gate closed behind her.

Randir was once more alone.

Captain Terrell commanded her troops once she entered the city. "You there, get back in formation! Remember, riflemen in front, swordsmen second, and heavy artillery behind them! We want to make as little movement as possible after we get there!"

Another Captain approached her. "Terrell, where have you been? Everyone has been looking for you."

She faced the Captain. "I am here on time and in my position. Captain, I would advise you to return your own formation and worry about your own troops." Though the other Captain was several years older, he still cowered under Terrell's glare and returned to his own position.

Terrell tried her best not to think about Randir at all. She did not know what she felt, but she knew she needed to stop feeling and start acting like a Captain.

The gates to the city opened wide for the troops to exit. There were nine battalions in Terrell's regiment, easily a few thousand soldiers. She marched ahead of her own troops and

halted them when they had reached their position. After several
more minutes, the rest of the army stood ready to march. A
massive Gate appeared in the water in front of them, and one
of the Captains started the march into Apolis. The Gate had
been summoned by several powerful mages from the Southern
Continent. After a few regiments, it was Terrell's turn. She gave
the order, and her soldiers followed her into the chilling water
of the South.

Randir observed the uniformed soldiers as they marched into the Gate. For the first time, he was beginning to realize this
was more than a battle between Maris and the Emperor of
Light. It was greater than the Y'mordi and the Guardians. This
battle would be about all of the nations of Gevás. He was wit-
nessing the beginning of a war.

He turned from the sight. Wars were nothing new to him.
He had led battles throughout his life, though most of them
had been during the Obsidian Wars. He remained an effective
General. The Shadows considered him their leader, and they
obeyed his command even now.

However, the only thing his mind could see at that moment
was Stehl's face. He shook his head, trying to dismiss the image. He twisted his face to see the sky, and a new face appeared
in his mind: the face of his deceased wife Ophelia.

Her soft, brown hair filled his vision, and he found his
hand reaching up to the sky in vain. "Ophelia..." he whispered.

The image faded.

"Ophelia, one day, I will come back to you. All things end,
and so will I. Be patient, my love. Then, I will tell you how sorry I am. I will tell you how much I wish things could have been
different." The image of Stehl intruded on his thoughts again.
This time, he did not force it out of his mind. He knew how
futile the effort would be.

He embraced *mysteria* and felt the vast amount of power he
had been saving over the years. There was not a limit to the
amount of *mysteria* a person had, but some people had a stronger storage than others did, so that some mages could cast

somewhat powerful spells with no work, while others had to spend years practicing that spell before it became effortless to use.

The stranger had made Teleporting seem easy. Randir had perfected that ability over the years, though it had taken a lot of time and effort. It was an extremely intense spell that utilized the form Gravity. He concentrated on the spell and allowed every atom of his being to connect to the space to where he wanted to go. The world blurred around him as he Teleported from the Eastern Continent to the icy plains of Helio.

The frost chilled him and forced him to shiver. Two Fires appeared beside his body to warm him and shield him from the cold. He walked toward Apolis. It would be several hours still before the dawn came. He wanted to enjoy his last moments in the night while he could. Y'tal would not treat him kindly when he returned.

The ever uncontended Prophet of Fire breathed in the frigid air and allowed his bare feet to step painfully on the frosted ground. He looked up and noticed that the last dawn he would see for a while was approaching.

Reflections of the Past

A ria focused on her breathing and forced out the noises that plagued her ears. There was a crowd in the arena, and a crowd was just what she had wanted. She had just not expected the people to be so noisy.

Her heart opened itself, allowing a sliver of *mysteria* to fill her being. Colors appeared through her eyelids. She could feel every heart in the stadium and sense every emotion. The sliver narrowed to only concentrate on the unseen duelist in front of her. The person's heart was near bursting with Light. Confidence, pride, curiosity, and excitement emanated from this one. She planned to use this person's emotions against him or her.

The voices quieted around her. One sound roared into the stadium, "Duelists, ready yourselves." Aria sensed the duelist in front of her open his or her heart to *mysteria*. She only allowed that tiny amount of *mysteria* to flow through her. Her abilities needed to remain a surprise to her rival.

"On my mark...three...two...ONE!"

However, neither of them made a move. She could sense the duelist's amusement and lack of interest. The mage considered this duel a joke. Anger started to rise up in her, but she smoothed out the emotion. Now was the time to focus.

Without warning, the duelist cast a spell of Light. Aria braced herself for the impact she knew was coming. The blast knocked her backward and almost out of the circle. Her heart sensed the laughter that filled the stadium. She stood, readying herself once more.

If two more blasts like that one hit her, she would lose the duel. To win, she would need to fight back as hard as this duelist was, if not harder. Still, she held only that small amount of *mysteria*. The duelist in front of her laughed even harder. His or her feelings of caution were fading, and even the feeling of curiosity had left. She felt the spell of Light rise again, and it hit her in the chest forcing her backward again.

When she stood this time, the stadium was in an uproar of utter amusement. She cast a spell of Fire that created a medium-sized fireball. It was by no means the best that she could do, but she needed to look like she was trying. The duelist dispelled it with an Ice spell, and he prepared his or her final counterattack.

This time, she dodged the spell and simultaneously grasped as much *mysteria* as she could. A wall of Force came to her aid and blasted through her enemy knocking him or her back, and she could sense the surprise that now dominated the duelist's heart. She did not stop though. Her hand waved upward, and vines sprouted from the ground, ensnaring the duelist.

The duelist cast a bolt of Lightning Aria blocked with a wall of stone that shattered upon impact. She bent low to the ground, placed both of her hands on the soil, and felt the earth shift beneath her, creating a gaping fault in the circle. The vines dragged the duelist into the crack. Sensing the duelist prepare another spell, she rapidly set the vine-covered mass alight with Fire. Though Aria could not see her spell, the Fire was a pure white, dazzling in its spectacular heat.

The earth began to close itself around the burning duelist. The person broke out of the spells and leaped back into the circle. Aria had expected this revival and counterattacked with a new spell: a Gate. As she cast this spell, the duelist created a far more powerful variant of the blast of Light that resembled lightning.

The Light went straight through the Gate and came out where the Gate ended, behind the duelist. The duelist's spell hit him or her from behind, knocking the duelist unconscious. As Aria sensed the Light of the duelist's heart weaken, she removed her blindfold to behold a crowd that was cheering her name in amazement.

The next thing she became aware of was the duelist she had defeated: Master Valdridge. She put one hand over her mouth in shock.

Mistress Leona used a Gate to appear in the arena and approached Aria with a proud smile on her face. "Very impressive, Aria," she whispered to the girl. She raised the volume of her voice using a simple Water spell, and her voice resounded throughout the stadium. "I now promote the Cadet Recruit Aria Newman to Wand Master 3rd Class Aria Newman."

When Aria thought the mass of people could not possibly be any louder, they proved her wrong. She had done it. She gazed around the stadium, and finally, her eyes met Matthew's own green eyes. Her eyes and smile widened as she waved to Draconis and Matthew. Her joy decreased when she realized Drage was nowhere to be found.

She collapsed into a chair when Draconis told her the news. Her face fell into her hands as she tried to make sense of it. "How, Draconis? How did this happen?"

The Golden Dragon snarled, "It was that filthy Y'mordi. Do you remember the servant and guard Ixion? He was one of *them*, the Lords of the Shadows."

Matthew could not believe it. "Ixion was one of the Y'mordi?"

The Golden Dragon nodded. "I am afraid so. I have no idea how he escaped his cell, but he did. Ixion had tried to attack the Emperor, and Mistress Daghda stopped him. I put him in a cell, and she offered to guard him overnight. She said it was likely he would try to escape."

Aria lifted her head from her hands, revealing a blank face that revealed no emotion. "She didn't come and watch me. This wouldn't have happened."

Matthew sat beside her and put a comforting hand on her shoulder. "Aria, I'm sure that she knew you were going to win this duel. That's why she didn't come." He had never seen Aria like this before. She seemed so cold and distant.

Mistress Leona approached. "I hate to interrupt, Wand Mistress Newman, but you have work to do before this night has ended." She noticed Aria's somber expression and felt a tinge of guilt. "Is everything alright?"

Aria glanced up at her. The creases in the phoenix robe straightened as she stood. "Yes, Mistress Leona. I am ready to see those who would follow me." As she began to trail after the Prophet of Nature, Matthew grabbed her shoulder again. She turned to face her friend. "What?" she asked, her voice becoming a snarl.

"Everything will be fine, Aria. We will find Drage soon, and after the battle tomorrow, we will have a really nice funeral for the Prophet. Try not to worry too much about everything right now. You have new responsibilities."

"Thanks, Matthew. I'll see you on the battlefield tomorrow." She turned from him without a second glance.

"You are not like the others," whispered the girl with the long white hair.

Draconis had hoped the short Guardian of Light would not start this conversation. After the trial, Draconis had decided to exit the city and inspect the troops. Lilian had volunteered to accompany him. He grumbled, "Oh? And how am I so different?"

Lilian's silver-rimmed eyes looked up at the Dragon as she said, "You are not an exile like me. The Emperor of Light has excluded you from the laws. You are free."

He winced as she mentioned his freedom. He looked over one of the battalions and was impressed by the formations. The

Emperor had gained several more allies for this battle. He could count the countries: Mashan Telis, Durot, Astra, Verdegoran, Norlante, and even Immyx.

The first thought for a reply was to say that he was not as free as it seemed, but he decided that that would be an ungrateful statement. He knew he owed the Emperor of Light a great deal yet. "I am only free because of my service to the Emperor. I owe him a debt."

Lilian nodded. Her eyes traced over the soldiers. "Oh, I see. Still, you must have done something truly wrong to owe the Emperor so much loyalty. Then again, he could just have done something truly spectacular for you, causing you to feel indebted to his kindness. Which is it, I wonder?"

The Golden Dragon's eyes narrowed as he surveyed the armies. He snarled at a nearby soldier who was talking while still in formation. "I would rather not discuss that topic right now, Lilian. The past is no longer a concern to me."

"That is a lie. Your heart cries that the past still concerns you."

"You have very sensitive *mysteria*, do you not?" replied Draconis with a hint of a snarl. He did not enjoy having his heart read by a child anima. "Here is some truth for you then. I was born and raised in Sharl Vran. My family was killed by a Black Dragon named Kusvor Cairon. By some stretch of luck, he allowed me to live. I knew I could not stay there any longer, so I left the world and ended up here in Gevás. The Emperor of Light Bral Helius found me starving and near death near Apolis and restored me to health. Bral made the Dragon's Clause to further help me, and in response to his kindness, I vowed to protect his bloodline, or more specifically, the Emperors of Light."

Lilian smiled. "Does that not feel a little better? It seems as if that was the first time you have talked about your past in a long time. Is this statement correct?" She cocked her head sideways as if she were an innocent puppy.

"Yes, to be honest, I do not talk about my past." He found himself smiling despite his annoyance at Lilian's prying. "I suppose it does feel comforting talking about it, but I cannot be thinking about it now. We have to prepare for the battle."

The girl maintained her smile as she scanned the formations. They heard orders being bellowed from the fronts of the battalions. The two came closer to the army from Astra. The petite army consisted of a few Dragons, several anima, and three or four griffins.

"Lilian," Draconis began. "What are you?"

"My true form is a white mare. I am much older than my human form shows. I was an apprentice to Maris before he turned to the Darkness." Her smile faded as they walked. Her bare feet crunched the frosted ground beneath her.

Draconis eyed her. "Are you sure you are going to be able to fight him tomorrow?"

She nodded. The Astran army marched into another area in the frozen plains. "Yes, he is not the same Maris anymore. He has allowed the Darkness to consume his heart."

His golden tail twitched. "Do you know how that happened? Do you know how the Darkness consumed his heart?"

The girl shrugged in her white gown. "I know the Y'mordi are the ones who manipulated him into using the powers of the Darkness, but the corruption was all his own doing, I believe. Everything has a heart: people, animals, plants, worlds, and even the Elements themselves. When someone uses *mysteria*, to some extent, he or she is submitting to the heart of that Element. At the same time, though, the person is controlling that heart. I fear that Maris has forgotten how to control his heart, and the Darkness has taken over it."

"I see..." Draconis replied. *Perhaps, the child is right. Perhaps, at his core, Maris was not as evil a person as we have all thought. Maris was just another exile and had been discriminated against by the same laws I fight to protect.*

A soldier approached Draconis. "Excuse me, sir, are you General Draconis of the armies of Helio?"

Though the Golden Dragon was flattered by the title, he shook his head in denial. "No, I am not a General. I am, however, the Guardian of the Emperor of Light and his Loyal Servant. Can I help you, soldier?"

The soldier nodded. "Perhaps you can. My name is Captain Terrell of the Emperor Regin's armies. I have heard occasional stories of the great Golden Dragon that serves the Emperor of Light, and I was wondering if I might have a word in private with you, sir."

"Certainly, Captain," responded Draconis. He turned to Lilian, "I shall return shortly."

She nodded and continued looking over the formations.

"How may I be of assistance, Captain Terrell?"

Terrell shuffled her feet. "Master Draconis, I do not mean to sound intrusive or rude, but can this conversation be off the record?"

Draconis nodded. "Proceed."

Terrell's tension relaxed at Draconis's welcoming nature. "I was wondering if you could give me any information on the secretive branch of the Emperor's military called the Enigma Brigade." Draconis's tail twitched. "You see, recently, the Enigma Brigade raided the Emperor Regin's castle recently and slaughtered most of the innocent people who worked there. The Captain's justification for this action was that he did not like politics and wanted to show his seriousness through more physical means."

The Golden Dragon clenched his claws. "The Enigma Brigade did this?" He was shaking with rage at even the possibility.

"Yes," replied Terrell. Her fists were clenched as well. "However, I would prefer that you not mention this to his Imperial Majesty. Do not think poorly of me, but I would like to bring the men involved to justice myself."

Draconis shook his head. "Forgive me, Captain, but if what you speak of is true, then I must alert the Emperor to this atrocity. Your job is to lead your men, not administer justice. I assure you, however, that these men shall be punished considerably should their crimes be verified. May I speak of this to the Emperor? Your name shall not be mentioned."

Though the answer did not please Captain Terrell, she grinned and saluted the Dragon. "Thank you very much, sir."

"At ease, Captain." He returned to Lilian, and the little girl stared up at him.

"She was telling you the truth until the end."

"Could you hear what she said?"

"No," remarked Lilian.

"It seems there may be more traitors in our midst than we had originally suspected. That matter shall have to wait until after the battle though," Draconis explained.

Lilian said, "Could you tell me a story? Of Sharl Vran?"

Draconis brightened at the thought of his home world, and he began to weave a tale that captured the elegance of the mountainous world of Dragons.

Marqest bowed before the Emperor of Light. "I pledge my allegiance to you, Lord Helius, Emperor of Light and King of Helio. As I was once a Loyal Servant, I now renew those vows. I serve the Light and am ever willing to assist."

The Emperor nodded his head in satisfaction. "That is sufficient, Master Marqest. You may rise as my Loyal Servant. The banishment that Emperor Mentiris once placed on you is removed and void. You are welcome in my Palace."

The Prophet of Water rose. His back cracked painfully from the strain, but he did not reveal his agony. "Thank you very much, your Majesty."

"No need to thank me, Master Marqest. However, I would now like to hear of the events that took place when my son and his friend Matthew found you." The Emperor sat back in his throne, anxious to listen to the Prophet.

"I am willing to inform you of what events have taken place, but I must at the same time warn you that there are certain truths that were revealed that concern you."

The Emperor's face tensed. "Concern me? What truths would these be, Master Marqest?"

Marqest hesitated. "Your Majesty, it's about your wife Elizabeth. It seems that she had two children before she married you."

John Helius smiled at the information. "I was already aware

of this news. Elizabeth loved me for several months before telling me she was already married and already had two kids. When she became pregnant with Dragenopn, she decided to leave her husband and marry me. I absolutely adored the girl that Elizabeth brought. Helen was her name. She looked just like her mother. I noticed early, however, that Matthew and Dragenopn were in constant competition, even for Elizabeth's love. Dragenopn was always the wild child, always eager, and always aggressive. Matthew, on the other hand, was quiet and reserved, yet Elizabeth had such strong affection for him."

"You claimed Helen as your own but not Matthew?"

"I loved Matthew, but I just could not accept him as my son. I truly did love him though."

Marqest had trouble accepting this brutal reality. Then, he understood. "You did not want him in line for the Crown."

The Emperor shifted his eyes. "No, I did not want him to be the next in line to be Emperor of Light. Law states that the eldest son takes the Crown, and that would have made Matthew the heir. Do not question my judgment, Master Marqest. I did what I saw to be right."

Marqest bowed again before telling the story in full. "Yes, your Majesty."

Matthew stood on the balcony that extended from his room in the Palace of Light. From this point, he could see the vast expanse of the city and the walls that protected it. Farther, he could make out the lights of the armies that were assembling.

The chilling current swept over him, making him shiver in his Astran coat. He had not changed yet, and his restlessness pained him. The battle that was supposed to be between Maris and the Guardians of Light had elevated to a massive war.

The thoughts that plagued his mind now were of Drage and Aria. Drage had disappeared. There were no signs of where he could have gone. He wondered how serious the Heartbind spell had become. The last time that Matthew had seen him, Drage had been in terrible shape.

Aria, however, had become close to the Prophet of Earth, and he knew that death would be affecting her tonight and even tomorrow. He hoped he had given her at least some comfort. With this new military position, Aria had a lot of power. Her work would last the entire night. Her motives were still a puzzle to Matthew.

He shook his head. Aria's face had lit up with such joy when she had passed the trial, but when she found out that the Prophet had been killed, her face had become stone. Matthew felt so sorry for her.

An idea came to him. He held up his raven staff and observed the crystal orb held in place by the twining wood. As he concentrated, the orb turned bright green.

Before he could attempt the spell that had come to mind, a voice spoke from behind him. "You would try to undo events that have already come into being? That action is against the laws of time. Even if you were to try, the force of time would crush you."

Matthew turned to see a man in a black robe. His face was completely masked by his long hood. However, he recognized the voice. "You're the one that saved us back on Earth…"

The figure stepped forward onto the balcony and leaned against the stone railing. "Yes, that was I. The Y'mordi were trying to kill you. I could not let them end the Prophecy so early."

Matthew eyed the stranger. "You were crazy that night. In all the time we've been in this world, I've never seen anyone fight the way you did on the beach." He turned back to the city and leaned on the railing with the stranger, enjoying the view. "May I ask you a question?"

"Certainly," replied the man in black.

"The night you brought us here, did you know all of this was going to happen? Were we just a part of your plan? Or someone else's? We could have lived our whole lives on Earth and never known about this world."

The figure sighed. "I did not plan for anything to happen. Your adventures were nothing of my making. I only helped out.

Remember though that the Prophecy did not limit what you did either. It is not a guideline for what you must do necessarily. Prophecies are merely observations of another time. They do not make that time."

Matthew's fingers traced the raven designs on the staff. He found the answers bringing up more questions than resolution. "How did you know what I was going to do?"

"Your spell?" inquired the stranger. "I can sense what a person plans to do with the *mysteria* he or she conjures. I knew about Mistress Daghda's death probably before you did, and I can assure you that trying to change the past is not the way to go. Time is more solid than you could possibly imagine, Matthew. It is impossible to alter its course once it has already happened. Through Time, you can observe the past and even help to fulfill certain paradoxes, but you cannot change what you already know to be true."

"May I ask you another question?"

The stranger laughed and nodded.

"Do you know where Drage is?" The man in black did not have an immediate response. The only sounds were the vehicles roaring in the city below, mingling with the occasional loud voices. Matthew repeated, "Do you?"

The stranger straightened and responded, "I do know where he is, but it is not our place to aid him. Rest assured, he shall be here in the morning in time for the battle. The Prophecy shall be fulfilled."

"Can you at least tell me if he is alright then?" pleaded Matthew.

"I can." The man turned back to the room. "He is badly injured right now, and the only reason he is still alive is that Sword. Reduced friction is not the only ability of the Sword of Destiny. Another of its abilities is the power to protect its chosen wielder. The pieces of the Great Spirit that reside in the Spirit Swords are awakening at last."

Matthew pounded a fist against the railing. "Why won't you help him? If your powers are so great, why can't you do something to get him out of whatever predicament he is in? You said he was in pain. How can you let someone suffer knowingly?"

Without turning back to face Matthew, he replied, "Matthew...everyone suffers. Not just in this world either. Earth, Gevás, Waldann, Menx, and even Sharl Vran, the world of Dragons. Everyone suffers. It is natural. My job is not to remove suffering from the worlds. My job is to stop both the Darkness...and the Light from dominating these worlds."

Though Matthew's expression of fury did not change, his tone softened. "What is your name?"

The figure smiled beneath his hood. He muttered, "Finally, the right question..." His robe billowed as he turned back to face Matthew. A pure black Gate appeared behind him. "I am known as the Wolf, the Shadow, the Remnant, and the Seeker of a place called Paradise." He stepped backward into the Gate, and as he did so, he said, "My name is Ace."

The Last Guardian

The ceiling of the cramped cell had caved in when the atmosdome shattered. Water had filled the freezing prison and had actually given him some warmth. A falling fragment of the ceiling above him had landed on his head, knocking him unconscious.

When he awoke, he thought he was dead. Then, he realized he was still in miserable pain. A shaking hand went to his forehead, and he winced as he felt a lengthy gash. He saw the room without his *mysteria*-enhanced vision. A blue glow came from a corner of the room. Now, the entire room was a low chamber filled with rubble.

"How...how am I still alive?" he murmured. His strength, if anything, had increased since the cell's collapse. He pushed his weight forward so he was supported by the joint effort of his hands and knees. He crawled to the corner that emitted that eerie blue light.

After pushing away some of the debris that surrounded the light, he managed to make out the steel shape that had been buried. It was the Sword of Destiny. It had a shimmering blue aura around its blade. Being so close to it gave him hope. Somehow, the Sword had ended up with him once more.

His eyes darted across the room, trying to plan a possible escape, but when he tried to stand, he collapsed again, pain splitting his head. His teeth clenched as he endured the waves of agony that came from his bleeding forehead. He lay there, cringing and clutching the Sword of Destiny close to his body, reveling in its warmth.

He managed to find sleep again. It was a dreamless sleep but a comforting one all the same.

A man in a black robe arrived on the island of the Obsidian Plains. He could breathe in the water of these Plains at last, now that it was no longer an atmosdome. The Y'mordi filth had protected the island well by filling it with air. He supposed that due to their powers of Darkness they could easily survive in such an environment.

This man had a job to do here. He was searching for a Guardian of Light, the one who had a heart of Light. That Guardian was the ultimate key to the Prophecy. The man had sensed it in the current.

As he surveyed the murky, ash-filled water, he became aware of other presences swimming in the sea above him: serpents. He clenched his teeth in worry. Serpents were mindless creatures that were easily controlled by the Darkness. He was nowhere near ready to face this many serpents at once. A mission like that would be one of suicide.

In the distance, he could make out the remnants of a once soaring tower. The cold water did not bother him as he searched in silence for the boy with the heart of Light.

When Drage woke, he felt frail and unable to move. The pain pounded in his head like a hammer. His eyes shut, and he opened his heart to the dark and almost sickening feeling of *mysteria*. A weak blast of Darkness shot upward through the surface of the broken cell. More dirt and rock fell on him, though none of it was massive enough to hurt him. It proved that whatever spells had been placed on his cell were gone.

He groaned as he used the piles of rock to help him stand. He knew if he stayed here any longer, he would probably die. His only hope was to try to get out despite his hunger and agony. Once he had managed to lean against the wall, he shot another blast into the ceiling. Holding the glowing Sword up to where he had blasted revealed that he had made a hole after all. It was dark outside. Opening his heart further, he enabled himself to see through the shadows.

After enlarging the hole, he found the next problem: how to climb out of the cell. He was having trouble standing, much less climbing or swimming. A sigh escaped his trembling lips as he decided to wait a while longer.

The man in black turned his head toward the sound of explosions. Dark blasts had erupted from the ground. That must be where the Guardian was. He looked up to see the serpents respond to the noise. Their undulating bodies darted toward the source of the spell.

The man fell forward so that he was balanced on feet and hands and then sprinted across the frozen ground. As he moved, the robe on his body fell away, and his skin sprouted black, silver, and white hairs giving him a warm coat of fur. His muscles expanded and became like steel machines. His face had stretched into a furry muzzle, and pale orbs of white were his eyes.

Once he reached the holes in the ground, he spun to find the first serpent mere feet from him. He leaped at the serpent and swiped at the scaly creature with his razor-sharp claws. It fell to the ground, unleashing a cloud of venomous blood into the water.

He fell back to all fours and prepared to strike the next serpent when a blast of Darkness shot out from between his legs and hit the next creature with such force that it disintegrated the serpent. The sight of the powerful spell encouraged the remaining serpents to flee into the murky water and out of sight.

The furry animal looked down at the hole beneath him and

saw a face lit by a blue glow.

"Help..." said the boy.

Several hours later, Drage woke once more to find he was no longer in his desolate cell. He was back on the surface. A blue fire lit the water in front of him, keeping him warm. Beside the flames, there was a pile of delicious-looking fish. However, no one was around. His dirty-covered hands snatched a fish, and he held it over the fire to cook it. When it was relatively warm, he bit into the soft mass. Regardless of the taste, it was the first food he had had in days. As he ate, he felt his strength returning to him.

The pile was half-gone when he stopped to survey his surroundings. He sat amongst the remains of the tower. The storm was gone along with the bubble of air that had surrounded the island. The black trees that had once stood here had been crushed like the tower, and the water was clouded from the dirt that had been stirred when the atmosdome broke.

An eerie howl pierced the night, and the memories of the past few hours rushed back to Drage. He put a hand to his forehead, and his skin found cloth wrapped around the gash.

Did that wolf save me?

As if the creature had heard Drage's thoughts, the lupine treaded into view of the blue fire and the Guardian that was huddled close to its heat. The beast stood on its hind legs and continued to walk. The fur fell from his body and became a fur coat around the human.

Drage's eyes widened, but he said nothing as the figure approached. The man sat on a rock near the fire. Finally, he spoke with a deep yet scratchy voice, "Are you Dragenopn Helius, boy?"

Drage swallowed and retorted, "Maybe I am. Who are you?"

The man brushed a hand through his grizzled hair as he laughed. "Yeah, I heard you had a mouth on you. So, you are Dragenopn then. My name is Kibou, though as you could imagine, I am often referred to as the Werewolf."

Drage did not trust the man. "What are you exactly?"

Kibou grunted. "I am an anima, an animal that has the ability to become a human at will."

"And how did you know I was here? Why were you looking for me?"

The Werewolf was becoming more and more aware of the youth's ingratitude. "Hmph, I can smell Darkness, so I merely followed the scent of Maris and of that Gate you made back in Astra. I came here to help you actually." He explained, "I found your brother Matthew in Astra after you left him. The last I saw of him, he was in good hands and looking for the Prophet Marqest."

"Matthew?" exclaimed Drage in happiness. "He's alright, then?"

Kibou nodded without saying another word.

Drage turned and looked into the hypnotic fire. His face softened. "Sorry, Kibou. I've been in that cell for a while. Thanks for saving me. I owe you, y'know."

A smile spread across Kibou's face. "It's alright. I merely wanted to see if I could help out with your curse problem."

Drage brightened. "Can you?"

Kibou began, "I might be able to help you, but I am not confident I have the ability. Can you open your heart to *mysteria* for me?"

He closed his eyes and focused on the Darkness that surrounded his heart. Its power washed over him. "Well?" Drage muttered. He was ready to be free of the curse.

The Werewolf shook his head. "I am sorry, but your heart has steeped too far into the dark depths. I think you are the only one who could possibly remove the curse. Dragenopn, your heart is strong without the use of Maris's Darkness. When you learn your own power, I think your own strength can overpower Maris's curse. You must learn to harness your heart's true power though. Only then will you be able to win this battle."

Drage sighed. "I am losing faith that I have such power. When I look inside myself, all I see are shadows."

"Everyone has shadows in their heart, boy. You just need to be able to distinguish between Maris's shadows and your own. Your Darkness is as much a strength to you as your Light is," Kibou said as he tried to comfort Drage. Deep down, Kibou pitied the boy. He realized Dragenopn had been through much already, probably more than Matthew had.

"What if I can't find my Light? I am the Prince of Light, yet I can't seem to find that power in myself. What emotions are connected to it? How can I use it?" asked Drage without looking away from the crackling fire.

"I am not going to pretend to know all the answers," grumbled Kibou. "Light and Darkness are two of the most interesting Elements. Many people have set standard emotions for them, and in many cases, those emotions work, but the overall agreement is that using Light and Darkness depends on the individual's perception of that Element. No two people see Light and Darkness in the exact same way."

Drage fell silent. In the distance, he saw tinges of color begin to spread across the horizon. The dawn was approaching.

Drage noticed the blue glow of his Sword was dimming. "It saved me..."

"What did?"

"I don't know how, Kibou, but this Sword saved my life. While I was in my cell, I should have died, but somehow, the Sword got into the room, and it gave me strength. It kept me alive."

Kibou nodded. "One of the Spirit Swords, eh? Which one is that one?"

Drage held the Sword high in the water to reveal its solid steel blade and hilt. "It's the Sword of Destiny. I was told it only allows someone with a great destiny to wield it, and somehow it chose me."

Admiration filled the Werewolf's core as his pupil-less eyes scanned over the blade. "That is a great Sword. I have heard the legends about it. You are lucky to have obtained such a weapon. It is even more spectacular that it chose to protect you as well."

"I just wish I knew why…"

"Bah!" grunted Kibou. "You humans always want to know why things happen. You're never content to just observe and learn. Isn't it enough to know that fish swim? Is it really necessary to question their actions? Have you really lost all instincts?"

Drage folded his arms. Again, he was silent. Over the past few days, he had become used to not speaking. For the first time in his life, he had learned how to think before he spoke. The light of the dawn illuminated the black particles that surrounded the island.

Kibou sighed and looked up to the remnants of the night sky. "The stars are fading, and war is upon Gevás at last. Maris has divided the world, Dragenopn. It will no longer be the same, especially if he wins."

"I know," Drage replied. "A part of this world is mine too, and I have to protect it. I never knew it, but a part of me has always lived here. I have to fight. It's my destiny."

Matthew, Draconis, Marqest, and Lilian went to stand by Aria's side at the head of her troops. Matthew said to her, "Hey, Aria, it's time. We need to be at the front of the army. You've helped your troops as much as you can. We need to get ready."

Aria made a final salute to her troops and followed the other Guardians to the Emperor of Light who stood at the front of the armies.

Draconis muttered to the Emperor, "Your Majesty, I think you should get back inside the city now. Things are going to get dangerous out here."

The Emperor gave Draconis a hard look. "No, Rexam. This time, I shall fight. I want you to promise me something, Rexam: protect my son if something goes wrong."

The Golden Dragon relented, "Of course. My promise remains. I shall protect the bloodline, your Majesty."

The Emperor nodded and turned to face the other Guardians of Light. "We now have five of the Guardians of Light present for the battle."

"Make that six," called a voice from behind them, closer to the armies. They all turned to see a man with red hair and a black robe.

Aria recognized the voice. "You are the man that helped us escape the island when we first got here."

Matthew added, "And the one who helped Drage and I escape Maris and Mali on the way here the first time."

The man's red hair swayed in the current. He raised a long hammer into a fighting position. "My name is Randir. I am here to help you fight Maris."

All eyes widened except for Aria's own blue eyes. With a violent frown, she lifted her wand to cast a spell of Lightning, but Marqest diverted the spell toward the sky with Force. He called, "Aria, stop!"

Lilian murmured, "He is telling the truth. He is one of us."

Aria cried out as Matthew tried to hold her wand arm back, "They killed her! It's their fault she died!"

"Perhaps," began Randir in explanation. "It would help for you to understand that I have not been with the other Y'mordi for some time now. Whatever any one of them did, I had no part in it. I disobeyed my orders. They consider me a traitor."

This justification calmed Aria only slightly. She turned away from him and faced the enemy armies that were coming closer and closer to Apolis.

Randir said to Matthew, "Where is the last Guardian? The battle is about to start, and we need that final person, unless the Emperor himself is a Guardian. I could have sworn that there was another young boy about your age who came with you."

Matthew likened this Y'mordi with the stranger named Ace he had spoken to last night. Making this connection made it easier to talk to him. "Yeah, my brother Drage is the last Guardian, but we don't actually know where he is right now."

The Y'mordi clenched his teeth. He had known he should have been looking for the Guardians. *Where could he be?*

The sun was over the horizon now. Both Drage and Kibou

could see all of the island's disaster now.

"This place is ruined," Drage said.

Kibou shook his head in sorrow. "This place wasn't always dark. This is the work of the Y'mordi over the years. During the Obsidian Wars, this place was spectacular. The grass used to be green, and flowers of all colors dominated these fields. At night, legendary creatures called fireflies lit up the water. It was beautiful once."

Drage smiled at the vivid description. A thought came to him. "Kibou, are you an Ancient?"

The elderly man sighed. "Yes and no. I am from another world, and the people there live a lot longer than the people here. I probably do not have many years left though. Maybe one day, I will tell you my story but not today."

Drage rose and stretched his arms. He felt much better now. "Alright, Kibou, sounds fair to me."

"Are you ready to leave?"

His black eyes traced the blue sky miles above them. "I think so. My destiny is waiting for me, and it is time to face it." He turned to face the Werewolf. "Listen. I'm sorry I have been a pest. Thank you for saving me. After this battle, look me up if you need a favor or something, okay? I owe you big time, Werewolf." He offered his hand.

Kibou grinned with one fang curling over his lower lip and shook Drage's hand with his own hair-covered hand. "It's a deal."

"Would you like a Gate to somewhere?" suggested Drage.

Kibou changed back into a wolf. Though his mouth did not move, Drage heard his scratchy voice in his mind. "No, thank you. I ride the current in search of those who would serve the Darkness." Without another word, the wolf sprinted across the island into the murky water beyond the ruins of the broken spire.

Drage summoned a black Gate. He stepped into it. Deep down, he knew he was not ready for a battle. He could not even control his own emotions. When he appeared in front of Apolis, a force knocked into him, and after a second, he realized it was Aria hugging him. Smiling, he hugged her back and repeated the gesture with his brother.

His father said, "Dragenopn, we do not have time for a proper reunion. We fight!" Drage turned to see the armies of Maris approaching with the dark sorcerer leading only meters away. The Emperor roared a foreign battle cry as he, his armies, and the seven Guardians of Light charged at the enemy.

The Prophesied battle was upon them.

Blood of the Great Servant

The battlefield was a mixture of varying colors: white for Helio, silver for Immyx, black for Maris, and so on. Dazzling white bullets streaked through the water, finding and piercing flesh. Flying beside the artillery projectiles, destructive spells exploded across the field. Above the battleground, vehicles darted through the water, shooting at both one another and at the land-based armies below. Occasionally, a decimated transport would detonate and crash down to the field, crushing several soldiers on both sides.

Ignoring the firefight above her, Captain Terrell fired upon the infinite amount of Shadows that met her troops. Wisps of Darkness emanated from the line where her soldiers fought the Shadows. She signaled for the heavy artillery, and a scorching hot blue laser shot from one of the rear cannons into the melee, dissipating many of the Shadows. She hoped the order had not hurt some of her own men.

A voice called out, "Captain, look!"

Without looking for the source of the voice, her eyes darted upward, and she saw the enemy naval transport that was headed their way. As she pointed to it, she yelled to her heavy artillery, "Naval transport, straight ahead! Fire when ready!" The transport came closer and closer to Terrell's regiment, and she saw the lights glow in the barrels of its lasers. "Fire!" she screamed again. The cannon fired, destroying the vehicle. Her joy faded as the debris headed toward Terrell and her troops.

Aria's wand barely deflected the dagger that flew at her with a spell of Force. She retaliated with a stream of white Fire. Ixion summoned a tree from the ground to block Aria's spell, but it exploded once the scalding spell hit it. He cried out as he threw two more daggers: one at Aria and one at Draconis. Both of the Guardians had singled him out from the other Y'mordi once the battle had started.

While Aria blasted the knife away from her body, Draconis struck the one near him with his own golden sword. He rushed the small man in a fury. As Ixion struggled to match the fluid strikes, Aria prepared her own attack. She concentrated on Fire and forced Ixion's daggers to turn white-hot.

Though he dropped the daggers, he avoided Draconis's attacks. Once he gained some distance, he used *mysteria* to create several long, thorn-covered vines that wrapped around Draconis's swinging arm and then the rest of his golden figure.

Before Ixion could turn to attack Aria, she unleashed a blast of high-powered Lightning that turned him into a blackened mass that clouded the water.

"One day, I'll kill you for real," muttered Aria as she dispelled the sharp vines that had ensnared Draconis.

Randir blocked the two katanas with one swipe of his hammer. Mali was forced back by the strength of Randir's deflection. Then, Mali counterattacked with a lengthy combo of attacks. His katanas whirled at Randir despite Randir's own strength.

"Don't you remember where your loyalties lie?" exclaimed Mali as they fought.

When Randir saw an opening, he shot a fireball at Mali that was slashed clean through by the shimmering blades. "Of course, I remember. However, you are not one to lecture me about loyalty, are you, Hector?"

Mali roared in fury and increased the intensity of his slashes, causing Randir to regret his words.

"Look, Mali," he explained between parries. "You cannot really think of me as a traitor just because I disobeyed Y'tal. Our original orders were to collect the blood of the Great Servants. I merely want to carry out those orders in the quickest way possible. I am being loyal to our true cause."

They both sensed a transport's inevitable crash near them. They separated and allowed the vehicle to crash through the space where they had just been fighting. When Mali jumped over the wreck to cast a spell at Randir, the red-haired Y'mordi raised a hand, and Lava erupted from the earth to melt Mali.

Right before the liquid death could touch him, Mali transformed into pure Light. When the lava returned to the ground, he materialized once more and released a blast of Light that Randir blocked with his hammer.

Mali landed in front of Randir when the hammer came flying toward him. He performed a backflip and then leaped high into the water. The force of the jump in combination with his *mysteria* allowed him to land on a naval vehicle overhead. Randir imitated the high leap and rode on the roof of another transport.

Marqest erected a wall of solid iron when the Force spell shot toward him. After he heard the powerful spell shatter against his wall, he used his own spell to blast the wall at the hapless Y'mordi.

As if it were a simple feat, she leaped to the top of the wall and jumped back to the ground with the wall never stopping in its strong momentum. Sarn smiled at the rush of the battle. She had been waiting years to have a fight like this. She had no intention of messing it up either.

Wind straightened her massive chain, so it acted like a staff, and she swung it with ease to attack Marqest. Despite Marqest's old age, he flowed around the battlefield as a veteran would.

Though the force of both of their blows varied, Sarn's chain met only Marqest's scepter.

She sidestepped away from the old man and waved her hand sideways, sending a series of sharp discs made purely out of Force toward Marqest. The orb at the end of his own scepter glowed blue as the current changed so rapidly and powerfully that the discs were redirected at Sarn.

She frowned in disappointment that the spell had backfired. She snarled as she leaped over the deadly discs. Marqest winced as the discs sliced an unfortunate soldier into bits.

Matthew and Lilian were fighting Sarn's twin Arnim. The woman in the brown robe wielded two pistols. As soon as she pulled the triggers for the guns, Matthew froze time for everyone but himself and Lilian allowing them to dodge the bullets. As he swung his staff backward to gain momentum, he unfroze time. His raven staff swung and knocked Arnim backward. She lifted a hand, and spikes of Earth aimed their pointed tips at Matthew's chest, but Lilian blasted through the dirt spears with large spells of Force.

Matthew used Time to increase his attack speed and unleashed a rapid combo of swirling strikes against Arnim, though she blocked each of them with her metallic pistols and an occasional Earth wall. Lilian emptied her heart to prepare for any spell. She did not want to risk hitting Matthew.

After Matthew pushed back from Arnim, Lilian created a shield of Wind around Matthew that deflected each bullet Arnim fired at him.

"Matthew, I will take it from here," grumbled a voice near them.

Matthew turned to see Draconis. He smiled up at the Golden Dragon.

Draconis continued, "Lilian and I can take care of this Y'mordi. Go and help Drage, Aria, and the Emperor."

Without asking any questions, Matthew complied and ran to his brother's side.

"Behold, your Majesty. The Third Obsidian War has begun. The nonhumans shall finally be liberated, and humanity shall bow before us. I have long dreamed of this day, and now, freedom is within my grasp."

Drage stood with his Sword in the starting position of the Dragon form. He had not used it in the battle against Ixion, and that mistake had cost him dearly. He would not make the same mistake twice. Inside, his heart struggled to fight off the dark influence of Maris's curse.

John Helius said, "Maris, you are a criminal. You have defied the law, and you shall be punished for your crimes. Will you submit?"

Maris drew his Behemoth, a massive Sword that required both of his hands. He lunged at the Emperor who had not even pulled out his own sword yet.

Drage sprang forward, parried the strike, and counterattacked. Maris shot a blast of Darkness at Drage, knocking him back to the ground.

John slashed at Maris with his own simple sword and also used the Way of the Dragon in his fighting. Every attack flowed into the next, giving the appearance of a dance on the battlefield.

While the two combatted, Drage fought in his heart. He could feel Maris's Darkness growing inside himself, trying to control him fully. It took his utmost concentration to fight that Darkness.

Aria appeared over him. "Hey, are you alright?"

Seeing her soft face comforted him. The struggle in his heart subsided, and he no longer required focus to keep Maris at bay. He rose. "Yeah, I'm fine. Let's help my dad though."

Then, before his eyes, Maris slashed his father's lower torso, causing him to collapse on the spot. "Dad!" he roared with pain in his chest. "Aria, get him to safety, and see if you can get someone to help him, a Prophet or something!" He ran at Maris.

Aria went to the Emperor and dragged him into a Gate.

Matthew came to help Drage once he saw Aria and the

Emperor of Light disappear. Together, their attacks pressed Maris so he had no opportunity for attack. In frustration, Maris retaliated with a spell of Darkness that surrounded all three of them in a sphere of pure Darkness. Here, Maris could see what others could not see. In this sphere, he could sense every movement and experience the world as if it were the brightest day.

He had not expected Drage to be able to experience it the same way.

Captain Terrell smiled as the barrier the Emperor of Light's sorcerers created around the regiment shielded them from the debris of the naval transport. "Forward!" she roared. She wanted to press this attack and wipe out the battalion of Shadows. Her eyes took in the scene.

The armies that were fighting for the Emperor of Light were pushing back Maris's armies. They were winning. She looked up at the naval battle and was shocked to see two figures above her fighting on top of one naval transport. She realized one of the fighters was Randir.

It did not take long for Maris to knock Matthew unconscious with a Dark blast. Matthew simply could not see in the Darkness that had trapped them.

Drage lunged at Maris in hopes that the sorcerer would not expect such a deviation from the Dragon form, and Maris spun around Drage, preparing to strike his back, but as Drage had practiced, he reached the Sword over his head and behind his back to block the attack. He spun to Maris and started a flurry of swift attacks that came with ease.

Maris and Drage were alone now in the shroud of Darkness. "You are brave, boy, but I would quit now, if I were you." Deep down, Drage knew it was a taunt. The closer Drage came to the Darkness, the easier it would be for Maris to control him. The taunt worked, and Drage became aware of the agonizing pain in his heart, Maris's curse. He hesitated in finishing his series of attacks, and the dark sorcerer took advantage of that hesitation.

Maris rushed forward with a single slash at Drage. Though Drage managed to block the attack, the Sword of Destiny flew outside the black sphere. Drage felt a Dark blast knock him back a few feet as he fell to the frosted ground. He did not have to look up with his black light vision to see the Behemoth pointed at his throat.

In that moment, Maris pitied the human in front of him. He seemed so weak and incapable. "I shall make this quick for you, so do not move, human."

The Behemoth rose into the water, and Drage closed his eyes, bracing himself for death. In his mind, he saw his life played like a video before him. Memories of Matthew, Aria, Helen, his mom, and even his adventures here in Gevás flashed through his mind.

By the time the Behemoth was on its descent, a part of Drage screamed against everything he had thought or felt during the past few days and even weeks. A part of him fought to live.

Randir jumped to the next passing transport to avoid Mali's ray of Light. When he looked behind him, the vehicle on which he had been standing had been reduced to cinders by the spell. Luckily, this transport was moving away from the crazed Y'mordi.

Then, Mali appeared through a Gate onto a transport that was right behind Randir. "You've got to be kidding me!" Randir exclaimed as he blasted a fireball at Mali. He released another, this time at the transport itself. It exploded, forcing Mali forward onto the same vehicle as Randir.

The two fought, swords to hammer, on the small transport, while the pilot was terrified as to what he should do. "We used to be friends, Randir, but you have changed too much. You no longer care about anyone else but yourself. So what if your wife died? We all lost something!"

However, this topic was the wrong one to bring up in the middle of a battle with Randir. The furious Y'mordi swung his hammer so forcefully that all three weapons flew down to the battlefield below them, but Randir did not stop.

He held his hand to Mali's heart, twisted his hand as if turning a doorknob, and then stood back. The motion had been so quick that Mali could not have done anything. Randir held his open palm out in front of him, wondering if he should finish his handiwork.

Mali pleaded, "Randir, please don't do it. Look…I did not mean to insult you or Ophelia. I never wanted it to happen any more than you did. It's just…when you lost her, I lost you, and we were best buds back in the day, remember?"

He brushed a hand through his red hair in frustration and confusion. "We're not what we used to be, Mali. I serve the Darkness, not Y'tal."

Mali nodded. "Perhaps you were right. I have wondered it ever since you left us. I pledged my service to the Dark Lord Dagan and the Darkness but never to Y'tal. Perhaps, you were right, Randir. Would you let me help you now?" Though Mali had started this conversation as a plea for his life, he believed what he was saying, and Randir could tell.

"Mali, I—"

The conversation was interrupted when a cannon shot split the water and bore a hole straight through Mali. Randir turned to see Stehl at the controls to the cannon. He could not decide whether to smile or weep.

The Behemoth met another Sword. Drage opened his eyes, wondering why he was not dead, and saw through his black light vision the Sword of Destiny had reappeared in his hands. His heart felt different. The part in him that had wanted to live had grown and filled him.

That life, that vigor, lessened the burden of Maris's curse so much that Drage could see his own heart for the first time, and what he saw amazed him.

"Maris, you are no longer a part of me," said Drage.

The Sword glowed bright blue, and a blast of the same color shot upward from the blade, sending Maris reeling backward. Drage stood and held the Sword in the ready position. "I know how to beat you now."

Drage closed his eyes and focused on his heart's true Element: Light. A small globe of Light the size of a quarter appeared.

Maris mocked, "Is that the best you have got?"

Drage shook his head without opening his eyes. The sphere grew until it dissipated the orb of Darkness that surrounded them, and it spread further yet. Every person on the battlefield shielded his or her eyes from the blinding Light that came from the center of the bloody battleground.

When the Light cleared, every Shadow had disappeared, leaving only humans and anima. All fighting ceased as everyone turned to stare at Drage and Maris. Drage's face revealed no surprise that the man he was fighting had turned into a giant black stallion. "Maris, you were not wrong in your desire for freedom. You were wrong in how you went about trying to get it. You committed crimes and hurt people. While you wanted to free some people, you were just as willing to limit others."

Maris's voice roared in outrage and even fear through the thoughts of every person on the battlefield, "How can you, an utter novice in the ways of *mysteria,* be stronger than me, the greatest sorcerer Astra has ever known?"

Randir approached the stallion and called, "You lost yourself in the Darkness. The problem was that the Darkness did not want you to win this battle."

The red-haired Y'mordi raised the monstrous Behemoth from its place on the ground and stabbed the dark horse, burying the blade to its hilt in Maris's flesh. Drage clenched his teeth. "No! You weren't supposed to do that!"

Randir revealed no expression as he turned to face Drage with his hand still on the heavy hilt of the Behemoth. He withdrew the blade, and Maris collapsed onto the ice-cold earth and felt his life slip away. His luck had failed him. Before he could do anything else, a blast of Darkness hit him from the side, and two Y'mordi appeared by Gate. The three Y'mordi dragged the horse into the Gate and vanished.

Lilian ran up to where Maris had been seconds before and knelt to the ground. She allowed the tears to come. "Maris...we did not plan for you to die. We wanted to help you, not kill you."

Draconis came up to Drage and put a claw on his shoulder. "Dragenopn, you need to come with me..."

"Dad..." Drage muttered.

Draconis summoned the Gate with a pained look on his face. He knew he had no choice.

Marqest and Lilian stepped into it first. Then, Drage said, "Draconis, what about Matthew? He's still unconscious."

The Golden Dragon looked to where Matthew's body was and cast a quick healing spell, and Matthew stood up in a hurry, dazed by the quiet nature of the still packed battlefield. The soldiers on both sides had revealed no reaction to what had just happened. Draconis felt like saying something, some form of dismissal, but the awkwardness of doing so prohibited him from acting on the urge, and he merely gestured for Matthew and Drage to step into the Gate.

Then, he followed them and entered the Palace of Light's Throne Room.

On the floor of the Throne Room, a man lay with a gash across his stomach. This man, an hour ago, had been the Emperor of Light, King of Helio, and the father of Helen, Matthew, and Dragenopn Helius.

Secrets and Stories

That night, a massive funeral service was held for the Emperor of Light John Helius, Prophet of Earth Linda Daghda, and the countless others who had died in the battle that morning. A grave had even been made for Maris upon Lilian's request.

After it ended, four people remained: Drage, Matthew, Aria, and Lilian. They stood in front of the colossal golden tombstone of John Helius. The stone bore his name and four years under it. They were his years of death and birth along with his years as Emperor of Light.

Matthew turned to Drage and saw the tears he was holding back. Matthew wondered if he should tell Drage about his own father but decided against it for now. Though it was comforting for Matthew to know he was at least partially related by blood to Drage, he knew Drage would focus on other matters.

"Drage…I'm so sorry…" he started. He did not know what else to say.

Drage shook his head. "We never really got to talk. We never did anything. When I met him, I was so happy I had finally found my father, and then, I left him. When I did come back, it was at the last minute, and I still couldn't save him. I wasn't strong enough to fight Maris."

Aria looked to Drage in sorrow. She stepped toward him and embraced him. "Drage, it wasn't your fault. You did everything you could, and you shouldn't be ashamed of that. You tried."

"Aria's right," agreed Matthew. "Your father cared about you, and I am sure he would be proud of you even now."

Drage only stood there in silence, looking out at the graveyard. The current pushed his white coat back to reveal the black shirt he wore underneath. His brown hair swayed in the current, while his tears chilled against his cheeks.

Matthew and Aria glanced at each other in worry. Though she had the Prophet to grieve, at the present, she was more worried about Drage. In his sorrow, Drage felt something grow deep within his heart. He had felt Maris's Darkness still attached to him even after the battle. Though he could no longer sense his presence or even feel the Darkness anywhere near as strong as it once had been, that Darkness had remained. The Light he had summoned during the battle had decreased the Darkness's power, but he could still feel its cold presence in his heart. He had chosen not to tell anybody. He was not ready to talk about everything that had happened to him since he had left Matthew on Astra.

"I met a Werewolf where I was," Drage started, clearing his throat. "He told me Darkness and Light were all based on individual perspectives. If everyone is doing what they think is right, then why do people have to die like this?"

Aria, Matthew, and Lilian did not respond. They could tell in his voice that it was a question more to himself and not for them. Even if it had been for them, they were not confident they could have given the right answer.

Matthew and Lilian thought about Drage meeting Kibou. Drage had changed so much since Matthew had last seen him, and he could tell it was not just because of John's death. Something had happened that had made Drage lose his usually joking nature, and Drage was not ready to talk about it.

Aria gave up. "Come on, Matthew, Lilian. Let's give him a moment." She motioned for the others to follow her out of the freezing cemetery.

The next day, Lilian went back to her small village in Astra. The law that exiled the nonhumans had not been removed, but that law's status depended on who the next Emperor of Light would be. Draconis and Marqest had both claimed the heir would be revealed soon, and the new Emperor of Light would be crowned within days.

However, Lilian was not worried about the laws. She just wanted to see her father and the other villagers again. Though she had not been gone for long, she had missed the cool waters and the anima she had cared for her whole life. As she approached the village, a voice cried out, "There's Lily!" It did not take long for the villagers to swarm around her in joy. Many phrases caught her ears, "I saw her on the battlefield at Apolis!" "The greatest anima ever!" "She sure showed those scum of the Darkness!"

She could not hide her joy and surprise at the myriad of compliments. Her father's warm face appeared in the crowd. She ran to him. Her father picked her up and whispered in her ear, "I have heard some good things about you, Lily. I have heard you fought one of the Y'mordi. Is this true?"

"Yes, father. That is true. I did not defeat her though. Actually, she escaped. I think it was Y'mir. She used guns and the Element Earth," she explained.

"That is fine," her father replied with a grin. "I am sure she learned not to go against you again."

The sound of howls reached the village. Wherever the wolves were, they were near the crowd. Cries rose from the villagers. "It's the Werewolf!"

Lilian instructed her father to put her down. "I must go to him for a moment. He wishes to speak with me." Though her father was frightened by the idea, he allowed her to leave.

She ran amongst the trees until she came to Kibou and his

pack of wolves. He sat on a fallen log in his lupine form. "It's about time you arrived, Lilian. I have been waiting for you."

"You helped Dragenopn, did you not?"

Kibou nodded. "Yes, he had been caught in a cell under the Y'mordi's hideout in the Obsidian Plains. The Y'mordi must have captured him after he left here. I merely got him out of the hole and gave him a little strength back."

Lilian shook her head. "You remain a mystery to me, Werewolf. I no longer think it logical to question your actions. So, tell me: What do you want with me now?"

The wolf sighed and responded, "I think I just wanted to let you know I would no longer be hunting here in Astra. We shall move southward and seek better hunting. I suppose you could return to your village and say that you took care of the Werewolf problem, that I would not be coming back."

"That is a possibility, or I could say you were simply misunderstood. I could tell them the truth."

Kibou grunted, "The truth can be a hard thing to believe sometimes, Lilian. Let them believe I'm a monster. Let me be a legend to them."

Lilian did not comment on Kibou's proposal, but she inquired, "Will you still hunt the Darkness? Now that everyone's loyalties have divided, tensions and fights will increase, as will the crimes of the world. You will be needed now more than ever."

"No, Lilian. I cannot keep seeking an end to the Darkness. I am too old to be doing this anymore. I will live as a wolf should live: without the logic of the human and the fire of its machines, but with the instinct of the beast and the natural splendor of the wild."

As usual, without waiting for a response, he ran into the woods with his pack following. Kibou had no intention of turning back into a human this time. Now, he was a wolf.

Randir hung by his arms, which were connected to the ceiling by enormous chains. His bare chest glistened with sweat and blood. All over his naked body were the stinging gashes

Y'tal had inflicted on him.

Though he had been instructed not to use *mysteria*, the sight of a Flame comforted him. It was the only light he had seen upon returning to the Palace of Shadows. His muscles burned from the stretching chains, and his cuts stung from his sweat. He tried to block out the pain; he would have days like this until the next Great Servant was found.

The door creaked open with a screech that filled Randir with terror. Y'tal had come again, and he braced his muscles to face the Dark spells, but only Mali stood in the doorway. The man in white staggered to the hanging man. "Randir..." he whispered.

Randir managed a cracked smile that caused blood to drip from his mouth. He was a ghastly sight in this chamber. "Mali, what are you doing here?"

"I have a way that I can help you, but it is not much. I don't have much time either. Y'tal could sense me down here any minute now. I have a plan: you are going to put yourself in a limited Stasis. It will be so powerful that only I will know how to release it."

Randir's eyes widened at the idea. "You mean—?"

Mali nodded. "Yes, your mind, heart, and body will be completely immobile, so the world will go by until we find the next Great Servant, and then you will wake up. It will feel like blinking, and the world will have aged while you will have not."

"Why are you doing this?"

"I wasn't just pleading for my life back on that transport. I meant what I said. You do not deserve to be punished for something so trivial. We pledged our loyalty to the Darkness and not to Y'tal. Now, listen closely..."

Stehl found herself thinking of Randir as soon as she entered the office of the terra. She could not understand why her thoughts kept returning to the Y'mordi. When she had saved him from that other Y'mordi with the white robe, he had stared at her so sadly. Then, he had had the same distant expression on his face when he had killed the villain Maris.

Her spells had worn off, and she was now clearly a female, but she did not change her armor. A secretary sat behind the front desk, typing some record or other into his computer. Stehl approached him and tried to get his attention, "Excuse me? I would like to register to join the terra. Do you have forms or something?"

"Yes, we do have forms. What is your specialty?"

"I'm a rifleman, sir," replied Stehl with a high voice that seemed so unfamiliar to her. The spells had deepened her voice when she had impersonated a man.

"You're a rifleman?" questioned the secretary with a raised eyebrow. "I'm sorry. I have honestly never met a female rifleman. If you go down that hallway, you will find an elevator. Go down to the eighth floor of the basement and ask for Captain Pan. He is in charge of most of the best riflemen we have. He should have some applications for you."

Stehl thanked the man and headed toward the elevator. She opened it and stepped inside. When the armies had returned to their own countries, Stehl had left the Emperor Regin to become a member of Helio's terra. The thoughts of Randir left as she thought of her new goal: eliminating the Enigma Brigade.

In her mind, she could still see the young man with the red hair so long it reached his waist, the man who had killed the woman that had raised Stehl. Though she had told Randir the truth that she had no family, her father's ex-wife had taken care of her when she was just a little girl. That woman had taught Stehl how to fend for herself and had led her to the black market mages that had cast the spells that had made her appear to others as a male. The woman had been a servant to the Emperor Regin…until Maksimilian had ordered his men to kill her along with the other innocents of the castle.

Stehl grinned in the elevator. The Enigma Brigade would pay for what they had done.

Drage had known what Marqest was going to say even as he saw the old man approaching. "Marqest, leave me alone. I do not want to talk about it now."

"You have no choice!" bellowed Marqest. He had been trying to find Drage all day, and Drage had been avoiding him all day. Drage had been wandering around the Palace of Light in hopes that he might find his father's room.

Marqest waved his scepter, and the doors at the end of the Throne Room closed. He waved it once more, and all other doors in the room shut as well. "Dragenopn, we must talk about this matter now!"

Drage turned to face the Prophet of Water. "What?" he asked as if he did not already know the answer.

"You are the heir to the Crown of Light. That throne is rightfully yours," Marqest said as he pointed to the towering chair. "You are the only one who can become the Emperor now."

Drage put a hand to his aching head. "No, Marqest, I can't do that. I could give you a million reasons. I am too young. I don't know the first thing about leading a kingdom. Most of all, I need to get back home. This is not my world."

Marqest retorted, "This is your world. Both of your parents were born here as were your siblings. You have friends here, just as you do on Earth."

"Why don't you bug Matthew about it? He's my brother, so shouldn't he also have a right to the Crown?"

Marqest hesitated. He did not want to say it, but he realized it was necessary. This boy was too ignorant of his own history. "He does, because your mother adopted him into your father's side. Dragenopn, Elizabeth is his real mother, and Helen's, as well."

Drage froze in thought. He stumbled for the right words and decided to change the subject. "Marqest, we're leaving tomorrow. I cannot lead this country. Isn't there an Emperor's Council? Have them assemble and decide what to do." He waved a hand and strode over to one of the doors.

When he found that the doors were still held by Marqest's spell, he summoned a Light spell that shot through a door, and he kept walking.

"Drage, Marqest has been looking for you everywhere!" called Matthew as his brother approached him and Aria in the Imperial Gardens.

Drage sat on the bench and ran his fingers through his hair. "Guys, I think we need to leave tomorrow."

Aria gaped. "Drage, why would we leave now? There is still so much to do here. The armies are expecting an attack by one of the enemy nations any day now. We cannot just abandon them!"

"She's right, Drage," Matthew agreed. "We're still needed here, and besides, aren't you supposed to…" He did not finish his sentence though, as Drage glared at him.

"So, when are you two planning on going back home? Apparently, we both have mom and Helen to go home to, while you have both your parents, Aria. How long are you two going to wait?"

Matthew and Aria exchanged glances. Matthew started, "Actually Drage, we were wondering what you thought about all of us staying here."

The idea was out in the open. Drage felt anger seep out of his body. He looked up at Matthew with his black-iris eyes and whispered, "You guys really want to stay, don't you?"

Matthew nodded.

Drage stood and paced on the cobblestone path of the Gardens. Aria sat down and looked at Drage, waiting. "Guys," he began. "I really do love it here. The place can be so beautiful sometimes, but…I really do miss home. When I was fighting Maris, he nearly killed me, but then, I thought of something: all the great times the three of us have had. When I was drowning in the Darkness of Maris's curse, I found Light in my memories of us. By doing that, I pushed away the curse, and my heart was able to shine. The Sword of Destiny came and protected me from Maris because it saw the Light my heart could wield." Drage sighed and decided to tell them what had happened to him.

"Drage, I didn't know…" was all Aria could say.

He had not enjoyed recounting his imprisonment in the Obsidian Plains, but he knew Matthew and Aria needed to hear it. Drage sighed and muttered, "Y'know, maybe I could stay here for a while, but I think I really need to go back home for at least a little while first."

Aria and Matthew were pleased. "That sounds like a plan," Matthew replied with a smile. He felt sorry for what Drage had gone through, but he also hoped Drage would feel better about it all soon.

"I think I am going to leave in the morning. As strange as it may sound coming from me, I really miss Mom and Helen."

"If the boy plans to leave, who are we to stop him?"

Marqest replied, "He is the heir to the throne, and that makes it our responsibility to make sure he is crowned."

"No," Draconis snarled. "If Dragenopn thinks he is not ready for this responsibility yet, then our duty is to guard the throne until he is ready. Until that time, the Emperor's Council shall watch over the affairs of Helio."

Because of his work in the first battle of the Third Obsidian War, Draconis had been promoted by Master Valdridge to be a member of the Council. Being a Prophet and Loyal Servant, Marqest had also been promoted, however.

"If the boy will not have the throne, then his brother will. This discussion is far from over, Draconis."

As the old man stormed off into the dusk, Draconis smiled. He knew Dragenopn was making a wise decision by choosing to return to Earth. John had claimed that Earth had a way of making people more strong-willed. The former Emperor of Light had talked so fondly of the unusual planet. If Dragenopn was not ready to be Emperor, it was fortunate he would be on Earth to prepare for that responsibility. That boy had learned much in his journey. Dragenopn would make a fine Emperor someday.

The next morning, Valdridge opened the Gate himself and stepped back.

Draconis embraced Drage, squeezing him in a tight Dragon hug. "Be careful on Earth, Dragenopn. I promised your father I would look out for you, and so I shall, so do not forget it."

Drage grinned. "Thanks, Draconis. I think I can be careful. I think I can hold out on the adventures until I come back." Then, Drage turned toward Matthew and Aria. He went to Aria first and held her, taking in the sweet scent of her brown hair. "Aria, I'm going to miss you so much."

She tried not to let the tears in her eyes show and held Drage even tighter. "I'm going to miss you too, Drage." She let him go and flashed him a coy smile. "Try to stay single for me, okay?" She winked at him and found it was futile to hold back her tears.

Matthew stepped forward to embrace him as well. "You might want to take Draconis's advice a bit and relax for a while before you do anything crazy again, Drage."

"Me?" Drage joked. "When do I ever do anything crazy?"

Matthew laughed. "You don't change, do you, Drage?" They both knew, however, that they had all changed since first coming here.

Drage turned to behold the shimmering Gate in front of him. This whole journey had started in a Gate, and now it would end in one. He walked toward the portal and nodded to Master Valdridge. His body was inches from the gap that connected the two worlds.

He looked over his shoulder to behold the golden walls of the Palace of Light and marveled at its magnificence. Then, his eyes stopped on the people who had come to see him leave. His promised protector, Draconis, stood there, grinning at the young Guardian of Light with his long tail wrapping around his massive golden-scaled legs.

His girlfriend Aria was turned away from him. She could not watch Drage leave. His brother Matthew held Aria to comfort her. His green eyes were fixed on Drage in his old Earthan clothes.

Drage called out, "Take care of her for me for a while, okay?"

Matthew nodded and called back, "You got it!"

Without another look back, Drage stepped into the Gate and felt the water change around him. The warmth of the Palace became the subzero cold of the lake. The ability to breathe in the water left him, and he choked on the salty sea as he struggled to swim upward.

When he broke the surface, he felt air hit him in the face. Water spewed from his lungs and mouth and was replaced by fresh air. He wiped his eyes as he floated.

Then, he saw it: the large house on the beach with glass windows. He was home.

Home

Weeks passed.

The roaring breeze rippled through his t-shirt as he stood on the old wooden pier. He felt the damp planks bend under his bare feet. The gentle waves hissed as they washed over the rocks and shells of the sandy beach. The sun shone down on him, warming his skin. His black eyes turned to the dazzling star, yet his eyes did not ache from the light. His heart embraced a power that filled his body with life, heightened senses, and a feeling of contention.

He raised his hands, and the lake glowed with a golden light. He knew it did not matter if someone looked: he had bent the light around the lake so no one could see what he was doing. The light grew and reached up to the sky, making a lake-sized, blinding column. Then, the spell broke as he clenched his heart. He could feel it. He felt the black thorns tearing into the pit of his heart. "You're still inside there, Maris." Looking up, he saw seagulls passing through the clouds. Their noisy calls faded into the distance along with their winged shapes. "I wish you guys could be here…" Drage murmured to the wind, as he imagined Matthew's and Aria's faces in the clouds.

His foot kicked a gray stone into the water, and he watched its round silhouette sink until it was no longer visible. He knew he would see them again. As his eyes stared out and watched the undulating waves, his mind imagined a world submerged in water that contained dragons, werewolves, magic, and even blue flames. He knew he missed that foreign world, and he would for a while yet. He was content with that longing. It would make it easier to stay there next time, and perhaps his leaving could be a more planned event instead of being practically pushed through a portal.

He glanced backward at the large white house. He had missed Helen and his mother more than he had thought. He had been so glad to see them after he had swum back to the shore in his drenched clothes. Of course, Helen and Elizabeth had been glad to see him too. Elizabeth and he had held a very long discussion about the events on Gevás, yet when Drage questioned her, he received answers that only gave him more questions than satisfaction. He thought back to their morning breakfast when Helen had given him another look of disapproval: she hated that she had no idea where he had been the past few months. Elizabeth and he had told her that he, Matthew, and Aria had gone to some Governor's School program at the last minute. She did not believe it, but Elizabeth and Drage insisted that's what it was.

His head turned back to look at the lake. Everything felt different than it had before Gevás. The water was different. School was different. The way he acted around Elizabeth had changed entirely, and at the same time, he felt more alone than ever. When he woke up in the mornings, he would smile, expecting to find Matthew in the room next door, but the room stayed empty. Still, despite the changes, he knew he felt at home here in Paradise Shores. Not even the Darkness could take that feeling away. With a shaking hand over his heart, he forced the idea that this place was his true home deeper into his mind. At the same time, the dark thorns snaked deeper into his heart.

www.ingramcontent.com/pod-product-compliance
Lightning Source LLC
Chambersburg PA
CBHW060532180626
46817CB00002B/542